Purgatory

He grimaced in the dark but he didn't realise it. His hands were shaking, hanging next to his body, but his eyes were still closed.

'That's the problem, when you can't get out of your own head. You think you're so clean. Because Silva was so dirty. We think in terms of black and white. Silva was a killer, dirty and black as sin. And I was the clean, white light of justice. And they encouraged me. Get him. They made me even cleaner. Get Silva for the girls, the two women he had thrown away on a rubbish tip like so much human garbage. Get him for the cop of Murder and Robbery with the hole in the forehead. Get him for the drugs, for his invulnerability, for his dirty, black soul.'

Joubert looked back and saw that he had made progress on the thin wire.

He gave a longer step . . .

D1413144

Dead Before Dying

Deon Meyer

Translated by Madeleine van Biljon

CORONET BOOKS

Hodder & Stoughton

Copyright © 1999 by Deon Meyer

Translation Copyright © 1999 by Madeleine van Biljon

First published in Great Britain in 1999
by Hodder and Stoughton
A division of Hodder Headline PLC
First published in paperback in 1999
by Hodder and Stoughton

The right of Deon Meyer to be identified as the Author
of the Work has been asserted by him in accordance
with the Copyright, Designs and Patents Act 1988.

A Coronet Paperback

10 9 8 7 6 5 4

All rights reserved. No part of this publication may
be reproduced, stored in a retrieval system, or transmitted,
in any form or by any means without the prior written
permission of the publisher, nor be otherwise circulated
in any form of binding or cover other than that in which
it is published and without a similar condition being
imposed on the subsequent purchaser.

All characters in this publication are fictitious
and any resemblance to real persons, living or dead,
is purely coincidental.

A CIP catalogue record for this title
is available from the British Library

ISBN 0340 73917 7

Typeset by Hewer Text Ltd, Edinburgh
Printed and bound in Great Britain by
Clays Ltd, St Ives PLC

Hodder and Stoughton
A division of Hodder Headline PLC
338 Euston Road
London NW1 3BH

Tutta la vita è morte
– Guiseppe Verdi

1

In the afternoon hush of the last day of the year, Mat Joubert thought about death. Mechanically his hands were busy cleaning his service pistol, the Z88. He sat in his sitting-room, leaning forward in the armchair, the parts of the pistol lying on the coffee-table in front of him among rags, brushes and an oil can. A cigarette in the ashtray sent up a long, thin plume of smoke. Above him, at the window, a bee flew against the glass with monotonous regularity, in an irritating attempt to reach the summer afternoon outside where a light southeaster was blowing.

Joubert didn't hear it. His mind wandered aimlessly through memories of the past weeks, among chronicles of death, his bread and butter. The white woman on her back on the kitchen floor, spatula in her right hand, omelet burnt on the stove, the blood an added splash of colour in the pleasant room. In the living room, the boy, nineteen, in tears, R3 240 in the pocket of his leather jacket, saying, over and over, his mother's name.

The man among the flowers, an easier memory. Death with dignity. He recalled the detectives and the uniformed men on the open industrial site between the grey factory buildings. They stood in a circle, knee-deep in the wild flowers thrusting up yellow and white and orange heads. In the centre of this judicial circle lay the body of a middle-aged man, small in stature. An empty bottle of meths was gripped in one hand, he was face down, cheek against the soil.

But his eyes were closed. And his other hand clutched a few flowers, now faded.

It was the hands that Mat Joubert remembered most vividly.

On Macassar beach. Three people. The stench of burning rubber and charred flesh still hanging in the air, the group of the law and the media forming a barrier downwind against the horror of multiple necklace murders.

The hands. Claws. Reaching up to the heavens in a petrified plea for deliverance.

Mat Joubert was tired of living. But he didn't want to die like that.

Using thumb and forefinger, he placed the fifteen stubby 9 mm bullets into the magazine one by one. The last one flashed briefly in the afternoon sun. He held the bullet at eye level, balanced between thumb and forefinger and stared at the rust-coloured lead point.

What would it be like? If you pressed the dark mouth of the Z88 softly against your lips, and you pulled the trigger, carefully, slowly, respectfully. Would you feel the lead projectile? Pain? Would thoughts still flash through the undamaged portions of the brain? Accuse you of cowardice just before the night enveloped you? Or did it all happen so quickly that the sound of the shot wouldn't even travel from gun to ear to brain?

He wondered. Had it been like that for Lara?

Her light simply switched off without knowing about the hand on the switch? Or had she known and in that fleeting moment between life and death seen everything? Perhaps felt remorse or gave a last mocking laugh?

He didn't want to think about it.

A new year would start the following day. There were people out there with resolutions and dreams and plans and enthusiasm and hope for this new era. And here he sat.

Tomorrow everything at work would be different. The new man, the political appointment. The others could talk about nothing else. Joubert didn't really care. He no longer wanted to know. Either about death, or life. It was simply one more thing to survive, to take account of, to squeeze the spirit out of life and lure the Great Predator even closer.

He banged the magazine into the stock with the flat of his left hand as if violence would give his thoughts a new direction. He thrust the weapon into its leather sheath. The oil and the rags went back into the old shoebox. He dragged on the cigarette, blew the smoke in the direction of the window. Then he saw the bee, heard exhaustion diminishing the sound of the wings.

Joubert got up, pulled the lace curtain aside and opened the window. The bee felt the warm breeze outside but still tried to find a way out through the wrong panel. Joubert turned, picked up an oily rag and carefully swiped it past the window. The insect hovered briefly in front of the opening, then flew outside. Joubert closed the window and straightened the curtain.

He could also escape, he thought. If he wanted to.

Deliberately he let this perception fade as well. But it was enough to have him make an impulsive decision. He'd walk across to the neighbourhood barbecue this evening. Just for a while. For the Old Year.

2

The first step in the rebirth of Mat Joubert was physical. Just after seven o' clock that evening he walked across the tree-lined street of the middle-class Monte Vista to the Stoffberg home. Jerry Stoffberg of Stoffberg & Mordt, Funeral Directors in Bellville. 'We're in the same business, Mat,' he liked saying. 'Only different branches.'

The door opened. Stoffberg saw Joubert coming into the house. They said hello, asked the ritual questions.

'Business is great, Mat. Profitable time of the year. It's as if many of them hang in there until just after the festive season,' he said as he put the beer which Joubert had brought into the refrigerator. The undertaker wore an apron announcing that he was THE WORLD'S WORST CHEF.

Joubert merely nodded because he'd heard it before and uncapped the first Castle of the evening.

The kitchen was warm and cosy, a centre of enthusiasm and laughter. Women's voices filled the room. Children and men traffic-patterned their way easily past female conversations and the ritual of preparations. Mat Joubert navigated his way outside.

His consciousness was internalised, his perceptions withdrawn like the retracted feelers of an insect. He was untouched by the warmth and the domesticity.

Outside the children moved like shadows through pools of light and darkness, divided into squads according to age but united in their carefree exuberance.

On the stoep teenagers sat in an uneasy, self-conscious no man's land between childhood and adulthood. Joubert noted them briefly because their clumsy attempts to appear at ease betrayed them. They had transgressed. He concentrated until he realised what they were trying to hide: the glasses on the stoep table were filled with forbidden contents. Two, three years ago he would've smiled about it, recalled his own stormy adolescent years. But now he simply withdrew the feelers again.

He joined the circle of men around the fire. Each one's passport to the group was a glass in the hand. Everyone stared at the lamb which, naked and without dignity, was turning on Stoffberg's spit.

'Jesus, Mat, but you're big,' Wessels, the press photographer said when Joubert came to stand next to him.

'Didn't you know he's Murder and Robbery's secret weapon?' Myburgh, Bellville's traffic chief, asked from across the fire. His luxuriant moustache bounced with each word.

Joubert's facial muscles tightened, showed his teeth in a mechanical smile.

'Ya, he's their mobile roadblock,' said Storridge, the businessman. They laughed respectfully.

Casual cracks and remarks were tossed back and forth across the sizzling lamb, all of it aware of and careful about Joubert's two-year-old loss – brotherly, friendly, fruitless attempts to rouse his quiescent spirit.

The conversation took a quiet turn. Stoffberg turned the spit and injected the browning meat with a secret sauce, like a doctor with a patient. Sport, quasi-sexual jokes, communal work problems. Joubert shook a Winston out of a packet in his shirt pocket. He offered it around. A lighter flared.

Members of the circle at the fire came and went. Stoffberg

turned the spit and checked the progress of the meat. Joubert accepted another beer, fetched another a while later. The women's kitchen activities had decreased. They had spilled over into the adjacent television room.

Outside the conversation was geared to Stoffberg's lamb.

'No use giving it another injection, Stoffs. It's dead.'

'I've got to eat before sunrise, Stoff. I have to open shop tomorrow.'

'No way. This liddle lamb will only be ready in February.'

'By that time it'll be mutton dressed as lamb.'

Joubert's eyes followed the conversation from face to face but he took no part. Quiet, that's how they knew him. Even before Lara's death he hadn't been a great talker.

The children's voices became softer, the men's louder. Stoffberg sent a courier to give the guests a call. The tempo of the party changed. The women called the children and walked out with plates laden with side dishes to where Stoffberg had started carving the lamb.

Joubert sucked at a Castle while he waited his turn. The alcohol had misted his senses. He wasn't hungry but ate out of habit and politeness at a garden table with the other men.

Music started up inside, the teenagers rocked. Joubert offered cigarettes again. Women fetched men to dance. The music grew steadily older but the decibels didn't. Joubert got up so as not to be left alone outside and grabbed another beer on the way to the living-room.

Stoffberg had replaced the room's ordinary globes with coloured lights. Writhing bodies were bathed in a muted glow of red and blue and yellow. Joubert sat in the dining-room from where he had a view of the dancers. Wessels's short body jerked spasmodically in imitation of Elvis. The movements of the teenagers were more subtle. Dancing past a red light, the body of Storridge's pretty, slender wife was briefly backlit. Joubert looked away. The daughter of the house, Yvonne Stoffberg's breasts bounced youthfully under a tight T-shirt. Joubert lit another cigarette.

Myburgh's fat wife asked Joubert for a traditional waltz. He agreed. She guided him skilfully past the other couples. When the music changed, she smiled sympathetically and let him go. He fetched another Castle. The tempo of the music slowed. Dancers moved closer to one another, entered the evening's new phase.

Joubert walked outside to empty his bladder. The garden lights had been switched off. The coals under the remains of the lamb were still a glowing red. He walked to a corner of the garden, relieved himself and walked back. A shooting star fell above the dark roof of the Stoffberg's house. Joubert stopped and looked up at the sky, saw only darkness.

'Hi, Mat.'

She suddenly appeared next to him, a nymphlike shadow of the night.

'I can call you that, can't I? I've done with school.' She stood silhouetted against the light of the back door, her rounded young curves moulded by T-shirt and pants.

'Sure,' he said hesitantly, surprised. She came closer, into the protected space of his loneliness.

'You didn't dance with me once, Mat.'

He stood rooted to the earth, uncertain, stupefied by seven Castles and so many months of soul searing introspection. He folded his arms protectively.

She put her hand on his arm. The tip of her left breast lightly touched his elbow.

'You were the only man here tonight, Mat.'

Dear God, he thought, this is my neighbour's daughter. He recalled the contents of the teenagers' glasses on the stoep.

'Yvonne . . .'

'Everybody calls me Bonnie.'

For the first time he looked at her face. Her eyes were fixed on him, shining, passionate and purposeful. Her mouth was a fruit, ripe, slightly open. She was no longer a child.

Joubert felt the fear of humiliation move in him.

Then his body spoke softly to him, a rusty moment which came and went, reminding his crotch of the rising pleasures of the past. But his fear was too great. He didn't know whether that kind of life had died in him. It was more than two years . . . He wanted to check her. He unlocked his arms, wanting to push her away.

She interpreted his movements differently, moved between his hands, pulled him closer, pressed her wet mouth to his. Her tongue forced open his lips, fluttered. Her body was against his, her breasts pinpoints of warmth.

In the kitchen someone called a child and alarms broke through Mat Joubert's rise upward, towards life. He pushed her away and immediately started towards the kitchen.

'I'm sorry,' he said over his shoulder without knowing why.

'I've done with school, Mat.' There was no reproach in her voice.

He walked to his house like a refugee, his thoughts focused on his destination, not on what lay behind him. There were cheers announcing the New Year. Fireworks, even a trumpet.

His house. He walked past trees and shrubs and flower-beds which Lara had made, struggled with the lock, went down the passage to the bedroom. There stood the bed in which he and Lara had slept. This was her wardrobe, empty now. There hung the painting she'd bought at the flea market in Green Point. The jailers of his captivity, the guards of his cell.

He undressed, pulled on the black shorts, threw off the blankets and lay down.

He didn't want to think about it.

But his elbow still felt the unbelievable softness, her tongue still entered his mouth.

Two years and three months after Lara's death. Two years and three months.

Recently, late in the afternoon, early evening, he stood in Voortrekker Road and looked up the street. And saw the parking meters which stretched for a kilometer or more, as far as he could see, on the arrow straight road. The parking meters so senselessly and proudly guarding them all, were empty after the working day. Then he knew that Lara had made him one – an irritation during the day, useless at night.

His body wouldn't believe him.

Like a neglected engine it creaked and coughed and rustily tried to get the gears moving. His subconscious still remembered the oil which waited in the brain, chemical messages of the urge which sent blood and mucus to the front. The machine sighed, a plug sparked feebly, a gear meshed.

He opened his eyes, stared at the ceiling.

A virus in his blood. He could feel the first vague symptoms. Not yet an organ which grew and strained against material with a life of its own. At first only a slow fever which spread through his body and slowly, like a tide, washed the alcohol out of his bloodstream, drove away sleep.

He tossed and turned, got up to open a window. The sweat on his torso gleamed dully in the light of a streetlamp. He lay down again, on his back, searched for a drug against longing and humiliation.

The yearning in his crotch and in his head was equally painful.

His thoughts were driven by a whirlwind, spilt over the barriers.

Emotion and lust and memories intermingled. Lara. He missed her and he hated her. Because of the pain. Jesus, but she'd been beautiful. Lithe, a crack of a whip, a tempest, a tease. A traitor.

The softness of a breast against his elbow. His neighbour's daughter.

Lara who'd turned him into a parking meter. Lara who was dead.

Lara was dead.

His mind searched for an escape in the face of this, shunted his thoughts into the disconsolate safety of a grey depression in which he had learnt to survive in the past months.

But for the first time in two years and three months Mat Joubert didn't want that as an escape hatch. The great driving-shaft had turned between the roughened ball-bearings, the valves moved in their cylinders. The machine had forged an alliance with Yvonne Stoffberg. Together they were fighting the approaching greyness.

Yvonne Stoffberg fluttered in his mouth again.

Lara was dead. He drifted down into sleep. A duel without a winner, a new experience.

Somewhere on the borderline of sleep he realised that life wanted to return. But he crossed over before fear could overcome him.

3

Detective Sergeant Benny Griessel called the Murder and Robbery building in Kasselsvlei Road, Bellville South, 'The Kremlin'.

Benny Griessel was the one with the ironical sense of humour, forged in the fire of nine years of crimesolving. Benny Griessel called the daily morning parade in The Kremlin's parade room the 'circus'.

But this was a cynical remark made during the time of the ascetic Colonel Willy Theal, of whom fat Sergeant Tony O' Grady had remarked: 'There but for the grace of God goes God.' O' Grady had laughed loudly and told no one that he had stolen the quip from Churchill. In any case none of the detectives had known it.

This morning was different. Theal, the Commanding Officer of Murder and Robbery had taken early retirement on December 31 and was going to grow vegetables on a smallholding in Philippi.

Coming in his place was Colonel Bart de Wit. Appointed by the Minister of Law and Order. The new black Minister of Law and Order. As from January 1 Murder and Robbery were officially part of the New South Africa. Because Bart de Wit was a former member of the African National Congress who had resigned his membership before accepting the command. Because a cop must be impartial.

When Joubert walked into the parade room at seven minutes past seven on the first of January, forty detectives were already seated on the blue-grey government issue chairs placed in a large rectangle against the four walls. The muted buzz speculated about the new man, this Bart de Wit.

Benny Griessel greeted Mat Joubert. Captain Gerbrand Vos greeted Mat Joubert. The rest carried on with their speculations. Joubert went to sit in a corner.

At exactly quarter past seven the Brigadier, in full uniform, came into the parade room. Behind him walked Colonel Bart de Wit.

Forty-one pairs of eyes followed him. The Brigadier stood up front next to the television set. De Wit sat down on one of the two empty chairs. The Brigadier greeted them and wished them all a Happy New Year. Then he started a speech but the detectives didn't give it their full attention. Their knowledge of human nature, their capacity to evaluate others was centred on the commander. Because their professional future was tied up with him.

Bart de Wit was short and slender. His black hair was thin in front and at the back on the crown. His nose was a beak with a fat mole on the border between organ and cheek. He wasn't an impressive figure.

The Brigadier's speech about a changing environment and a changing police force was nearing its end. He introduced de Wit. The commander stood up, cleared his throat and rubbed the mole with a forefinger.

'Colleagues, this is a great privilege,' he said and his voice was nasal and high-pitched like an electric bandsaw. His hands were folded behind his back, his short body was stiff as a ramrod, shoulders well back.

'The Brigadier is a busy man and asked that we excuse him.' He smiled at the brigadier who took his leave as he walked to the door.

Then they were alone, the new commander and his troops. They looked at one another, appraisingly.

'Well, colleagues, it's time we get to know one another. I already know you because I had the privilege of seeing your service files but you don't know me. And I know how easily rumours can spread about a commander. That's why I'm taking the liberty of giving you a short résumé. It's true that I've had no experience in local policing. But for that you must thank the apartheid regime. I was taking a course in Policing through Unisa when my political beliefs made it impossible for me to stay in my motherland . . .'

De Wit had a weak smile on his lips. His teeth were faintly yellowed but even. Each word was flawlessly rounded, perfect.

'In exile, among a valiant band of patriots, I had the privilege of continuing my studies. And in 1992 I was part of the ANC contingent which accepted the British offer for training. I spent more than a year at Scotland Yard.'

De Wit looked around the parade room as if expecting applause. The finger rubbed the mole again.

'And last year I did research at Scotland Yard for my doctorate. So I'm fully informed about the most modern methods of combating crime now being developed in the world. And you . . .'

The mole finger hastily sketched a square in the air to include all forty-one.

'. . . and you will benefit from that experience.'

Another opportunity for applause. The silence in the room was resounding.

Gerbrand Vos looked at Joubert. Vos's mouth soundlessly formed the word 'patriots' and cast his eyes upwards. Joubert stared at the ground.

'That's all as regards my credibility. Colleagues, we're all afraid of change. You know Toffler says one can never

15

underestimate the impact of change on the human psyche. But at the end of the day we have to manage change. The first manifestation is for me to tell you what I expect of you. If I prepare you for change you can facilitate it more easily . . .'

Benny Griessel banged the palm of his hand against his head just above the ear as if he wanted to get the wheels turning again. De Wit missed the gesture.

'I expect only one thing from you, colleagues. Success. The Minister appointed me because he has certain expectations. And I want to deliver the kind of input which will satisfy those expectations.'

He thrust his forefinger into the air. 'I will try to create a climate in which you can achieve success – by healthier, more modern management principles and training in the latest crime combating techniques. But what do I expect of you? What is your part of the contract? Three things . . .'

The forefinger acquired two friends held dramatically in front of de Wit.

'The first is loyalty. To the Service and its aims, to the unit and your colleagues and to me. The second is dedication. I expect quality work. Not ninety percent but one hundred percent. Yes, colleagues, we must also strive for zero defect.'

The detectives started to relax. The new man spoke a new language but the message remained the same. He expected no more than any of his predecessors. More work at the same inadequate pay. Results as long as his back was covered with the higher-ups. And his promotion was assured. They were used to it. They could live with it. Even if he had been a member of the ANC.

Joubert took the red packet of Winstons out of his pocket and lit up. A couple of others followed his example.

'The third is physical and mental health. Colleagues, I

firmly believe that a healthy body houses a healthy mind. I know this will make me unpopular in the short term but I'm willing to take the chance.'

De Wit knotted his hands behind his back and straightened his shoulders again as if expecting an attack. 'Each one of you will have to undergo a physical examination twice a year. The results remain confidential between us. But if the doctor finds certain . . . deficiencies, I expect you to correct them.'

The hands behind the back were released. The palms turned out as if he wanted to ward off an approaching attacker.

'I know, I know. It was the same at the Yard. I know how difficult it is to be fit all the time. I know your stress levels, the long hours. But colleagues, the fitter you are, the easier it is to overcome the obstacles. I don't want to be personal but some of you are overweight. There are those who smoke and drink . . .'

Joubert stared at the cigarette in his hand.

'But we'll tackle it together. Together we'll change your lifestyle, help you to get rid of your bad habits. Remember, colleagues, that you're the cream of the Service, you project the image both here and outside, you are ambassadors, PR's. But most important of all, you have a duty towards yourself to keep your body and mind in shape.'

Again the slight hesitation, the pause for applause. Joubert killed the cigarette. He saw Vos dropping his head into his hands. Vos didn't smoke but he had a beer gut.

'Right,' said Colonel Bart de Wit, 'let's handle today's workload.' He took a notebook out of his jacket pocket and opened it.

'Captain Marcus Joubert . . . Where is Captain Joubert?'

Joubert raised his arm to half-mast.

'Ah, we'll meet formally a little later on, Captain. Is it Marcus? Do they call you . . . ?

17

'Mat,' said Joubert.

'What?'

'Like in rug,' said a voice on the other side of the room and a few detectives gave a subdued laugh.

'I'm called Mat,' Joubert said more loudly. De Wit misheard him.

'Thank you, Captain. Very well, Captain Max Joubert will lead the back-up team for the coming week. With him are Lieutenant Leon Petersen, Adjutants Louw and Griessel, Sergeant O' Grady, Constables Turner, Maponya and Snyman. I'll get to know you all, colleagues. And Captain Gerbrand Vos led the back-up team over the festive season. Captain, is there anything you want to discuss?'

The professional life of a Murder and Robbery detective didn't leave much time for extended sympathy when a colleague lost his grip. There was comprehension because it could happen to anyone. There was gratitude because it hadn't happened to you. And there was sympathy which lasted for a month or two until the fated colleague became a millstone round your neck in the execution of your duty.

Two colleagues in Murder and Robbery had retained their sympathy for Mat Joubert for two years – each for his own reasons.

For Gerbrand Vos it was nostalgia. He and Joubert had started together at Murder and Robbery as detective sergeants. The two shining new stars. Willie Theal allowed them to compete, to strive for more and more accolades but they were promoted together to adjutant, to lieutenant. In the Force they were a national legend. The Afrikaans Cape newspaper, *Die Burger*, wrote a quotable piece about them on the centre page when they were promoted to captain simultaneously. Always simultaneously. The young reporter was obviously impressed by them both. *Captain Vos is the extrovert, the big man with the face of an angel, dimples in his cheeks, baby-blue eyes. Captain Mat Joubert is the quiet one, even bigger, with shoulders that will fill a doorway and the face of a hawk – brown eyes that can look straight through you*, she had written dramatically.

And then Lara's death came and Vos accepted that his colleague no longer wanted to compete. And waited for Joubert to complete the grieving process. Gerbrand Vos was still waiting.

Joubert was busy with the first case dossier of the morning. Seventeen more stood in three piles on his desk, yellow-grey SAP3 files which regulated his life. He heard Vos's purposeful tread on the bare grey floor tiles, heard that they didn't end at the office next door. Then Vos was in the door, his voice subdued as if de Wit was in the vicinity.

'General forecast deep shit,' he said. Gerbrand Vos used language like a blunt weapon.

Joubert nodded. Vos sat down on one of the blue-grey government issue chairs. 'Patriots. Patriots! Jesus, it makes my blood boil. And Scotland Yard. What does Scotland Yard know about Africa, Mat? And "colleagues" all the time. What kind of CO calls his people "colleagues"?'

'He's new, Gerry. It'll blow over.'

'He wants to see us. He stopped me at tea and said he wanted to see each and every one of us alone. I have . . .' Vos looked at his watch . . . 'to be there now. And you're next. We've got to hang together, Mat. We're the two senior officers. We've got to sort out this fucker from the start. Did you hear him on fitness? I can see us doing PT in the parking area every morning.'

Joubert smiled slightly. Vos got up. 'I'll call you when I've finished. Just remember: band of brothers. Even if we're not fucking patriots.'

'It's okay, it's only jam, Mat,' Vos said thirty-five minutes later when he walked in again. 'He's waiting for you. Quite friendly and full of compliments.'

Joubert sighed, put on his jacket and walked down the passage.

Colonel Bart de Wit had taken over Willie Theal's office and made it his own, Joubert saw when he knocked and was invited in.

The team pictures against the wall were gone. The dirty green carpet on the floor was gone, the sickly pot plant in the corner had disappeared. Three certificates of degrees conferred now hung against the newly-painted white wall. The floor was covered in a police blue carpet and in the corner was a coffee table on which a small plaque announced **I PREFER NOT TO SMOKE.** On the desk was a holder with four photographs – a smiling woman in glasses with heavy frames, a teenage boy with his father's nose, a teenage girl in glasses with heavy frames. The other picture showed de Wit and the Minister of Law and Order.

'Do sit down, Captain,' said de Wit and gestured at the blue-grey chair. He also sat down. A small smile instantly hovered.

Then he straightened the thick personnel file in front of him and opened it. 'What did you say? That they called you Max?'

'Mat.'

'Mat?'

'They're my initials, Colonel. I was christened Marcus Andreas Tobias. M.A.T. My father called me that.' Joubert's voice was soft, patient.

'Aaah. Your father. I see he was a Member too.'

'Yes, Colonel.'

'Never an officer?'

'No, Colonel.'

'Aaah.'

A moment's uncomfortable silence. Then de Wit picked up the staff file.

'I don't play my cards close to the chest, Captain. Not about my political views then and not about my work now. So I'm going to be painfully honest with you. Things haven't been going well. Since your wife's death.'

The smile on de Wit's face didn't match the seriousness of his voice. It confused Mat Joubert.

'She was also a Member, wasn't she?'

Joubert nodded. And wondered what the man across the desk knew. His stomach muscles contracted and doors closed in his mind as a precaution.

'She died in the course of duty?'

Again Joubert nodded and his pulse rate increased.

'A tragedy. But with respect Captain, since then things have gone badly for you . . .' He looked at the file again. 'One serious disciplinary warning and two petitions from seven NCO's. A decrease in the solving of crimes . . .'

Joubert stared at the photograph of de Wit and the Minister. The Minister was a half meter taller. Both were smiling broadly. It was a clear picture. One could see the mole.

'Do you want to comment, Captain?'

The curious smile on de Wit's face unnerved Joubert.

'It's all in the file, Colonel.'

'The disciplinary action.' De Wit read the document in front of him. 'The Wasserman case. You refused to make a statement . . .' He waited for Joubert to react. The silence grew.

'It's all in the file, Colonel. I didn't make a statement because Adjutant Potgieter's statement was correct.'

'So you were guilty of unbecoming conduct.'

'According to the definition, I was, Colonel.'

'And the two petitions from the seven NCO's that they didn't want to be with you on back-up again?'

'I don't blame them, Colonel.'

De Wit leant back in his chair, a magnate. 'I like your honesty, Captain.'

Joubert was astonished at the way the man could smile and talk at the same time.

'But I don't know whether it's going to be enough to save you. You see, Captain, this is the New South Africa. We've all got to make a contribution. Shape up or ship out. There are people in disadvantaged communities who have to be uplifted. In the Police Service as well. We can't keep dead wood in officers' posts for sentimental reasons. Do you understand?'

Joubert nodded.

'Then there's the question of my appointment. The pressure is heavy. Not just on me – on the new government. Everybody's waiting for the mistakes. The whites would love the black government to make mistakes so that they can say we told you so.'

De Wit leant forward. The smile grew.

'Here there are going to be no mistakes. Do we understand one another?'

'Yes, Colonel.'

'Shape up or ship out.'

'Yes, Colonel.'

'Ask yourself, Captain: am I a winner? Then you'll always be welcome here.'

'Yes, Colonel.'

De Wit sighed deeply, the smile in place.

'Your first medical examination is at 14:00 this afternoon. And a last point: the Service contracted two clinical psychologists for members who need it. I referred your file. They'll let you know. Perhaps by tomorrow. Have a good day, Captain.'

4

Premier Bank started out as a building society seventy-five years ago, but this kind of financial institution had become unfashionable.

So, like most other financial institutions, it broadened its scope a little. Now, in addition to home loans, its clients could also drown in overdrawn accounts, hire purchase, and every other conceivable method of squeezing interest from modern man.

For the average client there was the Ruby Plan with the pale mauve and grey cheque book and its imprint of a red precious stone. Those with a higher income and more debt, qualified for the Emerald Plan – and a green gem. But, above all, the Premier wanted all its clients to aim for the Diamond Plan.

Susan Ploos van Amstel saw the attractive man with the gold-framed glasses, the blonde hair, the deep tan and the steel-grey suit walking towards her teller cubicle and knew he was a Diamond Plan client.

Susan was plump, thirty-four years old with three children who spent their afternoons in a play school and a husband who spent his evenings in the garage tinkering with his 1962 Anglia. When the blonde man smiled, she felt young. His teeth were a flawless, gleaming white. His face was finely made but strong. He looked like a film star. A forty-year-old film star.

'Good afternoon, sir. How may I help you?' Susan gave him her best smile.

'Hi,' he said, and his voice was deep and rich. 'I heard that this branch has the prettiest tellers in the Cape. And I see it's true.'

Susan blushed, looked down. She was enjoying every moment.

'Sweetheart, won't you do me a great favour?'

Susan looked up again. Not an indecent proposal, surely?

'Certainly, sir. Anything.'

'Oh, dangerous words, sweetheart, dangerous words,' his voice loaded with meaning. Susan giggled and blushed a deeper red.

'But I'll leave that for another occasion. Don't you want to get one of those large old bank bags and fill it with notes – fifties and higher? I've got this large old gun here under my jacket . . .'

He opened his jacket slightly. Susan saw the grip of a weapon.

'. . . and I don't want to use it. But you look like a pretty and sensible girl. If you help me quickly, I'll be gone before anything nasty can happen.' His voice remained calm, the tone conversational.

Susan looked for the smile which would show that he was joking. It didn't arrive.

'You're serious.'

'Indeed, sweetheart.'

'Good God.'

'No, sweetheart, nice large notes.'

Susan's hands started shaking. She remembered her training. *The alarm bell is on the floor. Press it.* Her legs were jelly. Mechanically her hands took out the canvas bag. She opened the money drawer, started transferring the notes. *Press it.*

'Your perfume is delicious. What's it called?' he asked in his beautiful voice.

24

'Royal Secret,' she said and blushed, despite the circumstances. She had no more fifties. She gave him the bag. *Press it.*

'You're a star. Thank you. Tell your husband to look after you. Someone might steal you.' He gave a broad smile, took the bag and walked out. When he went through the glass door Susan Ploos van Amstel pressed the button with her toe.

'It could be a wig but we'll get an Identikit together,' Mat said to the three reporters. He was investigating the Premier robbery because his manpower was deployed in the Upper Cape, where a bag person had set a friend alight in a haze of methylated spirits; in Brackenfell, the scene of a shotgun robbery in a fish shop; and in Mitchells Plain where a thirteen-year-old girl had been raped by fourteen gang members.

'Only R7 000. Has to be an amateur,' said the reporter from *The Cape Argus* and sucked her ball-point pen. Joubert said nothing. Better that way when handling the media. He looked through the glass door of the manager's office where Susan Ploos van Amstel was telling her story to even more clients.

'The Sweetheart Robber. Could become a nice story. Think he'll try again, Captain?' the man from *Die Burger* asked. Joubert shrugged.

Then there were no more questions. The reporters excused themselves, Joubert said goodbye and sat down again. The Identikit people were on their way.

He drove the Service vehicle, a blue Sierra, because he was on standby. On the way home he stopped at the second-hand bookshop in Koeberg Road. Billy Wolfaardt stood in the doorway.

'Hi, Captain. How's the murder business?'

'Still the same, Billy.'

'Two Ben Bovas have come in. But I think you've got them.'

Joubert walked to the Science Fiction section.

'And a new William Gibson.'

Joubert ran his finger down the spines of the books. Billy Wolfaardt turned and walked to the cash register at the door. He knew the captain wasn't a great talker.

Joubert looked at the Bovas, put them back on the shelf, took the Gibson, paid for it. He said goodbye and drove off. On the way home he bought Kentucky chicken.

An envelope had been pushed under his door. He carried it to the kitchen with the paperback and the chicken.

The envelope had a drawing of flowers in pale pastel colours. He put down the rest of the stuff, took a knife out of a drawer and slit open the envelope. It contained a single sheet of paper with the same floral pattern, folded in half. It had a sweet smell, familiar. A perfume. He opened it. The handwriting was feminine and impressive, looped. He read:

> The hot embrace
> Of my deep desire
> Ignites the flame
> Of your hottest fire
>
> Taste me, touch me, take me
> Impale me like a butterfly
> My lovely love, oh can't you see
> To love me is to make me die.

It was unsigned. The perfume was the signature. He recognised it.

Joubert sat down at the kitchen table. Why was she fucking with him? He didn't need another night like the last.

He read it again. The unsubtle verses created visions in his head – Yvonne Stoffberg, her young body naked, underneath him, sweat gleaming on the full, round breasts . . .

He threw the poem and the envelope in the dustbin and muttering, walked to his room. Not another night like that. He wouldn't be able to cope. He threw his tie onto the bed, went to fetch the paperback and took it to the living-room.

He had difficulty in concentrating. After seven jerky pages he fetched the verses out of the bin and read them again, annoyed with his lack of discipline.

Should he telephone her? Just to say thank you.

No.

Her pa might answer and he didn't want to start anything.

Just to say thank you.

He'd thought the urge had died. The same time yesterday he still believed the urge was dead.

The phone rang. Joubert started, got up and walked to the bedroom.

'Joubert.'

'Radio control, Captain. Shooting incident at the Holiday Inn in Newlands. Deceased is a white man.'

'I'm on my way.'

5

The other colleague who hadn't given up on Mat Joubert was Detective Sergeant Benny Griessel.

Because, despite all his cynicism, Griessel drank like a fish. And completely understood Joubert's withdrawal. He believed that something had to give in the life of a Murder and Robbery detective where death was your constant companion, the source of your bread and butter.

For a little more than a year Griessel had watched Joubert sinking deeper and deeper into the quicksand of depression and self-pity – and not necessarily being able to pull out of it. And said to himself: rather that than the bottle. Because Benny Griessel knew the bottle. It allowed you to forget the shadow of death. But it sent your wife and two kids fleeing headlong, away from the abusive, battering drunk who made their lives hell on a Saturday night. And later, many other evenings of the week as well.

No, Mat Joubert had a better deal going.

Griessel was the first to reach the scene. He was of medium height with a Slav face, a broken nose and black hair worn rather long. He wore a creased blue suit.

Joubert pushed his way through the crowd of curious onlookers, bent under the yellow plastic band with which the uniformed men had cordoned off the scene and walked to Griessel who was standing over to one side talking to a young, blonde man. The uniforms had thrown a blanket over the body. It lay shapelessly in the shadow of a steel-blue BMW.

'Captain,' Griessel greeted him. 'Mr. Merryck here found the body and called the station. From hotel reception.' Joubert smelt the liquor on Griessel's breath. He looked at Merryck, saw the gold-framed glasses, the sparse moustache. A fleck of vomit still clung to his chin. The body couldn't be a pretty sight.

'Mr. Merryck is an hotel guest. He parked over there and was on his way to the entrance when he saw the body.'

'It was quite awful. Sickening,' said Merryck. 'But one has to do one's duty.'

Griessel patted him on the shoulder. 'You can go now. If we need you, we know where to find you,' he said in his faultless English. He and Joubert walked to the body. 'Photographer is on his way. I've asked for the pathologist, forensic and the fingerprint guys. And most of the others on standby. He's white,' said Griessel and pulled away the blanket.

Between two staring eyes lay the small blood-filled lake of a bullet wound, gaping, mocking, in flawless symmetry.

'But take a look at this,' said Griessel and pulled the blanket down further. Joubert saw another wound, a bloody blackish-red hole in the chest, in the centre of a stylish suit, shirt and tie.

'Jesus,' Mat Joubert said and knew why Merryck had vomited.

'Large caliber.'

'Yip,' said Griessel. 'A cannon.'

'Check his pockets,' said Joubert.

'Wasn't robbery,' they said virtually in unison when they saw the gold Rolex on the arm. And they both knew that this complicated the case infinitely.

Joubert's hand moved quickly over the lifeless eyes,

smoothing down the eyelids. He saw the defenselessness of the dead, the way in which all bodies lay, unmistakable, vulnerable, the hands and arms finally folded never again to defend that showcase of life, the face. He forced himself to keep his mind on his work.

Voices behind them, saying hi. More detectives from the back-up team. Joubert rose. They were coming to look at the body. Griessel chased them away when they blocked out the pale light of the street lamps.

'Start there. Walk the whole area. Every centimeter.'

The usual moan started but they obeyed, knew how important the first search was. Griessel carefully went through the deceased's pockets. Then he got up with a cheque book holder and car keys in his hand. He threw the keys to Adjutant Basie Louw.

'They're for a BMW. Try this one.'

Griessel opened the grey leather cheque book holder. 'We have a name,' he said. 'JJ Wallace. And an address. Ninety-six Oxford Street, Constantia.'

'The key fits,' said Louw and took it out carefully, so as not to leave his fingerprints in the car.

'A rich bugger,' said Griessel. 'We'll hit the headlines again.'

It was a young detective constable, Gerrit Snyman, who found the cartridge case half way under a nearby car. 'Captain,' he called, still inexperienced enough to get excited immediately. Joubert and Griessel walked towards him. Snyman lit the empty cartridge case with his flashlight. Joubert picked it up, held it against the light. Griessel came closer, read the numbers on the back.

'Seven comma six three.'

'Impossible. It's short. Pistol case.'

'There. You read it. Seven comma six . . . three. It seems. Might be badly printed.'

'Probably six two.'

Benny Griessel looked at Joubert. 'Must be. And that means only one thing.'

'Tokarev,' Joubert sighed.

'Apla,' Benny sighed. 'Fuckin' politics.'

Joubert walked towards his service vehicle. 'I'm going to radio the Colonel.'

'De Wit? All he'll do is to puke his fuckin' heart out,' and his grin shone silver in the street light.

For the moment Joubert had forgotten that Willie Theal would never visit a murder scene again. He felt gloom rising like damp.

The house in 96 Oxford Street was a large single storey set in huge grounds. The garden was a controlled lushness, impressive even in the semi darkness.

Somewhere deep in the house the doorbell sounded briefly overriding the sound of a television programme. The seconds ticked past. Inside their carefree time was decreasing, Joubert thought. The angels of death were at the front door. The tiding, like a parasite, was going to suck life, joy and peace out of their lives.

A woman opened the door, irritated, a frown of small wrinkles. Long, thick, auburn hair hung over one shoulder, covered part of the yellow-patterned apron and guided their gaze away from her eyes.

Her voice was melodious and annoyed. 'Can I help you?'

'Mrs. Wallace?' he asked. Then he saw the eyes. So did Griessel. A mismatched pair, the one pale blue and bright, the other in shades of brown, somewhere between light and dark. Joubert tried not to stare.

'Yes,' she said and knew it wasn't a sales ploy. Fear moved like a shadow over her face.

'It's James, isn't it.'

A boy of about ten appeared behind her. 'What is it, Mom?'

She looked round, worried. 'Jeremy, please go to your room.' Her voice was soft but urgent. The boy turned away. She looked back at the detectives.

'We're from the police,' Joubert said.

'You'd better come in,' she said, opening the door wide and taking off her apron.

Mrs. Margaret Wallace wept with the total abandon of helpless grief, hands in her lap, shoulders slightly bowed. Tears stuck to the yellow wool of her summer sweater and glistened in the bright light of her living-room's candelabra.

Joubert and Griessel stared at the carpet.

Joubert focused on the ball and claw of the coffee table's leg. He wanted to be in his chair in his own home, the paperback on his lap and a beer in his hand.

The boy came down the passage. Behind him was a girl somewhere between eight and ten.

'Mom?' His voice was small and scared.

Margaret Wallace straightened her shoulders, wiped the palm of her hand over her face. She got up with dignity. 'Excuse me.' She took the children's hands and led them down the passage. A door closed. The silence was deafening. A cry sounded. Then there was silence again.

They didn't look at one another because that would be an admission.

Eventually she came back. Her shoulders were still gallantly erect, as though she could contain her emotions physically. But they knew.

'I must call my mother. She lives in Tokai. She can help with the kids. I'm sure you have many questions.' Her voice was neutral like a sleep-walker's.

Joubert wanted to tell her that they would come back

33

later, that they would leave her with her pain. But he couldn't.

She came back within minutes. 'My mother is coming over. She's strong. My dad . . . I've asked the maid to make us some tea. I take it you drink tea?'

'Thank you but . . .' Joubert's voice was slightly hoarse. He cleared his throat.

'If you'll excuse me I'll stay with the kids until she arrives.' She didn't wait for an answer and walked down the semi-lit passage.

Joubert's pocket radio beeped. He looked at the LCD message on his screen: RING ADJ LOUW. There was a phone number attached.

He'd sent Louw and three other detectives to the hotel because the rooms overlooked the parking area. This was after the pathologist had mumbled over the body. And before Bart de Wit had turned up and called a media conference about a murder on which they had no information. He and Benny had fled to Oxford Street just after it started.

'The man is a clown,' Benny had said on the way. 'He won't last.' Joubert wondered if the OC had called in the NCO's one by one as well. And if de Wit was aware of Griessel's drinking problem.

'Basie wants me,' he said breaking the depressing silence and got up. He walked to the room from where Margaret Wallace had earlier made a call. He heard the maid clinking china in the kitchen.

It looked like a study. A desk with a computer and telephone stood in the centre. Against the back wall was a bookcase with hardcover files, a few books on business practice and a handful of Reader's Digest Condensed Books in their overdone mock leather bindings. The wall next to the door was covered in photographs and certificates. There was also a large cartoon by a local cartoonist. It depicted James Wallace – thick, black hair, luxuriant moustache, slightly bulging cheeks. The caricature wore a neat suit of clothes. One hand held a briefcase with the logo WALLACE QUICKMAIL. The other arm clutched a cricket bat, the hand held a flag with WP CRICKET on it.

Joubert dialled the number. It was the hotel's. He asked to speak to Basie and waited a few moments.

'Captain?'

'Yo, Basie.'

'We've found someone, Captain. Female, blonde. She says Wallace was with her in the room. But we didn't question her further. We're waiting for you.'

'Can you stay with her? Benny and I are going to be here for a while.'

'No problem, Captain.' Louw sounded keen. 'Oh, and there was another spent cartridge. Under the body.'

When Joubert walked out of the study, he glanced at the cartoon against the wall again. And knew that the insignificance of life was just as sad as the finality of death.

'He started business on his own,' said Margaret Wallace. She sat on the edge of the big, comfortable chair, her hands in her lap, her voice even, without inflection, controlled.

'He was awarded the contract to deliver the municipal accounts. It was tough at first. He had to import an adressograph and a computer from the United States but in those days every letter had to be inserted into the envelopes by hand, then sealed. I helped him. We worked through the night. Often. He sold seventy percent of the shares to Promail International two years ago but they stuck to the original name. He's still on the board and acts as a consultant.'

Joubert noted that she was still speaking about her

husband in the present tense. But he knew that it would change on the following day, after the night.

'Was your husband involved in politics?'

'Politics?' Margaret Wallace said, wholly uncomprehending.

'Was Mr. Wallace a member of a political party?' Griessel asked.

'No, he . . .' Her voice cracked. They waited.

'He was . . . apolitical. He didn't even vote. He says all politicians are the same. They only want power. They don't really care about people.' The frown on her forehead deepened.

'Was he involved in the townships? Welfare work?'

'No.'

'His company?'

'No.'

Joubert tried another tack. 'Were you aware of any tension at work recently?'

She shook her head slightly and the auburn hair moved. 'No.'

The unmatched pair of eyes blinked. She was fighting for control, Joubert knew. He helped her: 'We're sure there must be a logical explanation for this terrible thing, Mrs. Wallace.'

'Who could've done such a thing? Haven't we had enough death and destruction in this country already? James wasn't perfect but . . .'

'It could've been an accident, Mrs. Wallace. Or a robbery. The motive for this sort of thing is usually money,' Griessel said.

Or sex, Joubert thought. But that would have to wait.

'Do you know if anyone owed your husband money? Any other business ventures, transactions . . .'

She shook her head again. 'James was so responsible with

money. He didn't even gamble. We went to Sun City last year, with the people from Promail. He took along R5 000 and said that when that was gone, he would stop. And he did. The house doesn't have a mortgage, thank the Good Lord . . .'

Griessel cleared his throat. 'You were happily married.' A statement.

Margaret Wallace looked at Griessel and frowned. 'Yes, I would like to think so. We had the usual little squabbles. James loves cricket. And sometimes he comes home a bit tipsy after a night out with the boys. And sometimes I'm too sensitive about it. I can be moody, I suppose. But our marriage works, in its strange way. The kids . . . our existence revolves around the kids these days.' She looked in the direction of the bedroom where her mother had to be the comforter now.

The silence grew. Then Joubert spoke. He thought his voice sounded artificial and overly sympathetic. 'Mrs. Wallace, according to law you have to identify your husband at the morgue . . .'

'I can't do it.' Her voice was muffled and the tears were about to fall.

'Is there someone else who could?'

'Someone at work will have to. Walter Schutte. The managing director.' She gave a telephone number and Joubert wrote it down.

'I'll give him a call.'

They got up. She did too, but reluctantly because she knew the night lay ahead.

'If there's anything we can do . . .' Griessel said and he sounded sincere.

'We'll be fine,' said Margaret Wallace and started crying bitterly again.

*　　*　　*

The blonde sat on one of the hotel's bedroom chairs. Her name was Elizabeth Daphne van der Merwe.

Joubert sat in the other chair. Griessel, Louw and O' Grady were perched on the edge of the big double bed, arms folded, like judges.

Her hair was straw-coloured out of a bottle. Her face was long and thin, the eyes big and brown with long lashes, the nose small and delicate. Tears had drawn mascara tracks down her cheeks. But Lizzie van der Merwe had missed true beauty with a mouth that didn't match. Her front teeth were a bit rabbity, the bottom lip was small, too near the weakness of her jaw. Her body was tall and slender with small, high breasts under the white blouse. She had angular hipbones and wore a black skirt which showed too much of her legs in cream-coloured stockings ending in elegant high heels.

'Where did you meet the deceased?' Joubert's voice was wholly without sympathy now, his choice of words deliberate.

'I met him this afternoon.' She hesitated, looked up. The detectives all stared at her, their faces impassive. The long lashes danced across her cheeks. But no one reacted.

'I work for Zeus Computers. In Johannesburg. I phoned last week. We have new products . . . James . . . er . . . Mr. Wallace . . . They referred me to him. He is their consultant on computers. And so I flew down this morning. I had an eleven o'clock appointment. Then he took me to lunch . . .' Her eyes moved from face to face, looking for one which showed sympathy.

They waited in silence. Her lashes danced again. The lower lip quivered and placed more emphasis on the two front teeth she tried to hide. Joubert felt sorry for her.

'And then?' he asked softly. She embraced his tone of voice and focused the big eyes on him.

'He . . . We had wine. A great deal of wine. And we

talked. He said he was very unhappy in his marriage . . . His
wife doesn't understand him. There was something between
us. He understood me so well. He's a Ram. I'm Virgo.'

Joubert frowned.

'Star signs . . .'

The frown disappeared.

'Then we came here. I have a room here because I'm
staying over. I have another appointment tomorrow. With
someone from another firm. He left after six. I'm not sure of
the time. And that's the last time I saw him.'

The lashes fluttered again and the mascara tracks increased.

Basie Louw cleared his throat. 'What happened here? In
this room?'

She cried harder.

They waited.

She got up and went to the bathroom next door. They
heard her blowing her nose. A tap ran. Silence. Then the
nose being blown again. She came back and sat down. The
mascara tracks had disappeared.

'You know what happened. Here . . .'

They looked at her expectantly.

'We made love.' She cried again. 'He was so gentle with
me . . .'

'Miss, do you know anyone in Cape Town?' Mat Joubert
asked.

She took a tissue out of the sleeve of the white blouse and
blew her nose again. 'I have friends here. But I haven't seen
them for ages.'

'Is there anyone who'd be . . . unhappy if you slept with
other men?'

Her head jerked up. 'I don't sleep with other men . . .'

The eyebrows of the three detectives on the bed rose with
military precision.

'Don't you understand? There was a vibe. We . . . we were . . . It was beautiful.'

Joubert asked again: 'Miss, we want to know if you're involved with anyone else who would mind that you and the deceased slept together.'

'Oh, you mean . . . No. No, never. I don't even have a permanent relationship.'

'Do you belong to a political party or group, Miss van der Merwe?'

'Yes.'

'Which one?'

'I'm a member of the Democratic Party. But what has . . .'

Griessel didn't give her a chance. 'Did you ever have any connection with the Pan African Congress?'

She shook her head.

'Apla?'

'No, I . . .'

'Do you know anybody who belongs to these groups?'

'No.'

'What did the deceased say when he left here? Did he have another appointment?' Griessel asked.

'He said he had to go home, to his children. He is . . . was a good man . . .' Her head drooped. 'There was a vibe. So beautiful,' she said.

Mat Joubert sighed and got up.

6

He dreamt about Yvonne Stoffberg.

They were in the mountains. She ran ahead of him, her white bottom bobbing in the moonlight, her brown hair floating. She was laughing, skipping over river stones, past a rippling stream. He was also laughing, his hard-on rigid in the evening breeze. Then suddenly she screamed, a scream of terror and surprise. Her hands shot to her breasts, trying to hide them. Ahead of them on the mountain track stood Bart de Wit. Between his eyes there was a third eye, a staring, scarlet pit. But he could still speak: 'Ask yourself, Captain. Are you a winner?' Over and over again like a cracked record in that high, nasal voice. He looked round, searching for Yvonne Stoffberg but she had vanished. Suddenly, de Wit was gone, too. The dark invaded him. He felt himself dying. He closed his eyes. Long auburn hair drifted across his face. He was lying in the arms of Margaret Wallace. 'You'll be OK,' she said. He started crying.

At the traffic lights Joubert stared at *Die Burger*'s poster as he did every morning without seeing it. Then as the letters took on meaning, he was startled: CHINESE MAFIA BEHIND BRUTAL KILLING OF CRICKET FAN?

The lights changed to green and he couldn't stop next to the newspaper seller. He drove to a cafe in Plattekloof, bought a newspaper and looked for the report on the front page as he walked back to his car. He found it.

41

DEON MEYER

CAPE TOWN *A murder gang of the Chinese Mafia may possibly be behind the brutal slaying of a wealthy Cape Town businessman who was shot with a Tokarev pistol at a Newlands hotel last night.*

According to Col. Bart de Wit . . .

Joubert leaned against the car and looked up at Table Mountain. He sighed, not seeing how clearly the mountain was visible this morning or how the morning sun made a bright splash in the bay. Then he folded his newspaper, got into the car and drove off.

'What's beyond me, is why he had a bit on the side with a horse-faced blonde when he had a film star at home,' Griessel said.

Joubert wasn't listening. 'Have you seen the paper?'

'No?'

Then de Wit came in, ramrod straight, self-satisfied. The detectives fell silent.

'Good morning, colleagues. Beautiful morning, isn't it. Makes one grateful for the privilege of being alive. But there it is, we have to get on with the job. Before we discuss yesterday's cases . . . I've now met all the officers personally and we had productive discussions. Today I'm starting with the non-commissioned officers. I want to get to know you all as soon as possible. Mavis has a list. All the adjutants must check the time of their appointments. Right, let's discuss yesterday's cases. Captain Mat Joubert called me for assistance with a murder in Newlands . . .'

He looked at Mat and gave him a friendly smile. 'Thanks for the vote of confidence, Captain. Can you give us a progress report?'

Joubert was somewhat taken aback. He'd asked de Wit to come to the scene because it was standard procedure with

42

all murders that had a high publicity potential. Now the man was giving it a different interpretation.

'Uh . . . It's pretty thin, Colonel. The deceased certainly had extra-marital relationships. Today we'll check whether there's a jealous husband in the picture somewhere. Perhaps someone at his office . . .'

'You can drop that,' de Wit interrupted him. 'As I told the press last night, this is the work of a Chinese drug ring . . . Good piece in *Die Burger* this morning. If you dig deeply enough into the deceased's background you'll find the connection. I think the investigation can only benefit if you involve the Narcotics Bureau as well, Captain. Drop that jealous husband theory of yours. Interestingly enough, last year at the Yard we had two similar murders . . .'

De Wit broke eye contact with Joubert. Joubert stopped listening. There was an uncomfortable feeling in his belly as if an insect was scrabbling through his entrails.

Reluctantly he phoned the officer commanding Sanab – the SA Narcotics Bureau – after the morning parade.

'What have you appointed there this time, Joubert?' the voice at the other end asked. 'A clown? Cloete of Public Relations has just phoned me, asked whether de Wit had spoken to me. Cloete is mad as hell because your new boss chats to the newspapers himself. Cloete wants to know whether he can retire now and fish full-time. And what's this crap about the Chinese Mafia?'

'It's based on the previous experience of my commanding officer, Colonel. At this stage we have to investigate all possibilities.'

'Don't give me that official smokescreen, Joubert. You're just shielding de Wit.'

'Colonel, I would appreciate it very much if you and your staff would provide Murder and Robbery with any information which could cast more light on the possibility.'

'Ah, now I've got it. You're under orders. Awright, you have my sympathy, Joubert. If we uncover a Chinese smuggling ring in the next two hundred years, you'll be the first to know.'

The investigating officer had to be present during the post-mortem. That was the rule, the tradition – no matter what the state of the remains.

Joubert had never enjoyed it, not even in the good old days. But he could erect barriers between himself and the unsettling process which repeated itself time after time on a marble slab in a white-tiled room in Salt River where the dead lost the last remnants of dignity.

Not that Professor Pagel forced his scalpel and clamps and saws and forceps through skin and tissue and bone without respect. On the contrary, the state pathologist and his staff approached their work with the seriousness and professionalism which it deserved.

It was Lara's death which had destroyed his barriers. Because he knew she had also lain there. Images recalled from past experience had helped to reconstruct the scene. Naked, on her back, clean and sterile, her lithe body exposed to the world, to no effect. The blood washed from her face, only the small star-shaped bullet wound visible between the hairline and the eyebrows. And a pathologist explaining to a detective that it was characteristic of a contact shot, the point blank killing. Because the compressed gases in the gun's barrel landed under the skin and suddenly expanded, like a balloon bursting, the Star of Death was awarded, so often seen in suicide cases . . . But not in Lara's. Somebody else gave her the star.

Every time he walked down the cold, tiled passages of the mortuary in Salt River, his mind screened him the scene, a macabre replay he couldn't switch off.

Pagel was waiting in the little office with Walter Schutte, managing director of Quickmail. Joubert introduced himself. Schutte was of medium height with a deep voice and hair which protruded from every possible opening – his shirt collar, the cuffs, his ears. They walked to the theatre where James J Wallace lay under a green sheet.

Pagel stripped off the covering.

'Jeez,' said Walter Schutte and turned his face away.

'Is this James J Wallace?' Joubert asked.

'Yes,' said Schutte. He was pale and the line of shaven beard showed clearly on his skin. Joubert was astonished by the hairiness of the man. He took him by the shoulder and led him back to Pagel's office where Schutte signed a form.

'We'd like to ask you a few questions in your office later on.'

'What about?' Schutte's self-confidence was slowly reasserting itself.

'Routine.'

'Of course,' Schutte said. 'Any time.'

When Joubert walked back, Pagel switched on the bright lights, thrust his short, strong fingers into the transparent plastic gloves, took off the cloth covering the late James J, drew the arm of the large, mounted magnifying glass towards him and picked up a small scalpel.

The pathologist began his systematic procedure. Joubert knew all the mmm-sounds the man made, the unintelligible mutter when he found something important. But Pagel only shared his discoveries when he was quite certain about his conclusions. That's why Joubert waited. That's why he stared at the sterile washbasin against the wall where a drop of water pinged against the metal container every fourteen seconds.

'Head shot could've caused death. Entry through the left frontal sinus, exit two centimeters above the fontanel. The exit wound is very big. Softnosed bullet? Could be . . . could be. Must have a look at the trajectory.'

He looked at Joubert. 'Difficult to judge the caliber. Entry wound in the wrong place.' Joubert nodded as if he understood.

'Relatively close shot, the head shot. Two, three meters. The thorax shot probably equally close. Could also have caused death. Wound is typical. Additional signs less obvious. The clothes, of course. Heat absorbed. Powder particles. Smoke. Through the sternum. Bleeding absent.'

He looked up again. 'Your man was already dead, Captain. After the first shot. Doesn't matter which one it was. Dead before he hit the ground. The second one was unnecessary.'

Fuel for de Wit's Mafia mania, Joubert thought. But he remained silent.

'Let's go in,' Pagel said and picked up a larger scalpel.

Walter Schutte didn't get up when Joubert and Griessel were escorted in by the secretary. 'Sit down, gentlemen.' He swung a jovial arm at the modern leather and chrome chairs in front of the big desk with its sheet of glass. 'Tea or coffee? I'm having something so please don't hesitate.' The pale uncertainty in the mortuary had disappeared.

They both chose tea and sat down. The secretary closed the door behind her.

The morning wasn't far advanced but Schutte's beard already cast a shadow over his cheeks. His teeth flashed white when he gave a quick, bright smile. 'Well, in what way can I assist you?' Then the smile disappeared like a light that had been switched off.

'We'd like to know more about James Wallace, Mr. Schutte. You must've known him well?' Joubert asked.

'I met James for the first time two years ago, when

Promail appointed me here. He was a wonderful man.'
Wallace's voice was loaded with veneration.

'Is that what you called him? James?'

'Most of us called him Jimmy. But now it sounds so . . .'
Schutte flashed a gesture and a smile.

'What were his relations with the people at work?'

'We all liked him. Oh, hang on, I see what you're driving
at. No, Captain, you won't find his murderer here.' Schutte
waved both hands in front of him as if warding off an evil
spirit. 'We're like one big family, I always say. And James
was a part of the family. A much loved part. No, Captain,
look for your murderer somewhere else.'

'Do you know whether the deceased had any other
business interests?'

'No . . . I don't think so. Jim . . . James told me that all
his money was invested in unit trusts because he didn't want
to worry about it. As far as I know he only had Quickmail,
his cricket and his family.'

'Has your firm done any business for Chinese firms?'

Schutte frowned. 'No. What has that . . .'

Griessel interrupted him. 'Have you seen this morning's
Burger?'

'No.' Schutte was off balance.

'The way in which Wallace was murdered, Mr. Schutte –
it's similar to the modus operandi of the Chinese drug
dealers. Did he have any contact with people from Taiwan?'

'No.'

'The local Chinese community?'

'Not that I'm aware of.'

'Pharmaceutical companies?'

'There is one for whom we send marketing brochures to
the medical profession but Jimmy never worked with them.'

'Did he use drugs?'

'Never. It's an absurd idea. Jimmy wasn't the sort.'

'Mr. Wallace's politics. Did he have strong political opinions?'

'Jimmy? No . . .'

'Did you do business with any political group?'

'Not at any time.'

'Do you know how he and his wife got along?'

Schutte sat even straighter in his tall chair. 'You'll find nothing there, either, Captain.' His voice was reproachful. 'James and Margaret were the perfect couple. In love, successful, beautiful children . . . young Jeremy plays a fantastic game of cricket. No, Captain, you won't find anything there.'

Joubert realised that the time had come to free Schutte of his excessive respect for and protection of the dead.

The secretary brought in a tea tray with three cups and put in on the desk. She poured and they thanked her. When everyone had stopped stirring, Joubert asked: 'Do you know why the deceased went to the Holiday Inn in Newlands yesterday?'

Schutte moved his shoulders as if the question was obvious. 'James often had a beer there with his cricketing friends.'

'Mr. Schutte, how did the deceased get along with the women working here?'

'Very well. He got along with everyone.'

In the good old days, when Mat Joubert still performed his day's work with the zeal of the newly converted, he developed a technique for reluctant witnesses like Walter Schutte – the so-called Bull, as his colleagues called it. He would lean his big body forward, square and broaden his shoulders, drop his head like a battering-ram, lower his voice an octave and fix his eagle's eyes on the specific person. Then he would speak, pulling no punches, in a somewhat superior, threatening tone. It was melodramatic, overdone and feigned. But it worked.

But as Tony O' Grady said one day, a year or two ago, Joubert had lost 'the beat in his baton.' And with it the motivation to use The Bull.

Whether it was the flickering flame of sexual hunger ignited by Yvonne Stoffberg, or Colonel Bart de Wit's challenge to the remnants of his ego, Joubert would never know. When he switched to The Bull it was probably not a reasoned act but more than likely pure reflex.

The physical side of shoulders, head and eyes he managed but initially he had problems with the voice and the choice of words. 'Yesterday afternoon Jimmy Wallace spent the last hours of his life . . . on top of a blonde. I'm sure it wasn't his first . . . escapade. And . . . I know someone in the office must know about his escapades because someone had to protect him when Mrs. Wallace looked for him. You now have a choice, Mr. Schutte. You can go on telling fairy tales about Jimmy Wallace and how exemplary and wonderful he was. Then I'll have to bring in a team of detectives which will keep each of the employees busy for hours. Or you can help us and we'll leave as soon as possible.'

Joubert maintained his aggressive pose. Schutte opened his mouth and closed it again as if he couldn't find the right words.

'Jimmy . . . Jimmy had his little diversions.' The hands were quiet now.

Joubert leaned back in his chair – The Bull was no longer necessary.

'Mr. Schutte, you saw what James Wallace looks like now. We're trying to find the person who had a reason for doing that to him. Help us.'

'He . . . liked women.' Schutte glanced swiftly at the door as if he expected James Wallace there, eavesdropping.

'But he had two rules. No nonsense at work. And no long

relationships. Just once with each one. Into bed and that was it.'

Schutte's hands started to move again as if he was gaining momentum.

'You should've known Jimmy . . .' He gestured with his hands indicating a search for words. 'He attracted people like a magnet. Anyone. He was mad about people. We were in a restaurant in Johannesburg and he bet us that within twenty minutes he could convince the brunette in the corner to go to the ladies with him. We accepted the bet. We weren't allowed to look at them and he had to bring back a piece of evidence. Eighteen minutes later the brunette kissed him goodbye outside the restaurant. And when he sat down he took her panties out of his pocket. Red ones with a black . . .' Then Schutte blushed.

'We want you to think carefully, Mr. Schutte. Do you know of any of his relationships that might have resulted in conflict or unhappiness?'

'No, I told you he had no relationships. In his way he was very fond of Margaret. OK, occasionally he broke one of his own rules. There was a little secretary here, a young pretty number with big . . . But it only lasted a week. In all honesty I can't think of anything that would've made anyone want to murder him.'

Joubert looked at Griessel. Griessel shook his head slightly. They got up. 'We're sure there's a jealous husband somewhere who didn't like Wallace's rules, Mr. Schutte. Please phone us if you can think of something that would be helpful.'

'Of course, absolutely,' Schutte said in his deep voice and also stood. Solemnly they shook hands.

'I haven't seen The Bull for a long time, Captain,' said Griessel when they were in the lift on the way down to street level.

Joubert looked questioningly at him.

'The one where you lean forward like that.'

Joubert gave a lopsided, self-conscious grin.

'We all tried to imitate it,' Benny Griessel said, openly nostalgic. 'Those were the good old days.'

Then he realised that Mat Joubert might not want to be reminded of them and he shut up.

7

The doctor's reading glasses were perched on the end of his nose. Over them he stared at Joubert, grave and portentous.

'If I were a mechanic this would be the moment to whistle and shake my head, Captain.'

Joubert said nothing.

'Things don't look too good. You smoke. Your lungs don't sound good. You admitted that you drink too much. You're fifteen kilos overweight. You have a family history of cardiovascular disease. You work under stress.' The doctors linked his fingers on the desk in front of him.

The man should've become a public prosecutor, Joubert thought and stared at a plastic model of a heart and lungs which stood on the desk. It advertised some remedy.

'I'm sending the blood sample for tests. We must check your cholesterol level. But in the meanwhile we must consider your smoking.'

Joubert sighed.

'Have you thought of giving it up?'

'No.'

'Do you know how harmful it is?'

'Doctor . . .'

'It's not only that you're exposing yourself to diseases. It's the manner in which you'll die, Captain. Have you ever seen someone with emphysema? You should come to the hospital with me, Captain. They lie there in oxygen tents, slowly smothering in their own mucus, like fish on dry ground, unable to breathe.'

On the desk there was a penholder in the shape of a pill. It advertised another kind of medicine. Joubert folded his arms and stared at it.

'And those with lung cancer?' the doctor continued. 'Have you seen what chemotherapy does to one, Captain? The cancer makes you thin and tired, the treatment makes your hair fall out. The living dead. They don't want to look into a mirror. They're emotional. Adult men weep when their children sit next to the hospital bed.'

'I don't have children,' Joubert said softly.

The doctor took off his reading glasses. He sounded defeated. 'No, Captain, you don't have any children. But living a healthy life one does primarily for oneself. For your own mental and physical health. And for your employer. You owe it to your employer to be fit. Then you're alert and productive . . .'

The reading glasses were replaced on his nose.

'I'm not going to prescribe something before we have the results of the blood test. But I must urge you to think about the smoking. And you must exercise. And your eating and drinking habits . . .'

Joubert sighed.

'I know it's difficult, Captain. But weight is a dodgy issue. The longer you leave it, the harder it becomes to get rid of it.'

Joubert nodded but he didn't meet the doctor's eyes.

'I'm obliged to send a report of this examination to your employer.' Unaccountably the doctor added: 'I'm sorry.'

The Police College in Pretoria took every group of student constables to the Service's museum in Pretorius Street in the old Compol building. In general the visits were never a great success. The students spoilt it, in a manner typical of their age, by vying with one another in friskiness and unsophisticated humour.

That was why Mat Joubert only started loving the museum when years after his college days, he had to give evidence in a murder case in Pretoria. During the five days he had to wait before being called as a witness, boredom drove him there.

He moved from exhibition to exhibition, his imagination gripped. Because by then he had the experience and insight to know that every rusty murder weapon, every yellowed piece of documentary evidence had cost some long-forgotten detective hours of sweat and labour. With eventual success.

He'd been there again the following day. And Adjutant Blackie Swart had noticed him. Blackie Swart, face deeply lined, a chain smoker with a voice that sounded like boots on gravel, was the factotum of the museum – a post he had evidently acquired because he had worn the General down with his constant pleading.

He was fifteen when he joined the Force, he told Joubert in his broom cupboard office in the cellar. 'Did horse patrol between Parys and Potchefstroom.' Joubert was entertained for hours on end with anecdotes and police coffee, the brew that was made tolerable by a small shot of brandy.

Blackie Swart's life was on exhibit in the museum especially in the glass cases below the sign THE HISTORY OF CRIMINAL INVESTIGATION.

'I was part of it all, Matty, saw it happen. I first saw the museum when I came to fetch my twenty-five years from the General, here at headquarters. And I knew I wanted to come back one day. Then I took my pension at sixty with forty-five years of service and I went to Margate and for three months I watched my car rusting. Then I phoned the General. And now I'm here every day.'

Joubert and the old man chatted and smoked the day away. It wasn't a paternal relationship, a friendship rather, possibly because Blackie Swart was so wholly different to Joubert's father.

After the week in Pretoria they met sporadically. Both were bad telephone communicators but Joubert phoned occasionally, especially when he wanted advice about a case. Like now.

'The doctor says I must stop smoking, Uncle Blackie,' he said into the receiver, using the respectful Afrikaans way addressing elders.

He heard the hoarse cackle of laughter at the other end. 'They've been telling me that for the past fifty years, Matty. And I'm still hanging in there. I'll be sixty-eight in December.'

'I've got a funny murder here, Uncle Blackie. My OC says it's the Chinese Mafia.'

'Is that *your* case? *Beeld* quoted de Wit this morning. I didn't understand it, but then . . .' His voice became conspiratorial. 'I hear his black colleagues in the ANC called him Mpumlombini. De Wit, I mean. In the old days, in London.'

'What does it mean, Uncle?'

'Xhosa for Two Nose. The man evidently has a mole . . .' Blackie Swart chuckled.

Joubert heard a cigarette being lit at the other end of the line. Then Blackie had a long and prolonged coughing attack.

'Maybe I should also give up, Matty.'

Joubert told him about James Wallace.

'De Wit is right about the modus operandi, Matty. Chinese did it that way in London last year. But they have other ways as well. Fond of the crossbow. Dramatic stuff. Much more finesse than the American Mafia. But the Chinese aren't only involved in drugs. Look at credit card fraud. They're heavily involved in that. Trading in forged documents. Passports, driving licenses. Wallace had a mailing service. Did they send out banks' credit cards? He could easily have supplied the Chinese with the numbers.'

'His employees say he did no business with any Eastern companies.'

'Ask his wife. Perhaps they saw him at home.'

'He slept around, Uncle Blackie.'

'Could be, Matty. You know what I always say. There are two kinds of murder. The one where someone suddenly loses his temper and uses the first weapon at hand to hit or throw or shoot. And the other kind is the one which is planned. Head shot in a parking area sounds planned to me. And a man who sleeps around . . .'

Joubert sighed.

'Legwork, Matty. That's the only way. Legwork.'

He drove to Margaret Wallace's. He wondered how far she had travelled on her road of grief. Then, on the N1 between Bellville and the southern suburbs, he remembered his dream of the previous night for the first time.

He suddenly knew that for the past two years he had been someone in the process of drowning. He had struggled on the surface of his consciousness, too frightened to dive into the dark water. He could remember dreams which had come back to him during the safety of daylight. But he'd kept them deeply submerged while he drifted on the surface. But now he could plunge his head below the waterline, keeping his eyes open and look at his dream because Lara had been no part of it. Yvonne Stoffberg was there. How clearly he'd seen her body.

Would he be able to?

If dreams became a reality and she stood in front of him, an open invitation. Could he do it? Would the tool of love, so dulled, be able to function? Or was its blade too blunt to prune the past, allowing new growth?

The uncertainty lay like a weight, low in his abdomen, gripped like fear. His neighbour's eighteen-year-old daughter. Or was it seventeen? He forced his thoughts to the other characters in his dreams. What was Bart de Wit doing there? With the hole in his head. And Margaret Wallace? He was amazed by the mystery of his subconscious. Wondered why he hadn't dreamt of Lara. Wondered whether she would come back that night. The old monsters found their way into the pool of his thoughts. He sighed. And shot back to the safe surface.

The woman who opened the door had to be Margaret Wallace's sister. Her hair was short and redder, her skin lightly sprinkled with freckles, her eyes pale blue but the resemblance was unmistakable.

Joubert asked to see her sister.

'This isn't a good time.'

'I know,' he said and waited, uncomfortable, an intruder. The woman gave an annoyed sigh and invited him in.

There were people in the living-room speaking in hushed voices which stopped when he stood in the entrance hall, They looked at him, recognised the Law by his clothes, his size and his style. Margaret Wallace sat with her back towards him but followed the others' eyes. She got up. He saw that she had travelled a long way on her road. Her eyes were sunken and dark. There were lines around her mouth.

'I'm sorry to trouble you,' he said, made uncomfortable by the silence in the large room and the reproachful looks of all those present.

'Let's go out into the garden,' she said softly and opened the front door.

The southeaster was ruffling the tops of the big trees but

down below it was almost still. Margaret Wallace walked with her arms folded tightly across her breasts, her shoulders bowed. He knew the body language so well, the label of the widow, universally recognisable.

'Don't feel bad. I know you have a job to do,' she said and tried to smile.

'Did you see the newspaper?'

She shook her head. 'They hide it from me.'

'My superior . . . There's a theory . . .' His mind sought desperately for euphemisms, looked for gentle synonyms for death. He wished Benny Griessel was there.

'In Taiwan organised crime uses the same methods . . . in their . . . work. I have to pursue the possibility.'

She looked at him and the wind blew her hair over her face. She wiped it away with a hand, folded her arms again. She waited.

'Your husband might have done business with them, perhaps indirectly . . . With the Chinese. Would you know?'

'No.'

'Mrs. Wallace, I know this is difficult. But if there could be some explanation . . .'

'Haven't you found anything?' she asked, no reproach in her voice as if she already knew the answer. Her hair blew over her face again but she let it be.

'Nothing,' he said and wondered whether she would ever find out about Lizzie van der Merwe and the other women with whom James J had shared a night or two.

'It was a mistake,' she said. 'An accident.' Her arms unfolded, a hand comforted his upper arm. 'You'll see. It has to be.' Then she folded the hand away again.

He walked back to the house with her, took his leave. He drove home and wondered why the number of trees in a suburb equalled the per capita income of the breadwinners living there.

It was past seven but the sun was still high above the horizon. Joggers were sweating in the traffic fumes at the side of the road. He lit a cigarette and wondered what he was going to do about his health. Perhaps he should exercise. Jogging was out. He hated jogging. He was too big to jog. Swimming maybe. It would be nice to swim again. Not competitively. Just for fun. Forgotten memories surfaced. The smell of the swimming bath's change rooms, the footbath with Dettol in it, the fatigue after hours of practice, the taste of chlorine in his mouth, the adrenaline when the starter's pistol went off.

At home another letter had been pushed under his door. *Why don't you reply?*

The discomfort was back in his belly. By now he recognised it. There was a lane in Goodwood, behind the cinema in Voortrekker Road. They said that was where motorcycle riders did stuff. He was eight or nine. And every Saturday night he stared down the dark of the lane with a curiosity that threatened to consume him. Run, his mind told him. Run down it like the wind, just once. But the fear, the uncertainty about his own bravery, lay like a weight in his stomach. He had never risked the lane. He drove to Blouberg, bought chicken at Kentucky and ate it in the car while he stared at the wind-flattened sea. Then he drove home to read his book.

Late in the evening the telephone rang. He put William Gibson on the table next to the armchair, answered. It was Cloete of Public Relations.

'Are you still working on the Yellow Peril or can I feed the newspapers something else tomorrow?'

8

Cape Town – *Up to now the Police have been unable to establish any connection between the Tokarev murder and Chinese drug syndicates.*

De Wit read the report in a soft voice, a thin smile on his face. He put down the newspaper and looked at Joubert.

'Must we differ about this case in public, Captain?

'No, Colonel,' said Joubert and saw that the No Smoking sign had been moved from the coffee table in the corner to de Wit's desk next to the family photograph.

'Did you provide the information?' De Wit's voice was conversational, almost jolly.

'Colonel,' said Joubert tiredly, 'as investigating officer I reacted to a query from a colleague at Public Relations. It's in line with the procedures and regulations of the Service. I gave him the information in the light of the way I see the murder investigation at this stage. It's my duty.'

'I see,' said de Wit and again smiled slightly. He picked up the newspaper and slid his eyes over the report. 'You didn't deliberately make a fool of your commanding officer?'

'No, Colonel.'

'We'll never really know, Captain Joubert. But in the long run it probably won't matter. Thank you for coming by.'

Joubert realised he was being excused. He stood up, uncomfortable, uncertain about the other man's calmness, already aware that it meant something, predicted something.

'Thanks, Colonel,' Joubert mumbled at the door.

He was behind with his paperwork. He pulled the adjutants' files towards him but found it difficult to concentrate. He lit a Winston and sucked the smoke deep into his lungs. He wondered whether he'd deliberately made a fool of his commanding officer.

And he thought about the cunning of his sub-conscious and knew that he was not entirely innocent, Your Worship.

Dragging footsteps moved down the passage. Griessel walked past, his head bowed. There was something in his carriage which disturbed Joubert.

'Benny?'

The footsteps returned. Griessel's face appeared around the door. He was pale.

'Benny, is everything all right?'

'I'm OK, Captain.' The voice was remote.

'What's the matter, Benny?'

'I'm OK, Captain.' Slightly more expression. 'Probably something I ate.'

Or drank, Joubert thought but said nothing.

Griessel's face disappeared. Joubert lit another cigarette. He forced himself to concentrate on the work in front of him. Dossiers about death. An elderly couple in Durbanville. An unknown black body next to the train tracks in Kuilsriver. A woman in Belhar murdered with a screwdriver by her drunken husband.

Then he heard someone clearing his throat. Bart de Wit stood in front of his desk. Joubert wondered how he managed to move like a cat over the tiled floor.

He saw that de Wit wasn't smiling. His face was serious.

'I've got news, Captain. Good news.'

Joubert ground the gears of the Sierra and drove jerkily through the afternoon traffic. He wished he could express the astonishment and indignation which clung to him like a too tight piece of clothing.

De Wit had told him he had to see the psychologist.

'Your file has been referred.'

The passive form. Too scared to say: I referred your file, Captain, because you are a loser. And I, Bart de Wit, don't need losers. I want to get rid of you. And if I can't do it with the medical report, I'll do it in this way. Let's dig around in your head, Captain. Let's thrust a spoon into the stew of your head and stir it a little. Stand back, folks, because it might be dangerous. This man in front of you is slightly . . . off. Not all there. Mentally unbalanced. On the surface he looks normal. Somewhat overweight, somewhat untidy, but normal. But inside his head it's something else, ladies and gentlemen. Inside that skull a few circuits have shorted.

'Your file has been referred. There are appointments available . . .' He'd checked the green file. 'This afternoon at 16.30, tomorrow at 09.00, 14.00 . . .'

'This afternoon,' Mat Joubert had said hurriedly.

De Wit had looked up from the file, somewhat surprised, appraisingly. 'We'll arrange it.'

And now he was on his way. Because somewhere in a grey office with a couch for his patients, a bespectacled psychologist had had insight into his file. Had begun setting up the score card of Freud or Jung or whomsoever. What have we here? The death of his wife? Minus twenty. Disciplinary hearing? Minus twenty. And the slump in his work. Minus forty. He could have done something about that. Grand total minus eighty. Bring him in.

'We'll keep an eye on the situation, Captain. See whether the therapy helps.' A covert threat, concealed. But obviously de Wit's trump card.

Perhaps it was a good thing. God knows, his head had been muddled. Had been? Could one really judge the state of your own mind? How normal was he at Macassar when he'd looked at the burnt remains of the three, could hear their voices in his ears? The high, shrill, primal scream which the spirit utters when it reluctantly has to leave the body, the volume intensified by the screaming of flesh in the agony of death by fire, every pain receptor swamped by the intense heat.

Was that normal?

Was it normal to wonder then, for the umpteenth time, whether you shouldn't take the trouble to join the dead? Wasn't it better to have control over the when and the how? Was it wrong to be afraid of that unexpected moment when the mind realised it had a nano second left in the world? Afraid. Terrified.

And now de Wit was holding a sword above his muddled head. Let the psychologist fix the circuitry or . . .

He stopped in front of a tower block on the Foreshore. Sixteenth floor. Dr H Nortier. That was all he knew. He took the lift.

Joubert was pleased that there was no one else in the waiting-room.

It was different to what he'd expected. There was a couch and two chairs, comfortable and attractive, covered in a pink and blue floral. In the centre a coffee table held six magazines, the latest editions of *de Kat, Time, Car, Cosmopolitan, Sarie* and *ADA* magazine. Against a white-painted door which presumably led to the consulting-room,

there was a neat sign which read DR NORTIER WILL
WELCOME YOU SOON. PLEASE MAKE YOURSELF
AT HOME AND ENJOY THE COFFEE. THANK YOU.
The same sign was repeated in Afrikaans. There were water
colours on the other walls – one of cosmos, another of the
fishermen's cottages at Paternoster. In one corner there was
a table with a coffee machine. Next to it stood porcelain
coffee cups and saucers, teaspoons, a jar of powdered milk
and a bowl of sugar.

He poured himself a cup and the filter coffee smelt good.
Was the man a psychiatrist? Psychologists were 'mister', not
'doctor.' Was he so batty that he needed a psychiatrist?

He sat down on the couch, put the cup on the coffee table
and took out his Winstons. He looked for an ashtray. There
were none in the room. Irritation overcame him. How was it
possible for a psychologist not to have an ashtray in his
waiting-room? He returned the pack to his pocket.

He looked at *De Kat*'s cover. A man wearing make-up
adorned it. The front page teaser read NATANIEL – THE
MAN BEHIND THE MASK.

He wanted to smoke. He paged through the magazine.
Nothing in it interested him. The woman on the cover of
Cosmopolitan had big boobs and a big mouth. He picked up
the magazine and flipped through it. He saw a headline.
WHAT HE THINKS ABOUT AT WORK. He flattened
the pages there but realised the doctor could open the door
at any moment. He closed the magazine.

He was dying for a smoke. After all, cigarettes couldn't
harm the mind.

He took out the packet and put a cigarette between his
lips. He took out the lighter and stood up. There must be a
bin somewhere which he could use.

The white door opened. Joubert looked up. A woman
came in. She was small. She smiled and put out her hand.

'Captain Joubert?'

He put out his hand. The lighter was still in it. He drew back his hand and shifted the lighter to his left hand. 'That's right,' he wanted to say but the cigarette was still in his mouth. He blushed, pulled his hand back and removed the cigarette from his mouth putting it into his left hand. He put out his hand again and shook hers.

'There's no ashtray here,' he mumbled, blushing. and felt her hand, small and warm and dry.

She was still smiling. 'It must be the cleaning service. Come in and smoke here,' she said and dropped his hand. She held the white door for him.

'No, please,' he said, indicating that she had to walk in first, self-conscious and uncomfortable after his meaningless remark about the ashtray.

'Thank you.' She went in and he closed the door behind them, aware of her long brown skirt, her white blouse buttoned up to the throat, her brown brooch, a wooden elephant pinned above one of the small breasts. He caught a hint of feminine odour, perfume or her own, noticed her grace, her fragility and an odd beauty which he couldn't identify as yet.

'Do sit down,' she said and walked around the white desk. A tall, slender vase with three pink carnations stood on it. And a white telephone, an A-4 notebook, a small penholder containing a few red and black pencils, a large glass ashtray and a green file. He wondered whether it was his file. Behind her there was a white bookcase which almost filled the wall. It was full of books – paperbacks and hard covers, a neat, colourful, cheerful panel of knowledge and enjoyment.

There was another door in the corner, next to the bookcase. Did the previous patient leave through it?

He sat down on one of the two chairs in front of the desk.

They were television chairs, the adjustable kind, covered in black leather. He wondered whether he should've waited for her to sit down first. She smiled, her hands resting comfortably on the desk in front of her.

'I've never addressed anyone as "captain" in consultation,' she said.

Her voice was very soft as if she was speaking in the strictest confidence, but melodious. He wondered whether psychiatrists were taught to speak like that.

'I'm called Mat.'

'Because of your initials?'

'Yes,' he said, relieved.

'My name is Hanna. I'd be pleased if you called me that.'

'Are you a psychiatrist?' he asked nervously, impulsively.

She shook her head. Her hair was an almost colourless brown, tied back in a plait. The plait was visible with every movement of her head.

'An ordinary psychologist.'

'But you're a doctor?'

She tilted her head, as if she was slightly uncomfortable. 'I have a doctorate in psychology.'

He digested this information.

'May I smoke?'

'Of course.'

He lit the cigarette. It had bent when he'd clutched it in his hand earlier and it drooped sadly between his fingers. He sucked in the smoke and unnecessarily tapped the ash into the ashtray. He kept his eyes on the cigarette, on the ashtray.

'This is only the second week that I've been working with the Police,' she said. 'I've already seen a few people. Some were unhappy because they had to come. I do understand that. It's not pleasant to be forced into something.'

She waited for a reaction, got nothing.

67

'Psychological consultation doesn't mean that there's something wrong with you. Just that you need someone to talk to. Someone between work and home.'

Again she waited. Joubert kept his eyes away from her. Why did it sound like excuses to him? Why did it have to be a woman? It had caught him unawares.

'Your work creates a lot of stress. Every policeman should talk to a psychologist on a regular basis.'

'Was I referred because there's nothing wrong with me?'

'No.'

'Who decided that I had to come?'

'I did.'

He looked at her. Her arms were relaxed, only her hands occasionally made small gestures to punctuate her words. And her voice. He glanced quickly at her face. He saw the line of her jaw, straight and delicate as if it was fragile. He looked away again. She didn't look guilty. Only calm and patient.

'And my OC?'

'OC?'

'My commanding officer.'

'I get a whole pile of files every day from officers who think their men should talk to me. And only I recommend who should come.'

But it was still de Wit who had done the preliminary work. Filled in the forms. Written the motivation.

He became aware of the intensity of her gaze. He stubbed out the cigarette. He folded his arms and looked at her. Her face was serious.

Even more quietly than before she said: 'It's not unnatural to be unhappy about it.'

'Why did you choose me?'

'Why do you think?'

She's clever, he thought. Too clever for me.

He knew he wasn't mad. Or was that precisely what the crazies said? He was there because he was just a little crazy. The Great Predator was on his trail. And that sometimes made him . . .

'Because of my record,' he said resignedly.

She looked at him, a sympathetic half smile on her mouth. Her mouth was small. He saw that she wore no make-up. Her lower lip was a juicy morsel, a natural pale pink.

When she said nothing, he added: 'It's probably necessary.'

'Why do you think it's necessary?' Almost whispering. Only the musicality of her voice made it audible.

Was this the way she worked? You came in, sat down and lanced your own abscess, releasing the pus in front of the good doctor and she disinfected the wound and bandaged it. Where did he have to start? Did she want to know about his childhood? Did she think he'd never heard of Freud? Or should he start with Lara? Or end with Lara? Or with death? What about Yvonne Stoffberg? Do you want to hear the one about the detective and the neighbour's daughter, Doctor? Screamingly funny story . . . Because the detective wants to but doesn't know whether he can.

'Because my work is suffering.' A gutless reply. He knew it. And knew that she also knew it.

She was quiet for a long time. 'Your accent. I'm from Gauteng. It still sounds strange. Did you grow up here?'

He looked down, at his brown shoes which needed polish. He nodded. 'Goodwood.'

'Brothers and sisters?'

Wasn't that in his file as well? 'An older sister.'

'Is she still in the Cape?'

'No. Secunda.'

Now he looked at her when he spoke. He saw the broad

forehead, the big brown eyes, set wide apart, the heavy eyebrows.

'Do you resemble one another?'

'No . . .' He knew he had to say something more. He knew his replies were too brief.

'She . . . looks like my father.'

'And you?'

'Like my mother.' He was shy, uncomfortable. What he wanted to say sounded so commonplace. But he said it: 'Actually I take after my mother's family. Her father, my grandfather, was evidently also big.'

He took a deep breath: 'And clumsy.' He was annoyed because he'd added the last two words. Like a criminal deliberately leaving clues.

'Do you regard yourself as clumsy?' She said it automatically, a reflex, and in an odd way it made him feel better. At least she wasn't in complete control.

'I am.'

'Why do you say that?' More slowly, thoughtful now.

'I always was.' His eyes wandered over the bookshelves but he saw nothing. 'Since I can remember.' The memories dammed up against the dike. He took out a finger to let a few drops through. 'In junior school . . . I always came last in track events . . .' He was unaware of his wry smile. 'It worried me. Not in high school, though.'

'Why did it worry you?'

'My father . . . I wanted to be like him.' He pushed the finger back. The leak was sealed again.

She hesitated for a moment. 'Are your parents still living?'

'No.'

She waited.

'My father died three years ago. Of a heart attack. My mother a year later. He was sixty-one. She was fifty-nine.' He didn't want to remember.

'What did your father do?'

'Policeman. For seventeen years he was the commanding officer of the Goodwood Station.' Joubert could hear the wheels spinning in her head. His father was a policeman. He was a policeman. That meant whatever it meant. But she would be making a mistake.

'I didn't become a cop because my father was one.'

'Oh?'

She was so clever. She had caught him out. But not again. He said nothing. He dug his hand into his jacket pocket looking for his cigarettes. No, it was too soon. He took his hand out, folded his arms across his chest again.

'Was he a good policeman?'

Why this obsession with his father?

'I don't know. Yes. He was of another era. His people – the uniforms, white and brown – were fond of him.'

He hadn't even discussed his father with Lara.

'But I think they were scared of him.'

He had never spoken about his father to Blackie Swart. Or to his mother or his sister. Did he want to talk about him to anyone?

'He had a racial slur for every hue, for every racial classification in the crazy country. The Malay people were not Coloureds to him. He called them hotnots. To their faces. His hotnots. "Come along, my hotnot". And Xhosas and Zulus were not "Blacks". They were Kaffers. Never "my kaffers". Always "bloody kaffers". In his time there were no black constables, only black criminals. More and more as they moved in from the Eastern Cape looking for work. He hated them.'

He saw himself in the black armchair, the big man with the folded arms, bowed head and somewhat untidy hair, the brown jacket and trousers, the unpolished brown shoes, the tie. He heard himself speaking. As if he stood outside his body. Talk, Mat Joubert, talk. That's what she wants. Give her the skeletons. Let her dissect the remains of your life with her learning. Bleed out the filth.

'I also did at first, because he did. Before I started to read and had friends whose parents had different views. And then I simply . . . despised my father, his narrow, simplistic point of view, his useless hate. It was part of a . . . process.'

For a moment it was quiet in the dungeons of his mind. The pain pressed down on his shoulders. He was at his father's grave and he knew he'd hated the man. And no one knew it. But his father had suspected it.

'I hated him . . . Doctor.' He deliberately added her title, creating a distance. She wanted to know. She wanted to hear what specters were wandering about in his head. He would tell her. He would fucking tell her. Before her techniques and her voice and her greater knowledge winkled it out of him . . . 'I hated him because he was what I could never be. And because he resented it and threw it back in my face. He was so strong and . . . fleet-footed. On a Friday evening he would make the brown constables line up in the street behind the station. "Come, my hotnots, the one who reaches the lamp-post before I do, can go fuck this weekend." He was in his fifties and he always beat them. And I was slow. He said I was merely lazy. He said I must play rugby because that would make a man of me. I started swimming. I swam as if my life depended on it. In the water I wasn't big and clumsy and ugly. He said swimming was for girls. "Girls swim. Men play rugby. It gives you balls". He didn't smoke. He said it affected your wind. I started smoking. He didn't read because life was the only book one needed. Reading was for girls. I started reading. He was abusive. To my mother, my sister. I spoke softly to them. He said "hotnot" and "kaffer" and "coolie". I addressed them all as "mister". And then he went and died on me.'

Emotions expanded from the inside, in his chest. His body shook, independently, so that his elbows landed on his knees, his head between his hands. He wondered how she, when he . . .

Suddenly he wanted to tell her about death. The longing to do so spread through him like a fever. He could taste it, the relief. Speak about it, Mat Joubert and you'll be free . . .

He straightened and put his hand in his pocket. He took out the cigarettes. His hands were shaking. He lit one. He knew she would say something to break the silence. It was her job.

'Why did you choose the same career?'

'The detectives were separate from the uniforms at Goodwood. There was a Lieutenant Coombes. He wore a hat, a black hat. And he spoke softly. To everyone. And smoked Mills out of a tin. And always wore a waistcoat and drove a Ford Fairlane. Everyone knew about Coombes. He was mentioned in the newspapers several times, murders he'd solved. We lived next to the Station. I was on the stoep, reading, when he came past from the detectives' office in Voortrekker Road, probably on his way to see my father. He stopped at our gate and looked at me. Out of the blue he said, "You must become a detective". I asked him why. "We need clever people in the Force". Then he left. He never spoke to me again. I don't even know what became of him.'

Joubert killed the cigarette. It was half-smoked.

'My father said no child of his would ever work for the Force. Coombes told me to become a detective. He was everything I wanted my father to be.'

Tell her she's looking in the wrong place. This track leads nowhere. It wasn't his father who'd fucked him up. It was death. The death of Lara Joubert.

'Do you enjoy your work?'

Now you're getting warm, Doctor.

'It's a job. Sometimes it's pleasant, sometimes not.'
'When is it pleasant?'
When death is clothed in dignity, Doctor. Or when it's completely absent.
'Success is pleasant.'
'When is it unpleasant?'
Ding! You've just hit the jackpot, Doctor. But she wouldn't get the prize today.
'When they get away.'
Did she realise that he was hedging? That he was concealing, that he was too frightened now to open the sluice-gates because he'd forgotten how much water had been dammed up behind them?
'How do you relax?'
'I read.' She waited. 'Science fiction, mostly.'
'Is that all?'
'Yes.'
'You live alone?'
'Yes.'
'I haven't been here long,' she said and he noticed her nose – long and slightly pointed. It seemed as if the elements of her face didn't belong together but they formed a beautiful whole which began to fascinate him. Was it her fragility as well? He liked looking at her. And it gave him satisfaction that he found her attractive. Because she didn't know it. That was his advantage. 'And there are many things I still want to arrange. But one thing which is taking shape already is a social group – if one can call it that. Some of the people who consult me . . .'
'No thank you, Doctor.'
'Why not?'
It could hardly be difficult to get a doctorate in psychology. All you had to know was how to turn all remarks into questions. Especially questions which started with 'why.'

'I see enough crazy policemen at work.'

'They're not . . .' Then she smiled, slowly. 'They're not crazy and not all of them are men and not all of them are in the Service.'

He didn't react. Because he'd seen her face before she smiled. You, Doctor, are human like the rest of us.

'I'll let you know about our activities. Then you can decide. But only come along if you want to.'

Ask her whether she is part of this 'social group'. And a part of his head was amazed at his interest. For more than two years sexual urges had only come to him in vaguely remembered dreams in which he had uncomfortable intercourse with faceless women. And the real, living women who came his way were no more than sources of information which allowed him to do his work and go home to shelter between the pages of a book.

And now he had . . . an interest in Doctor Hanna. Well, well, well, Mat Joubert. The small, frail woman with the elusive beauty woke the man in you, the protective urge, the urge to possess.

'I'll think about it.'

9

On his way home he drove past the municipal swimming pool. The supervisor was a Black man.

'You can come and swim in the morning, sir. With the business club. In summer I'm here by half past five.'

'The business club?'

'Businessmen. Last year they asked the Council whether they could swim early in the morning, before work. Work too hard the rest of the day. Then the Council says OK and gives the early birds a name. Business club. From five thirty on weekdays, from six thirty on Saturdays and the seventh is a day of rest. Ninety Rand a season, September to May. You can pay at the cashier, sir. The lockers are twenty Rand extra.'

He fetched his cheque book from the car and paid. Then he walked to the swimming-pool. He stared at the blue water, unaware of the shouting, splashing mass of kids. He smelt the smells and remembered. Then he turned away. At the door he threw the red pack of Winstons into a dustbin.

He stopped at the cafe. The owner knew him and took Winstons off the shelf.

'No,' Joubert said. 'Benson & Hedges. Special Mild.'

At home no envelope had been pushed under the door. He fried himself three eggs. The yolks broke and ran. He ate them on toast. Then he sat down in the living-room with the William Gibson and finished the book.

Before going to bed he dug his swimming trunks out of a

cupboard. He rolled them up in a towel and put it on the chair at the door.

In the past few years he had come to hate weekends.

Saturdays weren't so bad because then Mrs. Emily Nofomela, his Xhosa cleaning lady, came in and the sounds of the washing-machine, clattering dishes and vacuum cleaner replaced the deathly silence of the house.

To be on duty also helped because it kept the boredom and the aimlessness of the weekend at bay.

When the alarm went off at a quarter past six, he got up purposefully, without realising that it was a milestone.

He was the only member of the business club who was utilising the Saturday morning. The change rooms were quiet and empty and he could hear the big pump of the swimming-pool outside. He pulled on his Speedo and realised it had become too small. He would have to buy a new one that morning. He walked out to the pool through the footbath and the smells and sounds released memories, fragments from his youth and it felt good to be back again.

The water stretched smoothly ahead of him. He dived in and started swimming, freestyle. It took exactly thirty meters to exhaust him.

An older, more experienced policeman would have bundled Hercules Jantjies out of the front door of the station, more like than not assisted by a hefty kick in the backside.

The problem was that vagrants often came in on a Saturday morning to complain about the joys and sorrows of their co-oppressed after the drunken bouts of the Friday evening. And if you had worked at the Newlands charge office for long enough, you eventually came to the conclusion that the best solution was to get rid of the appalling smell and the verbal assault on your ears which generally made no sense.

But the white constable's uniform was crisp and new, his enthusiasm still fuelled by the College lecturer who had said that the Police served everyone in South Africa.

He forced himself not to move away instinctively from the odour of an unwashed body and recycled methylated spirits and looked straight at Hercules Jantjies – at the small, brown eyes which skittered all over the place, the bluish-red of the skin which showed millions of tiny cracks inflicted by life, the toothless mouth, the stubble of beard.

'Can I help you?'

Hercules Jantjies stuck out his hand from under the worn, faded jacket. It held a piece of newspaper. He put it down on the table and smoothed it with a dirty hand. The constable saw that it was a front page of the *Cape Times*, a few days old. The headline read **Mafia Killing?** in large letters. Hercules Jantjies pressed a forefinger on the letters.

'Your honour, I came about this thing.'

The constable didn't grasp the import. 'Yes?'

'I want to give evidence, your honour.'

'Yes?'

'Cause why, I was there.'

'When it happened?'

'Just so, your honour, just so. An eyewitness report. But I want police protection.'

He hung onto the side of the swimming-pool. He was breathing heavily and his lungs were burning. A deep fatigue invaded his limbs and his heart was a rapidly pulsing worry in his chest. He had completed two lengths. He heard a voice and lifted his head, his mouth still open to gulp in air more quickly.

'Sir, inside there's a beeper which is beeping terribly.' It was the supervisor. He looked worried.

'I'm coming,' said Joubert and pressed his hands down on the edge to haul himself out of the water. He came halfway and then lay there, half in and half out of the water, too tired to make another effort.

'Are you awright, sir?'

'I don't know,' said Joubert, surprised at the deterioration of his body. 'I honestly don't know.'

Hercules Jantjies had the total attention of the three senior policemen in the office of the Newlands commanding officer, Adjutant Radie Donaldson. Joubert and Donaldson sat against the one wall on old brown wooden chairs, Benny Griessel leant against the wall. Jantjies was a reeking island against the other wall.

Donaldson still belonged to the old school of crime fighters who tackled all potential breakers of the law without kid gloves, irrespective of race, colour or political persuasion. That's why he directed a warning finger at Hercules Jantjies and said: 'If you're talking shit, you're dead.' Then, more suspiciously: 'Are you pissed?'

'Your honour, your honour,' Jantjies said nervously as though the moment had become greater than he'd anticipated.

'These men are from Murder and Robbery. They'll cut your balls off if you talk shit. Understand me?'

'Yes, your honour.'

His brown eyes glanced at the three policemen, his head slightly bowed. 'I saw the whole thing, your honour. But I want police protection.'

'If you're not careful you'll get police brutality,' Donaldson said.

'I was lying in the bushes, your honour, between the parking and Main Road.'

'Were you pissed?'

'No, just tired, your honour.'

'And then?'

'Then I saw her appear, your honour.'

'Her?'

'The one with the gun, your honour.'

'And then?'

'And she waited in the shadow and then the deceased came, God rest his soul and he saw her and he got a fright and he put up his hand, your honour. But she shot him and he dropped like a stone.'

'And then?'

'Then it was all over, your honour.'

'Where did the murderer go then?'

'No, then she jus' disappeared.'

'A woman? Do you mean to tell me it was a woman?'

'Not jus' an ordinary woman, your honour.'

'What do you mean?'

'It was the angel of death, your honour.'

Silence reigned in the office.

'Cause why I'm looking for police protection, your honour. Because now she's coming to fetch me.'

'What did she look like?' Joubert asked but his voice betrayed his disappointment.

'This long, black cloak, like Batman. And black boots and black hair. The angel of death. She came to me last night and she called me, like this, with her finger. Your honour, I know my rights in the new South Africa. I want police protection.'

Each and every cop knew the visions induced by Blue Train, not from first hand experience but from countless previous witnesses and accused. Despite the signs, they had remained hopeful up to now.

'Bastard!' said Donaldson and went straight for Hercules

81

Jantjies. Joubert stopped the station commander in the nick of time.

Early on Sunday morning Lieutenant Leon Petersen phoned. 'I think I have the fuckers who raped the girl, Captain. In Mitchell's Plain. But it's a gang thing. Fourteen of them. And they're not talking.'

Joubert drove there to help with the interrogation, compare alibis. Hours of listening to lies, sparring with teenage bravado and blatant provocation. But at 17:22 Lieutenant Petersen's patience eventually ran out. In interrogation room number two of the Mitchells Plain station he lost his temper and hit the youngest gang member on the nose and eye with his clenched fist. Blood spurted onto the table.

The brown child started sobbing. 'My ma's going to kill me, my ma's going to kill me,' he wept and began an admission which slowly bubbled up like a pot boiling over. In the corner Constable Gerrit Snyman sat with his notebook, scribbling as fast as he could.

10

'Twenty-three fucking kilograms, Mat. He's got rocks in his head. Do you know what he said to me? I've got six months for every five kilos. He's fucking crazy.' Captain Gerbrand Vos's red cheeks were scarlet with indignation. Joubert merely shook his head sympathetically. He was still waiting for his physical health session with de Wit.

'Jesus, Mat, I've always been heavy. It's part of me. How can a skeleton be a cop? Can you imagine it? In any case, fuck de Wit. He can't enforce it.'

Joubert smiled. 'He can, Gerry.'

'No way.'

'Police regulations. OC must see to it that all his people are fit and well at all times, and ready for action. Black on white. You can check it.'

Vos was quiet for a moment. 'We're Murder and Robbery, Mat, not a bunch of constables in a show-off unit. How fit must one be? I won't be able to run the Comrades but hell . . .'

Joubert remembered his swimming session of a few hours ago. It was no better than Saturday's: the stitch in his side after fifty meters of slow freestyle, the cigarette tar in his lungs which seemed to catch fire. After a hundred meters he'd clung to the side again, gasping for breath. He said nothing.

'Twenty-three fucking kilograms. I'll have to have my lips sewn together.'

*   *   *

He shuffled through the door of Premier Bank's branch in the Heerengracht. Slow, deliberate steps, the walking-stick tightly grasped in the left hand, the eyes fixed in deep concentration a metre beyond his feet. The wrinkles around his eyes and mouth were multiple, the contours of age.

He moved to the counter where the forms were kept, put his hand into an inner pocket and slowly and patiently took out a spectacle case. His hands trembled slightly when he opened the flap and unfolded a pair of black-framed reading glasses. He perched them on his nose. The hand went slowly back to the pocket and extracted a fountain pen.

He unscrewed the top, reached out a careful hand and picked up a withdrawal slip. With an uncertain hand he wrote letters and figures in the columns on the white paper with its mauve strip at the top.

When he'd finished, the fountain pen's top was replaced and carefully returned to the inner pocket. The glasses were folded, put into the case, the trembling hand returning it to the pocket. The right hand took the slip, the left hand the walking-stick. He began the weary walk to the cashier.

The Heerengracht branch of Premier Bank was not its largest. But to compete with all the other banks in the immediate vicinity, this branch was a flawless example of Premier's corporate identity; mauve carpets, wooden furniture painted pale grey, white walls decorated with advertising posters.

Joyce Odendaal's uniform was equally correct – a mauve jacket and skirt (trousers in winter) a white blouse with a frilled collar and a silver brooch which represented the logo – a sans serif PB. Joyce was twenty-two, attractive and the cashier of the month.

She saw the old man's jerky walk, the brown suit from another era, the gold watch chain which stretched from the waistcoat to the trouser pocket, the tie which the rheumatic hands hadn't been able to knot properly.

She sighed. She didn't like old people. They were deaf and stubborn and checked each transaction as if it was the bank's intention to cheat them. And they often made an unnecessary fuss about the smallest little mistake.

Nevertheless her 'Good morning, sir,' was friendly and she smiled. There was a slight gap between Joyce's front teeth. She saw the food stains on the tie and waistcoat and was grateful that she wouldn't have to watch him eating.

'Good morning, sweetheart,' he said and she thought that the voice sounded youthful. And the blue eyes set among the wrinkles also looked young.

'What can we do for you this morning?'

'A girl like you can help a man like me with many things,' he said in his youthful voice, 'But let's concentrate on what's possible right now.'

Joyce Odendaal's smile didn't waver for a second because she had no idea what he was talking about.

'Get one of those large money bags and fill it with fifty Rand notes. I've got a big, old revolver under my jacket which I don't want to use. You have such an attractive branch here.'

He opened his jacket to show her the weapon.

'Sir?' said Joyce, the smile uncertain.

'Come on, sweetheart, keep your foot off the alarm and let's get on with it. This old man is in a hurry.' He smiled. Joyce's right hand moved slowly towards her face. A forefinger slowly rubbed the skin under nose, her mouth by now agape. Then her hand started shaking. She lowered it again. The alarm button was four centimeters from her foot.

'What perfume do you use?' the elderly man asked in a calm, interested voice.

'You're the Fire,' she said without thinking and took a money bag. She opened her cash drawer and began taking out notes.

Joubert came back from the bank robbery and had to run to pick up the telephone in his office.

'Hold on for Dr Perold, please.'

He waited.

'Captain?'

'Doctor?'

'I don't have good news, Captain.'

Joubert's stomach muscles contracted. He wondered whether the doctor was staring at the telephone now with eyes narrowed over his reading glasses. Joubert waited.

'Your cholesterol, Captain. I sent the report to your commanding officer but I want to speak to you as well.'

'Yes.'

'It's high, Captain. Very high.'

'Is that bad?'

The doctor made a curious sound at the other end. 'That's an acceptable description of your condition, Captain. Combined with the smoking, the excessive weight and the family history, yes, I would describe it as bad.'

Should he tell the doctor that he had begun swimming on Saturday mornings?

'We must put you on medication. And a diet. Immediately.'

Joubert sighed. 'What must I do?'

He bought a collection of short stories, *The 1990 Hugo Award Winners* and a novel by Spider Robinson, strongly recommended by Willy. Children were playing cricket in the street in front of his house. He had to wait until they moved the cardboard box which served as wickets before he could get into his driveway.

The morning's swim had given him an appetite. There was a lonely tin of baked beans in tomato sauce in a corner of the cupboard,. He wondered whether it was bad for cholesterol. Tomorrow the dietician would be able to tell him. He took a Castle from the fridge. He had read somewhere that beer was full of healthy vitamins and minerals. He unscrewed the top, took the plastic holder with the cholesterol pills out his jacket pocket, put a pill on his tongue and swallowed it with a swig of beer. The beer was cold and made him shudder slightly. He walked to the living-room. He sat down and lit a Special Mild. The cigarette didn't satisfy him. Maybe he should go back to Winstons, only smoke less. Or did smoke also have an effect on cholesterol? He dragged deeply at the cigarette but it made no difference. He opened the paperback at the first story by Isaac Asimov.

There was a knock at the front door.

Joubert put the beer behind his chair and got up. He opened the front door.

Jerry Stoffberg stood on the stoep. And behind him Yvonne hovered.

'Evening, Mat.' Stoffberg wasn't as cheerful as usual.

Joubert knew why Stoffberg was there and he felt pressure building in his chest and for a moment wondered whether this was the first sign of a heart attack.

'Hello, Stoffs,' he said, his voice strained.

'May we come in, Mat?'

'Of course.' Joubert held the door for them. He noticed that the girl wouldn't meet his eyes and he knew what he had to say to Stoffberg. Nothing had happened. Stoffberg had to realise that. Up to that moment nothing had happened – yet.

They walked to the living-room in silence. Joubert's cigarette was still smoking in the ashtray.

'Do sit down,' he said but Stoffberg was already seated on the couch. His daughter sat down next to him as if she needed support. Joubert swallowed. The pressure in his chest increased.

'Mat, I'm sorry to bother you but an unfortunate thing has happened in our family.'

'Nothing happened,' said Joubert apprehensively and heavily swallowed the excess saliva in his mouth.

'Sorry?' Stoffberg obviously didn't understand. Joubert saw Yvonne frowning angrily at him.

'My sister's brother-in-law died last night. In Benoni. Heart attack. At thirty-eight. In the prime of life. Tragic.' He looked at Joubert's cigarette in the ashtray. 'He also smoked heavily, you know.'

A light went up for Joubert. For the first time he understood Stoffberg's attitude. It was the man's professional face. The undertaker on duty. The pressure in Joubert's chest disappeared.

'I'm sorry to hear that.' Yvonne's frown vanished.

'They want me to bury him, Mat.' Stoffberg was quiet for a moment. Joubert didn't know what to say. 'It's a great honour for me. Not a pleasant task. But an honour. The funeral is next Wednesday. But we have a problem. I need your help, Mat.'

'I'll do anything I can, Jerry,' he said feelingly.

'You see, Bonnie starts at the Technikon on Wednesday.' Stoffberg put his arm around his daughter and looked proudly at her. His voice lost some its gravity. 'Ja, Mat, pa's baby has grown up. She's going to study public relations.' Yvonne Stoffberg turned her face into her father's shoulder like a little girl and smiled sweetly at Joubert.

Stoffberg's voice regained its professionalism. 'She can't go with us, Mat. And all her friends are still on holiday. I can probably ask Mrs. Pretorius on the corner if she can stay with her but that redheaded son of hers . . .'

Stoffberg pressed the palms of his hands together in a pleading gesture. 'Then Bonnie suggested we come over and ask you whether she can stay here, Mat.'

He didn't realise immediately what Stoffberg was saying because he was considering the irony of Stoffberg's apprehension about the redheaded boy. Stoffberg interpreted the silence as hesitation.

'You're the only one we can trust, Mat. After all, you're a policeman. And it's only for a week. Bonnie said she could cook for you and keep house. And stay out of your way. It's only in the evenings, really. During the day she'll be at home. I'd really appreciate it, Mat.'

'Hell, Jerry . . .'

'Tell Uncle Mat you won't be in his way, Bonnie.'

She said nothing. She merely smiled sweetly.

Joubert knew what his reply was going to be. But he fought for his integrity.

'I often work at night, Jerry . . .'

Stoffberg nodded in grave agreement. 'I understand, Mat. But she's quite grown up, after all.'

Joubert could think of no other excuse. 'When are you leaving, Jerry? I'll have to give her a key.'

'Tomorrow morning,' Yvonne Stoffberg spoke for the first time, her eyes chastely fixed on the carpet.

He gave her a brief glance, saw her looking up quickly and smiling at him. He looked back at Jerry Stoffberg but avoided the man's eyes.

11

The water was as smooth as glass. Again he was the only member of the business club swimming that morning. He dived in and began with a breaststroke, slowly. He was looking for his rhythm. He didn't know whether he would ever find that old rhythm again. It was too many Winstons and Castles ago. A lifetime.

He tired more easily than on the previous two occasions. At least he had an excuse, he thought. A night of tossing and turning. Of wrestling with his conscience, caught between desire and a heavy feeling of guilt.

With his head on the pillow he could hear the beat of his heart. An increased rate. He had risen, sometime after one, and fetched the poem in the spare bedroom, under the William Gibson on a pile of paperbacks.

Taste me, touch me, take me . . .

He had to lie on his back and concentrate on other things. His work. De Wit. What was de Wit's agenda? Eventually sleep had overtaken him.

But he felt the tiredness in the morning. After two lengths of breaststroke he was finished.

De Wit came to Joubert's office, a green file in his hand. Joubert was on the phone to Pretoria.

De Wit knocked on the doorpost and waited outside. Joubert wondered why he didn't come in but finished his call. Then de Wit walked in. He had a smile on his face again. Uncomfortable, Joubert stood up.

'Sit down, Captain. I don't want to keep you from your work. Is Pretoria giving you problems?'

'No, Colonel. I . . . They haven't sent the ballistics report yet. About the Tokarev. I was chasing them.'

'May I sit down?'

'Of course, Colonel.' Why didn't he simply sit down?

'I want to discuss your physical health today, Captain.' Joubert understood the smile. It was one of triumph, he realised.

De Wit opened the green file. 'I've received your medical report.' He looked Joubert in the eye. 'Captain, there are the matters here you have to solve for yourself. I have no right to speak to you about your high cholesterol or your smoking habits. But I have the right to discuss your fitness. This report states that you're fifteen kilograms overweight. You don't have as many problems as some of your colleagues but it's still fifteen kilos too many. And the doctor considers you to be seriously unfit.'

De Wit closed the green file.

'I don't want to be unreasonable. The doctor says five kilograms every six months is not unreasonable. Shall we give you until this time next year, Captain? To monitor the progress? What do you think?'

Joubert was annoyed by the man's superior tone of voice, by his attitude of feigned friendliness. 'We can make it six months, Colonel.'

Because de Wit didn't know he had started swimming again. Joubert experienced a feeling of purpose. The long muscles of his legs and arms were pleasantly tired after the morning's swim. He knew he could keep it up. He would rub old Two Nose's face in it.

'We can make it six months. Definitely.'

De Wit was still wearing the small smile, almost a grimace. 'It's your choice, Captain. I'm impressed by your determination. We'll make a note of it.'

He opened the green file again.

The day took on its usual shape. He drove out to Crossroads. The mutilated body of a baby. Ritual murder. The radio on his hip scratched and buzzed and called him to Simons Town. The owner of a shop selling military artefacts had been shot with an AK. The splashes of blood and brains looked depressingly apt on an American Army steel helmet, a Japanese officer's sword and a captain's cap from a sunken U-boat.

In the afternoon he was five minutes late for his appointment with the dietician. He stopped in the parking area of the clinic. The woman was waiting for him.

She wasn't pretty but she was thin. Her fair hair curled about her head but her nose was crooked, her mouth small and humourless.

She shook her head in disbelief when Joubert told her about his eating habits. She used flash cards and posters to explain about fatty acids – saturated and unsaturated – about fibre and bran, animal fats and vegetable fats, calories, vitamins, minerals and balance.

He shook his head and said that he lived alone. His stomach contracted when he thought about Yvonne Stoffberg who would be waiting in his house that evening but he told the dietician that he couldn't cook, that he didn't have the time to maintain a healthy diet.

She asked him whether he had the time for a heart attack. She asked whether he realised what his cholesterol count meant. She asked how much time it would take to stop at a vegetable market, to put some fruit in his attaché case every morning.

Detectives don't carry attaché cases, he wanted to say but didn't. He admitted that it wouldn't be difficult.

And sandwiches? she asked. How much time did it take to wrap a whole-wheat sandwich in foil for the following day? And to swallow a plate of bran with skim milk in the morning? And to buy artificial sweeteners for all the tea and coffee in the office? How much time could it take?

Not much, he admitted.

Well, then, she said, we can start working. She took out a form which read THE DIET OF . . .

Her pen poised above the open space, she was the epitome of efficiency. 'First name?'

Joubert sighed. 'Mat.'

'What?'

The entrance hall of the Bellville South Murder and Robbery Squad had an area where visitors could wait. The walls were bare, the floor was covered with cold grey tiles and the chairs were civil service issue, made to last and not necessarily for comfort.

Those who waited there were the family, friends and relatives of murder or robbery suspects. So why offer such people comfort and amusement in a waiting area? After all, they were probably blood relatives of suspected criminals. This might well have been the thinking of the architects and administrators when the plans were being discussed.

But Mrs. Mavis Petersen didn't agree. The entrance hall was part of her kingdom, adjacent to the reception desk where she held sway. She was a Malay woman, slender and attractive and a beautiful shade of light brown. And she knew the pain of a criminal's nearest and dearest. That's why there were flowers on the reception desk of the Murder and Robbery building every day of the week. And a smile on her face.

But not now.

'Adjutant Griessel is missing,' she said when Joubert

came in and walked to the steel gate which gave access to the rest of the building.

'Missing?'

'He didn't come in this morning, Captain. We phoned but there was no reply. I sent two constables from the station in the van, but his house is locked.'

'His wife?'

'She says she hasn't seen him for weeks. And if we find him we might as well ask him where the alimony cheques are.'

Joubert thought it over, his fingers drumming on the desk.

Mavis's voice was suddenly low, disapproving. 'The Colonel says we don't have to look for him. He says it's Adjutant Griessels's way of answering him.'

Joubert said nothing.

'He's very different to Colonel Theal, hey Captain?' Her words were an invitation to form an alliance.

'Very different, Mavis. Are there any messages for me?'

'Nothing, Captain.'

'I'm going to try the Outspan. That's where we found him the previous time. And then I'm going home. Tell radio I want to know immediately if they hear anything about Benny.'

'Very well, Captain.'

Joubert walked out.

'Such authority,' Mavis said with raised eyebrows to the empty entrance hall.

The Outspan Hotel was in Voortrekker Road between Bellville and Stikland, an hotel which had acquired its one star under another management.

Joubert showed his plastic identity card and asked for the register. Only two rooms were occupied, neither by a Griessel. He walked to the bar, a dark room with a low ceiling and sombrely panelled in wood.

The first early evening clients were already leaning against the long bar counter, singly, uncomfortable, un-camouflaged by the anonymity conferred by numbers.

The smell rose in Joubert's nostrils. Liquor and tobacco, wood and people, cleaning materials and furniture polish – decades of it. It reached a tentacle deep into his memory and brought forgotten images to the surface: he, aged nine, ten, eleven was sent to call his father. Ten o'clock at night. The bar was filled with people and smoke and heat and voices. His father sat in a corner surrounded by faces. His father was arm wrestling against a big man with a red face. His pa was playing with the guy.

'Ahhh, my son's here. Sorry Henry, I can't look bad in front of him,' and his father pushed the man's arm down flat on the wooden table. The faces laughed amiably, full of admiration for the strong man, the keeper of law and order in Goodwood.

'Come on, Mat, let me teach you.' He sat down opposite his father, shy and proud.

Their hands clasped. His father acted, pretended that his son could easily beat him.

Again the onlookers laughed loudly.

'One day he'll really beat you, Joop.'

'Not if he jacks off too much.'

Joubert sat down at the Outspan's bar counter and remembered how he'd blushed, how embarrassment had overcome him. Did he have to tell Dr Hanna Nortier about that as well? Would it help?

Reluctantly the barman got up.

'Castle, please.'

The man served him with the smooth expertise acquired over years of experience.

'Three Rand.'

'I'm looking for Benny Griessel.'

The barman took his money.

'Who're you?'

'Colleague.'

'Where's your paper?'

Joubert showed the card again.

'He was here last night. Couldn't go home. I put him in the tank. I went to have a look after lunch and he'd gone.'

'Where does he usually go from here?'

'How should I know?'

Joubert poured his beer into the glass. The barman interpreted this as a signal and returned to his chair in the corner.

The beer tasted good, round and full. He wondered whether it had something to do with the surroundings. He lit a Special Mild. Would he ever get used to the mildness?

He knew he was hiding.

He smiled into the glass in his hand at the admission: he was looking for Benny in the bar – and he was looking for courage in the beer. Because there was a young body at home and he no longer knew whether he was capable.

He lifted the glass and emptied it. He put it down hard on the counter to attract the barman's attention.

'Another one?' Without enthusiasm.

'Just one. Then I have to go.'

12

He used his elbow to push open the door because he was carrying two large shopping bags – apples, pears, peaches, apricots, All Bran, oatmeal, skinless chicken, fat-free beef, skim milk, hake fillets, lowfat yoghurt, tins of tuna, dried fruit.

He could smell that she was there.

His house was filled with the heavy odour of roasting lamb. And other smells. Green beans? Garlic? And a baked pudding?

He heard the music.

'Hello?'

Her voice came from the kitchen. 'Here.'

He walked down the passage. She came out of the kitchen. She had a spoon in her hand. He saw the mini skirt, the lithe, beautiful legs, the high-heeled shoes. The other hand was on her hip, the hip angled. Her breasts were barely covered. Her stomach was bare and firm, pale flesh in the light of the late afternoon. Her hair had been brushed until it shone, her face was heavily made up.

Femme fatale of the kitchen. He recognised it in a flash as the theatrical flight of fancy of an eighteen-year-old. His embarrassment mingled with the knowledge that it was all for him. He could feel the beat of his heart.

'Hi,' she said, the voice of a hundred Hollywood heroines.

'I didn't . . . know that you . . . cook . . .' He lifted the bags in his hands.

'There are lots of things about me that you don't know, Mat.'

He simply stood there, a stranger in his own home.

'Come.' She disappeared into the kitchen. He followed her. The taste of the night was in his mouth.

Her portable radio and cassette player stood on the windowsill. It was turned to a local music station. She stood at the kitchen table. 'You're in the newspaper.'

He put the bags down on the table and looked at *The Argus* lying there.

'You're famous.'

He couldn't look at her. He picked up the newspaper. Lower down on the front page there was a headline DON CHAMELEON STRIKES AGAIN. He read:

As a blonde, middle-aged playboy, he escaped with R7 000 from Premier Bank's Bellville branch earlier this week. Yesterday he was a little, old man walking away with R15 000 from their offices in the Heerengracht.

But police have little doubt that it was the same man, because of curious similarities – the Chameleon was the epitome of charm, calling the tellers 'sweetheart' and asking them what perfume they wore.

According to police spokesman Lieut. John Cloete, one of the only clues they have so far is video footage of the second robbery, taken by a hidden bank camera.

'But it is obvious that the perpetrator is heavily disguised. There is little chance that anyone will be able to identify him from the video.'

Lieut. Cloete said one of the Peninsula's top detectives, Murder and Robbery Squad Captain Matt Joubert, had personally taken charge of the case.

Joubert stopped reading, replaced the paper on the table and sighed. He would have to phone Cloete. *One of the Peninsula's top detectives* . . . How would they know?

Couldn't even spell his name correctly. And de Wit wouldn't like it at all.

Yvonne had poured him a Castle while he was reading. She handed it to him, her slender hands and scarlet nails etched against the amber fluid.

'You're one behind.'

'Thanks.' He still avoided looking at her. He took the beer.

'I'm going to spoil you.' Suddenly she was next to him, against him. Her hands slid under his jacket, pulled him closer. She raised her face, offered her mouth.

'Say thank you,' she said. He kissed her. His one hand held the beer, the other touched the bare part of her back and he tightened his hold. She flowed against him like quicksilver. Her mouth tasted of beer and spices and he was astonished by the heat of her tongue. Her hands were behind his back, pulling up his shirt and sliding under the material to stroke his skin. Joubert was desperate to feel his hardness against her. He pushed the lower part of his body forward. She felt it and rubbed her stomach against him. His mind was in a whirl, his heart a lift – on its way up. But down there, where it mattered, was nothing.

'The food,' she said and fluttered her tongue over his lips. 'It'll burn.' She dug her pelvis hard into him, a serious promise. Her hands tucked his shirt in again, her body flowed away. She was slightly breathless.

He remained at the table, deserted and uncomfortable.

'I'm going to surprise you. But it's all a big secret. You must wait in the living-room. That's why I brought the newspaper.' Her voice had lost some of the theatrical intonation, held a measure of uncertainty now. She stretched out an arm to the windowsill and he saw her picking up a packet of cigarettes. She opened it and offered him one. Winstons. He hesitated for a moment, then took one. She extracted another one with her long red nails and put it in her mouth. Her lipstick was smudged.

He dug into his pocket, found the lighter, lit her cigarette and then his own. She deftly took a deep drag, blew a thin jet of smoke towards the ceiling, came to him and gave him a quick kiss on the cheek.

'Into the living-room with you.' Her voice had deepened again and the self-confidence had returned.

He smiled awkwardly, took the newspaper and the beer and walked to the living-room. He opened the newspaper, swallowed a mouthful of beer and dragged deeply on the Winston. It filled him with a deep satisfaction.

He hadn't known that she smoked. For some reason or another it made her even more exciting.

He stared at the newspaper. He felt her skin under his hand. Dear God, that youthfulness. Firm. firm, firm. He could feel the long muscles move when her hands were busy behind his back. And her pelvis rubbing against him.

He forced himself to read. Her heard her pottering about. She sang along with a rock number. Later she brought him another beer. 'You mustn't fall behind.' He assumed she was also drinking in the kitchen. 'I've almost done. When I call you must come.'

More activity in the kitchen, then a long stretch of quiet.

'Mat.'

'Yes.'

'Switch off the light. Then come here.'

He swallowed the last of his beer, folded the newspaper. He switched off the living-room light. There was a soft glow in the dining-room. He walked down the passage and entered the room.

Candles in two tall holders lit the table. There was a vase with flowers, two slender crystal glasses which reflected the candlelight, gleaming silver on the table, a silver ice bucket from which the neck of a bottle protruded.

She sat at the other end of the table. Her hair was piled high on her head. Large gold hoops dangled from her ears. Her scarlet mouth wore a small smile. Her slender neck, her shoulders, her arms and most of her breasts glowed rosily in the circle of light. The black dress glistened and clung. She rose with grace. He saw that her dress hung down to her ankles. She wore two thin gold bangles around her wrist. She walked to a chair at the top of the table and pulled it back. Her hip angled. A leg, the colour of ivory, slid out of the black.

'Please sit down, Mat.' She and the table were a picture out of a woman's magazine. It took his breath away.

'It . . . You look beautiful.'

'Thank you.'

He walked slowly to the chair. Had the beer caused the light-headedness? Before he could sit down she helped him take off his jacket.

'You can open the champagne.' She leant back, pressed a button on her cassette player. Soft music filled the room.

He reached for the bottle, pulled off the foil, unwound the wire and wiggled the cork.

'You've got big hands. Strong.'

The cork shot out. He poured sparkling wine into her glass. His hand shook and the foam overflowed the rim, spilling onto the white tablecloth.

'Sorry.' She giggled.

'To our first evening, Mat.' The glasses sang a high note as they touched. They drank.

'There's more champagne in the fridge. Have some more.' She emptied her glass and held it out to him to be refilled. He obeyed. They drank again. She dished up. Leg of lamb, rice, a rich brown gravy, baked potatoes, green beans with mushrooms and cream, cauliflower cheese.

'It looks . . . I didn't know you liked to cook.'

'Ag, it's just from a recipe book. I hope you like everything.'

'Everything,' he said. Tonight would be a farewell to all the wrong kinds of food. Tomorrow he'd speak to Yvonne about his diet.

'What did you think of my poem?'

'I . . . liked it very much.'

'Mr. Venter said I should do more writing. He was my English teacher last year. I showed him all my poems.'

'This one as well?'

'No, silly, of course not. Pour me some more champagne.'

They ate. Silence.

Then: 'I've been in love with you for more than a year, Mat.'

He swallowed some champagne.

'But I want you to know it's not because of being sorry about your wife.'

He took another swallow.

'There were a few guys in my class who were interested. Ginger Pretorius already has a job . . . His bike is very sexy and all that but he's so adolescent.'

She looked at him, unfocused. 'Didn't you suspect? Every time my parents invited you, I was there as well. I felt as if you didn't see me. I had to do something. Didn't you see?'

'No.'

'They say the time is over for women to simply sit around waiting. If I hadn't done something, we would still have been secretly in love. Are you pleased that I did something?'

'Yes.' There was a befogged window between Mat Joubert and reality.

'Tell me how you felt, that evening. Was I too aggressive? They say some men like it. Did you like it, Mat, hey did you?'

'Yes.' He looked at her, at the teeth so white in the candlelight, at her red lips, at the deep valley between her breasts where the black dress had shifted.

'For me it was a fucking rave.' She looked at him, saw his eyes on her breasts. 'Does it bother you if I swear, Mat?'

'No.'

'Do you like it?'

He listened to a single beat of his heart.

'Yes.'

She pushed her plate away, leant towards him. The top of the black dress unfolded like a petal. He could see the pink circle of one of her nipples.

'What else would you like, Mat?'

He slid his eyes away from the nipple, over her creamy neck up to her mouth, now half open. Her teeth shone. He wanted to tell her what he would like. His courage failed him. He swallowed more champagne, also pushed his plate away.

'A Winston.' He smiled ruefully.

She smiled back as if she'd heard the words but hadn't caught their meaning. She leant over and found the packet behind the radio. He lit cigarettes for both of them. She blew the smoke at the candles which flickered. He saw the nipple was now completely bare. Was she aware of it?

'Do you remember that I said everything was going to be a surprise?' He heard the faint slurring of some of her words and realised that she was drunk. For some or other reason this made his stomach muscles contract.

'Yes.' You're not completely sober either, Mat Joubert.

'Well, this evening you're getting the first course after the main course, Mat Joubert.' She got up slowly and moved

105

towards him. She sank down on his lap, her hands around his neck, the cigarette burning between her fingers. He put his cigarette in the plate on the table and placed the palms of his hands against her back, searching for the firm muscles of youth.

She kissed him in slow motion. Her mouth and tongue slid slowly over and into his mouth, like honey. His hand moved inch by inch towards her breast. His thumb and forefinger searched for the nipple. He felt it harden. He pressed his palm more strongly against the fullness. It was softer than he had expected.

She groaned. Her hand dropped, pressed against his abdomen, moved up, unloosened his tie, unbuttoned his shirt. Her tongue licked a line of fire across his chest, her teeth danced across his nipple. Suddenly he had an overwhelming need. He forced her throat back and dropped his lips to her breast. He sucked it into his mouth until it filled him from tongue to palate, the skin smooth and supple. He teased her with his tongue and she grew again, moaned, her hand between his legs again. He pushed his own hand to her leg, felt the strength of her muscles and visualised the pleasure that was waiting. He sighed shudderingly and moved his hand slowly to the centre of his interest. Her legs opened, her mouth on his again. He expected panties there but found none, only wetness. His fingers slid inside. She groaned and sucked his tongue.

And suddenly he was ready, a machine rescued from rust. The swelling in his groin changed to a rock hard erection, a fiery soldier on parade.

She pulled his hand away from her heat. 'This,' she said, and the hoarseness was real, 'is dessert.' She gave him a quick kiss and moved to her own chair with difficulty. She held her glass for more champagne. Her hair had come loose. She dragged deeply on the cigarette.

'I've never met anyone like you, Mat.' Her breast was still
bare. And he speculated about her experience, the fact that
this wasn't her first time. About the fact that she excited
him. About the fact that he was a vehicle for the achieve-
ment of a fantasy. But he didn't want to speculate any
longer. His heart leapt at the pressure in his trousers. The
bottle was empty. He got up, walked unsteadily to the
kitchen and fetched another one. When he came back
she was still sitting in the same position, elbows on the
table, cigarette between her fingers, the nipple almost
touching the tablecloth. He poured for them both.

'Were you shocked because I wasn't wearing anything.
Down there?'

'No.'

'I had nothing on below the mini this afternoon. It made
me so randy . . .'

She took a last puff of her cigarette, killed it. 'Does it
make you randy too?' Her hand dropped to her breast. Her
fingers quietly stroked the nipple.

'No one has ever made me so randy in my life,' he said
and knew that just for that moment it was true.

She put her hand on his and suddenly said softly: 'I'm so
pleased.'

She remembered: 'You must take the candles to the
living-room. That's where you're getting your dessert.'
She put Joubert's finger in her mouth, sucked it gently.
'Two kinds,' she said and smiled seductively but the alcohol
undermined the effectiveness. He didn't notice it.

He sat.

'Get up. I'll come in a second.' There was a momentary
silence then she giggled at the play on words. 'Take the
champagne, too.'

He got up.

'First fill my glass.' He obeyed, then took his own glass,

the bottle of champagne and the packet of Winstons to the living-room. When he came back for the candlesticks, she wasn't there. He carried the candles and saw that his shirt was unbuttoned down to his navel. He sat down on the carpet. He was filled with satisfaction, anticipation. In his imagination his finger slid into her again.

He heard someone knocking at the front door.

He couldn't believe it. The knock came again, more softly. A feeling of unreality came over him as if it was all part of a strange dream. He got up, uncertainly, and unlocked the front door, turned the handle, opened it.

Benny Griessel was leaning against the wall, chin on his breast, his clothes crumpled, his hair wildly untidy.

'Mat?' The voice was barely audible. 'I have to . . . talk.'

Griessel stumbled forward. For a moment Joubert wanted to stop him but then opened the door wider so that the man could come in.

'Benny, this is a bad time.'

'Must talk.'

Griessel staggered to the living-room, a road he knew. Joubert closed the door. His head struggled to find a solution. Quickly he walked to Griessel, turned him around, put his hands on his shoulders.

'Benny, listen to me.' He whispered, shook the shoulders.

'I want to die, Mat.'

'Benny.'

'Rather die.'

'Jesus, Benny, you're as pissed as a newt.'

Griessel started crying.

Joubert stared ahead, his hands still on the man's shoulders with not the vaguest idea of what to do. The sobs tore through the body of the figure in front of him. Joubert turned Griessel around, walked to the living-room. He'd make the man sit down, then warn Yvonne. He helped

Griessel as far as the couch. The sobs stopped when Griessel saw the candlelight. He looked at Joubert, frowned in an effort to understand.

'Is that you, Mat?' he asked his voice barely audible. Joubert wondered what demons were dancing in Griessel's skull. He pitied him.

Yvonne appeared in the door.

'Dessert,' she said, the word an announcement.

Her breasts and the dark love triangle of pubic hair were only too evident under the wisp of transparent nightgown. She was wearing high heels. In each hand she held a bowl of pudding. He arms were stretched out, an invitation to the other dessert.

She saw Griessel.

Griessel saw her.

'Mat?' Griessel repeated softly and then his head fell on his chest in an alcoholic and sensory stupor. Joubert's head swung back to Yvonne. His thoughts were formless and panicky.

She looked down at the way she had exhibited herself, saw herself the way they saw her. Her mouth thinned.

'Bonnie,' he said but he knew it wasn't going to work. She threw the bowl of pudding in her right hand at him. It hit his left shoulder, the smell of baked pudding and ice cream rising in his nostrils. It ran down his shirt and his bare chest. She swung round and walked down the passage, staggering on the high heels.

'Bonnie.'

'Fuck you!' she screamed and then a bedroom door slammed.

13

Drew Wilson was driving home in his CitiGolf. The radio was tuned to a late night chat show but he wasn't listening to it. He was tired. There was a dull throbbing behind his eyes and his back was stiff and sore from the long hours of sitting.

He didn't mind the tiredness because it was so good to be busy again. Even if you weren't working for yourself. It was good to be creative every day, to use your ingenuity and craftsmanship to mould the gold metal into something which would enchant a woman so that she, with true feminine charm, could convince the man in her life to buy it for her.

He fantasised about each one of his creations, about what kind of woman – or man sometimes – would wear it. With which outfit. To what occasion. Now and then, there were foreign tourists in the showroom but he tried to ignore them. They were never as beautiful or as stylish as in his dreams.

He lived in Boston in an old house with big rooms and high ceilings which he had restored. The driveway to the single garage was short but, as usual, he stopped to open the gate, got into the car again and drove to the garage doors.

When he put his hand on the car handle, someone, something stood next to him in the dark.

His head jerked and he saw the pistol.

'Oh God.'

Drew Wilson hadn't read a newspaper during the past week. The long hours and the pressure at work simply hadn't left time for that. He didn't know about the death of James J Wallace. But he saw the face behind the pistol.

The physiology of shock is predictable. The brain signals orders to prepare for action, for fast, urgent activity. Adrenaline pumps into the bloodstream, the heart rate increases, blood vessels expand, lungs pump.

He, however, could only remain seated behind the steering-wheel because the muzzle of the strange gun was against his skull, just above his right eye. But his body was forced to react. So he trembled, his hands and his knees shook with fear.

'I . . .' he said and a tear rolled slowly down his cheek to the black moustache on his upper lip.

'I . . .'

Then the bullet penetrated his skull, the heartbeat ceased, the blood vessels narrowed and the lungs collapsed – the adrenaline wasted forever.

Radio control woke Mat Joubert at 4:52. His voice was hoarse, his mouth dry. He searched clumsily for pencil and paper when the woman began speaking. She gave the facts in a neutral voice – the address, the sex, who had been notified.

'Looks like more Chinese, Captain. One in the head, one in the chest,' she added in a conversational tone and said goodbye. He mumbled and put back the receiver.

He had slept very little and the champagne and beer had turned his head into a mushy cement mixer. He sat up and rubbed his eyes. He groaned and thought about Benny Griessel in the living-room. He thought about Yvonne Stoffberg and groaned more loudly.

It hadn't been his fault.

How could he have foreseen that Griessel would arrive?

He had followed her, down the passage but she had banged the bedroom door in his face and locked it.

'Yvonne, I didn't know . . .'

He voice was shrill and hysterical. 'My name's Bonnie.'

'I didn't know he was coming here.'

'Who opened the fucking door?'

Good argument. There were noises behind the bedroom door – a banging and shuffling.

'Someone knocked. I had to.'

The door had opened. He face appeared. Anger and hate had changed her mouth, narrowed her eyes. By now she was wearing a pink track suit.

'You could've ignored it, you fucking stupid cop.' She'd banged and locked the door again.

He'd sunk down on the floor next to the door. Now the drunkenness was a burden which prevented him from thinking of ways to convince her. But her final words had taken the starch out of him. He was still sitting there when she jerked the door open some time later. Her suitcase was in her hand. She stepped over him and stormed down the passage to the front door. There she hesitated for a moment, threw down the case and walked back to him and said with the same thin mouth: 'I'll leave the key here tomorrow when I fetch my other stuff.' Then she left with her suitcase. He saw the firm bottom in the tight pink track suit pants disappearing around the front door and briefly wondered if she was wearing underwear. He'd remained sitting there, his mind dulled, liquor a sour taste in his mouth, only a vague yearning left between his legs.

Sometime during the night he'd climbed into bed and now he felt old and tired. And in Boston a second man was lying with a shattered head and a smashed heart. He got up with a groan. First of all he had to look after the man in the living-room.

He wanted coffee but there was no time. He hastily brushed his teeth but it didn't remove the foul taste in his mouth. He washed his face, dressed and walked down the passage. In the dining-room the remains of their meal lay cold and unappetising. In passing he saw the cigarette stub which had smoldered in the plate. The disappointment of the evening's fiasco swept over him again.

Griessel was snoring on the living-room couch. Joubert found the packet of Winstons on the small table and lit one. He'd go back to Special Milds a bit later. His mouth tasted of stale liquor. He shook Griessel's shoulder lightly. The snoring stopped.

'Mat,' Griessel said, surprised.

'Come on, Benny, I've got to go.'

Slowly Benny sat up, his head in his hands.

'Another Tokarev murder. In Boston. But you're not coming with me.'

He pulled Griessel to his feet and marched him to the front door, then to the Sierra. They got in and drove off.

'De Wit gave me an ultimatum, Mat.'

Joubert said nothing.

'I must leave the bottle or I'm out.'

'And you gave him your answer.'

They drove on in silence.

'Where are you taking me?'

'To the cells at the Edgemead station, Benny.'

Griessel looked at him like a wounded animal.

'You've got to stay dry now, Benny, until I can find help for you.'

Griessel stared ahead of him. 'De Wit warned you, too.'

'Yes, Benny, he warned me as well.'

Mrs. Shirley Venter was a tiny sparrow of a woman who constantly used her hands while she spoke very fast and in a high voice. 'Shame, what a way to go. In any case, I get up at four o'clock every morning. I don't have the luxury of a maid. Bob goes to work early during the week and it gives me time to make his breakfast and to feed the dogs and put the washing in the machine. I don't believe in these automatic things. I have a twin tub Defy, seventeen years old and not a thing wrong with it. In any case, I switched on the kettle for coffee because Bob likes percolator coffee and it takes a while and then I saw a car with its lights on in front of Drew's garage but you can see it's difficult to see clearly through that window because Bob hasn't trimmed the hedge for a long time.'

She turned to her husband, a man in late middle-age with heavy shoulders, thick lips and a mouth slightly agape under an Adolf Hitler moustache.

'Bob, you'll have to trim the hedge, my darling.' Bob gave a low grumble and Joubert didn't know whether it implied assent or not. They were standing in the kitchen among the unwashed dishes and the laundry surrounded by the smell of fried bacon. Joubert leant against a kitchen cupboard, Basie Louw sat at the kitchen table drinking coffee.

'In any case then I saw the lights on the garage door but I went on making the coffee and put the percolator on the stove and put out the cups. Bob doesn't get up until he's had one cup in bed. And I put in the washing and then I looked out of the window again and the car's lights were still shining on the garage. Then I thought, no, something's wrong. So I went to tell Bob and he said I must leave the neighbours alone but I said Bob, everything's not all right, a car doesn't stand in front of a closed garage for ten minutes. So Bob went to have a look. I still said he must take a stick or something because one never knows but he just walked out. He still played prop forward for Parow until he was forty-three, didn't you, darling?'

Bob made a noise again.

'And then he found him there and there was blood all over the place and Bob said he thinks the car was still idling until early this morning because that was why the lights were still so bright. And then he came to tell me and I let the Flying Squad know. One nought triple one. I keep the number next to the telephone since that *911* was on the TV. Shame, we were so shocked. What a way to go.'

Her voice was a knife scraping Joubert's frayed nerves. He looked longingly at Basie Louw's coffee. Basie had arrived before he did. When evidently there had been something left in the percolator.

'You didn't hear the shots? Noises, voices, cars racing away?' He looked at Bob Venter in the hope that he would reply.

'There are always cars here backfiring, not like the old times when it was a quiet decent suburb. But now Bob and I keep ourselves to ourselves, mind our own business. And we sleep well. Only the rich have time to lie awake at night,' the woman replied.

Joubert accepted it as a negative response to his question. 'Mr. Venter, did you notice nothing odd when you went out?'

Bob Venter growled again and moved his head a few millimeters from side to side.

'What do you know about the deceased?'

It was as if Shirley Venter had been waiting for the question. 'Drew Wilson was a lovely boy. And so artistic. You must see the inside of that house, it's nicer than mine. And quiet. You never heard a sound from there. He always greeted me and smiled and worked so hard, especially lately . . .'

'What did he do, Mrs. Venter?'

'He makes those little bits of jewellery, you know. In any

case, when he moved in here I took a tray over and when I came back I said to Bob what a nice boy . . .'

'Do you know where he worked?'

'Benjamin Goldberg's in Adderley Street. It's a very fancy place and the stuff is so expensive. I went there once when I was in town just to go and say hello to him but it was just high brows and credit cards. In any case, when he moved in I took a tray over and came and told Bob that he was such a nice boy and you know, first impressions are what usually count because it was true. Quiet and friendly.'

'Was he unmarried? Divorced?'

'Unmarried. I always said Drew doesn't need a wife. You just go and have a look inside. It's nicer than my house.'

Bob Venter growled something unintelligible.

'Bob, you can't say that,' she said. 'Don't take any notice of Bob. Drew was only arty. In any case . . .'

'What did you say, Mr. Venter?'

'Bob, drop that story.'

The man growled again. Joubert watched his lips. He deciphered the words. 'He was a queer,' said Bob.

'Bob thinks anybody who hasn't played rugby for thirty years is queer. He was just arty. He was given other talents. Don't take any notice of Bob.'

'He was a queer,' Bob said with finality and folded his thick arms across his chest.

'He was just arty,' Shirley said and fished a tissue from inside the neckline of her dress.

He went to fetch Griessel at the Edgemead police station. The constable who unlocked the door looked uncomfortable and turned his gaze away. Griessel walked out to the car in silence.

Joubert drove. 'How do I get you into the sanatorium which helped you the previous time, Benny?'

'Drop me at the front door.'

'Will you go?'

Griessel rubbed a dirty hand over the stubble on his face. His voice sounded tired. 'Will it help, Mat? When I come out I'm dry but they can do nothing about the . . . about the work.'

Joubert said nothing. Griessel interpreted it incorrectly. 'God, Mat, I dream in the night. I dream that it's my children lying dead. And my wife. And me. With blood against the walls and AK shots through the head or guts spilling out onto the floor. They can't take it away, Mat. I dream even when I'm sober. Even if I don't drink a drop.'

'De Wit forced me to see a psychologist.'

Griessel sighed as if the burden had become too heavy.

'Perhaps she can help you too, Benny. Take away the dreams.'

'Perhaps.'

'But we have to let you dry out first.'

They drove in silence on the M5 to Muizenberg where the sanatorium was situated. Joubert took out the Winstons, offered one to Griessel and pressed in the Sierra's lighter. They smoked in silence for a while.

'A Tokarev again?'

'Yes. Two shots. Two empty cartridges. But the thing has changed. Victim was possibly homosexual.'

Griessel audibly expelled smoke. 'Could make it easier.'

'If it's the same murderer. I've got a feeling about this thing, Benny.'

'Copycat?'

'Perhaps. And perhaps it's the start of bigger things.'

'A serial?'

'I've got that feeling.'

'Maybe,' said Benny Griessel. 'Maybe.'

* * *

118

Joubert explained about Griessel's dreams. He said that his colleague was also willing to undergo psychological treatment.

'But he'll dry out first?'

Joubert nodded. De Wit rubbed the mole and stared at the ceiling. Then he agreed.

Joubert thanked him and reported the second Tokarev murder. De Wit listened without interrupting. Joubert told him about Drew Wilson's neighbours who suspected that he was homosexual. Wilson's employer and colleagues had verified this.

They had all sat or stood among the work tables of the goldsmiths – Benjamin Goldberg, three other men and a woman. They were sincerely shocked. The woman cried. They couldn't think who would've done a thing like that to Drew Wilson. Yes, he was gay but hadn't had a relationship with another man for the past five or six years. He really tried, occasionally even taking out a woman. Why? Because Drew Wilson's mother had threatened suicide.

Joubert wiped the sweat off his upper lip.

'Any drugs?' de Wit asked, assuming a hurt expression in advance.

Joubert thought how odd it was that his concentration was always better after a heavy drinking session. Possibly because only then did the mind have the ability to concentrate on only one thing at a time. He took a deep breath and kept his voice calm and even: 'I'm going through Wilson's house with a team now, Colonel. We'll look for drugs as well.'

'But that's not all.'

He heard the barely concealed reproach in the other man's voice. Overdone patience crept into his voice. 'Colonel, I don't know how matters stand at Scotland Yard but white murders in the Cape are few and far between. And six

119

or seven times out of ten male homosexuals are involved. We'll have to investigate that in depth.'

De Wit's smile broadened slightly. 'I'm not sure that I understand you rightly. Wallace, you told me recently, played around with women and now you tell me Wilson did the same thing with men. Are you telling me there are two different murderers?'

Joubert's mind searched for cross references. De Wit's smile was different from anything he'd ever encountered. It was the man's way of handling conflict, his way of releasing tension. But it confused the person on the receiving end. Maybe it was meant to do just that.

'No, Colonel, I don't know. It could be a copycat. If a murder gets a lot of publicity . . .'

'I'm aware of the phenomenon, Captain.' The smile.

'But I think it's too soon for that.'

'Did the victims know one another?'

'I'll check on that.'

'Very well, Captain.'

Joubert rose half-way out of his chair. 'Colonel . . .'

De Wit waited.

'There's one other matter. The article in the *Argus* about the bank robber . . .'

'I see your friends at Public Relations think highly of you, Captain.' De Wit leant forward and added softly: 'Keep it that way.'

14

I t was the first time that Detective-sergeant Gerrit Snyman had had to search a house without the knowledge
of the owner. It made him feel uncomfortable, like an
intruder.

In Drew Wilson's bedroom, at the bottom of the built-in
cupboard next to a neat row of shoes, he found a thick
photograph album with a brown cover. He knelt in front of
the cupboard and opened it. Photographs were pasted in
neat rows, each one with a caption – some witty, some
nostalgic. The feeling of discomfort grew because here
Drew Wilson was still alive in timeless moments of happi-
ness, birthdays and awards, parental love, friendship. Detective-sergeant Gerrit Snyman didn't consider the
symbolism of the photo album for a single second, nor
for the same brief space of time, did it occur to him that
everyone left only the happy moments for future generations and took the grief and the pain, the heartbreak and the
failures to their graves.

This was because the life of Drew Wilson as illustrated by
the photographs changed in a way that upset the young
policeman. Then he recognised someone in a photo and an
involuntary whistle escaped him. He got up in one smooth
movement and hurried to where Captain Mat Joubert was
going through a chest of drawers in another room.

'Captain, I think I might have something here,' Snyman
said modestly. But his face betrayed his shock and excitement.

Joubert looked at the pictures. 'Isn't that . . .' and he tapped a finger on a photo.

'It is, Captain, it is,' Snyman said enthusiastically.

'Shit,' Joubert said. Snyman nodded as if he agreed.

'Well done,' said Joubert. He tapped Snyman on the shoulder with a clenched fist.

Snyman saw the shine in Joubert's eyes and smiled because he saw it as his reward.

'We must cover all the bases,' Joubert said thoughtfully. 'But first of all you must fetch him.'

Mat Joubert knew it was impossible to know from the start whether a suspect was lying. Some wore the signs of guilt like beacons on their faces, others could hide it with the greatest of ease.

He looked at the man opposite him clad in a multicoloured, V-necked track suit and expensive running shoes. The man was big and broad-shouldered. He was attractive with a square jaw and black hair which curled at the nape of his neck. At the neckline of the track suit curly hair was clearly visible. A gold cross on a thin chain nestled in the hair. There was a serious expression his face, a controlled frown between the heavy black eyebrows, an expression of grave co-operation. Joubert had seen it before. It could mean anything because all this suspect had been asked to do was to accompany Snyman to Murder and Robbery because 'he might be able to help them with an investigation.' Who knew what thoughts were churning behind that attractive frown?

Snyman sat next to the suspect, his place there earned by his good work. Bart de Wit sat somewhat behind the suspect, against the wall, an observer by personal request.

Joubert pressed the button of the tape recorder. 'Mr Zeelie, you're aware of the fact that we're recording this conversation?'

'Yes.' A small muscle next to the mouth twitched the upper lip.

'Have you any objection?'

'No.' His voice was deep and masculine.

'Please give us your full name for the record.'

'Charles Theodore Zeelie.'

'Your profession?'

'Professional cricketer.'

'You regularly play for the Western Province senior team?'

'Yes.'

'As a Province cricketer you must've known the late Mr. James Wallace well?'

'I did.'

Joubert watched him closely. Sometimes precisely the exaggerated ease was a sign, the forced lack of concern a mask for guilt. But Zeelie kept to the exact opposite – the tense frown, the serious helpfulness.

'Tell us about your relationship with Mr. Wallace.'

'Well . . . er . . . acquaintances, I'd say. We saw one another from time to time generally at the get-togethers after the match. We chatted. I liked him. He was a . . . flamboyant man. Acquaintances. We were no more than acquaintances.'

'Are you positive?'

'Yes.'

'You never discussed your personal life with Mr. Wallace?'

'Er . . . no . . .'

'You had no reason to dislike Mr. Wallace?'

'No. I liked him.' The seriousness of the issue deepened the frown on Zeelie's forehead.

'Never got annoyed with him?'

'No . . . not that I can remember.'

Joubert leant forward slightly and stared straight at the man in front of him. 'Are or were you ever acquainted with a Mr. Drew Joseph Wilson of 64 Clarence Street, Boston?'

Shock spread like a veld fire over Zeelie's face – his jaw clenched, the eyes narrowed. The left hand on the arm of the chair trembled.

'Yes.' Barely audible.

'Would you please speak more clearly for the sake of the tape recorder.' Mat Joubert's voice carried the civility of the victor. 'Would you like to tell us about your relationship with him?'

Now Zeelie's voice was trembling as well as his hand. 'You must forgive me but I don't see what that has to do with this.' It became an appeal.

'With what, Mr. Zeelie?'

'Jimmy Wallace's death.'

'Oh, so you reckon you can help us with the investigation into the murder of Wallace?'

He didn't get it. 'I'll do everything in my power but . . .'

'Yes, Mr. Zeelie?'

'Leave Drew Wilson out of it.'

'Why?'

'Because he has nothing to do with it.' Zeelie was recovering from the shock.

Joubert leant forward again. 'Oh but he has, Mr. Zeelie. Drew Joseph Wilson was killed at approximately 22:00 last night. Two pistol shots, one in the head, one in the heart.'

Zeelie's hands gripped the arms of the chair, his knuckles white.

'James J Wallace died in the same way. And we suspect that the same weapon was used.'

Zeelie stared at Joubert as if he were invisible. His face had blanched. The silence lengthened

'Mr. Zeelie?'

'I . . .'

'Yes?'

'I want an attorney.'

Joubert and Snyman waited outside the interrogation room for an hour-and-a half while Charles Theodore Zeelie consulted with his attorney. De Wit had asked to be called again and went back to his office.

The longer the conversation inside lasted, the more certain Joubert became that Zeelie was his man.

Eventually the grey-haired attorney appeared.

'If my client is completely open with you, I want the assurance that his evidence will be kept totally confidential.'

'In court nothing is confidential,' Joubert said.

'It won't come to that,' said the attorney and Joubert's confidence ebbed. He asked for de Wit to be called. The OC agreed to the attorney's request. They went into the room. Zeelie was pale, his eyes on the floor. They sat down at the table.

'Put your questions,' the attorney said.

Joubert activated the tape recorder, cleared his throat, not certain of the correct words. 'Did you have . . . a relationship with Drew Joseph Wilson?'

Zeelie's voice was low. 'It was a long time ago. Six, seven years. We were . . . friends.'

'Friends, Mr. Zeelie?'

'Yes.' Louder, as if he wanted to convince himself of that.

'We have photographs in an album which . . .'

'It was a long time ago . . .'

Only the faint whirr of the tape recorder was audible. Joubert waited. Snyman sat on the edge of his chair. The attorney stared at the wall. Bart de Wit rubbed his mole.

Then Zeelie started speaking in his deep, attractive voice, softly, almost tonelessly.

'He didn't even know who I was.' He thought for a moment, spoke as if he was alone in the room.

'I was thumbing a lift from campus to town. Drew picked me up. The previous year, during matric, I'd played for Border and the newspapers made a big thing of it when I came to Cape Town. He asked me who I was and I said he ought to know. He smiled and said that all he knew was that I was the most beautiful man he'd ever seen.'

Zeelie became aware of the people around him again. He looked at Joubert. 'No . . . I didn't know that I was gay. I didn't really know what it meant. I simply liked Drew very much . . . the attention he paid me . . . his company, his cheerfulness, his zest for life. I told him I was a student and a cricketer and that I was going to play cricket for South Africa. He laughed at my self-confidence and said he knew nothing about cricket. He said he was a goldsmith and his dream was to have his own establishment where he could make his own designs, not simply things meant for fat, rich tourists. We talked. We couldn't stop talking. In town he invited me for coffee at a street cafe. And said he would wait for me and take me back to campus. He came to visit, a week later. He was older than I was. So clever. Wise. He was so different from the other guys at cricket. He invited me to his home for dinner. I thought it was only friendship . . .'

He looked at de Wit and Snyman, seeking a sympathetic face. 'At first it was just . . . right. With Drew it was neither dirty nor wrong. But it began to bother me. We discussed it. He told me it was never going to be easy. But it was different for him. I started playing for Western Province. Every time a schoolboy asked me for a signature, I wondered how long it would be before someone found out. I think I did . . . I was scared. My parents . . .'

He gave a deep sigh, his head on his chest, eyes fixed on the writhing hands on his lap. Then he looked up.

'One evening, after a match, I met a girl. Older. And sophisticated, like Drew. And . . . decisive. She took me to her flat. I was . . . relieved, thrilled. I didn't think I would be able . . . But I could. And enjoyed it. That was the beginning of the end because it offered a way out . . . Drew immediately noticed that something was wrong. I told him. He was furious. Then I . . . ended the relationship. He cried. We talked all night. But it was over.'

The hands in Zeelie's lap relaxed. 'I admit that I loved him. Those photographs don't show the love. But the tension became too much. And the woman . . . I wanted to be normal. I wanted to be a hero in my own eyes . . .'

He rubbed a hand through his black hair.

'Carry on.'

'During the first two weeks he often phoned Residence. But I never returned the calls. A few times he waited for me in his car, wrote letters. I also saw him at matches a few times. Then I think he accepted it. It was over.'

'When last did you see him?'

'Lordy . . . Two years ago? At the airport. We were coming back from Durban after a match against Natal. His mother was on the same flight. We said hello, had a brief conversation. It was very . . . normal.'

'And you never saw him again?'

'No.'

'Mr. Zeelie, where were you last night between 20:00 and 23:00?'

'At Newlands, Captain.' Calmly, no bravado.

'Anyone able to confirm that?'

'It was an day-night match against Gauteng, Captain. I took two for twenty-four.'

15

He was tired enough not to care what the other neighbours might say. He knocked loudly at the Stoffbergs' front door. He heard her footsteps, then she opened the door. When she saw him her face changed. He knew he'd come to no purpose.

'Could we talk about last night?'

She stared at him with dislike, almost pity. Then the humiliation became too much for him. He turned and walked back to his house.

Behind him he heard her closing the door.

He walked home in the dusk of early evening but already felt shrouded in darkness.

He sat in his armchair in the living-room but without a book. He lit a Winston and stared at the blue-grey smoke pluming to the ceiling.

Perhaps de Wit was right. Perhaps he was a loser. The Great Loser. The counterweight to success. Maybe he was the refuse tip of the gods where all the dark thoughts and experiences, adversity and unhappiness could be dumped like nuclear waste. Programmed to absorb the shadows like a sponge so that there could be light. Death, the great predator, was following the bloody tracks of Mat Joubert, saliva dripping from its fangs to fall onto the black soil. So that humanity could be free.

Like Charles Theodore Zeelie. He had walked out a free

man. 'You'll keep your promise?' he'd made quite certain one last time.

'Yes.' Because even without promises Murder and Robbery didn't like to expose their dead ends, their failures, in the media. Charles Theodore Zeelie had been relieved. The strong face had regained its colour, the hands had relaxed, the frown smoothed from the forehead by the invisible hand of innocence.

He quite understood why they had asked him to come. He wasn't annoyed with them. If he could help . . .

Relieved. Friendly, almost lighthearted. Untouched by the death of a man who had made him experience self-hatred. And love.

Charles Theodore Zeelie had walked out free. But not Mat Joubert.

De Wit had made no comment, only directed that smile at Joubert. Had a smile of pity replaced the victorious one?

On the sixth floor of a block of flats in Sea Point which looked out over the vast cold expanse of the Atlantic Ocean, he had visited Mrs. Joyce Wilson, the mother of Drew Joseph Wilson.

She replied calmly to Joubert's questions, the grief firmly under control. A woman who cared for her appearance, tall and strong and impressive, her attractiveness arrived at by her own hand, not due to genetic factors. Gallant and straight-backed in her painfully neat flat. Yes, Drew her beloved and only son had been gay. But he had changed. It was more than six or seven years that he had let it go.

Tell her it's wishful thinking, Mat Joubert. Tell her. Let her feel the darkness too. Share it. Spread it around a little. But he'd said nothing. He left her alone to cry in her bedroom where no one could see her.

He'd been to see Margaret Wallace again as well. With the pain in her eyes which hadn't yet disappeared. You're almost there, lady. Open your heart. Leave the back door of your mind permanently open so that death can come in, the black wind can blow through your skull. You're on the right road, lady. Life has disappeared from your eyes. Your skin, your mouth look tired. Your shoulders are carrying a heavy load.

No, she had never heard of Drew Wilson. She didn't know whether James had known him.

And her body language inferred that she didn't care.

And here sat Mat Joubert. The Great Loser. The man with the physician and the psychologist and the dietician. He made a sound in the back of his throat, jeering at himself, at the thought, the concept that a thirty-four-year-old captain and detective couldn't seduce the eighteen-year-old daughter of an undertaker.

How pathetic.

Benny Griessel's face rose in his mind again. At the moment when Yvonne Stoffberg appeared in the doorway, a fanfare of flesh, his late night dessert.

Benny Griessel's face.

Joubert smiled. And suddenly saw his self-pity from another perspective – at first only a glimpse, then with disillusion. And he smiled at himself. And at Benny Griessel's face. Joubert looked at his burning cigarette and saw himself as he was at that moment – in his reading chair, staring at a cigarette and with a smile meant only for himself and he knew he had another chance.

He stubbed the cigarette and got up. He fetched his diet sheet and the recipe book the dietician had given him. He walked to the kitchen: 60 grams of chicken (no skin) 60 millilitres fat-free meat sauce, 100 grams baked potato, 150 grams carrots, broccoli. Two units of fat.

Jesus.

He took out pots and pans, started the preparations, his

head re-thinking the two murders. Eventually he sat down at the table, ate the food slowly. *Chew food slowly. This allows the stomach to signal the brain when it is full*, said the diet sheet. But the telephone rang twice before his plate was empty.

The first time he answered it was with his mouth full of broccoli. 'Wawert.'

'Captain Joubert, please.' A man's voice.

Joubert swallowed. 'Speaking.'

'Good evening, Captain. Sorry to bother you at home. But that colonel of yours is a terror.'

'Oh?'

'Yes, Captain. Michaels here, at the laboratory. It's about SAP3 four slash two slash one slash ninety-five. The Wallace murder.'

'Yes?'

'The weapon, Captain. It's not . . '

'Are you calling from Pretoria?' still trying to get a grip on what was going on.

'Yes, Captain.'

'Which colonel are you talking about?'

'De Wit, Captain.'

'What has he got to do with this?'

'He phoned us, Captain, this afternoon. And crapped on our heads from a dizzy height. Said his people were working their fingers to the bone while we sat on our hands.'

'Bart de Wit?'

'Yes, Captain.'

Joubert chewed on the information.

'In any case, Captain, that Tokarev of yours . . '

'Yes?' But he was still amazed by de Wit's call and the fact that the commanding officer had told him nothing about it.

'It's not a Tokarev, Captain. I don't know who thought that one up. It's a Mauser.'

Suddenly Joubert was part of the conversation again. 'A what?'

'A Mauser, Captain. But not just any old Mauser. It's a Broomhandle.'

'A what?'

'It's a pistol, Captain.' Michael's voice had taken on the patient tone of a teacher. 'The Mauser military model, M96 or M98, I'd guess. 7,63 mm caliber. The cartridge cases are typical. Rimless with a bottleneck. I can't imagine why you thought it's a Tokarev. The . . .'

'The caliber,' Joubert defended Griessel's guess.

'No, Captain, sorry, but hell, there's a huge fucking difference. In both cases it should make your job much easier.'

'Oh?'

Michaels became impatient. 'The Mauser, Captain. It's old and it's rare. There can hardly be that many people in the Cape who own one. Firearm records.'

'How old?'

'Almost a hundred years, Captain. 1896 or '98. Most beautiful thing the Germans ever made. But you'll know it, Captain. Broomhandle. Slender wooden stock. Boer officers carried it. Long barrel, magazine in front of the trigger.'

Joubert tried to visualise the weapon, and somewhere an image stirred, a vague memory. 'Looks almost like a Luger?'

'Luger's grandfather, Captain. That's the one.'

'Where would they find ammunition for it? After a hundred years?'

'It shoots Tokarev but it could hurt it. Pressure ratios differ. But the guy still has a supply, Captain. Your murderer. Even his cartridges are old. '99. Maybe 1900. You must get him. He's fucking shooting Africana to hell and gone.'

'The ammunition is also a hundred years old?'

'Unbelievable, isn't it.'

'And it's still effective?'

'In those days they built to last, Captain. Occasionally you'll get a misfire. But most of them are still in working order. The guy can wipe out the whole of Cape Town.'

'You think it's a man?'

'Definitely, Captain.'

'Oh?'

'Mauser kicks like a fucking mule, Captain. Takes a man on a horse.'

16

He swam with enjoyment for the duration of one length. When he turned, kicking against the wall of the pool and swam back, fatigue sent its feelers through his muscles again.

He strove for the weightlessness, the efficiency. He swam more slowly, then faster, rested, tried again but it evaded him.

When he climbed out of the water he was hopeful about the swimming for the first time.

On that Thursday, the tenth of January, the chief sub-editor of *Die Burger* had a small stroke of luck. Subs, the people who, among other things, have to think up the headlines in a newspaper, occasionally like an alliteration or a play on words to jazz up their work and, as his luck would have it, the words Mauser, murder and maniac all started with the same letter.

That apart, the newspaper had decided to devote the main story on the front page to the murders. There were two reasons for that decision. The first was that the usual sources of information had nothing of note to offer that morning. No more people than usual had died in the townships, the various colours of the political rainbow had made no new serious referrals to one another and the government wasn't involved in a new scandal. On the international front it was quiet too, even in the Middle East, Eastern Europe and Ireland.

The second reason was the murder weapon. The Mauser Broomhandle.

After he had seen the photographs of James J Wallace and Drew Joseph Wilson lying on his desk the previous evening, the crime reporter of *Die Burger* had started playing around with a theory.

Both had black hair and black moustaches. They vaguely resembled one another. Both were in their late thirties.

The reporter had also telephoned Lieutenant John Cloete of the SAPS Department of Public Relations and asked whether it might be possible that the Service was dealing with a mass murderer who had his knife – Tokarev – out for mustachioed, black-haired men this side of forty.

It was Cloete's duty to keep the Service in the media's good books. And if a crime reporter had some stupid theory or other, Cloete listened to it and promised that he would come back to him.

The previous evening he had called Mat Joubert away from a slice of skinless chicken breast, carrots, potato and broccoli to ask him whether the reporter was onto something.

Joubert was fully aware of journalists' habit of grabbing at straws and he sympathised with Cloete.

'We're exploring all avenues,' he'd said because he knew that that was what Cloete wanted to tell the reporter.

Cloete had thanked Joubert.

'There's something else, John,' Joubert said before Cloete could put the phone down.

'Yes, Captain?'

'The murder weapon.'

'Yes, Captain?'

'It's a Mauser Broomhandle.'

'A what?'

Joubert had told him. As much as he could remember.

'Keee-rist,' Cloete had said because he knew the press. And he knew . .

'And then there's another thing, John.'

'Yes, Captain?'

'Don't let the newspapers refer to me as "one of the Peninsula's top detectives"'.

Cloete had laughed, promised and returned the reporter's call. 'Captain Mat Joubert says they're exploring all avenues.'

Then Cloete told him about the Mauser.

Sensation, the reporter knew, was often contained in the minor details of a story. The condition and colour of a pair of underpants, for example. The colour of a couple or the difference in colour. Or, as in this case, the age of the murder weapon.

The Mauser was manna from heaven. Old, rich in history, with a touch of controversy about it – dating from the Anglo-Boer War which might give it a right-wing colour. It had a strange, exotic appearance. That was why *Die Burger*'s front page looked the way it did that morning. In the newspaper's attractive modular make-up, the main story, photographs and a graphic box in a large square had been etched against a salmon-coloured background. And the headline? Two words, alliterative, in big sans serif letters: MAUSER MURDERER. And below it, in smaller serif, the sub-heading: MANIAC MAY STRIKE AGAIN.

Joubert read the newspaper in his office.

His week of back-up duty was over. He now had a three week breathing space before he had to lead a back-up group again. That was why he had the luxury of a newspaper on his desk that morning. He read the copy and shook his head over the inventiveness of a journalist who could make front page news out of the make of a weapon, a theory and a vague statement from the Police.

But he didn't mind. Publicity was one of the great allies in the solving of crimes. Some criminals had even given themselves up as a result of a newspaper report stating that 'the Police net was tightening'. And as for the impact of television . . .

He read the report and looked at the photographs of Jimmy Wallace and Drew Wilson. He knew he didn't have one single solid clue and he was certain that this wasn't the last Mauser murder. Maybe the reporter was right. Maybe it was a man who came home to catch a black-haired man with a black moustache with his wife. And was now shooting such men to boost his ego.

Mat Joubert, armchair psychologist.

Never mind, he said to himself. Another few hours and he would be back with the real thing, his own personal physician of the soul. The one and only Dr Hanna Nortier, interrogator, surgeon of the psyche, healer of sick soul.

'We'll see one another on Thursdays, Captain,' she had said. He suddenly realised that he was looking forward to it.

What could that mean? He lit a Benson & Hedges Special Mild. It still didn't taste like a Winston. He folded the newspaper and looked at his watch. Half past eight. Perhaps the people at Records were at work by now. He picked up the receiver and dialed the number. The time had come for them to start looking for a Mauser.

Ferdy Ferreira didn't read *Die Burger* on Thursday, January 10. Or on any other day. Because reading a newspaper was too much trouble.

And he had enough trouble in his life. Like his wife. His wife was Trouble with a capital T.

'Ferdy, walk the dogs.'

'Ferdy, look for work.'

'Ferdy, you eat too much.'

'Ferdy, beer has given you that gut.'

'Ferdy, the least you could do is to help me clear the table.'

'Ferdy, I'm on my feet all day long. And what do you do? You sit.'

He especially liked sitting in front of the television. From the moment his wife caught the Golden Arrow at the bus stop in front of the Old Ship Caravan Park until it ended with a religious broadcast in the evening.

Ferdy's lack of knowledge of the murders was due to the fact that there was no way the SABC could give its attention to every murder in the country. After all, it was a national news service which covered only major events. That's why there had been no mention at all of the death of James J Wallace and that of Drew Wilson. So in a certain sense it could be said that the SABC news service carried some guilt for the death of Ferdy Ferreira.

Not that they would ever know.

Joubert knocked at the door of the dilapidated house in Boston and considered the fact that it was only two blocks away from the late Drew Wilson's. His heart rate increased and he slid the palm of his hand over the Z88 to reassure himself that it was still there.

The fax from Records had stated that there were sixteen registered Mauser Broomhandles in the Cape Peninsula.

Joubert had divided the list of names between himself and Gerrit Snyman because there was no one else: the detectives who were not on back-up were in court as witnesses – conclusive evidence that they had done their work successfully in the past year. Snyman was new. And Mat Joubert . . .

The door opened. A woman stood there, large, middle-aged and ugly. Her features – the eyes, the mouth, the nose –

were uniformly small and unattractive in the centre of her face so that she resembled a reptile.

'Mrs. Stander?'

'Yes.' Impatiently.

He introduced himself and explained why he was there. They had to check every Mauser in the Peninsula to see whether it had been fired.

'Come in.' She turned and walked down the passage. Joubert saw that her shoulders were broad and thought she looked like a murderer. He could see her in his mind's eye, this hunk of a woman in front of James J Wallace and next to Drew Wilson's car.

She hesitated at the sitting-room door. 'Wait here,' she gestured with her hand and walked on down the passage. He walked into the sitting-room and sat down in a chair, ill at ease. And he was vaguely amused by his discomfort. His job was to seek out murderers without discrimination – beautiful and ugly, fat and thin, old and young. It was only in films and on television that the murderer was always an aesthetically unattractive stereotype.

But when he heard Mrs. Stander's heavy footsteps in the passage again, he kept his hand close to his service pistol and balanced his body so that he could get up easily.

She had a wooden chest in her hands. She came to sit next to him and wordlessly offered the chest.

He took it. He saw the carving on it – a scene of Boer soldiers on their horses, the fine detail of the animals, of the men's hats and waistcoats and firearms, precisely and lovingly etched into the wood. He touched the small work of art, amazed.

'My grandfather made it on St Helena,' the woman said. 'He was an officer. And a prisoner of war there, of course.'

He opened the chest.

He'd seen the drawing, the graphic representation of the

Mauser in *Die Burger* that morning, remembered its shape and appearance. But the graphics hadn't prepared him for the metal and the wood, the curves and contrasts of the weapon.

It didn't look like a murder weapon.

The line of the barrel, the angle it formed with the slender stock was feminine – a soft, sensual curve. The magazine, square, chunky and blunt, was an abruptness in front of the trigger, like a male sexual organ, unattractive but effective. He lifted the Mauser out of the chest. It felt lighter than it looked. WAFFENFABRIK MAUSER OBERNDORF he read on the frame. He turned the pistol over, looked down the barrel, sniffed in the odour of black metal and dark wood.

He knew that this wasn't the weapon.

'You must oil it,' he told Mrs. Stander who sat forward in her chair, her eyes never leaving his face. 'There's rust in the barrel. You must oil it well.' Then he placed the weapon carefully and respectfully back into the chest.

When he drove to Paarl, to the next Mauser owner on his list, he speculated about the murderer. Why this weapon? Why choose a pistol which attracted attention like a beacon burning in the night? Why use ammunition which was a century old, and could leave you, at that heartstopping moment, in the lurch? Was it a political statement after all? 'The voice of the Boer is not stilled.'

Two victims, one English-speaking, a ladies' man, one Afrikaans-speaking, gay. 'Our Boer voice is not stilled and we still shoot the English and queers.'

No, it was too simple. Too one-dimensional. It might be a statement but on another level. A way of attracting attention. Of saying: 'I'm different. I'm special.'

The other seven names and addresses on his list took him to two retirement homes, three pensioners and two amateur weapon collectors. He saw four different Mauser Broom-handle models, each subtly different from the other, each one with its own chilling charm.

He found no suspect on his list.

In the late afternoon he drove back to Cape Town. In the city, at a stoplight on the way to Dr Hanna Nortier's consulting rooms, the *Argus* paperboy stood next to the car. Joubert read the headline with ease:

BLAST FROM THE PAST.

17

When he followed her through the door he noticed that she was wearing a dress in a plain design, dark-blue material patterned with small red and orange flowers. It covered her to below her knees. He could see the muscle and bone of her shoulders and wondered who her dietician was.

They sat down.

He saw that her frail beauty was pale today, the smile polite but not warm, slightly forced.

'And how is Captain Mat Joubert?' she asked and opened his file.

What should he say? 'Fine.'

'Have you come to terms with the fact that you're consulting a psychologist?'

'Yes.' Not the whole truth because he'd looked forward to the visit. He'd chewed over this peculiarity between visits to Mauser Broomhandle owners in the Cape. He'd speculated, considered possibilities, because there wasn't one reason only. After the previous visit it seemed as if the abscess in his head . . . the pressure had decreased and the grey curtain between him and life had taken on a paler hue.

Then there was the other tale, Dr Hanna. The heart-rending story of the Fucking Stupid Policeman and the Undertaker's Daughter. A thriller in one short act with a twist in the tail. Psychologist's dream, Dr Hanna. So many nuances to investigate. Self-image, sex . . .

He surprised himself when he realised that he wanted to speak to Hanna Nortier about it. About his relief that his sexual urge still existed. About the humiliation. He wanted to know whether he had been programmed for humiliation.

But there was another possibility which he'd discovered, another potential reason why Mat Joubert was looking forward to his second visit to his personal head doctor. And that was the doctor herself.

She paged in the file in front of her. It bothered him. Couldn't she remember what he had told her the previous time? Had the blood he'd spilt on her carpet washed out so easily? She looked up at him. He saw the tiredness around her eyes and had a sudden insight: he was the eighth or the tenth or the twelfth patient of the day who sat opposite the slender woman spewing out the bitterness of their lives.

'You said very little about your mother during the first session.' Her head was still bent over the file. He heard her voice and it sounded like a musical instrument. He put his hand into his coat pocket, took out the Benson & Hedges, lifted the packet's lid, saw the cigarettes in their neat rows. His big fingers always found it difficult to extract the first cigarette from a new packet. He pinched the filter between thumb and forefinger and pulled. The cigarette slid out, Joubert changed his grip on it and put it into his mouth, then realised she was waiting for him to speak.

'My mother . . .'

Why had he looked forward to this visit? He put his hand into his pocket, brought out the lighter, let the flame shoot up, sucked in the smoke. He noticed that his hand was shaking slightly. He put the lighter back into his pocket. He looked at her.

'How do you remember her?'

'I . . .' He thought about it.

'As a child, I mean.'

As a child? How did one remember anything as a child? Episodes, fleeting incidents which made such an impression that you recognised their shape and content even when they lay under a thick layer of dust on the shelves of your memory.

'My mother was pretty.'

He was six or seven when he realised it for the first time. It was in Voortrekker Road, that main artery of his youth. The church's building fund or missionary money was at low ebb again and the sisters of the community had organised a pancake stall on the sidewalk – every Saturday morning. He'd begged his mother to take him along, the promise of soft pancakes with unmelted cinnamon sugar crunching under his teeth a prospect which inspired him to make a complete pest of himself. She gave in in the end, simply to keep him quiet. There were four or five other women at the sidewalk stall early in the morning. The street was still quiet with the sun rising at the eastern point of Voortrekker Road, as if the road determined its orbit. He sat away from them, his back against a shopfront, his arms around his knees, his head on his arms. He was sleepy, already sorry that he had come, his expectations of pancakes disappearing in the face of the women's business-like attitude. He'd closed his eyes and heard his mother's voice. It was different, not the way it usually sounded. This made him look up at her. There she stood behind the table, busy unpacking and arranging, her hands skilful and sure while her face reflected the gold of the early morning sunlight. She was speaking. The other women were listening. And laughing. His mother, the woman reduced to quiet self-effacement by the abusive shouting of her husband, was amusing the women. That morning he'd caught a glimpse of someone he would never really get to know.

'I think they'd forgotten about me,' he said to Hanna

Nortier. 'And my mother was imitating someone. I don't know who it was – another woman probably. There on the sidewalk, just after seven in the morning. She walked a little way up the pavement, turned and became someone else – her walk, her bearing, the way she turned her head and neck, her hands and arms. "Who am I?" she asked. The other women laughed so much they couldn't speak. "I'm going to wet myself," one said. I remember that because I was shocked. Between the gales of laughter they shouted the name of the woman, the one my mother was imitating. And then they clapped. My mother bowed with a smile on her face and the sun shone and then I saw my mother was beautiful with her smooth skin and her red cheeks and her shining eyes.'

He was silent. The cigarette had burnt down to almost nothing.

'I only remembered it when we buried her.'

She wrote in the file. Joubert stubbed the butt in the ashtray and wiped a hand across his upper lip. He smelt the tobacco and smoke on his fingers, an unpleasant smell.

'Maybe I was disappointed in her. Later. Because she never confronted my father. That she hadn't left him because of his tyranny and abusiveness and drinking. She was so . . . passive. No. It was more than passive. She . . . On Friday evenings when my father was in the bar she never spoke about it. She never said: "Go and fetch your father from the bar for supper." She used to say: "Go and look for your father." As if he might have been somewhere else. And when I came back and said that he didn't want to eat, it seemed as if she didn't hear me. As if she had an inexhaustible capacity to deny reality, to create her own.'

'How much of that did you inherit?' Her tone of voice was sharper, almost accusatory. He realised that it was the first psychological introspection she had expected of him.

Joubert tried to consider it. But she released him, her voice gentle again. 'Was it easy for you to take out girls? Later?'

Somewhere in his head a soft alarm sounded. Where was this leading? His mother. His girls?

'No.'

He was reluctant to face that memory, the awkwardness, the gnawing uncertainties of puberty, the period he came to terms with with such difficulty. He saw Hanna Nortier's frailness. How could she understand? 'I was large, Doctor – even at school.' Not simply tall. Big. He knew he wasn't as at ease with his body as other boys – the fly halves, the wings, the sprinters. Others pranced like high-bred race horses; he, with heavy, dull movements, fought his war against gravity. He was convinced that it disqualified him from associating with girls. Eight years after matriculation he met a school friend who asked him whether he'd known that she was in love with him at school. He couldn't believe it.

'I never had a girl friend. The one who went with me to the matric farewell . . . my mother and her mother fixed it. Like an arranged marriage.'

'Did it bother you? That you didn't have a girl friend?'

He thought about it.

'I read.'

She waited.

'Books create their own reality, Doctor. In books there are no clumsy heroes. And there are always happy endings. Even when the hero makes mistakes, in the end he always gets the heroine. I thought that all I had to do was to be patient. And until then the books were enough.'

'Your first girl?'

Alarm bells rang. The process had been exposed. His mother, his girls, the way to Lara Joubert. And dear God, he didn't want to talk about Lara.

'Lara,' he said softly and looked at the hands in his lap, the thick fingers which twitched and struggled with one another. There were others, before Lara. The secret loves of his teenage years which made his heart beat and his palms sweat. A PT teacher, a new girl from another school, the dark, somber Greek girl with the strong scent in the cafe on the corner of Rhodes and Voortrekker.

But they never knew about his passion, his dreams and fantasies. Lara did.

He felt Hanna Nortier's eyes on him. Then he heard her voice, soft, almost inaudible, deeply comprehending. 'You don't want to discuss her.' It was a question and a statement, a form of sympathy offered – and a challenge.

He was touched by the emotion in her voice. He felt the weight of the memory of Lara which lay on his mind. His mind was shouting: Tell her, Mat Joubert. Throw off the black ballast which forces the prow of your soul to meet every grey breaker head on. Open the hatches. Toss overboard.

He can't tell her everything.

He shook his head, back and forth. No. He didn't want to talk about Lara.

'We can do it slowly.' Her voice still filled with comprehension.

He looked up at her. He wanted to hug the frail body of Hanna Nortier with great gentleness, cover the etched shoulders with his big hands so that she didn't look so vulnerable. He wanted to hold her against him with sympathy and care, like a bulwark, a lifebelt. He was filled with emotion.

'How did you meet her?' The words were barely loud enough to reach his ears.

He was quiet for a long time. At first to get his emotions under control. Then he cat-footed through his memory banks as if too heavy a tread would trigger the wrong recollection. The emotion was like a magnifying glass, an acoustic booster, multiplying the clarity of his memory. He saw the image in his mind's eye, heard the sounds as if he were there. At first he had to draw back, then inch forward. Lara's face in front of him, that first time. She opening the door, her short straight black hair, her black eyes which blazed like searchlights with her lust for life, her smiling mouth, one eye tooth slightly askew, her body so lithe, so lively under the bright red dress. She had looked him up and down and said: 'I didn't order an extra large,' closed the door, then flung it open again with the laugh which flowed over him like music. Then she put out her hand and said: 'I'm Lara du Toit.'

'It was a . . .' Joubert searched for a more dignified word, found none. 'It was a blind date.'

He was looking at Hanna Nortier now, at her eyes, her nose, her mouth – his toehold in the precipice of memory.

'Hans van Rensburg arranged it. He was a sergeant at Murder and Robbery. They shot him at a roadblock on the N1 in 1992. She was still a uniform then, at the Sea Point station but Hans was investigating a murder there and met her. He said he'd seen just the right girl for me. One who would do all the talking. Because I was too useless and too scared of women to get anywhere, ever, he said. He phoned her and talked her into it. And so I drove to her flat. She shared a one bedroomed flat in Kloofnek with a girl friend because they were both so poor. Lara slept in the sitting-room, the other one in the bedroom and men were only allowed in the kitchen. Then she opened the door and she was beautiful. Then she said we must walk to the flicks because it was a lovely evening. Walk, the whole way down Kloofnek to the Foreshore. We hadn't even reached the street when she took my hand and said she liked being touched and people might think I was her brother if we didn't hold hands. She laughed at my shyness and at the way I blushed. Then she became serious because a man who could blush was a marrying man, and then she laughed again.'

He heard the laughter of his dead wife, the laugh of that first day and he remembered how they had walked back later that evening up the first rise of the mountain, the Cape night windless about them. Lara du Toit had spoken to him as if he mattered, as if it was worthwhile sharing her secrets with him. He feasted on her laughter, on the touch of her hand which like some small animal was never still in his, on her eyes, her mouth, her deeply tanned skin, unblemished, shining like polished copper.

He remembered how he'd climbed into his ancient Datsun SSS and later hadn't been able to recall the trip home. How he, in the tree-lined street in Wynberg where he rented a room behind the main house, had lifted his head to the heavens and given one mighty shout because the joy in him was too much to contain.

And then Mat Joubert wept for the first time in seventeen years – a wordless, soundless emotion, only the wetness dripping out of his eyes betraying it. He turned away from Hanna Nortier and wondered when the humiliation would end.

18

Benny Griessel was shaking. His hands, his arms, his shoulders, his legs.

'I know, Mat. That's the worst. I know. I know what's coming. It scares me so badly.'

Joubert sat on the single chair in the small room, Griessel on the bed with its grey blanket. The walls were bare, plastered and painted white up to head height, then brown brick to the ceiling. Next to the bed stood a wooden table without a drawer. A red Gideon bible lay on it. A cupboard stood against the wall next to the washbasin and lavatory.

He looked for the old Benny Griessel, the witty, cynical man with the slight liquor breath. This one's face was drawn with fear, his skin grey, his lips blue.

'Tonight the demons will come, Mat, the voices and the faces. They tell me they're hallucinations but I don't know the difference when they come. I can hear them calling and I can feel their fingers and you can never get away because you're too slow and there are too many of them.'

Benny Griessel doubled over and a spasm shook his body.

'I'll find you another blanket, Benny.'

'Blankets won't stop them, Mat. Blankets won't stop them.'

He telephoned Gerrit Snyman when he got home.

'Nothing, Captain. There are some which are so rusted

that they'll never shoot again. And the guy who lives in Table View has a helluva collection of weapons, Captain. His Mauser looks as if it was made yesterday. Oiled and polished. Almost too much, as if it could've been the murder weapon. But the man has an alibi for both murders.'

Joubert said that he had found nothing either, thanked Snyman for his work and said goodbye.

He walked to the living-room with a few pieces of fruit, a knife and a plate and sat down in his reading chair. He quartered an apple, carefully cut out the cores.

Two days, he thought. For two days the Benny-Griessel-coitus-interruptus had been his number one humiliation. Now it had been supplanted. By his stupid blubbing in front of Hanna Nortier.

She's a psychologist, he told himself. She's used to it.

But he wasn't. He wasn't used to the humiliation.

She had handled it well. She hadn't said anything. She had stood up and walked around the desk, crossing the invisible divide between psychologist and patient, and come to stand next to him. She had put her hand on his shoulder. She stood like that until he, his head still turned away from her, had with one angry movement wiped the wetness off his face with the sleeve of his jacket. Then she had walked back, sat down and waited until he was in control.

'We'll talk some more next time,' she had said softly. He had got up and walked to the door, forcing himself not to run.

And now, with a quarter of an apple in his hand, he knew the humiliation in front of her was the greater of the two. Because if he placed Dr Hanna Nortier and Yvonne Stoffberg next to one another on the scale of femininity, he was stunned. How could he have been so aroused? Now, compared to Hanna Nortier, Yvonne Stoffberg's beauty had become shallow, her sensuality lessened in value.

For a moment he felt sorry for Yvonne. Then he remembered the firmness of her back muscles, the texture of her breast in his mouth.

Yes, set against the Doctor she was common, ordinary. But she had made Mat Joubert's blood race.

Ferdy Ferreira hated his wife's two dogs.

Especially now at twenty to six in the morning, the sun barely up.

One reason was that in his view their mobile home, the Plettenberg, was too small for two adults and two corgis

Another reason was the attention and love which Gail Ferreira gave the dogs. When she came home, late in the afternoon from the coal company's offices where she was the bookkeeper, she greeted them first. Their names were Charles and Diana but she called them her angel faces.

The main reason, however, for Ferdy's hatred, was that he had to take the dogs for a walk on the beach every morning. 'Before six, Ferdy, so that I can say bye bye to them before I get the bus.' This then, was the pecking order in the Ferreiras' Plettenberg in Melkbos Strand's Old Ship Caravan Park: first Gail, then the dogs, then Ferdy.

'Ferdy, the dogs,' Gail said, busy dressing in front of her cupboard. She was a woman of average height and build, in her mid-forties, but her voice and her decisive attitude created the illusion of a big woman.

Ferdy sighed and got out of his single bed, divided from Gail's by a bedside table. He knew it was useless to argue. It only made things worse.

And the corgis sat moodily at the bedroom door as if they, too, weren't looking forward to the walk.

Ferdy dragged his left foot every morning.

'Don't drag your foot like that.'

'It's sore, Flash,' Ferdy said in a whining voice. Gail's

nickname at school, derived from 'Jack the Flash' referred to her speed and adroitness on the hockey field. He still called her that occasionally.

'There's not a thing wrong with it,' said Gail.

Ferdy Ferreira had contracted polio as a child. His left foot was affected but only insofar as it needed a slightly thicker sole to his shoe and gave a subtle list to his walk. But Ferdy had learnt to use it as a weapon with only qualified success.

Ferdy sighed, as he did every morning, and got dressed. He took the dogs' leads out of the broom cupboard in the kitchen and walked back to the bedroom, the list heavily emphasised in a useless play for sympathy. The dogs were still sitting in the bedroom, their eyes fixed on Gail. Ferdy clipped the leads to their collars. Charles and Diana growled.

'I'll be going now.' He sounded hurt, his voice martyred.

'Be careful with my angels,' was Gail's reply.

He walked down the caravan park's tarred road to the main gate on the west side. He greeted old Missis Atkinson who lived in the park permanently on site seventeen with eleven cats. The corgis strained towards the cat smell. Ferdy jerked them back with satisfaction, using more force than was necessary. The corgis growled.

He walked them through the gate. The black gatekeeper was probably still sleeping in the little wooden hut. They walked across the tarred road, over the empty piece of land which lay next to the Little Salt River which flowed into the sea there.

He didn't see the orange of the eastern horizon or the blue-green of the Atlantic Ocean in front of him or the long stretch of white beach or the car parked on the empty piece of land. Because he was thinking of other things. George Walmer had acquired three new videos. Pure porn. He was bringing them later.

Between the brown soil of the informal parking area and the stretch of beach there was a low dune – an irregular sandbank a meter or two high with occasional clumps of Port Jackson bushes or *vygie* ground cover.

Ferdy aimed for his usual route to the beach, a pathway worn through the dune. The corgis wanted to smell a plant. He jerked them back. They growled.

Ferdy saw the figure coming towards him but didn't find it odd. There were people on the beach at that hour quite often. Some jogged, some walked, some stared at the sea.

Ferdy only really saw the figure when the Mauser appeared from under the blue windbreaker. He assumed that it was a joke and wanted to laugh but then the big pistol was aimed at him and he saw the face and fear gripped his guts in a painful grasp.

'I'm a cripple,' he said, his eyes wild.

The corgis growled at the figure in front of them.

The Mauser, gripped in both hands, was aimed at his head. He saw the tension in the trigger finger, the set of the killer's jaw, the purposeful eyes and knew that he was going to die. Ferdy dropped the corgis' leads and sprang forward in an effort to save his life.

The shot thundered across the beach, an echo of the waves. The lead bullet broke his bottom right incisor, tore through his palate, just above his upper teeth, punched through the lower bone of his eye socket and broke through the skin just in front of his left ear. He staggered back, then dropped down into a sitting position. Pain shot through his head. The blood dripped warmly down his cheek. His left eye wouldn't focus.

But he was alive.

He looked up. His left eye. There was something seriously wrong with his left eye.

But with his right eye he saw the big pistol in front of him again.

'I'm a cripple.'

He didn't see the trigger finger tightening again. But he heard the mechanical metal sound.

Jammed, he thought. The thing won't shoot. Its innards have seized up. And Ferdy Ferreira though he was going to live.

The Mauser disappeared in front of him. He saw another pistol. Toy pistol, he thought, because it was so small.

He saw the strangest thing. The corgis stood with trembling upper lips and bared teeth, growling at the executioner. Then Charles rushed forward. Ferdy heard a shot. Another shot.

The dogs wanted to protect him, he thought and he was overcome with emotion. The little pistol was in front of him but he didn't hear the last shot.

Joubert drove to work from the swimming-pool in his own car, a yellow Cortina XR6, one of the monuments to the days when he still competed with Gerbrand Vos. He worried about the fact that after exercising for a week, he still couldn't swim more than four lengths before he was forced to rest.

Perhaps I'm in too much of a hurry, he thought, and lit a Special Mild. His diet also had to get off the ground. On the seat next to him was a blue and white Pick 'n Pay plastic bag. In it was his lunch which he had made himself that morning: whole wheat bread with low fat spread, lettuce leaves, tomato and cucumber slices. No salt.

He stopped at Murder and Robbery and Mavis came running out. He knew there was trouble before he even heard what she was saying.

*   *   *

The news editor at the SABC offices in Sea Point heard from the crime reporter of the radio team that the Mauser murderer had claimed a third victim.

The news editor read the newspapers. He knew this saga had the local newspapers on the hop. He could just imagine what they would do with number three. Now there was irrefutable evidence that the Cape could boast a serial killer. And that was good enough for national television. So the news editor telephoned the television reporter at home and the camera man at his flat. He gave them their brief.

'If anyone had a motive for killing Ferdy it was me,' said Gail Ferreira.

She sat in an armchair in the Plettenberg's sitting-room. Gerbrand Vos sat opposite her on a two-seater couch. He was on back-up duty that week. Joubert sat next to him, the two large detectives squashed together on a couch which was too small. But there was no other seating.

Each one held a cup of tea.

'What do you mean, Mrs. Ferreira?' Vos asked and lifted his cup to his mouth.

'Because Ferdy was bad news.' She said it forcibly and stressed the last two words. She sat up straight, with her knees together, her teacup held on her lap. Joubert noticed that she wasn't a pretty woman. Her black hair was liberally laced with grey. It was short and curly. Traces of a skin complaint in youth were still visible under the make-up. The corners of her mouth turned down naturally which gave her a permanently surly expression.

'Why do you say that?' Vos asked.

'Because he could never keep a job. Because he was lazy. Because he felt too sorry for himself. You see, Captain, Ferdy had polio, and his right foot was slightly affected. But there was nothing wrong with him. Only in his head. He thought the world owed him a living.'

She brought the cup to her lips.

'What kind of work did he do?' Joubert asked.

'He was a carpenter when he worked at all. He was clever with his hands. But according to him, his bosses were never good enough. He always said he had to work for himself. But he was useless. He went on a course once to learn to start his own business but nothing came of it. Then they advertised for carpenters for the factories in Atlantis and we moved here but it didn't last long. He complained that the Black carpenters got the best jobs and preferential treatment and he couldn't work under bosses like that. Now he sits at home every day, in front of the television, and he and that worthless George Walmer of the club watch blue movies the moment my back is turned.'

Vos put his cup down on the little table in the middle of the room.

'But you didn't kill him, ma'am. Therefore there must be someone else who had reason to . . .'

'Captain, Ferdy was too useless to make enemies,' Gail Ferreira said with finality.

'Have you ever heard the name James Wallace, Mrs. Ferreira?'

'No.'

'Jimmy Wallace?'

'No.'

'Drew Wilson?'

'No. Should I have?'

'The same murder weapon was probably used in their murders, ma'am. We're looking for a connection.'

'Were they also bad news?' she asked seriously.

The detectives didn't reply – Gerry Vos because he saw the question as rhetorical and Joubert because he was wondering whether the wife of Ferdy Ferreira didn't have something there. Both James J Wallace and Drew Wilson had been bad news. Each in his own way.

But then Gail Ferreira showed that she wasn't wholly without feeling. 'The house is going to be empty,' she sighed and put her cup on the table.

The detectives looked up, faintly surprised.

'Who's going to bark at me when I get home?'

19

The television news team was too late to shoot, in their somewhat tactless parlance, the gruesome remains of Ferdy Ferreira. They were too late at the murder scene to record the Police ballistics team, laboratory team, video unit, photographer and dog unit.

However, the cameraman found a blotch of blood in the sand where Ferdy's head had rested after the pistol had punched a hole through it. He made a recording of it. He also held the camera low over the white sand and walked through the gap in the dune in an attempt to get dramatic material of Ferdy Ferreira's last steps this side of the grave.

Then he and the reporter drove to the Old Ship Caravan Park and waited with the newspaper reporters in front of the Plettenberg. The television team didn't like that. They usually got preferential treatment at news events. The cameraman set up his tripod, screwed the Sony Betacam SP onto it and focused on the front door of the Plettenberg.

Joubert and Vos came out. Gail Ferreira said goodbye to them at the front door. The policemen walked to their cars. The reporters hurried after them.

The camera lens followed the procession. The microphone on the camera didn't pick up Vos's words, however: 'Fuckit, now the TV's here as well. You can keep the case, partner. The going's getting rough.'

The reporters reached them and asked for information.

'You know you must work through PR,' Joubert said.

'Just the basics, Captain, please.'

'The Brigadier wants to know what we're doing,' said Colonel Bart de Wit and nervously rubbed his mole. His smile was very vague. 'He heard from PR that the television was there as well.'

Joubert and Vos were sitting opposite him.

'Whether it's a new government or not, everything remains the same. Isn't it amazing the way the entire Force shits its pants every time the TV covers something,' said Vos and shook his head sadly.

De Wit's smile disappeared and Joubert's heart swelled with pride in his colleague.

'Captain, that was totally unnecessary. The Service's image is at stake here.'

'With respect, Colonel, it's the Minister and the Commissioner and the Brigadier's image. Because when the newspapers write something, it's fuckall. But just let the TV guys show an interest . . .'

'Captain Vos, your language does not become an officer. And we aren't here to do the work of PR. The Brigadier wants to know what we're going to do.'

Joubert saw that de Wit had regained his self-possession and his voice was heavy with that sarcastic intonation. 'We're investigating the case, Colonel.'

'But not well enough, Captain. This is the third murder and you don't even have a clue. Every theory bombs out. First the man who sleeps around. Then the homosexual. What's it this time? Lesbians?'

He knew de Wit was trying to humiliate him in front of Vos. He wanted to say something, retain his dignity but his mind refused to formulate the words.

'That's unfair, Colonel. With a serial there never are any clues,' Vos defended his colleague.

'Do you know something about the murders we don't know, Captain?'

'One doesn't have to be psychic to know that it's a serial, Colonel.'

'There was a gun of a different caliber involved in the Melkbos murder. Doesn't sound like the same modus operandi to me.'

Joubert found words. 'He knows his Mauser and his ammunition are not a hundred per cent dependable. One jamming and you're in trouble . . .'

'That's for fucking sure,' Gerbrand de Vos helped.

'And there was a jamming this morning. Only one 7,63 cartridge case.'

De Wit said nothing.

'We'll know if it's the same murderer tomorrow, Colonel.'

'Oh?'

'The ballistics guys in Pretoria are on the jump, Colonel. Because you evidently phoned them. I must thank you.'

'It's my job, Captain, to support my staff.' Then his tone of voice changed. 'But what do I tell the Brigadier?'

'I'm doing my best, Colonel,' Joubert said softly.

'But is that enough, Captain?' de Wit asked and smiled.

'He wants to nail you, Mat. And you're taking it lying down?'

Vos's hand was on Joubert's shoulder. They were walking down the passage on their way to their offices.

Joubert said nothing because he thought it hadn't gone too badly. At least he'd made a contribution, had had something to say. Usually he simply sat there . . .

'He's got no right to jerk you around like that.'

'Yes, Gerry.'

Vos stopped in front of his office door. 'You'll have to take him on, Mat. You know that?'

Joubert nodded.

'I'm with you, partner. All the way.'

He mumbled his thanks and walked to his office. The ochre-coloured SAP3 case files were piled up on his desk. He sat down. On top of the pile the two files slotted into one – Wallace's and Wilson's. He pushed the pile to one side and opened the two dossiers. Each dossier had three sections. Section A was for applicable evidence which could be used in court. Both files were pretty thin. Pictures taken by the pathologist. The forensic report, the ballistic findings, pictures of the scene.

Section B held his notes about the questioning and other corresponding matters. There were his summaries of conversations with Margaret Wallace, Walter Schutte, Zeelie . . .

In Section C he had made notes of everything he'd done in each investigation. His actions, those involved, the times when they occurred – everything written down in his untidy scrawl.

He took a new, clean SAP3, took out his notebook, unfolded the report of the uniformed constable who was first on the scene and started giving substance to the Ferdy Ferreira file.

His thoughts drifted back to de Wit's question. *But is it enough, Captain?*

Was it? Would someone else be able to slot in the pieces of the bloody puzzle to form a picture? Would someone who didn't have a grey veil between himself and the world, have asked better questions? Shown a sharper insight into human actions? Found a suspect in the narrow range?

He looked at the dossiers. The work wasn't bad. Without the former enthusiasm. But that was improving. Better than those dark, dark days of the disciplinary trial and the detectives who had refused to work with him. Better than . . .

He wanted to think about it. Examine the reasons.

The telephone rang. He picked up the receiver. 'Captain, it's time for the fame game again,' said Cloete of Public Relations.

'Oh?'

'The TV guys want an interview. And you know how important they are to us.'

20

The bank robber walked into Premier Bank's Milnerton branch at 15:32. There was a bounce in his step. He looked like Elvis Presley today. His black hair was combed back with a curl in the floppy lock, he had sideburns and heavy eyebrows above the dark glasses. He was dressed with a certain flamboyance in a pair of white trousers, white shoes, a white shirt and a white jacket.

But his cravat and the weapon under his jacket were black.

'Hello,' he said to Rosa Wasserman, a fat nineteen-year-old brunette with nervous problems.

'Good afternoon, sir,' said Rosa, 'Can I help you?'

Today the bank robber was doing his thing to the beat of rock and roll which only he could hear in the concert hall of his head. But there were observable signs, like the right foot tapping away, the voice which imitated the deceased king's.

'Indeed, sweetheart. Fetch us one of those large bank bags and fill it with fifty Rand notes. I've got a large old gun under my coat and I don't want to use it.'

The edge of the white coat was lifted slightly. Rosa heard the word 'sweetheart', saw the black stock of the gun. She turned to stone, her mouth at half cock, accentuating her double chin.

'Keep the foot off the alarm as well. Come on, sweetheart, let's boogie.'

Rosa's pulse rate had increased dramatically. So had the tempo of her breathing. The bank robber saw it.

'What perfume do you use? It smells delicious.'

This didn't work with Rosa Wasserman. He saw panic striking her – the hands shook, the bosom heaved, the eyes grew wild, the nostrils distended, the double chin developed a life of its own.

'Seems like I should've brought my Mauser,' said Elvis and with this one brief sentence changed his status permanently.

Rosa sometimes glanced at *Die Burger* in the morning before her father paged through it. She knew about the Mauser murders. Her fear of the man in front of her intensified. She put her hands over her ears as if she didn't want to hear the shot that would end her life.

She screamed with every ounce of power in her large body and pressed the alarm with determination.

When the lengthy scream stopped, the robber recovered. 'Sweetheart, you'll pay for this,' Elvis said and turned towards the door.

The alarm didn't ring in the bank itself, only on the computerised control panel of a security firm. Rosa's yell had petrified everyone else in the bank. They stared at her, not at the man in white. The bank robber walked out of the door. Rosa pointed to him and shrieked again. The other people in the bank followed her pointing finger, heads turning in surprise, but the robber had disappeared.

Joubert drove from Premier Bank in Milnerton to the sanatorium. He was annoyed. The newspaper reporters had asked endless questions. He knew they would go to town with this story. One look at *The Argus* poster was indication enough:

DEAD BEFORE DYING

MAUSER
MURDERER
ON THE
RAMPAGE.

Fortunately the attempted bank robbery was too late to hit today's newspapers. Television hadn't even heard about it. But tomorrow all hell would be let loose. Joubert had told the small group of reporters that it didn't necessarily indicate a connection between the bank robbery and the Mauser murders. The robber might have said it for effect. That wasn't what they wanted to hear.

'But you can't exclude the possibility of a connection, Captain?'

'No.'

They all scribbled in their notebooks.

Rosa Wasserman had changed from a pathetic bundle of fear into the woman of the hour. It was she who had blurted out the information to the reporters that the bank robber had spoken of 'his Mauser.'

'And he threatened me with death.'

Benny Griessel would've loved it. This circus. Benny would've shared his usual ironic perspective on the media with him.

Joubert stopped in front of the redbrick building and walked in. At Reception he told them he wanted to see Benny Griessel. The two nurses looked meaningfully at one another.

'I don't think that's a good idea, sir.'

He was annoyed by the decided tone of her voice. 'Why not?'

'He refused medication.' She saw that the man opposite her didn't grasp what it meant. 'We don't think Adjutant Griessel wants to see anyone at present.'

169

'I don't think you have the right to make decisions for him, nurse,' Joubert said aggressively.

The nurse stared at him through her pebble-lensed glasses as if she was weighing him up. Then she said softly: 'Come along, then.'

They walked in a direction opposite to where Benny's room was, she leading, he on her heels, pleased at having overcome bureaucracy.

They walked along silent passages and then up steps.

He heard the sounds long before they reached the door.

Griessel's voice, vaguely recognisable. Cries of pain. The bellowing of an animal filled with a deadly fear. A plea for help, for mercy.

Joubert's walk slowed. He wanted to stop. The nurse turned, took him by the sleeve of his jacket and pulled him closer – her method of punishment.

'Come,' she said. He didn't look at her. He walked towards the door, the sounds resonating in his head.

There were six hospital beds. Only on one, in the corner, a figure lay. Joubert stopped in his tracks. In the semi-darkness Griessel's black hair was visible above the white of the sheets. Heavy leather straps stretched across him from one side of the bed to the other. Benny Griessel's body jerked under the buckles, spasmodically, like convulsions before death. The noises emanated from deep within his bowels, regular and jolting with each exhalation of breath.

The nurse stood next to him. She said nothing. She merely looked at Joubert.

'I'm sorry,' he said quietly. 'I made a mistake.'

Then he turned on his heel and walked quickly down the grey passage. The sounds of Benny Griessel's tortured soul still sounded in his ears long after he had reached his car.

* * *

Margaret Wallace sat in the television room with her family. Her mother, her son and her daughter were there. They were having their meal in front of the set because the silence and unease at the dinner table upset them all.

'In the news tonight,' the news reader said, his face serious, and gave the headlines. Margaret didn't listen. The news reader reported a new political crisis, a drought disaster in Northern Transvaal and then . . . 'A third victim of the Cape's Mauser murderer but the police are still baffled.'

Margaret looked up and saw the photo of Ferdy Ferreira. Then the news reader supplied the rest of the events.

Didn't she know that face?

'You want me to switch it off, Maggie?' her mother asked.

Margaret shook her head. She looked at the screen while shots were being shown about politics and agriculture but searched her mind for a file which would supply a connection between man and place.

'In what seems to be developing into a major serial killer scare, the Cape's Mauser murderer struck for the third time this morning. The victim was 54-year-old Mr. Ferdy Ferreira of Melkbosstrand. Police say the antique murder weapon, a hundred-year-old Mauser Broomhandle pistol, is the only connection between this murder and the deaths of businessman James Wallace and jewellery designer Drew Wilson who both died from close range gunshot wounds during the past ten days.'

While the news reader uttered the words, the visuals which the cameraman had shot in the dunes appeared – the camera moving over the sand, ending in the patch of blood which had soaked into the sand.

Margaret looked away because it still reminded her . . .

Then she heard a voice she knew and looked up again.

Captain Mat Joubert's face filled the screen. His hair was still too long and somewhat untidy. His shoulders sagged as if bowed down by an invisible weight. His tie was too thin. His English accent was acceptable.

'The only connection seems to be the murder weapon. We have no reason to believe that the victims knew one another,' the big policeman said. At the bottom of the screen the caption read CAPT M.A.T. JOUBERT MURDER AND ROBBERY SQUAD.

The reporter's face appeared. 'But Mr. Ferreira and his two dogs died of gunshot wounds made with a smaller caliber?'

'Yes,' Mat Joubert replied. 'We believe the murderer carries a small caliber firearm as back-up because the Mauser seems to have been fired first but it did not prove to be fatal.'

'Captain, do you think the Mauser murderer will strike again?'

'It's impossible to say,' said Joubert and he looked uncomfortable.

Then the photo of Ferdy Ferreira appeared on the screen with two telephone numbers next to it. The news reader said: 'Anyone with information that could assist the police in their investigation, can call . . .'

Margaret stared at the picture of Ferdy Ferreira. She knew she had seen him. But where? How?

Should she phone the detective?

No, not until she remembered.

On the thirteenth floor of an apartment building in Sea Point a thirty-two-year-old woman sat in front of the television.

Her name was Carina Oberholzer. Since the visuals of the Mauser murderer she had seen nothing else that was show-

ing on the screen. She rocked back and forth in the armchair, ceaselessly, a human metronome. Her lips murmured
one word, over and over again: 'Lord, Lord, Lord,
Lord . . .'

Carina Oberholzer was re-living a piece of her past. The
images she recalled would take her life before the night was
over.

The forty-six-year-old man was watching the news bulletin
with his beautiful wife. His name was Oliver Nienaber. His
four sons, the eldest in matric, the youngest in standard
four, were somewhere in the large house, busy with their
own affairs. Oliver Nienaber had spent the past three weeks
in Pretoria. He too, had been very busy. He hadn't read the
newspapers. The news visuals of the Mauser murder was
like a hammerblow to his chest. But he stayed calm so that
his wife wouldn't notice.

He looked for solutions, weighed the implications, recalled
incidents. Oliver Nienaber was intelligent. He could think fast
even when fear gripped him like an evil spirit. That was why
the man had made such a success of his calling.

He got up after the weather report. 'I still have some work
to do,' he said.

His wife looked up from her needlework and smiled at
him. He saw the flawlessness of her blonde beauty and
wondered if he was going to lose her. If he was going to lose
everything. If he was going to lose his life.

'Don't work too late, darling,' she said.

He walked to his study, a large room. Against the walls
hung the photographs, the certificates. His rise. His triumph. He opened his slender attaché case of real grey
buffalo hide and took out a thin black notebook and a
fountain pen. He made a list of names. *Mac McDonald,
Carina Oberholzer, Jacques Coetzee.*

Then he skipped a few lines and wrote the name *Hester Clarke*. He put the notebook on his desk and reached for the new Cape telephone guide next to the telephone. He paged to M. His finger moved quickly down the columns. It stopped at MacDonald Fisheries. He underlined the number, then wrote it down. Then he paged to O looked for Carina Oberholzer's number and wrote that down. He had trouble with Jacques Coetzee's number because there were a great many J Coetzees and he didn't know the precise address. At Hester Clarke's name he left only a question mark. Then he took a bunch of keys out of the attaché case, walked to a corner in the study, unlocked the safe and took out the big Star 9 mm pistol. He checked the safety catch and put the pistol, the notebook and the pen back into the case.

Oliver Nienaber stood quite still, with the attaché case in his hand, his head bent, his eyes closed. It seemed as if he were praying.

Joubert knew he wouldn't be able to read. The evening was hot and the southeaster made sad noises as it blew around the corners of the house. The front veranda faced north. There the wind was only audible in the trees. He sat down on the slate-tiled floor, his back against the wall and lit a cigarette.

He wanted to laugh at himself.

Had he really thought he would be able to bury Lara?

Just because he had thought about the ripe body of a eighteen-year-old for a few days? Because he was 'consulting' a psychologist?

It wasn't the first time that he had heard the sounds torn out of Benny Griessel.

He knew those sounds. He had made them himself. Not with his voice but in his head. In that hazy past when he still hated the pain and the humiliation. Before he had become addicted to it.

Tell your psychologist, he thought. Tell her you're as addicted to the darkness of your soul as Griessel is to the bottle. But there is a difference, Doctor. You can take Mat Joubert out of the dark but you can't take the dark out of Mat Joubert. It had become part of his flesh, his body had grown around it as a tree will take a length of barbed wire into its trunk to have it forever scratching and tearing and causing the sap to bleed.

He heard Lara's laugh again, the one he played over and over again on the tape recorder while he banged his head against the wall – over and over again until the blood ran into his eyes.

Griessel's pain tonight had been a blessing in disguise. It had brought Joubert to his senses.

He should have realised it the day before, when Hanna Nortier asked her last question. When he'd realised that he would have to speak about Lara, when he'd realised that he would not be able to tell the doctor everything.

He was Lara Joubert's captive. And the key to his cell was there, within reach, so invitingly within reach. Just tell the good doctor everything. The whole truth, Nothing but the truth. Tell the doctor that part of Lara's death which only he knew about – and he knew he would be freed. Share that hour with Dr Hanna Nortier and he could shake off the burden, tear the dark curtain.

It was half past twelve when he had reached the tape recorder, down in the cellar, and pressed the button to turn the cassette. With the earphones illegally on his head, he'd looked round to check whether anyone could see him, certain of his right to break the law in this way. Press the button. Unsuspecting. In the execution of his duty.

PLAY.

He wouldn't be able to tell Hanna Nortier.

Joubert leant his head against the wall and shot the cigarette into the dark.

He couldn't even tell it to himself, he thought. How many times hadn't he tried to look at it anew. To look for excuses, mitigation, a way out. To consider other interpretations.

But nothing would work.

He had burnt the cassette. But the voices were still on tape. In his head. And he could no longer press the play button. Not even for himself. It was too fucking painful.

He leant sideways to get his hand into his trouser pocket, took out his cigarettes, lit another one.

Come on, Doctor Hanna, he thought. Could you really sweep up the debris of a human being and fit them together, apply the wonder glue and say that he was whole again? The cracks would be visible forever so that only the lightest touch would be enough to shatter the whole into fragments once more.

What was the use of that, Doctor?

Tell me, Doctor, why shouldn't I put the cool maw of my service pistol into my mouth and blow the last copy of the tape, together with all the ghosts collected up there, into eternity?

Carina Oberholzer sat at her dressing-table, writing.

She wrote as the tears ran down her cheeks and dripped onto the blue notepaper.

Carina Oberholzer didn't write why the Mauser murderer was busy sending people into eternity with one pull of the trigger. She didn't want to. She couldn't. All that her mind allowed her was to write. *We deserve it*. And then she wrote that they mustn't stop the murderer. And that they mustn't punish the murderer.

She wrote down a name and surname with a shaking hand, but it was quite legible.

She added the words *Mama, forgive me* although her father was still living, and signed the letter: Carrie. Then she put the pen down next to the paper and walked to the window. She opened it wide, lifted her foot and put it on the sill. She hoisted herself up into the frame, balanced briefly, and then she fell.

She fell soundlessly, except for the material of her skirt which fluttered softly in the wind, like a flag.

Later, when the wail of a siren sounded above the city's roar, the wind shifted. It blew gently through the open window on the thirteenth floor and like an invisible hand picked up the single sheet of blue notepaper and let it slip down the thin dark space between dressing-table and wall.

Joubert sat on his front stoep and looked up at the pale stars which glimmered above the suburban sky and didn't know how to react to his newly found insight.

Yet he knew something had changed.

A week or two, a month, a year ago the concept of a pistol in his mouth had been so logical. Not a yearning, only a logical way out which would have to be used like a tool for a specific task. Now, when he thought about the moment of truth, when the hand had to pick up the gun and the lips had to open and the finger had to contract, Mat Joubert still wanted to live for a while.

And he briefly considered the reasons why things had changed: The Triumph of the Great Erection? The many aspects of Hanna Nortier?

But then his thoughts wandered.

He was going to be a cripple, he thought. The poor man's Ferdy Ferreira. He would have to take Lara Joubert with him – if he couldn't tell Hanna Nortier everything. He would have to drag the load of pain with him for the rest of his life.

Could he do it?

Perhaps.

He got up off the stoep's cold floor, stretched his arms and felt the muscles of his back and his shoulders, the vague, pleasurable lassitude of muscles which had been exercised in a swimming pool.

Perhaps, he thought.

He turned, walked into the house, locked the door behind him and walked to the spare bedroom looking for something to read. The paperbacks lay in an untidy heap.

He would have to put up bookcases, he thought and stood in the doorway for a moment, staring, contemplating. He was aware of an urge to set the books in order, to arrange them according to authors, each one neatly in its allotted space.

He walked into the room, went down on his knees next to the pile and picked up the top one.

21

D r Hanna Nortier lay on a sofa. He sat next to her on a
chair. He stroked her colourless hair with soft mechanical movements. His heart was filled with love and pity
for her. He spoke to her. He emptied his heart. The tears
poured down his cheeks. His hand shifted to her breast,
small and soft as a bird, his fingers kneaded the tissue
carefully under the material. He looked at her. He saw that
she was pale. He realised that she was dead. But why was he
hearing shrill sounds emanating from her? The alarm. He
opened his eyes. The green figures of the instrument said
6:30.

He got up immediately and drove to the swimming pool.
He swam seven purposeful lengths before he needed to rest.
When he felt better he did two more lengths, slowly.

Joubert bought a newspaper when he stopped for a packet
of Special Milds mainly because of the front page headlines.
TELLER LIVES IN FEAR OF MAUSER the biggest one
read. And a smaller sub-heading: IS SWEETHEART
ROBBER THE SERIAL KILLER?

He read the reports in the car in front of the cafe. The
main news was the bank robber's reference made to Rosa
Wasserman but there were also other, smaller reports about
the crimes. In one the reporter, using dates, tried to trace a
connection between the murders and the bank robberies. In
another he quoted a Dr AL Boshoff 'well-known Cape

criminologist and lecturer in Criminology at the University of Stellenbosch' on the psyche of the serial killer.

Joubert finished reading and folded the newspaper. His mouth thinned. He had never worked on a case which had engendered so much on-going publicity. There had been the kidnapping of a deputy minister's child in '89. The case was solved within hours but the press had had a two day orgy. And the axe murderer of Mitchells Plain in '86. The newspapers wrote for weeks. But chiefly on the inside pages because the victims were not white.

He switched on the engine and drove to Bellville, to the big hardware shop in Durban Road.

Why did he find the reporter's copy about the dates and the similarities between the crimes so unacceptable? Was it simply a premonition, an opinion honed by experience?

No. It was the differences which the reporter had ignored. The bank robber was an exhibitionist. He played for the main pavilion with his dramatic disguises and showy dialogue; the pet name and the questions about perfume. The bank robber was a coward who kept his gun hidden under his coat and relied on the fear of women.

The Mauser murderer was cool and clinical.

It couldn't be the same man.

Or could it?

He was annoyed by his own indecisiveness. 'Fighting crime is like playing golf, Matty,' Blackie Swart had said once. 'Just as soon as you think you've got it made, it sideswipes you again.'

He had made a casual drawing for his bookcase the previous evening. He explained briefly to the salesman what he was looking for. The salesman was enthusiastic. He showed Joubert the various kinds of do it yourself bookcase kits on the market. Some sets were packed in such a way that the buyer could assemble it in five minutes without drilling a single hole, sawing one plank or hammering in one nail.

Joubert wanted to do more with his hands. He had developed a certain dedication to the task since the previous evening. He wanted to smell sawdust and use the electric drill which had been gathering dust in the garage for almost three years. He wanted to sweat and measure and fit and make pencil marks on the wall and on the wood.

He and the salesman decided on a more primitive patent: long metal strips which had to be screwed to the wall vertically. Metal struts hooked horizontally onto the strips. The wooden shelves which Joubert would have to measure and saw, rested on the supports.

He bought bits for the drill and screws and plastic envelopes into which the screws would be sheathed. Sandpaper, varnish, paint brushes, a new tape measure, and a three point plug completed his purchases because he couldn't remember whether the electric drill still had a plug.

He paid by cheque and did a quick sum in his head to see how much he'd saved by not buying one of the luxury do it yourself models. Two black men helped him carry the stuff to his car. He tipped them five Rand each. Some of the planks and the metal strips were too long for the interior of the car or the boot. He let them stick out of the window.

He drove to the Bellville Market to replenish his stock of fruit and vegetables and ate an apple as he drove home.

When he arrived Emily was already doing the laundry. He went to say hello to her, and asked after her children in the Transkei and her husband in Soweto. He told her the spare bedroom would soon be a very tidy room. She shook her head in disbelief.

His enthusiasm for the task was great. He opened the garage door and chose the tools. Everything, except a few screwdrivers and the lawnmower, was covered in a thick layer of dust.

Some of the tools had belonged to his father. His father, who had used them hastily but with precision and impatience. 'No, they must teach you at school how to use these things. Here you'll just get hurt. And your mother will be cross with me.'

Joubert walked to the second bedroom again to use his new tape measure. He made a new sketch on paper. He fetched another apple in the kitchen and went to fetch the drill and the metal strips. The electric drill had no plug. He put on the new one with a feeling of deep satisfaction. He measured where the holes for the screws had to be made. Then it occurred to him that he needed a spirit level.

No, he wasn't going to drive out again. He would measure carefully, using the corner of the room as a guide-line. He started working.

When he had drilled all the holes, he fetched the portable radio out of Lara's night-stand. There were always new batteries in her drawer. He looked. They were still there. He slotted them into the radio and switched it on. He turned the tuner past a few music stations until he found RSG, the Afrikaans station. Two men were delivering a cricket commentary. He carried the radio to the garage because he had to do the sawing.

The radio played a cut of boeremusiek. It recalled memories. His father never listened to cricket. But in the time before television he listened to rugby commentaries on a Saturday afternoon. And swore at the commentators and the players and the referee when Western Province lost. After the game, before they switched to other stadiums for summaries, there was always a snatch of boeremusiek or a band. That was the signal for his father to go and have his Saturday evening drink in the bar of the Royal. And

Joubert had to lay the fire because on Saturday evenings they had a barbecue. Sometimes he had to keep feeding the fire with rooikrans logs until late at night because his father allowed no one else to barbecue the meat. 'It's a man's job.'

At the start he had enjoyed fetching his father in the bar. He had liked the warmth of the place, the camaraderie, the good-natured friendship, the respect the people there had for his father.

He started sawing. The sweat ran down his forehead. He wiped it away with the back of his hand and left a dirty mark on his face.

Over the sound of the saw he heard the commentator say: 'Zeelie from the opposite side. He's at the wicket now. And Loxton plays that one defensively back to the bowler . . .'

Zeelie, the great white hope as suspect. He had never asked Gail Ferreira whether her husband had known Zeelie. But he was reasonably certain what the answer would be.

Three inexplicable murders. With nothing in common. A family man, gay and a cripple. A promiscuous heterosexual, a conservative homosexual and a blue movies addict. Married, unmarried, married. Businessman, goldsmith, unemployed.

There was no connection.

There was one connection – the bare fact that there was no connection.

A murderer who without any pattern, without rhyme or reason, in the late afternoon, early morning or middle of the night, pulled the trigger and took a life. How did he choose his victims? Eeny, meeny, miny, mo . . . Or did he see someone in the street and follow him home because he didn't like his face or clothes?

It had happened before. Here. Overseas. It drove the media crazy because people wanted to read about it. It woke a primitive fear: death without reason, the most fearful of

all fates. And the Police were powerless because there was
no pattern. The great crime prevention machine's fuel was
the observable pattern, like an established modus operandi
or a comprehendible motive. Like sex. Or avarice. But if the
observable pattern was missing, or its octane too low, the
great machine came to a sighing halt. Its tank empty. It had
trouble in re-starting.

And if the driver was Captain Mat Joubert to boot . . .

All he needed was one small lead which didn't disappear
like mist before the sun when you gave it a sharp look. Just
one. A small one.

He picked up a plank to take to the spare room to fit it.
Before he was out of the garage he heard Zeelie bowling
Loxton for a duck.

22

The news editor of *The Weekend Argus* paged through the Saturday edition. He was looking for follow-ups for the Sunday edition – news which hadn't had the last bit of blood squeezed out of it. So that he could assign reporters to do just that.

He paged from the back to the front, past the copy on page six under the small headline SEA POINT WOMAN DIES IN FALL.

He didn't read the details because he knew the contents. He had, after all, checked the new reporter's work.

A 32-year-old Sea Point secretary, Ms Carina Oberholzer, sustained fatal injuries when she fell from her thirteenth storey flat in Yates Road.

Ms Oberholzer, an employee of Petrogas in Rondebosch, was alone in her flat at the time.

According to a police spokesman, foul play is not suspected. 'We believe it was a tragic accident.'

The news editor turned to page two where there were a few run on stories about the Mauser murder. Tucked into the unattractive non-modular page make-up, there was a half column photo of Captain Mat Joubert.

And, as he told the crime reporter of *The Argus* sometime later, it rang a bell somewhere. He picked up the receiver next to him and dialed an internal number, waited until someone answered.

'Hi, Brenda. I need a file, pronto, please. M.A.T. Joubert.

Captain, Murder and Robbery.' He thanked her and rang off. Eight minutes later the brown file landed on his desk. He shifted the telexes in front of him out of the way, opened the file and quickly paged through the contents as if he was looking for something. Then he gave a sigh of relief and extracted a somewhat yellowing *Argus* report and read it.

He got up, the copy in his hand and walked to the crime reporter's desk in the general news office. 'Did you know that this guy's wife died in the line of duty?' he asked and handed over the evidence.

'No,' said Genevieve Cromwell who, despite her name, was a unprepossessing, unattractive woman. She shifted her glasses.

'Could be a nice story. Human interest angle. Two years after, still pursuing justice, still wearing the tragedy, that sort of shit.'

Genevieve's face brightened. 'Yeah,' she said. 'He might have a new girlfriend.'

'Don't go starry-eyed on me,' the news editor said. 'Let's do something so comprehensive that there's nothing left for the others. Talk to him, his boss, his friends, his neighbours. Hit the files, dig a little.'

'He's a nice man, you know.'

'I've never met him.'

'He's a nice man. Sort of shy.'

'Get that fucking romantic look off your face, dear, and get going.'

'And handsome, too, in a big cuddly bear kind of way.'

'Jesus,' he said, shook his head in disgust and walked back to his office. But Genevieve didn't hear her boss blaspheming. She stared at the ceiling seeing nothing.

Joubert made his second little error when he was putting a screw through the metal strip into the wall.

When it still had a quarter way to go, the screw refused to budge. He decided to give the screw a little help with a few taps of the hammer. This was a wrong decision because the hole he had drilled earlier simply wasn't deep enough.

When he tapped the screw with the hammer it broke, plastic envelope and all together with a hefty piece of plaster.

Joubert, who wasn't in Gerbrand Vos's league, said something which would've cheered his colleague's heart. Emily, ironing in the kitchen, heard it. She smiled and put her hand in front of her mouth.

Cloete of Public Relations phoned just after a quarter past five on the Saturday afternoon.

Bart de Wit was playing chess with Bart Jnr. But he didn't mind the invasion of his time because he was losing.

'Sorry to bother you at home, Colonel, but the *Argus* has just phoned me. They want to do a major story on Captain Joubert. Because he's investigating the murders and the bank robberies. Interview with you, with members of his team, with him, his previous cases, the whole tutti.'

De Wit's first thought was that the newspaper knew something.

It could happen. He thought. Reporters dug up information in impossible places. And now they were suspicious.

'No,' de Wit said.

'Colonel?'

'No. Under no circumstances. Over my dead body.'

Cloete's heart sank. He waited for the Colonel to offer some explanation. But Bart de Wit said nothing. Eventually Cloete said he would inform the *Argus* and said goodbye. Why had he ever accepted this post? It was impossible to keep every officer and every member of the press happy at the same time.

He sighed and phoned the reporter.

Joubert had all four screws secured to the wall.

He stood back and had a look. The hole where the plaster had fallen off the wall was unsightly. He saw that not all the strips were level. His eye, without the spirit level, had not been all that accurate.

You are not a handy man, he acknowledged resignedly. But once the books were on the shelves it would virtually cover the strips. But right now he needed a cigarette. And a Castle . . . No, not a Castle. A pear?

'What's happening to you?' he said loudly.

'Mr. Mat?' Emily asked in the kitchen.

Bart de Wit Jnr won the game easily because his father's thoughts were not on chess.

His father's mind was working at top speed. The big question was whether the newspapers knew about Joubert's psychological treatment and the black marks on his record. And if they knew, how did they know?

But if he presumed that they might not know, what were the chances of their finding out?

They're like hyenas, he thought. They would gnaw and bite at the bone until it snapped and they could get to the juicy marrow of the story which they would then suck with a great noise.

Whether they knew or not, he was going to take Captain Mat Joubert off the investigations. On Monday morning.

Not a pleasant task but it was part of a leader's work. Sometimes sacrifices had to be made so that the law could take its course.

Rather give the cases to Gerbrand de Vos.

It was like a weight off his shoulders. He felt relieved. He applied his concentration to the board in front of him.

'Checkmate,' said Bart Jnr and rubbed his finger alongside his nose. There was no mole there.

He took Mrs. Nofomela to the bus terminus at Bellville station by car and drove home. He was physically tired, he felt dirty and sweaty and he was hungry. The more he thought about his hunger, the more it grew.

He decided that he needed a good meal. Not junk food. He would go to a decent restaurant. For a steak, thick and brown and juicy, a fillet which melted in the mouth with . . .

No, he would have to stick to fish. For the diet. Kingklip. A large, fat slice of kingklip with lemon butter sauce. No, sole, the way they prepared it at the Lobster Pot – grilled, with a cheese and mushroom sauce.

His mouth filled with saliva. His stomach growled like far-off thunder. When last had he been this hungry? Really hungry, with that slight light-headedness, that sharp readiness for the taste of food, the pleasure of satiety? He couldn't remember.

He bathed and dressed and drove to the restaurant. When he sat down he knew it had been the wrong thing to do.

It wasn't the eyes staring at the big man sitting alone which upset him. It was the sudden realisation when he looked at the couples who sat at tables talking softly and intimately, that he was alone.

He gobbled his sole because he wanted to get away. Then he drove home. He heard the telephone at the door. He walked quickly, with a heavy tread and picked up the receiver.

'Hello, Captain Joubert?'

He recognised the voice. 'Hello, Dr Nortier.'

'Do you remember that I spoke about social groups?'

'Yes.'

'Tomorrow morning we're going to the Friends of the Opera's preview of *The Barber*. It's at eleven o' clock in the orchestra's practice room at the Nico. You're very welcome to join us.'

Her voice sang and danced over the electronic distance between them. He saw her features in his mind's eye.

'I . . . er . . .'

'You don't have to decide now. Think about it.'

'I'm busy building a bookcase.'

She sounded surprised and impressed. 'I didn't know woodwork was your hobby.'

'Well . . . er . . .'

'Well, perhaps we'll see you tomorrow.'

'Maybe,' and said goodbye.

He looked at his watch. It was half past seven. Which meant that she didn't have a very busy social life on this Saturday evening, either.

It made him feel better.

23

Oliver Nienaber was reading the Sunday edition of the *Weekend Argus*.

He was in bed, his wife next to him. She was reading the newspaper's *Magazine*. It was part of their Sunday morning ritual. Except that since the day before yesterday Oliver Nienaber had been reading his newspapers with far closer attention than usual. That was why he saw the small report about Carina Oberholzer.

Now Oliver Nienaber urgently needed to get up. He needed to move, he wanted to run away, away from the things that were happening. The timing couldn't have been worse because he was about to achieve his ideals, make his dreams come true. Things were going so well, with him, his family, his business.

And now the Mauser murders and the death of Carina Oberholzer.

We believe it was a tragic accident, the police were quoted in the newspaper. He didn't agree. He had a strong suspicion that it was no accident. How it could've happened he couldn't imagine. Because it was difficult to imagine . . .

Again he felt the tightening in his chest as if a giant hand was pressing down on it.

He would have to speak to MacDonald. And Coetzee.

Then it struck him. MacDonald or Coetzee might well be the 'accident.' Mac was big enough to fling a woman like Carina Oberholzer out of her window with one hand. But why would he . . .

Coetzee? What about Coetzee? No. It made no sense.

It made no sense. He got up, purposefully.

'What now, darling?' his wife asked and creased the flawless, smooth, creamy skin of her forehead.

'I've just remembered a call I have to make.'

'You never relax,' she said with more admiration than reproach and went back to the magazine she was holding.

He walked to his study and dialed the number of Mac-Donald Fisheries. There was no reply. It's Sunday, idiot, he told himself. He would drive to Hout Bay tomorrow. He had to discuss this affair.

It made him uneasy. It was irritating. It could spoil everything.

Margaret Wallace didn't read the Sunday papers. Especially now, after her husband's death.

But she caught a quick glimpse of the front page of the *Sunday Times* which her mother had bought. There was a report about the Mauser murders with a smallish photo of Ferdy Ferreira next to it.

She went to sit in the summer sun on the swing seat in the garden with a cup of coffee. The sun, its warmth, seemed to lighten her pain.

Where had she seen that face before?

Think carefully, she thought. Think systematically. Start with Jimmy's work. Think, because it might help to catch the scum who had taken Jimmy away. And perhaps that would relieve her enormous grief. If only she knew why someone had wanted to do it to him, to her, to them.

He had finished sawing the planks. He placed them on the metal struts, arranged the shelves so that his paperbacks would fit.

His thoughts were even busier.

The Barber?

Was that the name of an opera? He thought so. Some-where there was a brain cell with the information which was wrestling against the dark. How silly human beings were, he laughed at himself. He could've asked what *The Barber* was. 'Dr Hanna, please explain to this fucking stupid policeman what *The Barber* is, please.' And more than likely she would've enjoyed it and he would've known by now. But human beings were odd. They didn't want to be caught out. Live a lie and resist being caught out at any price.

If it was an opera he didn't want to go.

It was Sunday Afternoon music. Those hours which were sheer torture when he was at high school, when the silence in the house was palpable, a noiseless sound when he had the radio in his room on very softly so that it wouldn't disturb his parents and some or other fat woman yelled as if she was being assaulted – morally or immorally.

He had cut the one plank too short.

How on earth had he managed that? He had measured each one so carefully. That meant that there was one plank short. He wouldn't be able to finish today.

If he went, he would be able to see Hanna Nortier.

Revel in her strange attractiveness.

But the others. The other crazies. He didn't want to follow her to the opera with a herd of rabid sheep. 'Hey, there's Doc Nortier with her patients. Hello, Doc. Shame, look at that big number with the dull eyes. Shell-shocked, probably.'

Suddenly he remembered Griessel. He would have to . . . visit was the wrong word. He would have to see him.

Then he might as well . . .

And he decided to go to the bloody opera preview and then go and see Benny afterwards. If it was possible.

*   *   *

Hanna Nortier stood in the passage of the orchestra's practice room, a frown on her face.

He saw that she was informally dressed and his stomach contracted. He was wearing grey trousers and his black blazer with the crest of the Police College's swimming team on the pocket. And a white shirt with a maroon tie. She looked small and slender and defenceless in her long navy skirt, white blouse and white sandals. She smiled when she saw him, an odd expression on her face because the frown was still there and competed with the smile.

'No one else has come,' she said and looked past him at the entrance.

'Oh,' he said. It was a possibility he hadn't considered. He stood next to her, uncomfortable. The blazer was slightly tight across the shoulders. He folded his hands in front of him. Hanna Nortier was dwarfed next to him. She still looked frowningly at the entrance, then at her watch, an overdone gesture which he didn't see.

'They're going to begin now.' But she remained where she was, uncomfortable.

Joubert didn't know what to say. He looked at the other people who were walking through the door at the end of the passage. They were all informally clad. There wasn't a tie in sight. He felt everyone staring at him. At him and Hanna Nortier. Beauty and the Beast.

She took a decision. 'Let's go and sit down.'

She walked ahead of him, down the passage and through the door. It was a large room, almost as big as the Olympic swimming pool in which he suffered every morning. The floor was contoured into steps, like a flat amphitheater, which ran from a low centre and divided to rise on both sides of the middle aisle. Chairs covered the contoured steps. Almost every seat had already been taken. Below, in the centre, there was a piano, a few chairs and some stainless steel music stands.

He followed her, looked at his black shoes. He saw that they weren't shined. He wished he could hide them. It felt as if the audience's eyes were fixed with his, on his drab shoes. And his tie.

Eventually she sat down. He sat next to her. He glanced around him. No one was looking at him. People were chatting to one another, wholly relaxed.

Should he tell her that he knew nothing about opera? Before she wanted to discuss it and he made a fool of himself. Perhaps he should.

'Well,' she said and smiled at him. Without the frown. He wished he could get rid of his frustrations so easily, immediately and totally. 'You're the one I didn't expect, Captain Mat Joubert.'

Tell her.

'I . . .'

A collection of people filed through the door. The audience applauded enthusiastically. The arrivals sat down on chairs against the wall at the back of the piano. One man remained standing. The applause died down and the man smiled. He began speaking.

It seemed as if he and Drew Wilson would've liked one another, Joubert thought.

The man spoke about Rossini. His voice wasn't loud but Joubert could hear him clearly. He gave Hanna Nortier a quick glance. She was fascinated.

Joubert took a deep breath. It wasn't as bad as he'd thought.

The speaker spoke with great enthusiasm. Joubert began to listen.

'And then at thirty-seven, Rossini wrote his last opera. *Wilhelm Tell*,' the man said.

Ha, Joubert thought. The Great Predator also feasts on the flesh of the famous.

'For the remaining forty years of his life, he wrote no other opera – unless one could describe the *Stabat Mater* as such. Was he lazy? Was he tired? Or had the creative urge simply dried up?' the man asked and was quiet for a brief moment.

'We will never know.'

Not the work of the Predator, Joubert thought, but Rossini remained his blood brother. Except that he had beaten the composer. He was only thirty-four and he was already tired, his creative juices exhausted. Would the brain behind great compositions like *The State versus Thomas Maasen* and gripping works like *The Case of the Oranjezicht Rapist* never solve a classical crime again?

We will never know.

Or would we?

The speaker was talking about *The Barber of Seville*. Joubert burnt the full name of the opera into his mind. He didn't want to forget it. If Hanna Nortier spoke about it, he didn't want to make a fool of himself at any price.

'It's curious that the Italians almost hissed the first performance of *The Barber* off the stage,' the speaker said. 'What a humiliation it must've been for Rossini.'

Joubert smiled inwardly. Indeed, friend, I can understand it. I know humiliation.

The man spoke about the libretto. Joubert didn't know what it meant. He absorbed each word, looked for clues. He decided it had to mean the story.

'We are privileged to have the well-known Italian tenor, Andro Valenti, as Figaro in this year's production,' said the man with the soft voice and turned round. Behind him another man stood up. The people clapped and Valenti bowed. 'Andro will sign the first aria, "Largo al factotum", for us. You all know it.'

The manner in which the audience applauded made it clear to Joubert that they all knew and liked it.

He watched the Italian. The man wasn't tall, but broad in the shoulder and chest. He stood easily, hands relaxed at his sides, feet planted wide. A young woman had sat down at the piano. They nodded at one another. The Italian smiled when the notes sounded from the piano. He took a deep breath.

Joubert was startled by the intensity of Valenti's voice. It was like a radio suddenly switched on, its volume turned up too high.

The Italian's voice filled the room. He sang in his own language and often repeated the name, Figaro. The music was light and rhythmical, the melody surprisingly pleasant to his ears. And Valenti sang with abandon.

Joubert was fascinated by the man's attitude, his enthusiasm, his self-confidence, his voice which made the wooden floor under Joubert's feet quiver, the ease with which he sang. But there was something else, something which made him feel guilty, something like an accusation. He tried to identify it, had difficulty in ridding himself of the positive hold the music had on him.

The Italian was enjoying it. This was his profession and he did it well and he enjoyed it without reservations.

How very different from Captain Mat Joubert.

He was suspicious. Was this why Hanna Nortier had brought him here? Was this a secret, sophisticated form of therapy?

The man's voice and the sweet exuberance of the melody invaded him again. It filled Joubert with a curious longing. He concentrated on the music, allowed the longing to grow in his sub-conscious, nameless and formless.

It struck him just before Valenti completed the aria. He also wanted to get up and sing, stand next to the Italian and roar so that he, too, could feel the euphoria. He wanted life to glow in him like a great burning brand. He wanted to do his work with the disdainful commitment of total efficiency. He longed for enthusiasm, for passion, for those rare moments of intensity when one felt that life was laughing with you. He longed for life. He was tired, and sick of death. He had such a yearning for life. Then the audience applauded. Mat Joubert also clapped. Louder than anyone else.

They had coffee at a restaurant.

'Did you like it?' she asked.

'I know nothing about opera.'

'One doesn't have to know anything about something to enjoy it.'

'I . . . er . . .' He was very aware of the fact that she was The Psychologist, The Weigher of Words. He dropped his head and shoulders. 'It was lovely, at the beginning. But later . . .'

'You felt like a child who had eaten too many sweets?'

He didn't understand her immediately. She explained. The first one was delicious, sweet and tasty. But then it became too much.

'Yes,' he said, surprised that she understood it so well.

'It's a sensory overload. You should be pleased that it wasn't Wagner.'

'The name sounds vaguely familiar,' he said. 'Has he got a criminal record?'

He surprised himself with his attempt at humour, the manner in which he handled his own ignorance and her superior knowledge.

She smiled. He caught a glimpse of her personality because the small smile was a mere movement of her pretty, delicate mouth. Her eyes wore the traces of a frown. There was a withdrawn quality about her as if she was aware of every emotion and the reaction of others to her personality. He wondered whether this was the price she had to pay for the knowledge in her head. Every thought was measured against a paragraph in a textbook.

'I'll lend you a CD of *The Barber*. If you listen to it and get used to the music and get to know it you'll be able to bear more.'

'I don't have a CD player.' Lara had bought the music centre which stood in his living-room, on a police salary. It had an unknown name, was a special offer at Lewis Stores but it was good enough for Lara's Abba records and later BZN. Sometimes she turned up the sound to an ear-splitting volume and danced in the dark room, alone, while he sat in a chair and watched her and knew that when she had finished . . .

And he had wondered if the neighbours weren't going to complain about the loud music but he couldn't wait for the energy in her body, absorbed through the music, to be unleashed on him. Later, after her death, he had wondered about those moments when she, filled with the rhythm of the music, had mounted him on their double bed. Was the man in her head and the one between her thighs the same person? Or was he the means with which she acted out a fantasy, her black hair with the auburn lights over her face, her eyes closed, her breasts shiny with the sweat of love, her hips heaving like the sea, ceaselessly, until deep sounds indicated the moment of orgasm, rhythmic, rhythmic, faster, faster, uhm, uhm, uhm, uhm and she gasped and she came, unaware that his own climax had already been reached and that he was watching her with his consuming love, and gratitude for his luck, storing each millimeter of her unbelievably lithe body in his memory.

Hanna Nortier had said something he hadn't heard and

he blushed at his thoughts and his mouth which hung slightly open because of the intensity of the memory.

She saw that he hadn't heard. 'I'll tape it. You have a cassette player?'

'Yes,' he said.

'And a television.' It wasn't a question.

'No.' He wasn't going to tell her that he had given the television to his cleaning woman because he'd sat in front of it night after night, like a zombie, while one American sitcom after the other rolled across the screen and the canned laughter had rubbed his nerve ends raw, and each stupid story of each stupid programme with its own stupid moral had been a re-arrangement of his own stupid life.

'Then you didn't see yourself on television on Friday night?'

'No.'

He didn't want their meeting to turn into a therapy session. He and a pretty woman together in a restaurant. So different to last night. He wanted to keep up the appearance. What other people were seeing, a couple.

'The media are really giving it a run for its money,' she said and he realised that she also wanted to avoid their professional status.

'Ja. Seems as if other news is low on the ground.'

'Did you see yesterday's *Burger*?' He could just think that she must be desperate – because the man didn't have either a CD player or a television.

'Yesterday's, yes.'

'Do you think it's the same person? The murderer and the robber?'

He took a deep breath, his uncertainty willing him to close the door in her face, to give her a brief reply, afraid that he might not be able to motivate it, afraid that he might make a fool of himself in front of this small, pretty woman.

'I doubt it,' he said and began speaking, slowly and carefully. He told her about the murders, one by one, about the suspects and the intrigues and the dead end streets. He forgot about himself when he explained patterns and criminal behaviour and his earlier experiences. His monologue became a proof of himself, an argument for the defence, that he was still worthy of his vocation. That he still had a reason for existence.

She asked questions, dared him in a subtle manner to answer questions, tested the validity of his arguments with slender fingers. His eyes remained on her face, on the cheekbones that seemed so frail beneath the pale skin, on the eyes, the eyebrows, created to frown, the line of her jaw, immeasurably perfectly drawn.

'You read what they said? About the woman in the bank? About how brave she was? She's a heroine. That's not true. I think she was scared and the robber had a fright. The Mauser murderer wouldn't have been frightened. He would've shot. It's not the same person. To shoot someone at point-blank range with a large pistol needs . . . it needs a certain absence. Sometimes murderers and robbers are the same. But this robber is different. He's a clown. The disguises, the sweetheart nonsense. I simply can't believe it.'

'Are you going to speak to the criminologist?'

He was still too involved in his argument to grasp her meaning.

'The one they quoted? Who said the mass murderer's acts were a revolt against society. Dr Boshoff, I think.'

He shrugged his shoulders. He hadn't considered it.

'Don't you think it would help to get to know the psyche of the murderer?'

How could he explain to her that the examinations he wrote for sergeant and lieutenant and captain had contained nothing about the psyche. He only knew how to ask questions, how to look for the numbers in the spider's web of the law's thousand and one rules, to add them up until the sums made sense. Until the books balanced and he asked for a warrant of arrest and went to hammer on someone's door with the face of an executioner.

'I don't know. That's your field.'

'It can't do any harm. They've got all that data and research results. They teach it to the students. It would be a good thing if it could be used somewhere.'

'Perhaps I should,' he said.

The same nurse was on duty. 'I've come to ask how Sergeant Griessel is,' he said politely and carefully.

Her eyes were large behind her glasses. 'He asked for medication last night.' It sounded as though she had forgiven him.

'May I see him?'

'He's sleeping. He won't know that you're here.'

He accepted her word. He thanked her and turned away. Then he stopped. 'Why didn't he want medicine before?'

'He said he didn't deserve it.'

He just stood there and looked at her while the gears in his head slowly shifted.

'Are you a relative?'

'No,' he said. 'Just a . . . friend.'

'They are like that sometimes. They fight it for so long. The bottle. They think that the next time round it'll be easier to remember how bad it was to leave it.'

'Thank you,' he said without thinking and walked out.

There were still books which had to be arranged on the shelves. And his shoes. He wanted them shining. By evening.

24

He wasn't alone in the swimming pool this morning. The business club was there in full force, possibly because people were back from their holidays.

He swam grimly.

The bloody diet. He'd been hungry last night. Was it the conversation with Hanna Nortier, or the physical effort with the bookcase which had sharpened his hunger? But he would not eat fattening foods even though he yearned for Russians and chips and toasted egg and bacon sandwiches from the bloody cafe. He would lose the weight and show Bart de Wit and the doctor and the psychologist . . .

So he smoked. As if his stomach would get nourishment through the tubes of his lungs. Food or cigarettes. Last night he had smoked the Special Milds without satisfaction, one after another until his mouth was dry and his tongue tasted foul, while he considered the curious relationship between The Detective and The Psychologist and wondered whether he was falling in love. Suddenly you're a sexual whirlwind, Mat Joubert? One randy young thing you couldn't even get into your gunsight and you're busy with the next one. Don Juan Joubert. What has happened to your grief and pain? Do you really think you can escape Lara Joubert?

He had mocked himself, one section of his mind a spectator, watching his life passing, commenting and laughing at the owner of a video machine and a pile of cassettes.

Let's play one for you, Mat Joubert. See, there's your dead wife, Lara. There, at the dressing-table, the brush being dragged through her hair with irritable strokes. Watch the biceps and the triceps of her arm bunching under the tanned skin with each stroke. Watch the breasts bobbing, her bare breasts which you can see in the mirror, small annoyed little tremors which made the nipples dance. Listen to her voice. 'Jesus, Mat, we spend every weekend at home.'

There you are, lying on the bed, a book on your chest. 'That place's music deafens me,' you say weakly, a pathetic defence. Look at her turning towards you, look at her glowing with life. Look at her ardour. That was the way one should live. With every fibre of your being feeling, experiencing, expressing itself. 'I'll go alone. As God is my witness, Mat, one day I'll go alone.'

There were images as well. Before her death, after her death. Was the demon who orchestrated the libretto of his dreams, also the mad scriptwriter in his head?

Now he swam even more grimly to escape too many cigarettes, his fear of his mind which he didn't understand.

He swam more lengths than he had ever swum before. And that made him feel slightly better.

The forensic report lay on his desk. He opened it. Mauser Broomhandle. The ammunition old.

His phone rang. De Wit wanted to see him. He got up, took the report with him. Gerbrand Vos stood in front of de Wit's office.

'I just want to have a quick word with Captain Joubert,' de Wit said to Vos. He held the door for Joubert, walked in and sat down. Vos remained outside.

'You must understand me clearly, Captain, it's nothing personal. But this Mauser number is getting out of hand. The Brigadier's coming here at eleven. He wants a complete report. And the media. They're running with the murders. And it's my duty to protect you.'

'Colonel?'

'I'm afraid someone might talk, Captain. People are people, even here. I want to take you off the case before they find out.'

'Find out what, Colonel?'

'About your psychological treatment, Captain. The Force can't afford it. Can you imagine how the newspapers would react?'

De Wit said it as if Joubert's psychological treatment was a transgression for which he could be held directly responsible.

'I don't understand, Colonel.'

The nervous smile was back on de Wit's face. 'What don't you understand, Captain?'

'How they would find out. Surely only you and I and the psychologist know about it?'

The smile disappeared for a moment, then re-appeared. 'The Service pays the psychologist, Captain. There are clerks who do the documentation, who send through files . . . Listen, it's a preventive measure. It's nothing personal.'

Joubert was caught unawares. He collected the loose threads of counter arguments, tried to arrange them. De Wit got up. 'I'll just let Captain Vos in.'

He opened the door, called Vos, sat down again. Vos sat down next to Joubert.

'Captain Joubert and I have just agreed that you must take over the Mauser investigation, Captain,' de Wit said.

Joubert's thoughts scurried between the walls of his skull, looking for a way out, panic-stricken. He had to stop this. It was an urge for survival. It was his last chance. But he found no argument. He found calm.

'No, Colonel,' he said.

205

Vos and de Wit looked at him.

'We didn't agree, Colonel,' he said, controlled and with precision.

De Wit's mouth opened and closed.

'Colonel, the reason you gave for removing me from the investigation is not acceptable.' He turned to Vos. 'I'm with a psychologist, Gerry. I'm ashamed of it but perhaps it's a good thing. The Colonel is afraid the newspapers may find out about it. That's why he wants to hide me. But I'll carry on, Colonel, until I'm officially relieved of my duty, and through the correct channels.'

'Captain . . .' de Wit said, his face heavy with perturbation. He couldn't find the words to match it.

Vos gave a broad smile. 'The Mauser thing is enough to make one fuckin' loony tunes, Colonel. I don't want it.'

'You . . .' De Wit looked at Vos in disbelief, then at Joubert and back at Vos.

There was a knock at the door.

'Not now!' de Wit shouted. His voice threatened to crack. He looked at the officers in front of him again. 'You have . . .'

The knock at the door was louder.

'Not now!' de Wit screamed with recognisable hysteria. He shook his head as if he'd walked into a spider's web. He shook his mole finger at Joubert and Vos. 'You're conspiring against me.' The finger shook. So did his voice.

The knock at the door was insistent.

De Wit jumped up. Behind him his chair fell over. He walked to the door and jerked it open. Gerrit Snyman stood there.

'Are you deaf?' De Wit was a soprano.

'Colonel . . .'

'I said not now.' De Wit started closing the door.

'There's been another murder, Colonel,' Snyman said

quickly before the wood could reach the frame. The door came to an abrupt halt. All three looked at Snyman.

'They're looking for Captain Joubert on the radio. A man in Hout Bay, Colonel. Two shots. Two 7,63 cartridge cases.'

They stared at Snyman as if they were waiting for him to say he was only joking. De Wit cooled down, slowly almost imperceptibly.

'Thank you, Constable,' he said, in his normal bandsaw tenor voice. Snyman nodded and turned away. De Wit closed the door. He walked back to his chair, picked it up, set it in place and sat down.

Joubert considered his words as he started speaking, only aware that the Mauser investigation was his life-line and that he had to give de Wit a way out of this confrontation. 'Colonel, there is no conspiracy. Captain Vos and I couldn't have known beforehand what you were going to tell us. But I'm asking you to reconsider.'

He realised that it wasn't enough. Nor for a man like de Wit. He knew the time had come to save himself, to grab at the straw. 'Colonel, you were right when you said that my record for the past few years hasn't been good. Perhaps you were also right about my attitude which was wrong. Even towards the Mauser case – I could've put in more by now. But I give you my word. I'll give it all I've got. But don't take it away from me.'

He heard himself, how close he was to begging. He didn't care.

De Wit looked at him. His hands were on the table. His right hand moved slowly up to his face. Joubert and Vos knew what its destination was.

'I can't stop the press if they find out,' he said when the finger reached the mole. Joubert was grateful that the smile remained absent.

'I know, Colonel.'

'And if they find out the Commissioner will take you off. You know that?'

'Yes, Colonel.'

De Wit pointed his mole finger at Joubert. 'You must realise one thing. You've had your last chance.'

'Yes, Colonel.' He was grateful that de Wit was using the opportunity for peace. And to regain lost esteem.

'You're going to be watched like no other policeman has ever been watched. And I'm not referring to the media, I'm referring to me.'

'Yes, Colonel.'

'One slip-up, Captain . . .'

The phone rang. De Wit's eyes were still fixed warningly on Joubert. He picked up the phone. The smile suddenly reappeared. 'Good morning, Brigadier.' He waved a hand at Vos and Joubert, dismissing them. The officers got up and closed the door behind them. They walked down the passage.

'Thanks, Gerry.'

'It was fuckall.'

The walked in silence, their footsteps hurried on the bare tile floor. Vos stopped in front of his office door. 'Mat, may I ask you something?'

Joubert nodded.

'How the fuck do you suddenly get your shoes so shiny?'

First of all he had the whole area cordoned off – the plot, the small wooden house, the sidewalk and a part of the street.

He was astonished by the beauty of the surroundings. The street was a contour against the slopes of Karbonkelberg, the wooden-frame houses in an uneven row a picture postcard of Cape beauty. It wasn't a place for death.

He had placed the local station's uniform personnel at the garden gate with instructions that for the present only the pathologist and the forensic unit were to be allowed access to the scene of the murder.

Fat Sergeant Tony O' Grady had waylaid Joubert and Gerrit Snyman in Murder and Robbery's parking area. 'Can I come with you, Cappy? This thing fascinates me. And Captain Vos says it's OK.'

Now the three were looking at the corpse. They couldn't get too close because blood lay in a wide pool around the body. But they could see that Alexander MacDonald had been a big, rugged man, with thin red hair, a red beard and huge hands and feet. In his last moments he'd worn nothing except a pair of shorts. Even in death the bulk of his chest and upper arms was impressive.

They could also see that the murder of Alexander Mac-Donald was somewhat different from the previous ones.

The one shot was through his neck where the blood had spouted onto the wall, the few pieces of furniture and eventually, spilled over the floor.

The other was between his legs, more or less where his sexual organs had been.

Fat Sergeant Tony O' Grady's mouth was full of his staple food. It was his escape and his downfall. It was also the reason for his nickname, Nougat. He trod carefully between the pool of blood's tributaries and said: 'This is new, Cappy. This is new.'

Joubert said nothing. He looked at the room, the way the body was lying.

'Doesn't look like an accident, the shot between the balls.' He bit off another piece of nougat. 'Wonder if he was shot there first? Must be fucking sore, hey Cappy?'

'Looks as if he was shot at the door. First in the neck, I think. Look at the blood against the wall here. Carotid artery spouts like that. Then he fell. Then he gave him the second shot.'

'Right up the prick, poor bastard.'

A uniformed constable called carefully from the small front veranda. Joubert peered around the door. 'Here are a lot of people from Murder and Robbery looking for you, Captain,' said the constable and pointed to the street. Joubert's eyes followed the pointing finger. Eight unmarked police cars had suddenly filled the street. The detectives stood at the garden gate like a rugby team posing for a group photo. He walked to them

Murder and Robbery's only officer of colour, Lieutenant Leon Petersen was the group's spokesman.

'The Colonel sent us, Captain. To help. He said the District Commissioner had phoned the Brigadier and the Brigadier had phoned him. They're suddenly wide awake about this . . .' He indicated the house '. . . thing. He said the Captain needed more people, the Brigadier must get detectives from all the stations, especially for the ground-work. But we're here to help.'

'Thank, Leon.'

It was the press, he knew. The pressure was increasing on everyone – from unimportant captains up to generals. Reputations were being laid on the line. The smell of blood was going to drive the press crazy.

He explained to the group of detectives that he wanted to keep the house and the plot clean until the laboratory team arrived. He sent them in pairs down the street. Perhaps the neighbours had seen something. Maybe they knew some-thing about the deceased.

The Police video unit was the first to arrive. He asked them to wait. They moaned. He beckoned the uniformed sergeant. 'Where's the woman who found the body?'

'In the back of the police van, Captain,' said the sergeant.

'In the back of the van?'

'Just to make sure, Captain,' the sergeant said, aware of Joubert's disapproval.

'Bring her here, please.'

She was a black woman, big and heavy. Her mouth was stiff with anger about the treatment she had received. Joubert held the garden gate for her.

'I'm sorry about the inconvenience,' he said in Afrikaans.

'I only speak English.'

He repeated the sentence.

She shrugged her shoulders.

He walked around the house with her to the back door. On the stoep there was an old couch and two old steel and plastic kitchen chairs. 'Please sit down,' he said, then called Snyman and O' Grady. When they were all present he asked her what her name was.

'I didn't do it.'

He knew that, he said. But they had to have it for the witness forms.

Miriam Ngobeni, she said.

Her address?

The informal settlement, here in Karbonkelberg.

What precisely happened this morning?

She had come to work as usual at about half past seven. But the door was open and her employer was there, lying in all that blood. She had a fright and ran to the neighbour.

Had she seen anyone? Someone who looked suspicious?

No. Could she leave now?

If she would answer a few more questions, please.

According to the uniformed police the man's surname was MacDonald. Did she know his first name?

Mac.

Did she know where in the house he kept his personal documents, like an ID book?

No. Not in the house. Probably on the boat.

The boat?

One of the two fishing boats lying in the harbour. MacDonald's fishing boats. She had never seen them but every day she had to try and wash the stink of fish out of MacDonald's clothes with her hands because he didn't have a washing machine. You couldn't leave the clothes in the laundry basket for one day. The smell . . .

Did MacDonald live alone?

She thought so. Sometimes, on a Monday morning, there were signs of a big parties. Empty bottles and cigarette butts and liquor stains and burn marks on the tables and the chairs and the floors and the few loose carpets. Sometimes the bed in the main bedroom . . . But apart from that she knew of no permanent woman. She seldom saw him. Often only on Saturdays when she came to fetch her money. And then she waited at the door.

What was he like?

White.

What did she mean?

He was difficult, always threatening and complaining that he paid her too much and that she stole his liquor and took the change out of his pockets.

So she hadn't liked him?

Not so. That's the way white people are.

Thank you very much for her willingness to answer questions. Could someone take her home a bit later?

Please not.

Joubert explained the pattern of the investigation of the house to her. He asked her whether she was willing to wait until it had been completed. He said she had to look through the house to see if anything was missing.

Must she sit in the van again?

No. She could sit on the back stoep if she wanted to.

She nodded her assent.

They walked round to the front gate. The press had arrived. A horde. In a single glance he counted ten, mostly reporters and photographers. The cameras flashed. 'Is there a suspect?' one called out. It became a chorus. They rushed towards the gate. The uniformed constables stopped them.

'Forensics are inside, Captain,' the constable at the gate said.

'Thank you. Tell your sergeant to keep the press out, please.'

He sent O' Grady and Snyman to the harbour to have a look at the boats and to talk to the crew. Then he walked into the house and told the forensic team that they had to search the entire house and the plot as well. They complained. He said they had to hurry because he was allowing no one else into the area until they had finished. They moaned again.

He stood at the window and looked outside. The appearance of a murder scene, he thought. They all looked alike. Township or downtown. A group of curious onlookers, avid for details, talking to one another behind their hands in hushed voices as if they thought they could wake the dead. The uniforms' yellow cars with the blue lights. The red and white turning lights of the ambulance. Sometimes, if there was enough hysteria, the press – a moving, noisy mass, almost like a mobile stock exchange. Sometimes the next of kin were also on the stage of death, a small group who clung quietly to one another and hoped for guidance to avoid the bitter knowledge.

He saw the pathologist making his way past the people at the hedge and reaching the gate where he showed his plastic card to the uniform. Then he walked over the neglected lawn and entered the house.

He whistled through his teeth, then saw Joubert.

'Messy,' said Professor Pagel. He saw the second wound in Alexander MacDonald's groin. 'And a new twist, I see.'

'Yes,' said Joubert and sighed. 'A new twist.'

Outside the photographer, the video unit and the dog unit had arrived. They would have to wait. They wouldn't like it but they would have to wait.

He lit a cigarette and walked out. His radio on his hip suddenly spoke loudly. De Wit wanted him urgently. He thought he knew why.

25

T he District Commissioner was a General-Major, a short, square man with black hair which he wore well-oiled and combed straight back. He also had a black Charlie Chaplin moustache. The Chief of Detectives was a brigadier, a tall, large man with a bald patch. They looked like a South African edition of Laurel and Hardy. With one difference: Bart de Wit did not find their presence amusing in the least. The smile on his face was present but Joubert decided that beyond reasonable doubt, it was a nervous smile.

They were in the General's office. The office was large and attractive, the walls panelled in dark wood, a large desk at one end and a circular conference table at the other, with ten chairs around it. They sat at the table. Joubert had been in the office before, more than three years ago, after an award parade at which he had been honoured. The office hadn't changed, he noticed. But a great many other things had.

The General wanted to know if the latest murder had supplied any new clues. Joubert told him about the circumstances, the shot in the groin.

'That's a new one,' the General said.

'Indeed,' de Wit grinned.

'We've installed a temporary investigation office at the Hout Bay station, General. The men are still busy doing the legwork, the neighbours, the crew of the boats. We're looking for relatives and friends.'

'What else?'

De Wit's hopeless gaze was fixed on Joubert. Relax, Two Nose, he thought, I have things under control.

'I would like to send men to all the arms dealers in the Cape, General,' Joubert said.

'Haven't you as yet?'

'We first tried to trace all the licensed Mausers in the Western Cape, General. It yielded nothing. Now we have to talk to dealers and gunsmiths. Maybe someone somewhere had a Mauser Broomhandle serviced.'

'Makes sense,' the General said.

'Undeniably,' said the Brigadier.

'Of course,' de Wit said.

'But will it help? People must show licenses if they want to have weapons serviced.'

'The dealers are only human, General. A few fast Rands are often more effective than the rules. If we apply enough pressure . . . Even if they don't have a name and an address, they might remember what the person looks like.'

'Then we'll have a description at least,' the General said. He turned to the Brigadier. 'Would you assist in getting Captain Joubert more manpower, Pete? As long as necessary.'

The Brigadier nodded enthusiastically.

'There's something else, General,' Joubert said. 'The other weapon in the Ferreira murder. We still haven't had the ballistic report. If we know the caliber and what kind of weapon it was, we can ask arms dealers about that as well. Maybe, if we're lucky, someone had both weapons serviced at the same time.'

'You'll have your report within the hour, Captain. Believe me.'

Joubert believed him.

'And if there's anything else moving too slowly to suit you, let me know. Or if you need more men. Got that?'

'Thank you, General.'

'What else?'

'I'm going to see all the relatives of the previous victims, General. With the new murder . . . perhaps they'll remember something.'

'Fine. What else?'

'I'm seeing a doctor in Criminology at the University of Stellenbosch, General. I . . .'

'The one who was in *Die Burger*?'

'Yes, General, I . . .'

'Why?'

'I want to put together a profile by tonight, General. Everything we know. It's not much but we have to take the chance. We think it's a man because the weapon is large. Perhaps the doctor can help to compile the profile. I want to give it to the press. Maybe someone knows somebody with a Mauser and a small caliber handgun.'

'It's a shot in the dark.'

'Indeed,' said the Brigadier.

De Wit nodded and grinned.

'I simply want to make sure that I'm doing everything possible, General.'

'Might just work.'

'More like than not,' said the Brigadier.

De Wit nodded.

'What about the bank robber?'

'General, I firmly believe the robber has nothing to do with the murders.'

'Tell that to the newspapers.'

'All we can do is to put a policeman in every Premier Bank branch in the Peninsula – in civilian dress, General. And hope that the man strikes again. But the manpower . . .'

DEON MEYER

'Captain, if we've made an error of judgement and it proves that the robber and the Mauser guy are the same person, you and I will be selling insurance by morning. Every station can afford a few men. I'll speak to Brigadier Brown. Then you have to talk to Premier.'

'Thank you, General.'

'Is that the lot?'

'For the moment, General.'

'What about a medium?' de Wit asked.

'A what?' the General asked on behalf of everyone else.

'A medium. A spiritualist. The English refer to them as psychics.'

'You mean someone with second sight? A fortune teller?' the Brigadier said.

'Are you serious?' the General asked disbelievingly.

'General, they often use them in England. While I was there they solved two murders like that. One was a body they couldn't trace. The site which the psychic indicated was no more than five hundred meters from where the body was found.'

'Do you want the Minister to sh . . .' The General controlled himself. 'There's no money for a circus like that, Colonel. You should be aware of that.'

De Wit's smile was a mask. 'It needn't cost us a cent, General.'

'Oh?'

'Sometimes these people do the work for free. It's like a marketing ploy. Publicity.'

'Mmm. I don't know. Sounds like a circus to me.'

'The media would like it,' Joubert said. The others looked at him. 'It would give them something to write about, General. Take the pressure off us so that we can get on with it.'

Joubert caught a glimpse of de Wit's surprise.

'That's true,' the General said. 'But on one condition. It doesn't cost us a cent. And the psychic doesn't reveal that we called him in.'

'Her,' de Wit said.

'The best psychic in England is a woman, General.'

'Indeed,' said the General.

'But surely we have psychics here,' said the brigadier.

'It's just that I know her. And the publicity value of a foreign person . . .'

'Imagine that,' said the Brigadier.

Joubert said nothing.

The man in the overalls, with the thick neck and a head as bald and as round as a cannonball walked through the crowd of detectives and uniforms looking for someone. He could hardly believe that the Hout Bay station could be so busy. He asked where Captain Mat Joubert of Murder and Robbery was. In that storeroom, someone replied. It's the investigation office, someone else said.

He tried getting in through the door. The room was full of people and smoke. In one corner, sitting at a table, was a big man with hair that was too long and too untidy to be a detective's. It tallied with the description he'd been given. He walked towards him. The man had a cigarette in one hand and a pen in the other. He was talking to a fat man in front of him.

'They must divide the Peninsula into sectors, Nougat. And not skip an arms dealer or a gunsmith, no matter how small. Now we're just waiting for the bloody ballistics report.'

'Here it is,' said the man with the cannonball head and handed Joubert a brown envelope.

Joubert looked up in surprise. 'Thank you,' he said. 'Did the General send you?'

'Yes, Captain . . .'

Joubert looked at his watch. 'He's a man of his word.' He tore open the envelope and read the report.

'.22 Long Rifle. According to the marks on the case and the cartridge, a Smith & Wesson Escort, the so-called Model 61.'

'Point two two. Shit. Common as muck,' Nougat said.

'It does help us, though. They must question the dealers, Nougat. Has someone bought a Smith & Wesson and perhaps had a Mauser serviced. Or bought .22 long ammunition. Or had a Smith & Wesson and a Mauser serviced. Or just a Smith & Wesson . . .'

'I catch your drift.'

'Anything, Nougat. We're looking for needles in a haystack. That doesn't mean asking a few simple questions and going on to the next shop. They must do it properly. Apply some pressure. Threaten with inspections. The Mauser isn't licensed.'

'Leave it to me, Cappy. We'll get our man.'

'Woman,' said the man with the cannonball head.

'What did you say?' asked Joubert, slightly irritated.

'I think it was a woman, Captain.'

'Oh?'

'The Model 61 is a woman's weapon, Captain.'

'And who are you, if I may ask?' said Nougat O' Grady.

'I'm Adjutant Mike de Villiers. From the armoury. The General phoned me and asked me whether I'd look through the ballistic report and bring it to you. He said you could ask me questions, if you want to. I . . . er . . . I know something about guns, Captain.'

Joubert looked at the man opposite him, the round head, the absence of a neck, the blue overalls covered in gun oil marks. If the general had sent him . . .

'What do you know about the .22, Adjutant?'

Mike de Villiers closed his eyes. 'Smith & Wesson made the Escort for the female market. In the seventies. Short grip, small weapon. People spoke about the "Model 61". Fitted easily into a handbag. Semi-automatic pistol, five in the magazine. Not a great success, especially the first produced which had a weak safety indicator. Smith & Wesson built a magazine safety mechanism into the second model, in '70 but owners had to take the pistol back to the factory for adjusting. Four models between '69 and '71. Good penetration capacity, better than the Baby Browning. Accurate at short distance. Jamming rare but not impossible.'

Mike de Villiers opened his eyes.

Joubert and O' Grady stared at him.

'That doesn't mean a man won't use it,' Joubert said, still bemused.

The eyes closed again. 'Short grip, Captain, very short. Small weapon. Your finger won't even fit into the trigger-guard. Doesn't fit into a man's hand, doesn't fit a man's ego. A man looks for a large gun – 9 mm, .45 Magnum. Statistics show that eighty-seven percent of handgun murders are committed by men with large calibers. Shooting incidents by women are rare, generally in self-defence, generally small caliber.'

The eyes opened, slowly, like a reptile's.

O' Grady's jaw had come to a halt and dropped slightly. Joubert frowned.

'But the Mauser is a man's weapon.'

'I don't know anything about the Broomhandle, Captain. If it was made before 1918, I'm not interested,' de Villiers said.

'Is Captain Joubert here?' the leader of a group of uniforms who had walked through the door called out.

'Here,' Joubert said and sighed. The place was a mad-house.

'Did the Captain want to know anything else?'

'Than you, Adjutant. I know where to get hold of you if there's anything else.'

De Villiers nodded, said good-bye and quietly left.

'Looks like a lizard, talks like a computer,' said O' Grady. 'Man's a fucking genius.'

Joubert didn't hear him. His thoughts were frustrated, confused by the new information. 'Nothing in this investigation makes any sense, Nougat. Nothing.'

He phoned Stellenbosch University and asked to speak to Dr AL Boshoff.

'Anne Boshoff,' a woman's voice answered. He sighed quietly. Another female doctor.

He explained who he was and asked whether he could speak to her that afternoon, explaining that it was urgent.

'I'll prepare in the meanwhile,' she said.

He closed the station commander's door. 'How peaceful the silence is,' said Lieutenant Leon Petersen.

O' Grady wiped his handkerchief over his forehead. 'All we need is air conditioning,' he said. Next to him sat Gerrit Snyman with his notebook in front of him.

'Get on with it,' said Joubert.

'His full name is Alexander MacDonald, born in Humansdorp on April 8, 1952. Unmarried, no dependants. He is the sole owner of two fishing trawlers, the High Road and the Low Road. According to his documents he still owes the bank R110 000 on the Low Road. He had a contract with Good Hope Fisheries and delivers solely to them. John Paulsen is the skipper of the High Road. He's worked for MacDonald for eighteen years. He says the man was good-hearted but had a terrible temper. When we asked him who would have had reason to murder MacDonald, he said he could think of at least two hundred with no effort. Mac-Donald never drank at sea but when they were in the harbour . . . He has a criminal record. Driving under the influence, Hout Bay '88; assault with intent to cause severe bodily harm '89; fifteen complaints of disturbing the peace since '79. One conviction for deliberate injury to property. He and a few crew members smashed up a bar in Simons Town. And here's an interesting one. An accusation of rape was laid by one Eleanor Davids two years ago. She later withdrew it. The investigating officers suspected that Mac-Donald threatened her with violence but couldn't prove anything.'

'A difficult customer,' Petersen said.

'A chat to Eleanor Davids could be interesting,' Joubert said.

'That's the idea, Captain, that's the idea.'

26

He drove to Stellenbosch, late for his appointment with Dr Anne Boshoff.

The district manager of Premier Bank, in his luxurious office, had been impatient. The robber was bad for business, bad for the bank's image. All the negative publicity. Nor was he impressed by the SAPD's plans. A plainclothes policeman in every branch? What would happen if a policeman scared the robber? He could start shooting. Premier Bank didn't want to expose its clients or its employees to danger.

Patiently Joubert had explained that the members of the Force were very aware of the danger and that confrontation with the robber would be handled with great circumspection.

The district manager had said that he saw examples of the Police's circumspection on television every evening.

Joubert had sighed, stood up and said that he would mention Premier Bank's attitude at the press conference.

The district manager also sighed and said Joubert must sit down. He had to consult head office.

Head office couldn't decide, either. They wanted to call a meeting to discuss it. Joubert said he had to go to Stellenbosch. He had left Dr Boshoff's telephone number. The bank must inform him when a decision had been reached.

He took the N2 and drove too fast. The big, white Sierra kept his thoughts on the traffic. The road was quieter after the R300 exit. He didn't want to think about the investigation too much, about de Wit's attempt to replace him, about the meeting at the General's, about the adrenaline of the chase which, like an old, almost forgotten friend, was rearing its head again. Because he didn't know whether any of it was worthwhile. Tomorrow or the day after, the excitement would die down. Then he would be alone again, with only his thoughts and his memories.

He forced his mind back to the appointment ahead. What was he going to say to Dr Boshoff? *I'm here because my psychologist suggested it? She's a pretty, frail woman with sad eyes and I think I'm in love with her because I told her something about my father which I've never told anyone else. Because she's the first person in more than two years to whom I can talk without being scared of that overdone, artificial sympathy of those who don't really care. That's why I'm here, Dr Boshoff.*

No. He had to get a profile. Not only for the newspapers but for himself. He couldn't chase a phantom. He was looking for a face. A person with a disturbed mind who took other people's lives.

Anne Boshoff's office was in an old, restored gabled house. In front, in the neat garden, there was a sign: CRIMINOLOGY DEPARTMENT, UNIVERSITY OF STELLENBOSCH. He parked the car and got out. The afternoon was warm and windless. He took off his jacket and hung it over his shoulder. He adjusted the Z88 in the leather holster on his belt.

Two male students were walking ahead of him on the pavement. The looked at the police vehicle with curiosity, at him and the gun. They saw him opening the garden gate.

'I knew that paper was too difficult,' one said. 'Lock them up.'

Joubert grinned and walked onto the cool veranda. The

front door was open. He walked in hesitantly. The front entrance was deserted. He saw nameplates on doors. He walked down the passage. Right at the end he saw Anne Boshoff's door. It was open. He peered inside.

She sat in front of a computer, her back to him. He noticed her short, black hair, shorter than his own. He saw her neck, a part of her shoulder.

She became aware of him and turned.

He saw her face, the high forehead, the eyes set wide apart, the cheekbones, broad in an almost Eastern manner, mouth wide and full, the strong jaw. She looked measuringly at him from head to toe with dark, bright eyes.

'I'm Mat Joubert,' he said, aware of his discomfort.

'You sounded like an old man on the telephone,' she said and swivelled the chair round. He saw that she was full-bodied, her dress short. He tore his eyes away from the well-shaped, tanned legs.

He stood between the door and the woman. She got up. She was tall, almost as tall as he was.

'Let's sit down,' she said and walked to a small desk in the corner of the large room. He saw the muscles of her strong legs moving under the skin. Then he looked away at the rest of the office. It was untidy. There were piles of books everywhere. The small bookcase behind the desk was spilling over. A racing bicycle stood against one wall. The only chair in the room was the one at the computer. Against another wall, under the window, there were cartons filled with documents. She turned and sat down on one of the cartons, the long legs stretched out in front of her. Her ringless hand indicated another carton.

'Make yourself at home.'

He shifted the Z88 into a more comfortable position on his hip and sat down.

'It is it true what they say about men who carry large guns?'

He looked at her. Her mouth was wide and red and smiling.

'I . . . um . . .' She was so extremely sexy.

'Great answer,' she said.

'Well, I . . .'

'What do you want from me, Mat Joubert?'

'I . . .'

'About the murder case, I mean.'

'Yes, I . . .'

'The statistics? They could help. Could give you a picture. But it's an American picture. They set the pace for mass murderers. And we follow in their footsteps. Little America, that's what we are. So, the figures might help you. Do you know how they've increased in the past twenty years? Exponentially. It's an accusation against Western civilisation, Mat Joubert.' She looked at him when she spoke, a focus, a direct, spotlight of a focus, a beam, a ray.

'Is . . .'

'The statistics say your murderer is a man. A middle-class man with the weight of his background on his shoulders. Why a man? Because most of them are. They're the sex who have problems in accepting the prison of middle-classness. We live in an era in which we teach our sons that they must achieve, be better, become rich. And if they can't . . . Why middle-class? Because most people are. Isn't it curious? In previous ages the small handful of mass murderers came from the lowest classes. Slaves and prostitutes and the scum of the earth. In our time it's the middle classes. Sometimes lower middle-class like Charles Starkweather, sometimes upper middle-class like Ted Bundy. Their background? It can vary. Do you know how many mass murderers were adopted children? Kallinger. Bianchi. Earle Nelson. And illegitimate. Now some psychologists are of the opinion that Ted Bundy killed because he knew he was an illegitimate child. David Berkowitz was adopted and illegitimate. And so many were orphans or taken by Welfare. Fish. Kemper. Olson. Panzram. Bonin. And then they murder to assure themselves of a small place in the community. Tragic, isn't it.'

He wrote. It kept his eyes and his hands busy.

'But do you know what bothers me, Mat Joubert? The weapon and the victims. The Mauser is too blatant. Too macho. A statement. It bothers me. Here sex is raising its horrible head. That long barrel. I checked. Ian Hogg's book *German Pistols and Revolvers*. That long barrel. A phallic symbol. A male symbol. This is a man with a problem. All the victims are male. It bothers me. A man with a problem who kills other men. But the victims aren't gay . . .'

'They . . . One was,' he said loudly.

'One? Just one, Mat Joubert? Are you sure? Do you know for certain?'

'Wallace was . . . promiscuous but heterosexual. Wilson was homosexual. Ferreira . . . I don't know. He liked blue movies, his wife said. And MacDonald, the one we found this morning. He'd been charged with rape. But the woman withdrew the case.'

'You see – you can actually speak,' she said in a mock serious tone, frowning and he wondered whether there was something this woman could do that didn't make him think of sex.

'It sounds to me as if they were all closet queens, Mat Joubert. Do you know how many men suppress their homosexuality with promiscuity? And the rape. Perhaps he wanted to prove his masculinity to himself. Come on, I bet you your murderer is going to be gay. It fits. The Mauser. It's a statement. A sexual statement. By a homosexual man.'

'From the middle classes. Who was adopted,' he said and frowned as she had frowned earlier on.

'The captain has a sense of humour,' she said to her bike. She looked at him again.

'What are you doing this evening? You're too precious to get away.'

'Doctor, the problem is . . .'

'Please don't call me doctor. Call me anything. Call me sexy. But not doctor. Do you think I'm sexy? Where do you get your name? Mat? An abbreviation of Matthew?'

'Yes,' he said to save time.

'Yes, I'm sexy or yes, it's short for Matthew?'

Somewhere on her desk the telephone rang. She got up smoothly and gave one long step. She scrabbled under the books and documents. He watched the muscle of her calf tensing and relaxing and was amazed by its perfection.

'Anne Boshoff,' she said in an irritable voice. 'Just a moment.' She held out the receiver. 'For you, Matthew.'

He got up, put his notebook down on the carton and took the receiver. It was the district manager of Premier Bank. Head office had agreed that the Police could deploy members of the Force in their branches. But they urgently requested that the SAPD consider the lives and safety of the bank's personnel and clients. Joubert assured him that they would.

'May I use the phone?' he asked and looked round. She was sitting on a carton again, her legs crossed, paging through his notebook.

'Your handwriting is awful. The long loops of your "y" and "j" and "g" indicate that you're sexually frustrated. Are you? You're already using the telephone, Matthew. Just carry on.'

He dialed the number and tried concentrating on the call. He patted his shirt pocket in search of a cigarette. Then he remembered that they were in his coat pocket. He wanted to smoke. He wanted to do something with his hands to hide his dreadful discomfort and his awkwardness. De Wit answered his telephone in the manner prescribed by the circular of the office of the district commissioner. 'Murder and Robbery. Colonel Bart de Wit, good afternoon.'

He told de Wit about Premier Bank's decision. De Wit promised to liaise with Brigadier Brown about the arrangements.

'Where are you, Captain?' de Wit asked.

'In Stellenbosch, Colonel. With the crimina . . . criminologist.'

'The press conference has been scheduled for 18:00. In the general's office. Please don't be late.'

'Very well, Colonel.'

He looked at his watch. He would have to hurry.

'Freudian slip, Matthew?' Anne Boshoff asked. Her knees were together now, almost chaste.

'No, it's a press conference . . .'

'I'm speaking about the criminal you so very nearly mentioned. Tell me, was it Bart de Wit to whom you spoke?'

He nodded.

'I know him. He was in Unisa's department. I attended a few conferences where he was also present. Good example of a small man. His nickname was Kilroy. Kilroy the killjoy. He looks exactly like Kilroy, the little graffiti man who peers over the wall. Kilroy was here. With his nose. He just doesn't have the hormones. Didn't try it on, at even one conference. It made a girl think.'

'May I have my notebook?'

'Tell me, Matthew, are you absent or is it merely your way of putting crooks and villains at ease?' She handed over the notebook. He took his jacket, took out a cigarette and lit it.

'Do you know how bad that is for your health?'

'It's a Special Mild.'

'Oh. So that doesn't cause cancer.'

'Doctor,' he said firmly, 'the weapon used in the Ferreira murder was a Smith & Wesson Model 61. According to one of our weapons experts, it's typical of a gun a woman would use.'

'And?'

'It doesn't match your theory, Doctor . . .'

'Doctor. You sound like a vicar. Call me Anne. And drop the doctor bit. I like it when men are rude to me. It keeps me in my place. Of course it matches my theory. If you have a Mauser, you already have a large pistol, no matter how small your prick is.'

'Are you certain it's a man?'

'Of course I'm not sure. It could be a woman. It could be a lesbian chimpanzee. I can only tell you what the law of averages says. I don't have an ashtray. You'll have to open the window.'

'I must go.'

'You're so beautifully tall and big. Your body, I mean. I like big men. Small ones carry too much inferiority. Bodies too small for all the hormones.'

He was confused. He looked at the window to avoid the legs and the full breasts.

'You look like a bear. I like bears. I think a person's looks have a great influence on their personality. Don't you agree?' Her eyes were still fixed on him, her concentration aimed at him like a weapon. He looked at her and then away. He hadn't the vaguest idea of what to say.

'Do I make you uncomfortable? Are you the kind of man who likes more subtle women?'

'I . . . er . . .'

'Are you married, Mat Joubert?'

'No, I . . .'

'Neither am I. I'm divorced. One of those heartrending affairs which didn't pan out. He was . . . is a surgeon. We're still friends. That's it. Now you know.'

'Oh.' He knew he had to get the conversation under control. He decided to be decisive. 'I . . .'

She interrupted him. 'I hate social games. I hate the artificial manner in which people communicate. The superficiality. I think one should say what you want to say. Say what you mean. People don't always like it. Especially men. Men want to be in control, they want to play the game according to their rules. The love game, especially. Why go through all the pretence first? If I think a man is sexy, I want to say so. If a man wants me, he mustn't take me to an expensive restaurant first and send me flowers. He must take me. Don't you think it saves time?'

He looked at her legs. 'I know a eighteen-year-old student in Monte Vista who agrees with you,' he said and felt better.

'Tell me about her. Is she your lover? Do you like them young? I'm thirty-two. Does that disqualify me?'

'She's not my lover.'

'Why do you sound disappointed about it?' She didn't give him a chance to reply.

'You're very different from what I imagined you to be, you know. A Murder and Robbery detective. I imagined this hard, sophisticated man with a scar on his face and cold, blue eyes. And here you are. A big, shy bear. And absent. You look absent to me, Mat Joubert. Are you?'

'A little,' he said and felt it was a victory.

'Do you know one lives only once?'

'Yes . . .'

'You must grab it.'

'I . . .'

'Every day, every moment.'

'I must go.'

'Do I exhaust you? Many people say I exhaust them. But I do have friends. I can prove it.'

'In a court of law?'

She smiled. 'I'm going to miss you, Matthew.'

He put his cigarettes, pen and notebook in his coat pocket.

'Thank you very much for your time, Doc . . . Anne.'

'You see, we're making progress. Hang on, I'll walk out with you.'

They walked in silence down the house's passage, over the veranda into the sunlight. He saw her gleaming skin brown and bright, her open shoulders, her legs. He saw her buttocks moving under the mini dress.

She looked round, caught him looking. 'Will I see you again?'

'If there's anything else . . .'

'I'll see you again, Matthew Joubert. That's a promise.'

27

T he press conference had been moved to the entrance hall of Police Headquarters because there were too many people.

'You're late,' Cloete of PR said when he caught sight of Mat Joubert. He looked worried and panicky. 'There are two TV teams present from overseas stations. And one from the SABC. And one from M-Net – they were making a programme for *Carte Blanche*. There are newspaper people here I've never seen before.' Then he hurried away to inform the General that Joubert had arrived.

The press formed a semi-circle. The bright television lights shone on a small table. The General sat at the table. Next to him sat the Brigadier and de Wit. The General crooked a finger at Joubert. 'Found anything?'

Had he found anything? He had tried to think on the way back to Cape Town. But Dr Anne Boshoff lay like a shadow over his thoughts. He wondered whether women with a double 'f' in their names were all the same. Bonnie Stoffberg, Anne Boshoff. Did the extra 'f' stand for . . . He'd shaken his head at his inability to rid his mind of sex. Barely in love with Hanna Nortier and now you want to lie between the other clever doctor's legs. Raging bull. From conscientious objector to Ramblin' Rambo in just more than a week. Yes, General, I've found something. Something I can't handle very well.

'I think so, General.'

'Good. I'll begin and then introduce you.'

No. He wasn't prepared. He couldn't tell them they were looking for a middle-class homosexual who had possibly been adopted or illegitimate.

'Dames en here . . .' the General said loudly and the media scrambled for cameras and notebooks. More bright lights were switched on.

'Dames en here.' No quiet.

'Can you speak English?' someone called. Camera motor drives whirred. Flashlights went off.

'Dames and here, dankie . . .' Cloete had jogged round to the General and whispered in his ear. The General looked annoyed. Then he nodded.

'Ladies and gentlemen, thanks for being here. Let me start by saying that the South African Police Service are doing everything they can to apprehend the ruthless murderer who are killing people without apparent reason.'

Is, Joubert thought. The murderer who *is*.

'We regard this matter in a very serious light and are allocating as many people as we can to assist with the investigation. I cannot tell you everything we are doing, because some of it is part of our strategy to catch the person or persons involved. What I can tell you, are that the investigating officer, Captain Mat Joubert, have as many policemen at his disposal as he needs. We have already given him all available staff from Murder and Robbery. If necessary, we will also give him more. This now has become the biggest manhunt the Cape has ever seen. We will not rest before the person or persons responsible for these thoughtless murders is apprehended. Now, I leave you in the hands of Captain Mat Joubert. Afterwards, I will answer your questions. If you have any.'

Then the General announced: 'Captain Joubert.'

Joubert walked round the table. The press buzzed. The

General got up and offered him his chair. The lights shone in his eyes. The cameras clicked again. He could see no one beyond the lights. He sat down. The bunch of microphones in front of him was intimidating.

'Good afternoon,' he said and hadn't the faintest idea of what else to say.

The press waited.

Begin with this morning, he thought, panicking. After all, he had spoken in front of people before. But there were so many here.

'E . . .'

His heart thudded in his chest. His mouth was dry. He was breathing too quickly.

'As you know . . .'

He heard his own strong Afrikaans accent. His heart beat faster.

'. . . the Mauser killer struck this morning for the fourth time.'

His notebook. Where was his notebook? He felt in his inside pocket. It wasn't there. Had he taken it back from Anne Boshoff? The other pocket. Felt in the other pocket. He found it. The relief was brief. The silence was heavy in the hall. Someone giggled, someone coughed. He took out the note-book and opened it. He saw that his hands were shaking.

'The victim . . .'

De wiektum. Fucking stupid policeman.

'. . . was forty-one-year-old Alexander MacDonald of Hammerhead Street in Houtbaai . . . er . . . Hout Bay.'

Someone called his name. He ignored it.

'The perpetrator used a weapon similar to the previous . . .'

'Captain Joubert . . .'

'Just a moment,' the Brigadier said next to him. Joubert was confused.

Then he saw a figure moving past the lights, towards the table. It was Petersen.

'Excuse me, Captain. I'm sorry. But we've found something. This very minute.'

The General joined them. 'Who the hell are you?' he asked in a lowered tone.

'Lieutenant Petersen, of Murder and Robbery, General.'

'They've found something, General,' Joubert said. He heard the buzz of the press increasing in volume.

'It better be important, Lieutenant,' the General said.

'Indeed,' said the Brigadier.

'One of the neighbours, General,' Petersen said in a whisper. 'He saw a car at the murder scene this morning. A new five series BMW.'

'And?' said the General impatiently.

'He said it was early. He was on his way to the bus stop. Then he saw a man getting out of the BMW and walk into MacDonald's house. And minutes later the BMW raced past him.'

'Did he see the man? Recognise him?' The General had trouble in keeping his voice down.

'Barely. He said it happened too quickly. But he saw the registration number. It was easy to remember. CY 77.'

'Fuckit!' said the General. 'Find out who it is.'

'We already have, General. That's why we're here. We want Captain Joubert to come with us.'

'Fuckit,' said the General and cleared his throat.

'Ladies and gentlemen. Quiet please. Ladies and gentleman.' One could hear a pin drop. 'Our efforts has paid off.'

Have, Joubert thought. *Have* paid off.

'We now received fresh information and I think a suspect will be arrested in a matter of hours. We will now excuse Captain Mat Joubert who will follow up this new lead.'

Joubert got up with the buoyancy of total relief. The

press shouted questions but Joubert walked to the door past the group, with Leon Petersen.

'Please, ladies and gentlemen, please, can I have your attention,' the General shouted.

Then Joubert and Petersen were out of the door.

'To whom does the BMW belong?' Joubert asked.

'Oliver Sigmund Nienaber.'

For a moment he was speechless. He stopped in his tracks. '*The* Oliver Nienaber?'

'The very same. "No one cuts your hair better or cheaper. I promise."'

'Fuckit,' said Joubert and felt like a general.

The house was high up against the rise of Tygerberg, with a view across Bellville and the Cape Flats, to the Hottentots-Holland range. It was built on three levels, a modern building of white-painted concrete and glass. They stopped in front of the three-door garage.

'Rich, because of woman's vanity,' Petersen said.

They walked up the stairs next to the garage. The front door was large. Joubert pressed the doorbell. The couldn't hear it ring. They waited.

The front door opened. A black woman in a neat uniform appeared.

'Can I help you?'

Joubert showed her the plastic card on which his photo, the police crest and his details were shown. 'We're from the Police. We would like to see Oliver Nienaber, please.'

Her eyes widened. 'Please come in,' she said and turned round. They walked into the entrance hall. She disappeared down the passage. They heard women's voices while they studied the modern painting against the wall. Then a blonde woman appeared. They recognised her. Mrs. Antoinette Nienaber, nee Antoinette van Zyl, star of such unforgettable movies as *A Rose for Janey*, *Seven Soldiers* and *A Woman in Love*. And today, as so many magazine and newspaper articles repeated over and over again, she was still happily married to the hairdresser king, owner of a chain of salons, the head of Hair Tomorrow, Oliver Nienaber.

She was still beautiful enough to take their breath away. She gave them a friendly smile. 'Good evening. May I help you?'

Joubert coughed. 'Mrs. Nienaber, I'm Captain Joubert and this is Lieutenant Petersen. We're from the Police's Murder and Robbery squad and would like to speak to Mr. Nienaber.'

Her smile widened. 'Of course. Please come in. He's playing snooker with the boys.' She walked ahead and Joubert thought that she must be close to forty but that there was nothing wrong with her body.

He stood in the doorway of a large room. 'Oliver, someone to see you.'

They heard his voice. 'At this time of the evening?'

His wife didn't reply.

'You carry on. Play for me, Toby, We can still win.'

'OK, Pa.'

Oliver Nienaber came through the door. The well-known face which could be seen virtually every day in full-page advertisements in the newspapers with the equally well-known words: NOBODY CUTS YOUR HAIR BETTER OR CHEAPER. I PROMISE. And his flamboyant signature and the big logo of Hair Today. And usually, at the bottom: NOW OPEN AT . . . George. Or Laingsburg. Or Oudtshoorn. Or Kimberley.

'Good evening, gentlemen,' he said jovially. 'I'm sorry, but I don't cut hair in the evening.'

'They're from the Police, darling,' said Antoinette Nienaber softly. She introduced them. 'Take them to the study and I'll organize something to drink. Tea? Coffee?'

They all wanted coffee. Nienaber led them to his study. He didn't sit behind the desk. The room was big enough to have a corner for a couch and armchairs. 'Please sit down. I don't have a visit from the Police every day.'

Joubert saw the framed certificates and photos and newspaper advertisements against the wall.

'The same advertisements for the past six years. And they're still working,' Nienaber said as he followed Joubert's eyes.

'How many salons do you have now?' Joubert asked.

'The sixty-second opened its doors in Cradock last week. And now we're going to Gauteng. If I can find a good local manager. How about it? Don't you feel like it?' Nienaber spoke to Joubert, ignored Petersen completely. He was relaxed and comfortable but Joubert knew it meant nothing.

'Mr. Nienaber . . .'

'How can I help you?'

'We're from Murder and Robbery . . .'

'Goodness, it sounds serious.'

'Does the name Alexander Macdonald mean anything to you?'

'MacDonald? MacDonald? You know, I meet so many people . . .'

'Mr. MacDonald is the owner of MacDonald Fisheries, a small concern in Hout Bay with two fishing trawlers. Big man. Red hair,' Petersen said.

'What's his name? Alexander? Why does it sound vaguely familiar?' Nienaber stared at the ceiling and rubbed his ear.

'You didn't visit anyone with that name today?'

'Not that I can recall.'

'You are the owner of a new dark red BMW with the registration CY 77?'

'That's right.' No sign of worry.

'You used the vehicle today?'

'I use it every day.'

'To your knowledge the vehicle wasn't used by anyone else today?'

'No . . . Could you tell me . . . Has my car been stolen?'

'When last did you see your car, Mr. Nienaber?' Joubert asked.

'This afternoon, when I came home.'

'And at what time did you leave this morning?'

'Six o' clock. I think it was around six. I always like to be in the office early.' His face began to show concern. 'Would you like to tell me what this is about, please?'

'You weren't . . .'

'Knock, knock,' Antoinette Nienaber said at the door, a tray with coffee mugs in her hands. Nienaber sprang up. 'Thank you, love,' he said.

'Pleasure,' she smiled, as relaxed as before. 'Is everything OK, darling?'

'Just fine.'

'Do help yourselves to biscuits,' she said and walked out. Nienaber held the tray for the detectives in silence. Then he sat down. 'You have to tell me what this is about.'

'You weren't in Hout Bay between six and half past six this morning?'

'No, I've told you . . .'

'Think carefully, Mr. Nienaber,' Petersen said.

'Heavens, sergeant, I know where I was.'

'Lieutenant.'

'Sorry. Lieutenant,' Nienaber said and there was a lot of irritation in his voice.

He doesn't like Petersen asking the questions, Joubert thought. Rich, racist bastard.

'Do you know about the Mauser murders which have been committed in the Cape recently, Mr. Nienaber?'

He shrugged his shoulders. 'Yes. I mean . . . I read the newspapers. There was something on television.'

'Do you possess a Mauser Broomhandle, Mr. Nienaber?'

'No. You can't possibly imagine . . . What's going on here?'

'Can you explain why your car, a dark red five series BMW with the registration CY 77 was seen this morning in front of the house of Alexander MacDonald, the latest victim of the Mauser murderer?'

Nienaber sat up straight, almost rose. 'How would I . . . No. You're cops. You've heard of false number plates. I told you I was in the office just after six this morning.'

'Can anyone verify that?'

'That I was there? No, that's why I go in so early. So that I can be alone and get work done.'

'So you were at work at six o' clock?'

'Yes.' Relief. These people were going to believe him.

'And it's not near Hout Bay?'

'That's correct.'

'Then you have nothing to be concerned about, Mr. Nienaber,' Joubert said and saw the man opposite him relax in his chair.

'That's right,' said Nienaber.

'But we would like to ask you a favour.'

'Yes?' Suspicious.

Joubert gave the truth a slight twist. 'It would help us a great deal if we could clear up the matter beyond any doubt. We believe you weren't near Hout Bay today. But we have an eye witness who says that he saw your BMW and a man who looked very familiar. Won't you please accompany us to Murder and Robbery? We have what we call an identification room. We get a group of people together who have the same build and colouring as you have. And the eye witness must identify the person whom he thinks he saw. As you're innocent . . .'

Oliver Nienaber had turned pale.

He sat staring at them for a long time.

'I think I must phone my attorney.'

28

Oliver Nienaber lied to his wife before he accompanied the detectives to the Murder and Robbery building in Kasselsvlei Road. He told her the Police needed his help with a case. 'Nothing to be worried about.'

They waited in silence for Nienaber's attorney to arrive, the three of them at a table on which cigarette burns were the only evidence of previous conversations.

The attorney came rushing in, a very short man in his forties, with a very large head, thick lips and virtually no jaw. He protested in the habitual manner of practitioners of his profession, about the treatment his client was receiving but Nienaber shut him up. 'I'm here of my own free will, Phil.'

The attorney sat down, unclipped the clasps of his expensive attaché case, took out a writing pad, removed a pen from his coat and looked up at Joubert.

'You may carry on,' the attorney said, as if it now carried his official approval.

Joubert said nothing, merely raised his eyebrows.

'I was at Alexander MacDonald's house this morning, Phil. The guy who was shot by the Mauser murderer.'

'Sheesh,' the attorney said and pursed his fleshy lips.

Nienaber looked at Joubert. 'He phoned me. Last week. On Tuesday or Wednesday. I can't remember. He wanted to know whether I didn't want to open a salon in Hout Bay. He had money to invest. He wanted to buy a building in the

245

main road, something like that. But he was looking for tenants first . . .'

'MacDonald?' Petersen asked.

'Yes,' said Nienaber. 'I didn't really . . .'

'Alexander MacDonald? The fisherman? Big redhead?' There was a edge to Petersen's voice.

'Well . . . I didn't know what he looked like the . . .'

'The man was in debt to the tune of R100 000 and he phones you out of the blue to ask whether you want to open a salon in a building he didn't even possess?'

'If you'll give me a chance to finish my story, Lieutenant,' said Nienaber, the 'lieutenant' heavily loaded with sarcasm.

'We're listening,' said Joubert.

'I told the man I didn't do business like that. I mean, I'd never even heard of him. And in any case I didn't want to establish a salon in Hout Bay. So I said no. But he phoned again the following day. Same voice. English, with an accent. You know like that guy from Wales who does the Four Nations rugby commentary . . .'

'Five,' the attorney said.

'Huh?' said Nienaber.

'Five Nations.'

'No,' said Nienaber. He held up his fingers, counted. 'England, Wales, Scotland and Ireland.'

'Sheesh, Oliver, you work too hard. Add France to that lot.'

'But France . . .'

'Alexander MacDonald,' said Joubert and leant forward, his shoulders broad across the table, his head lowered as if he was going to rush them, his voice a growl like a large dog's.

'I'm sorry. Then he phoned again. The next day. Same story. Didn't I want to open a salon if he bought the building.'

'Which building?' Joubert asked.

'I don't know which building.'

'He must've mentioned the name of the building.'

'He did. Marine Plaza, something like that. I can't remember. I didn't even write it down. I don't do business like that.'

'And then?'

'Then I said no again. Then I heard nothing more from him. Until last night. Then he phoned me at home. Same old story, the building and the salon. Then I said to him: "Listen, mister, I'm not interested in your building, not tonight nor any other time." Then he said: "I'm going to crush your balls. Dutchman." Just like that. And other stuff. I'm going to cut off your . . . your . . . penis and stuff it in your ear. Just like that . . .'

'Wait a minute, just wait a minute,' Petersen said, angrily. 'Here we've got a sailor, a man who had been locked up for assault and malicious damage to property who speaks about "penis?"'

'Listen, Lieutenant, I can't remember precisely which words . . .'

'Gentlemen,' the attorney said placatingly. 'Gentlemen, you can't expect my client to remember the ipsissima verba of a telephone conversation which happened twenty-four hours ago while you interrogate him like a criminal here. He's under pressure. He's a human being. Please.'

'He's a liar,' said Petersen, got up and turned his back on Nienaber.

'Very well. He used filthy language. Is it necessary for me to repeat the filth?'

Nienaber's voice formed a halo.

'Do your best,' said Joubert and leant back, suspecting that Petersen wanted to play the tough cop role.

'In any case, he made a great many filthy remarks and I

put down the phone. Then, half an hour later he phoned again. Said he was sorry he'd carried on in that way. Wouldn't I just have a look. It was a fantastic building. And he would charge me an extremely cheap rental. He was very convincing. Then I thought it would be easier to get rid of him in the cheapest possible way. Have a look at the building. I mean, it was cheaper than changing my telephone number. But then I told him I didn't have the time. And he said what about early in the morning. Before work. Then I said it was OK, what about tomorrow morning because I wanted to be shot of the whole thing. I simply wanted to get rid of the man. Then we decided on six in the morning. At his home. And we could use my car. He said his car stank too much. Of fish. So I drove there this morning. But I was late because I couldn't find the address at first. And when I got there he was lying in the doorway and he'd been shot right in the . . . the . . .' .

'Penis,' said Petersen and turned back to Nienaber.

'That's right. In the penis.'

'Sheesh,' said the attorney.

'You're lying,' Petersen said.

'You can't say that,' said Nienaber.

'I can say exactly what I like.'

'He can't say that.' Nienaber turned to the short attorney.

'I insist that you treat my client with respect.'

'With respect, Oliver, you're lying.'

'He can't say that,' Oliver complained and looked at Joubert who was leaning back in his chair, a sneer on his face. The scene in front of him was faintly unreal.

But Petersen was angry now. Angry, because Nienaber had ignored him in the first place and then sarcastically called him 'lieutenant.' Angry, because the man was rich and superior and blatantly lying.

'I can, Ollie. You're lying. And I'm going to catch you

out. I'm going to lock you up. And throw away the key. And what's going to happen to your pretty little wife then, Ollie? Huh? While you're behind bars, Ollie? Who's going to scratch her when she itches, Ollie?'

'Leon,' Joubert said warningly because he suddenly recognised the tone of voice. He remembered the Sunday afternoon in Mitchells Plain when Petersen had a go at the young gang member who was also lying, smashed his face, Petersen had a temper, a bad one . . .

'Fuckin' rich asshole whitey is lying, Captain,' Petersen said, the whites of his eyes huge. His hands were shaking.

'No, no,' said the attorney and waved an admonishing finger.

Nienaber was half-way out of his chair, his face contorted. 'Hotnot,' he said, the charm of the newspaper advertisements unimaginable. 'You hotnot.'

Petersen jumped over the attorney and hit Nienaber on the cheek in one, smooth, quick movement. Nienaber fell backwards in his chair. His head hit the bare tiled floor with a dull thud and then he rolled out of the chair.

Joubert had jumped up even before the blow fell but he was too late. Now he grabbed Petersen's shirt and jerked him back while the attorney dived down to his client and spread protective arms over him. 'No, no, no,' he shouted, his big head tucked into his shoulders as if he expected more blows.

Petersen let out his breath and relaxed in Joubert's grip. 'Never mind, Captain, I won't hit him again.'

'Get an ambulance,' said the attorney from the floor, his arms still extended to ward off another attack. 'I think he's dead.'

Joubert kneeled next to them. 'Let me see.' The attorney was reluctant but moved away. Joubert saw that Nienaber's cheekbone was already swollen and discoloured. But his chest moved up and down in a perfectly healthy manner. 'There's nothing wrong with him,' said Joubert. 'Just a bit faint.'

'Get an ambulance,' said the attorney. 'And get your commanding officer.'

Joubert knew what that meant. And he knew what the upshot would be: de Wit would give the case to Gerry. SALON BARON SUES STATE FOR MILLIONS. De Wit would have to give the case to Gerry. He would have no choice. Joubert sighed and his shoulders sagged. Petersen saw it and he grasped something of the attitude.

'I'm sorry, Captain.'

'Will someone get an ambulance! Now!' the attorney pleaded and ordered at the same time.

'It's not necessary,' said a voice from the floor.

All three stared at Nienaber who slowly sat up.

'We're going to sue them, Oliver,' said the attorney. 'We'll strip them of everything. He . . .' A finger pointed at Leon Petersen. 'He'll never find another job in this country.'

'No,' Nienaber said.

Silence.

'Drop it,' Nienaber said. 'Let's just drop the whole thing.' He got up with difficulty, his right hand touching the bruised cheek. The attorney immediately rushed to his assistance, pulled Nienaber upright, helped him to straighten the chair, carefully helped him to sit down.

'They don't stand a chance, Oliver. It was brutality in its worst form. Under the new government . . . They'll both be looking for work.'

'I'm prepared to drop it, Phil.'

'Sheesh, Oliver.'

Nienaber looked up at Joubert. 'Are you prepared to leave it?'

Joubert said nothing. His mind was at a standstill, he was holding his breath. He merely stared at Nienaber. Petersen stared at the wall.

'Let's go, Phil,' said Nienaber and he walked to the door. The attorney grabbed his attaché case, his notepad and his pen and hurried after him on his short legs. Nienaber opened the door and walked out. The attorney followed him, slamming the door behind him.

Petersen lifted his head slightly and massaged the hand that had hit Nienaber. 'I'm sorry, Captain.'

'It's OK, Leon.' Joubert sat down at the table and took out his cigarettes. He lit one and blew a thin plume of smoke towards the ceiling.

'It's OK. I also think the fuckin' rich asshole whitey is lying.'

29

They drank coffee in the tea-room at half past eight on the Monday night. They sat next to one another, elbows resting on their knees, both hands curved around the coffee mugs. Rows of cheap steel and plastic chairs were stacked against the wall waiting for the seating rush in the morning.

'I've fucked up everything, Captain.'

Joubert sighed. 'That's true, Leon.' He swallowed a mouthful of the coffee which had been brewing in the big urn for too long. 'You'll have to do something about that temper of yours.'

'I know.'

Petersen stared at the contents of his mug, the muddy colour, the steam which formed a transparent wisp. 'God, Captain, there's so much trouble. My wife . . .'

His head dropped. He sighed deeply.

'What is it, Leon?'

He looked up at the ceiling as if searching for help. He blew out his breath slowly.

'My wife wants to leave me.'

Joubert did not say anything.

'She says I'm never at home. She says my daughters need a father. She says a step-father in the house is better than an own father who they never see. And she says in any case there's never any money for anything. You work like an executive and get paid like a gardener, she says.

Can I tell you something, Captain? Something private?'
He looked at Joubert and carried on before Joubert could
reply. 'Do you know when last my wife and I . . . You
know . . . Months. And now Bart de Wit tells me I must
spark because Blacks must get up the ladder, show it's not
just affirmative action. Now, suddenly, I'm a "Black."
Not Coloured anymore, not Cape Malay or Brown, but
Black. Instant reclassification. And I must spark. Now I
ask you, Captain, what else do I do? I've been sparking
for fucking years but my pay slip is still waiting for
affirmative action. And not just mine. All of ours. White.
black, brown. All the troubles, all the murders and deaths
and rapes, all the long hours with fuckers shooting at you
and rich whiteys who act as if you're not there and your
boss who says you must spark and the union which says
don't worry, things will be fine and a wife who says she
wants to leave you . . .'

Petersen took a large swallow of his coffee.

He sighed again. Then there was silence.

'We'll get him, Leon.'

'No, Captain, I've fucked it all up.'

'Temporary set-back.'

'What now, Captain?'

They heard hurried footsteps in the passage.

'I'm going to have him followed.'

They looked expectantly at the door. A sergeant peered
round it. 'Captain, Gerrit Snyman on the phone. He's
holding on. You can take it in my office, Captain.'

Joubert put down the mug on the big table in the centre of
the tea-room and hurried out with him. In the sergeant's
office he picked up the receiver. 'Gerrit?'

'I've found Eleanor Davids, Captain.' Excited.

'Who?'

'The woman who accused MacDonald of rape.'

Joubert struggled to remember. Snyman interpreted the silence correctly.

'Two years ago, Captain. She withdrew the charge.'

'Oh. Yes.'

'She's a prostitute, Captain.'

'Oh?'

A little more interest.

'And she owns a Smith & Wesson Escort, Captain.'

His heart jumped.

'She says she has an alibi, Captain, but I think she's lying.'

'We're on our way, Gerrit.'

'Great, Captain.' Then Snyman spoke more softly, confidentially. 'She's a pretty strange lady, Captain. Coloured, but the hair has been dyed pure white and the clothes are all black. High boots, pants, shirt. A cloak, even . . .'

This long black cloak like Batman. And black boots and black hair. The angel of death. Hercules Jantjies. The vagrant. In the Gardens police station. Joubert remembered it. *Ipsissima verba*, as the thick-lipped attorney would say. *Black hair.*

'Gerrit,' he said hurriedly.

'Captain?'

'You said her hair is white.'

'As snow, Captain.'

Perhaps Hercules Jantjies had grasped a part of the truth despite his meths haze.

'Where are you?'

'Charlie's Little Devils Escort Agency, Captain. Galleon Parade, Hout Bay.'

'Stay right there. Leon and I are on our way.'

The little devils were painted on the window facing the street, two of them, large and red, with long lithe legs, slender waists and big, voluptuous breasts. Above the roguish buttocks a tail grew, ending in an arrow point. Under the long, blonde hair there were two little horns. Above them, the name: CHARLIE'S LITTLE DEVILS.

Snyman perched self-consciously on a slightly worn armchair in the reception area as if he wanted to leave in a hurry. Joubert and Petersen shared the couch. It matched the other chair in which Eleanor Davids sat. Her legs, encased in black leather trousers, hung over the arm of the chair. She wore black boots which reached to her knees. A long cigarette dangled from the black lips. At the back of the reception area the owner sat, a young Greek with long curly hair and an unbuttoned shirt. He was concentrating on a paperback in front of him but Joubert knew his ears were pricked.

Eleanor denied having known of any of the other Mauser victims.

'Only MacDonald. And I say good riddance.'

'The rape?' Petersen asked.

'He was a flippin' animal, that one, brother,' she said and took the cigarette out of her mouth with fingers ending in long, black-painted nails. She spoke slowly, intimately, unworried.

'What happened?'

'He phoned for a girl. One night, over a weekend. Friday. Saturday. Said he wanted brown bread. Then Mike took me there in the van. Mike went in with me, to get the fee and to suss out the place. Then he left. And then MacDonald took me, brother, and all he wanted was love. I was still trying to hold him off but he grabbed me here and grabbed me there and tore my clothes, brother, and he forced himself on me. That's not how I do business, brother. We must negotiate first. It's not just grab and fuck. But he was an animal, bro', he said he'd paid and he wanted it right away.'

'And then?'

'Then he took what he wanted, brother.'

They waited in silence. She took a deep drag on the cigarette, killed it half-smoked in an overflowing ashtray with calm, deliberate movements.

'I phoned Mike when he'd finished, told him he had to take me to the charge office first. Mike didn't want to but I insisted. Then I laid the charge.'

'You withdrew it later.'

'Mike gave me a bonus.'

'And then you shot him on Saturday, sister.'

She smiled slowly, her teeth uneven and yellow. 'You're cute, brother. You must come for a freebie.'

'You possess a firearm.'

'Of course, bro'. In my line of business . . .'

'May we see it?'

She stood up slowly, swung the black cloak theatrically over her shoulder.

'What's with the cloak, sister?'

'One must give the product a unique package, brother.'

She walked with precise steps on her high heels to a door next to the reception desk. She opened it, left it open. The three detectives looked into another room where four women were seated, one with a magazine, one doing her make-up, two chatting. Then Eleanor Davids closed the door, a handbag in her hand. She took out a pistol, small and black, and gave it to Petersen.

Petersen turned it in his hands. 'It's an Escort, sister.'

She sat down again, lit another cigarette, shrugged her shoulders.

'So am I, bro', so am I.'

'This is the Mauser murderer's other pistol.'

'It's not me, brother. I'm bad but I don't kill.'

'You'll have to come with us, sister.'

'I know my rights. I have an alibi.'

'You think the magistrate will take your word?'

'No, but he'll probably take the word of a policeman.'

'Sister?'

'Ask Hatting, the desk sergeant at the Bay's station which evening of the week he gets his brown bread, brother. On the house. Sunset to sunup.'

Hatting was a middle-aged man, balding, which he tried to disguise by combing the few remaining hairs over the bald patch. He was in civvies because the station commander had called him in.

'I'm going to lose my pension,' Hatting said and he looked old and frightened and defenceless.

'It won't go any further, Sergeant,' said Joubert and looked at Petersen, Snyman and the Hout Bay OC. They all gave affirmative nods.

'My wife is deceased, Captain. It's been twelve years.' No one said anything. Hatting rubbed his hands and stared at the floor, his face contorted with regret. 'The children go back to boarding-school on Sunday afternoons, Captain . . . dear God, the Sunday evenings.'

They sat in an uncomfortable silence. But Joubert had to make sure.

'Sergeant, are you very sure that Eleanor Davids was with you until after seven on Monday morning?'

Hatting merely nodded. He couldn't look at Joubert.

'The whole night?'

Nod. Then silence again.

'Never again,' said Hatting and he wept.

Griessel's eyes were deeply sunken into their dark sockets, his skin the blueish-yellow of the very ill but he listened to Joubert's every word, craving for normality, the routine, the life outside. Joubert sat on one iron bed, on a bare mattress.

Benny sat on the other, his legs drawn up. The sanatorium was quiet, a mausoleum.

'Snyman will follow Nienaber, from tomorrow morning. With Louw relieving him in the evening. That's all we've got, Benny.'

'Can't be him.' Griessel's voice was vague as if he was speaking from a distance.

'I don't know, Benny. Hairdresser. I was . . .' He had to think when he had been at Anne Boshoff's. Today? It felt like yesterday or the day before. He remembered her and his discomfort and he wanted to laugh at himself and tell Benny Griessel about her but he merely gave a slightly embarrassed smile. 'I saw a beautiful woman today, Benny. A doctor in criminology. She said that the murderer could be queer. Nienaber is married but he's a hairdresser . . .'

'My nephew is a hairdresser in Danielskuil and he's screwed every farmer's wife in the area.'

'It's all I've got, Benny. Because Nienaber is lying. I don't know why or about what but he's lying. He's slippery, Benny. As an eel.'

Joubert looked at his watch. It was half past ten. The nurse had said only fifteen minutes.

'I want to come and help, Captain.'

'Come when you're ready.' He got up. ''Night, Benny.'

Joubert walked down the ward. His footsteps echoed off the walls. He had almost reached the double doors when he heard Griessel calling him.

'Mat.'

Joubert stopped, looked back.

'Why don't you ask her out? The doctor.'

He stood in the semi-dark and looked at the figure on the bed.

'Maybe, Benny. Sleep well.'

*   *   *

259

A block away from his house he stopped at a stop street, his window open so that the smoke of the Special Mild could waft outside. He heard the big motorcycle before it stopped next to him. The driver, in a black safety helmet, looked straight ahead, a passenger clung to him.

Joubert looked up, curious, instinctively, and saw the eyes of Yvonne Stoffberg through the narrow opening of her helmet.

Then the motorcycle revved up and drew away from his car. Joubert's mind put two and two together. Ginger Pretorius's Kawasaki, just before midnight on a Monday night. Yvonne Stoffberg's eyes.

There was something in the way she looked at him, something in the frown, the sudden manner in which she looked away. Perhaps it was only his imagination, he thought when he drove away from the stop street. But it seemed as if she was slightly self-conscious. 'I can do better than Ginger Pretorius,' is what he thought she wanted to say.

And then he knew he wasn't going to follow Griessel's advice. He wasn't going to ask Anne Boshoff out.

Because he wanted Dr Hanna Nortier.

30

Margaret Wallace woke just after three in the morning with the realisation that Tuesday was garbage removal day – and that she would have to lug the garbage bags from the kitchen door to the front gate on her own. Early. They usually came before six. Last week her brother-in-law had still been there to lend a hand but she was alone now. Without Jimmy. Tomorrow it would be two weeks. And there were so many things to do. A thousand things. Too many.

She got up, put on her dressing-gown and went to the kitchen, knowing that sleep would elude her. She switched on the kettle, unlocked the back door, took the garbage bin by the handle and manhandled it to the gate, a long and tiring job, by the light offered by the garden lights and the street lamps. But it gave her satisfaction. In future she would have to be self-sufficient. Jimmy would've expected it of her. She owed it to the children.

At the front gate, she removed the garbage bags from the bin, placed them on the pavement, dusted her hands and turned back to the kitchen, dragging the empty dustbin.

She remembered Ferdy Ferreira.

Without warning, without encouragement, her memory suddenly released the information, between the gate and the kitchen.

The man on the television. The third victim. Ferdy Ferreira. She remembered where she had seen the face

261

before. He'd been here, in their house, one evening. She was busy in the kitchen when the doorbell had rung. Jimmy had answered it. They had gone to the study without her seeing the man. But when he left, she thought, I saw him hobbling through the living-room, slightly lame. He had looked up and met her eyes, a man with a sad face, like a large, faithful dog's. But he hadn't greeted her, simply kept on walking to the door.

A long time ago. Four years? Five?

She had asked Jimmy who the man was. 'Just business, my sweet.' Some or other explanation, vague, lost in the mists of so many people who had come and gone, traipsing through her house, Jimmy's business acquaintances, instant friends, cricket people . . .

But Ferdy Ferreira had been there. And tomorrow she would phone the big policeman with the unseeing eyes and tell him.

Perhaps it would help.

He was already swimming just after six, knowing that it was going to be a long day, determined to make an early start. He counted the first two lengths and then became enmeshed in a search for solutions. What did he have to do today? Oliver Nienaber. Suspect number one. Gerrit Snyman was probably parked in front of the expensive house by now, ready for the first round of follow-the-hairdresser. The autopsy. Find out whether the pathologist had been able to establish the time of death. That might pin Nienaber down . . . despite Petersen's blow. Talk to the previous victims' relatives about MacDonald. Who had known him? Where? The bank robber. Ask Brigadier Brown whether people had been deployed in all Premier Bank's branches by now.

Two more days before he would see Hanna Nortier again, he thought. Only two days.

He wanted to ask her out. Where to? 'Drink in the canteen, Doc?'

Ha.

Dinner by candlelight in a good restaurant, one of those in Sea Point with the heavy curtains, perhaps one of the new ones in the Waterfront which everyone was talking about? No. Not for a first time – it would be too intimate, too much him and her.

Flick? Perhaps. What? 'Seen *Rocky VII*, Doc?' Maybe one of those European numbers with the sub-titles which showed in the southern suburbs? No. Too many bare breasts and blatant sex. She would get a wrong impression about him.

Joubert suddenly realised that he had sub-consciously kept count and that he had completed eight lengths. And he wanted more.

He couldn't believe it. Eight lengths. How about that? Eight fucking lengths.

Who needed to give up smoking? He turned the way he'd been taught all those years ago, in one smooth movement, his feet kicking against the swimming pool wall. He slid through the water until his big body broke surface and his arm stretched and his head turned to inhale and he tilted his chest for the next stroke upwards and the next. Left, right, left, breathe, right, left, right, breathe . . .

He swam another four lengths, rhythmically, easily, while his heart beat deep in his chest, a thrust. His satisfaction grew until he knew after the twelfth that it had been great and it was enough. He hauled himself effortlessly out of the pool and dripping water, walked to the change room. The long room was still empty at that time and the temptation was suddenly overwhelming. He bellowed: 'Baaa!'

One sound, explosive, an echo in the building. The shout which resounded in his ears was an embarrassment but the feeling enfolded him like a cloak even when he got out of the car at the Hout Bay police station, passed the voices of the journalists, walked up the stairs and through the big wooden door.

But it melted away when he saw the District Commissioner, the Chief of Detectives and de Wit.

They said good morning, the eyes of the three senior officers fixed hopefully on Joubert. His own revealed nothing. They walked to the ops rooms and closed the door.

Joubert told them everything – up to the point of Petersen's blow. And he began to lie. 'We had to let him go.'

'You had to let him go,' the District Commissioner said without intonation, stunned.

'We thought about the reputation of the Force, General, in these difficult times. Our image is at stake. Oliver Nienaber is a well-known personality. If we lock him up, we must have sufficient evidence. And we haven't. One witness who saw him at the scene of the murder. The pathologist hasn't even established whether MacDonald was murdered at more or less that time. We have no proof that Nienaber owns a Mauser. His story . . . It might well be true. But our image, General. If we charge the wrong man now . . .' Joubert stressed the image, knew that it was the one strong point in his argument.

'Ye-e-es,' the General said thoughtfully.

'But I have a team following Nienaber, General.'

'What do we tell the press?' the Brigadier asked. 'After last night's drama at the news conference they're like hyenas who've smelt blood. *Die Burger* even says someone might well be charged today. Where do they get hold of such nonsense?'

Silence fell on the room.

'Don't we have anything else, Captain?' the General asked but knew the answer.

'We have a great deal of follow-up work to do today, General. It might produce something.'

'We have to sound positive in front of the media. I'll say we've had a breakthrough and are following up new leads now. That's virtually the truth.'

'The medium,' said de Wit making his first contribution. The others stared at him. 'She's arriving tonight. Madame Jocelyn Lowe.'

'We can't tell the press that, Bart.' The Brigadier sounded irritated.

'I know, Brigadier. Nor will we. But the Madame has a press officer. And the press officer said she was sending faxes to the local newspapers this morning. From London.' De Wit looked at his watch. 'I promise you, our lack of success won't be the main copy this afternoon.'

'I hope you're right, Bart,' the General said. 'Let's go and speak to the vultures.'

While the General spoke to the media, Joubert stood to one side. He listened but his thoughts were still concentrated on the things that had to be done. Here and there he caught press questions: 'When is an arrest going to be made?' 'Is there a connection between the murders and the bank robberies?' The usual stuff. And then a new one. 'General, have you heard that the so-called field marshall of the Army of the New Afrikaner Boer Republic said that the Mauser was a voice calling the Afrikaners to the service of their nation?'

'No,' said the General.

The reporter paged back in his notebook. 'I quote: "The Mauser is the voice of our forefathers, the echo of their blood, spilt for freedom in two wars against overwhelming odds. It is a trumpet call for the uprising of the nation, a war cry from a forgotten era when Afrikaner pride was still pure and true".'

The whole press group was silent. So was the General.
Joubert looked at his shoes which shone in the sharp
sunlight.

'I'll ask Captain Joubert to answer to that,' said the
General.

Joubert looked at the expectant faces, speechless for a
moment. His panic grabbed at words, selected, discarded,
chose others until he started to speak, carefully. 'We cannot
summarily exclude any motive for the murders. To be frank,
we investigated political motives from the start. But I have
to tell you that there has been no reason up to now to
believe that any political groups are directly or indirectly
involved in this.'

'But you don't discount it altogether?' asked a radio
reporter, the microphone extended.

'We don't discount *anything* at this stage.'

The group realised that the impromptu news conference
was over and began dispersing. The television teams packed
up their equipment, photographers unscrewed their flash
lights. Joubert walked up the steps, back to the ops room.
He had to get hold of the pathologist.

Professor Pagel, the pathologist, complained about O
Grady. 'The man has no respect for death, Captain. I would
prefer you to be present in future. I find his kind of gallow
humour unprofessional.'

Joubert mumbled an apology then asked about the time
of MacDonald's death.

It's difficult, Captain. You know I can't give an exact
time.' Always the academic carefulness, honed by a thou
sand cases as witness for the state. 'But it looks like 6:00
with a sixty minute margin either way.' Then he began
explaining what he ascribed it to. Joubert was saved by a
voice from the charge office shouting his name. He excused

himself and trotted off. The constable held out a receiver. He took it.

'Joubert.'

'Captain, this is Margaret Wallace.'

'Good morning, Mrs. Wallace.'

'Captain, I don't know whether this is going to help you at all, but I think Jimmy knew one of the victims.'

He heard her using the past tense and knew she had passed through the Portal of Night and now knew the texture of the landscape on the other side.

'MacDonald?' he asked.

'No. The other one. From Melkbos. Ferreira, I think.'

And suddenly Joubert's heart beat faster because this was the first probable link. Along with Oliver Nienaber's lie, the first sign of a breakthrough. 'Where are you?'

'At home.'

'I'm on my way.'

Margaret Wallace invited him to a breakfast nook at the big swimming pool behind the house and made him sit down while she went to make tea. Then she came back with a pretty tray with porcelain cups and saucers and a banana loaf which was freshly cut and spread. She put it down on the white PVC table. 'Jimmy loved banana loaf, you know. But I stopped making it. I don't know why. It's just one of those things. Life moves on, past things like banana loaf. With the kids growing up, you start worrying about their favourite foods, their needs.'

She poured the tea. Joubert heard the birds in the trees, the fluid whispering from pot to cup, saw her slender hands with the delicate freckles, the wedding ring still on her left hand.

'And then yesterday I wanted to make banana loaf. Isn't it strange?'

267

He looked at her, saw her looking at him with her mismatched eyes but he didn't feel like replying.

'Would you like some?'

He nodded but immediately added guiltily: 'I'm on a diet.'

She smiled. Her teeth were white and even and he saw that she had a pretty mouth. 'You? Do you really need it?'

'Yes.'

'What does your wife say?' Still amused.

'I'm not married.' And then for no rhyme or reason: 'My wife is dead.'

'I'm so sorry.' There was a silence which caused the sun to darken and drowned out the garden sounds, to lie on the table between them like a tangible divide. Suddenly they were partners, buddies who knew the road up to here but didn't want to meet one another's eyes, too frightened that the other would cause the pain to return.

In silence they poured milk, added sugar, stirred the tea with tinkling sounds. She told him about Ferdy's visit, but her eyes were on the cup and saucer, her voice flat. He wondered how good her memory was, after four or five years, until she mentioned the visitor's limping walk.

'He had polio.'

'Oh.'

He asked her whether Ferdy Ferreira had ever been there again. If there was nothing else she could recall. If she had ever heard of Alexander MacDonald. All her replies were in the negative. He quickly swallowed his tea. Then he asked her for a photograph of the late James J Wallace. 'A recent one, if possible. Please.'

'Why?'

'To show the relatives of the other victims.'

'You think it means something? That Ferdy Ferreira was here?'

'I want to find out.'

She was away for a while, then came back with a photo, gave it to him without looking at it. He hurriedly stuffed it into his pocket and excused himself. She walked to the door with him and smiled when she said goodbye but the gesture was meaningless.

Uncle Zatopek Scholtz didn't like the Tygerberg shopping centre. He didn't like the American riverboat theme in the big atrium, he didn't like the crowds, the loud music and the smell of instant food. He wanted to go back to his farm beyond Malmesbury but his wife had insisted that he stop there on his way back from the auction because Woolworth's was having a sale of underwear and their bras were the only ones she could wear.

That's why Uncle Zato, as everyone called him, was sitting in the Nissan truck in the parking area until he remembered that he didn't have more than two or three Rands in cash on him. He had to put in petrol and buy tobacco for one of the farm hands.

Uncle Zato took his Premier cheque book out of the glove compartment, got out, carefully locked the truck, straightened his jacket and walked to the shopping centre. He knew there was a branch there. He took his time, unhurried – a sixty-five-year-old man in a tweed jacket, a short-sleeved blue shirt, beige shorts, long beige socks and brown Grasshoppers. He walked past the rows of cars, through the automatic doors to the centre's banking area and went to the Premier branch. He opened his cheque book at a desk, wrote out a cheque and joined a queue, moving forward until his turn came.

He slid the cheque under the glass and looked up at the very young teller with her long black hair and her sulky mouth.

'Give it in twenty Rand notes, sweetheart,' he said and put his hand in the pocket of the tweed jacket to take out his purse.

The teller only heard the last word and saw the movement which unbuttoned the jacket and the man's hand moving inside it.

She kicked the alarm button with a panicky foot and screamed.

Constable Vusi Khumalo was caught unawares. He was in civilian dress, standing at the window of the bank, staring outside, where a pretty black woman was mopping the floor of the shopping centre. Then he heard the scream and his hand went to his belt and he yanked out the Z88, swung round, saw the teller and the man with his hand inside his jacket.

Khumalo was a good cop. He had had his baptism of fire in the townships of Cape Town in the stormy days of 1994 and in the past month had successfully passed his sergeant's examination. And the book said spread your weight on two legs set wide apart, extend the pistol in front of you with both hands, eye behind the gunsight and shout in a loud, commanding voice. Get respect, let them know who's in control.

'Don't move or I shoot,' his voice rising above the shrilling of the alarm and the terrified screams of the onlookers, his weapon aimed at Uncle Zato's forehead.

The innocence of the Malmesbury farmer was conclusive. If Uncle Zato was a bank robber he would undoubtedly have stood still, immobile so that there could be no suspicion about his intentions.

But he'd had a fright, turned round quickly, saw the black man with the pistol and instinctively wanted to hold his purse in his hands, keeping it safe.

Uncle Zato pulled his purse out of the inside pocket of his jacket.

Khumalo moved the pistol a few centimeters and pulled the trigger, dead certain that the man with the jacket wanted to take out a firearm.

The 9 mm round ripped through Uncle Zato's shoulder, broke the clavicle and tore the sub-clavicle artery. He fell back against the counter, his blood spouting in a thick stream against the wood panelling. He had two minutes to live before too much of his life's fluid pumped out onto the floor.

Between the screams and the exclamations of clients and banking personnel, only Vusi Khumalo, moving forward and bending over Uncle Zato, heard the flabbergasted words: 'What are you doing?'

'You wanted to rob the bank,' Khumalo said.

'No,' said Uncle Zato but darkness was overcoming him and he couldn't understand anything any more.

'I think we must stop the bleeding,' a calm voice said next to Constable Khumalo. He looked up, saw a young black man in a short white coat.

'Are you a doctor?' asked Khumalo and moved away so that the man's hand could reach Uncle Zato's shoulder to block the red flow.

'No,' said the young man. 'I'm still learning.' And he saved Zatopek Scholtz's life.

31

J oubert and de Wit sat in the luxurious office of Premier
Bank's district manager. The view to the north, over the
harbour and Table Bay was breathtaking. None of the three
men saw it.

The district manager of Premier Bank stood right in front
of Joubert and wagged his finger at him. 'You promised me
discretion. Discretion. Discretion is a much loved and
respected client who is fighting for his life in Tygerberg's
Intensive Care Unit. Discretion is the chairman of my board
of directors who is waiting for me to return his call.
Discretion is my managing director who is having a cor-
onary. Discretion is a phone call from the media every seven
minutes. Discretion is a bank robber who's still somewhere
out there with a bloody great pistol while the discreet people
of Murder and Robbery tell me they're sorry.'

Sweat dripped off the district manager's face and his high,
bald head shone under the concealed lighting of the office.

'You must understand . . .' said Colonel Bart de Wit and
lifted a finger of his own.

'No, I don't have to understand anything. This fat fart
. . .' the district manager's finger shot in Joubert's direction,
. . . 'gave me the assurance that nothing would happen. But
he'd forgotten to assure me that you would deploy a crowd
of kaffer constables with cannons in my branches. He . . .'

Joubert got up, his body virtually touching the district
manager's, his face only inches from the man's nose.

'Listen,' Mat Joubert said.

The district manager stepped back, kept his mouth shut.

'Listen carefully,' said Mat Joubert. 'If you speak to me or speak to him,' and he indicated Bart de Wit, 'you speak politely. And if you ever refer to my men again as kaffer constables, I'll smash your face.'

The district manager looked pleadingly at de Wit. De Wit looked at Joubert. There was a small, confused smile on the Colonel's face.

'Anyway,' said Joubert. 'I can't be that fat any more. I'm on a diet.'

Then he sat down again.

No one said anything. The district manager stared at the carpet. He sighed deeply, walked slowly to his chair. He sat down.

'I'm sorry. I'm sorry. The stress . . .' He took a corporatively correct handkerchief from the top pocket of his coat and pressed it against his forehead. 'The stress,' he said. Then he looked up. 'What now?'

'Obviously we'll relieve Constable Vusi Khumalo and do a complete investigation of the whole incident,' said Joubert. 'And this evening we'll assemble all the policemen who have to do duty in Premier Bank branches. We'll drill them. Safety, caution, public interest. We'll give them a short course which they must impart to every branch member tomorrow morning. Crisis management. Self-control. Emergency planning.'

De Wit nodded his head enthusiastically.

'And from tomorrow the whole operation will be under the command of one of the Peninsula's top detectives.'

De Wit and the district manager looked at him expectantly.

'His name is Benny Griessel.'

*   *   *

'No, Captain. I mean I approve of your reaction to his racist and discriminatory remarks. But Benny Griessel?'

They walked to Joubert's car.

'Colonel, I'm sorry. I should've discussed it with you first. But I only thought of it some minutes ago. In that man's office.'

'Griessel is lying drunk in hospital,' de Wit said.

'I was there last night, Colonel. He's dry. He needs something, Colonel. He must be kept busy now. He must regain his self-respect. This is just the right thing.'

'The right thing? With all the stress?'

'Benny can handle stress, Captain. It's death he can't handle,' Joubert said quietly.

They walked in silence to the white Sierra. Joubert unlocked the passenger door for de Wit, walked round and got in. The car was unbearably hot inside. They turned down windows. Then Joubert switched on the engine and they drove off to the N1.

Bart de Wit stared at the road through the front window. His finger rubbed the mole nervously, over and over again. He didn't speak. Joubert sighed and concentrated on his driving.

They had already passed the N7 exit when de Wit looked at Joubert. 'We're no longer in control of this thing, Captain. Neither you nor I. The whole case has developed a life of its own. All that remains is to pray. Because, Captain, the truth of the matter is that my head is at stake. There are many eyes in the Force who are watching me. Old Two Nose, they say. Old Two Nose won't make it. He was given the post because of his buddies in the ANC. He didn't deserve it. All I really wanted, Captain, was to prove them wrong.'

Then de Wit was silent until they turned into Kasselsvlei Road.

'You can give Benny Griessel the opportunity, Captain.'

'Thank you, Colonel.'

'Who knows. Maybe someone will gain something from this mess.'

Joubert closed the special ops room in Hout Bay and shifted the investigation to head office, back to Murder and Robbery. He sent people to Gail Ferreira and to Alexander MacDonald's employers for photographs of the victims. He had the SAPS photographers make copies. Then he called in his team to the parade room. 'Thank you very much for the trouble you took with the arms dealers and the gunsmiths,' he started his address. 'Unfortunately we found nothing which we could follow up. But there's still hope.' They looked at him expectantly.

'There is a possibility that the victims knew one another.' A few men drew in an audible breath.

'You'll be divided into teams of two. Each team will get a set of photographs of all the victims. Leon Petersen and I will visit the relatives, you'll take the neighbours, colleagues and acquaintances. Start with the names on the notice board but you're responsible for extending the list. Anyone who lived near a victim. Contacts at work. Drinking pals. Anyone. We want to know if they knew one another.'

He ran his eyes over them. They were listening attentively, already caught up in the excitement. Tonight they'll tell their families 'I'm working on the Mauser case'.

'There's something else, more difficult,' Joubert continued. 'There might be a homosexual connection.'

A few muted whistles and the odd remark.

'This doesn't mean that you immediately ask each and everyone whether so and so was queer.'

They laughed. Joubert lifted his hand until silence fell

again. He spoke urgently.

'If the press finds out there'll be chaos. I urge the senior member of every team to act responsibly. Ask your questions carefully. Very carefully. There's no direct evidence. But we have to investigate it. You're aware of the way in which the newspapers are carrying on. The name of the Force is at stake. But don't forget the relatives of the victims. It's hard for them. Don't make it harder with tactlessness and loose talk. Are there any questions?'

'Is it true that Oliver Nienaber is a suspect?' someone called from the back. Joubert shook his head. The rumour was spreading.

'No longer,' he said with finality. That rumour had to be squashed. 'Any more questions?'

'Case of beer for the team who cracks it?'

'Ten cases,' said Joubert and received a standing ovation.

He and Petersen found nothing from the relatives, no matter how long or how seriously the people stared at the photographs of the other victims. They had all shown the same reaction. A negative shake of the head and the inevitable: 'I'm sorry but . . .'

He dropped Petersen at Murder and Robbery that afternoon and drove to the sanatorium. The nurse directed him to a recreation room on the third floor. When he walked into the room he saw Benny Griessel sitting at a table with five other people – three men and two women. They were playing cards.

'Raise you forty,' said Griessel and tossed two twenty cent pieces into the kitty in the centre of the table.

'Gawd,' said a woman with greasy hair and a long cigarette between her fingers.

'You must have a flush.'

'Pay if you want to find out,' Benny said mysteriously.

Joubert went to stand behind him. No one took any notice of the new arrival.

'Raise you ten,' said a human skeleton with watery blue eyes and shot in twenty cents.

'I fold,' said an elderly woman next to him. She put her cards down. A pair of queens.

'So do I,' said a man with a network of thin red and blue ink stretching from his shoulder to his wrist – an elegant dragon, breathing fire.

'Raise you another forty,' said Griessel.

'Too rich for my blood,' said the human skeleton. 'It's your game.'

Griessel got up, leant over the table and raked in the money.

'Show us what you had,' the woman with the cigarette said.

'I needn't,' said Griessel.

'Be a sport,' said the dragon.

'I bluffed,' said Griessel while he pushed the money over the edge of the table with a cupped hand, to let it fall tinkling into his purse. Then he put the purse down and turned over the five cards.

'Not even a pair,' the elderly woman complained.

'You're too clever to be an alky,' said the skeleton.

'He's only a stupid cop,' said Joubert. 'And he starts working tonight.'

Griessel thanked him from the recreation room to the deserted hall but Joubert remained stern. For fifteen minutes he laid down the law until the sergeant held up his hands. 'I've heard it all before. From my wife, my brother, Willie Theal. And it didn't help, Mat. I've got to be OK in here,' and he slapped a palm on his chest. 'I've done a lot of thinking over the past few days. And I know I'll manage for a week or two. Then I'll go the same road unless I do something. I need that head doctor of yours. If my head is in shape, I can leave the liquor. And I want to leave it. But she must help me.'

'That's a great idea, Benny.' Then he brought Griessel up to date on both investigations – the Mauser murders and the Sweetheart robber – while Griessel packed his stuff into a large paper bag. They walked down the passages together. To Reception.

'And now you must take over the bank robber, Benny. Tonight. You must talk to the people. It's your team.'

Griessel said nothing until they came to the entrance hall. 'Are you leaving, Griessel?' the nurse behind the desk asked.

'Yes, Sister.'

'Are you scared, Griessel?'

'Yes, Sister,' he said and signed the release form.

'That's good, Griessel. It keeps one dry. Keep him out of here, big boy.'

'Yes, Sister,' he echoed Griessel meekly. Then they walked down the steps together, to the car.

The great hunger struck again just after four, in his office where he was busy checking the lists and tabulations on the investigation, looking for more possibilities. His hunger was a sudden realisation that broke his concentration like thunder – contracting, noisy guts, a trembling hand, a curious light-headedness and the certain knowledge that he wanted to eat now, seated at a table armed with a knife and fork and attacking a plate of food boldly and com-mitedly: a thick, juicy steak; a steaming potato baked in foil, with sour cream; cauliflower with a rich cheese sauce; green beans with tomato and onion; a gem squash in which butter gently melted while he shook salt and pepper over the lot.

He saw the food so clearly, the impulse to get into his car right away and drive to a restaurant so strong that he had reached the door when he had to stop himself physically by banging his hand against the frame.

'Big boy,' the nurse had called him.

'Fat fart,' the district manager of Premier Bank had said.

He sat down at his desk and lit a Special Mild. His stomach rumbled again, a long drawn-out sound with multiple crescendos.

He looked for the dietician's number, found it in his notebook and dialed. She answered before the end of the first ring. He identified himself. 'My diet isn't working.'

She bombarded him with questions until she was satisfied. 'No, Captain, your diet will work if you stick to it. You can't keep to your programme in the morning and evening only. The midday meals . . .'

'I work during my lunch hour.'

'Make your lunch in the evening, Captain. And take it to work.'

He said nothing, shaking his head at the unfairness of it all.

'Dieting is hard work, Captain. It's not easy.'

'That's true,' said Joubert and gave a deep sigh.

There was a long silence during which only the static on the telephone line was audible. Eventually the dietician said: 'You can crook once a week. But then you must crook cleverly.'

'Crook cleverly,' Joubert said hopefully.

'All I can suggest is that you fetch *A New Generation* here.'

'A what?'

'*Cookbook for a New Generation*. From the Heart Foundation. With that you can crook cleverly. Once a week.'

'*Cookbook for a New Generation*,' he said later and felt like a fool. Hunger made his guts rumble again.

32

We all know what fat looks like on the human body it said on page eleven of the cookbook.

Ain't that the fucking truth, said Joubert and shifted uncomfortably on the chair in his kitchen. The book lay on the table in front of him, next to the ingredients for the recipe the dietician had recommended.

'What do you feel like?' she'd asked after she had given him the book.

'Steak.'

'You're stubborn.'

'I'm hungry,' he'd said with finality.

'Try the beef fillet with mushrooms. Page 113. But read the whole introduction first so that you understand your calories and unsaturated fats. And eat a small portion. There's no point in cooking it in a healthy way and then eating the whole dish on your own.'

He had stopped at Pick 'n Pay and with the book open at page 113 he'd walked the aisles until he had all the ingredients he needed.

What you might not know, he read on, *is that over and above the fat you can see around your waist, or on your thighs and breast, people who are overweight also build up interior fat. Fat usually forms around the interior organs especially in the lower body and around the intestines, kidneys and heart.*

In his mind's eye he saw his organs, each one wrapped in its own yellowish-white fat and he shuddered.

THE FOLDED SKIN TEST, one of the headings read. *An easy and quick way to measure your fat is to pinch a fairly large piece of stomach skin between your thumb and forefinger. If it's thicker than 2.5 cm then you're fat – and you can be sure that the fat is spread right through your body.*

He put the book down on the table, leant back, pulled his shirt out of his trousers and grabbed a pinch of stomach skin. He gave it a measuring eye.

Shit. Could it be true?

He got up and went to look for his new measuring tape. He found it in the study where the books were packed on the skew shelves. He walked back to the kitchen, sat down, pinched the skin of his stomach with his left hand and measured with the right.

More than four centimeters. And he was giving it a bit of leeway.

Crossly he closed the cookbook with a slam.

Crook cleverly.

He couldn't afford to crook cleverly. Not with four centimeters of stomach skin. Not with organs encrusted with thick layers of fat.

He sighed, put the cookbook aside and picked up his diet sheet. *120 grams grilled fish. 250 ml mashed potato, tomato and onion salad. 1 unit fat.*

One unit of fat. He looked for the key at the end of the programme. He could choose between small amounts of margarine, salad dressing, mayonnaise, peanut butter, avocado pear, small olives, thin cream or a strip of bacon. He chose the salad dressing and started his preparations.

'The report on Eleanor Davids's Escort is here, Captain,' said Snyman and handed the sheet of paper to Joubert.

'It's negative,' he said without glancing at it.

'Yes, Captain.'

He sighed. 'Thanks, Gerrit.'

He turned. It was time to go and watch *The Return of Benny Griessel*.

Joubert stood unobtrusively in the door of Murder and Robbery's parade room. Griessel mustn't think he had come to check on him.

Griessel stood on a chair next to the TV set, addressing the twenty-two uniformed people.

'In the file you'll find photographs taken by the security cameras in the branches of the bank and an Identikit of what our artist thinks the robber might actually look like. But these are only pointers. And it could be dangerous, as we learnt from this morning's incident. For heaven's sake don't confront every possible suspect who vaguely resembles the Identikit with a firearm. Use your common sense. Think. And think again,' Griessel said and he smiled at the faces in front of him.

Joubert saw that the traces of the past week lay heavily on Griessel's face, on his bulky body which had shrunk visibly. But his voice was clear and enthusiastic.

'The media still don't know that we have people in every branch. We told them Khumalo was there by chance to draw money. That means that the robber doesn't have to suspect anything. But he's nobody's fool. He'll check out the scene very well before he robs. He'll be careful. I know thinking isn't covered by a police salary but do it for your country. Think before you hang around looking like a cop who's a plant. Move around. Fill in bank forms. Pretend to be drawing money. Go to the inquiries desk. Lieutenant Brand of Internal Stability will speak to you shortly about crisis management which you must share with the personnel in your bank branch. Tell them they must be in on the act. They must treat you like a client. Nothing more and nothing less . . .'

Joubert turned away and walked down the passage on his way home.

Griessel didn't need his help. He walked out, into the night, towards his car.

Oliver Nienaber grinned behind the wheel of his dark red BMW.

The police must think him a fool. He had already noticed it the day before, quite by chance, when the white Opel Kadett followed him all the way home. The idiot had to jump a red light to keep up. And later he had noticed him again on the quieter roads of Plattekloof. Early this morning he had seen the red Sierra in the street, just below his house.

Now, at a quarter to six in the morning, the N1 wasn't busy enough for an unobtrusive tail. He could see the Ford far back in the rear-view mirror.

They were wasting their time, he thought. He was innocent. He wasn't the hunter, he was the prey. And now they were unwittingly giving him protection.

If it hadn't been for the little brown lieutenant he would've gotten away with his lie. Lord, but he'd done some fast thinking. On Monday in that interrogation room. But that was why he was where he was today. Quick thinking. From hair stylist to millionaire in six, seven years.

That tale about MacDonald phoning him about the building had simply risen unbidden in his mind. Needs must when the devil drives.

Need. The whole Monday had been filled with need. From the moment he'd seen Mac lying in the door of that pitiful wooden house with blood against the wall and blood on the floor and his neck which had been blown away and the shot between the balls, he had needed to feel safe.

He had wanted to speak to him. He hadn't known at

what time Mac went to sea and had hoped that he was early enough. He'd stopped in front of the door, opened the gate and then he saw the man lying there, big Mac. Big Mac with the biggest penis he'd ever seen in his life. He could remember that.

'Mac, you've got a prick like a pole,' Ferdy Ferreira had said. The late Ferdy. The late, lame fool.

'A penis,' said Oliver Sigmund Nienaber loudly and snorted with laughter. That was the word which had caught the attention of that little lieutenant.

Fuckin' hotnot. He rubbed his cheek. It still hurt. But it had been worth it. A small price to pay.

'I fell,' he had told his beautiful wife.

'With what did you have to help the Police?' she'd asked.

Think fast. 'Oh, it was about a black cleaner who used to work for us. They've charged him with child abuse. They wanted to know whether we'd noticed anything.'

'Couldn't they have asked about it here, darling?'

He had merely shrugged. 'But they should clean those steps of theirs. All the dirt makes them slippery. I slipped and fell against the door frame.'

This morning Antoinette had fetched some of her make-up base to disguise the purplish mark on his face.

'There, darling, that looks better.'

He turned off again, to Wynberg, drove to the Main Road. Just before driving into the parking garage of his building, he looked to check whether he could still see the Sierra. But there was nothing. Never mind, he thought, they'll probably park somewhere around here where they have a clear view. He stopped in his parking bay RESERVED FOR MD HAIR TODAY.

He set the numbers of the combination lock on his attaché case and opened it. The Star pistol lay on top. He closed it again, gave the lock numbers a routine spin with his thumbs. He wouldn't need the pistol now that the Police were giving him free protection. He got out, pressed the button on his key holder for the central locking system of the BMW and walked to the lift. The door was open. He walked in and looked at his watch. Six o'clock. Dead on time. As usual. With the exception of Monday morning. He pressed the button for the sixth floor. The doors closed soundlessly.

Snyman parked opposite the Servier Building in the Main Road in such a way that he could watch the building's entrance and that of the parking garage. He opened the lunch box next to him and took out a flask of coffee and a packet of sandwiches. He wasn't hungry but the coffee would taste good now. He unscrewed the flask's cup, poured the steaming liquid into it and sipped slowly and carefully.

The coffee burnt his lips. He swore and blew on the brown surface of the drink.

He leant back in the comfortable seat of the Sierra.

It might just be a long day.

Nienaber stared at the floor of the lift as he habitually did and only looked up when the doors opened.

He saw the executioner immediately.

Feet slightly apart, arms extended, the firearm held in both hands, aimed at him.

He knew the executioner had waited for him, had watched the lights above the lift. B for basement, M for mezzanine, 1,2,3,4,5,6. He knew all this in a micro second.

Quick thinking, Oliver Nienaber. That's why you are where you are.

He also knew that the Star in his attaché case was too far away, useless. But he could talk. He could negotiate. He could think.

He lifted his hand in a 'stop' gesture.

'You . . .' he said but by then the cartridge had penetrated the palm of his hand and was unstoppably on its way to his brain.

At a quarter to seven on the Wednesday morning, Joubert sat on the wooden bench of the swimming pool's changeroom. His elbows rested on his knees, his head hung down, water dripped onto the cement floor and he knew he would have to leave the cigarettes.

His lungs were burning. He knew it was the layer of tar, the black, sticky, dirty, gummy layer which smouldered in his lungs after the swim, which caused his inability to cross the fitness threshold permanently. He could feel it with every breath he tried to draw after five, six lengths this morning. With every new swing of his arm, every rhythmic kick of his legs, the clearer the image became of the muddy encrustation in his lungs which stood between him and the energy-supplying oxygen.

Mat Joubert, human garbage carrier. Full of fat and soot.

No matter that it was Special Mild, sooner or later he would have to stop. They had no taste, in any case.

He took a decision.

He got up suddenly, purposefully, and walked to where his clothes were hanging on a peg. He took the white and grey packet and the lighter out of his coat pocket, walked to the big, black garbage bin in the corner, lifted the lid and forcefully threw the smokes into it.

The bin had been empty. He stared at the packet and the lighter lying there.

I've done with it, he thought. Forever.

Solemnly he closed the garbage bin, turned, and walked to the showers.

On the way to Kasselsvlei Road he saw the *Cape Times*

poster: MAUSER: UK PSYCHIC FLIES IN TO HELP.

The paperseller held the newspaper in such a way that Joubert could read the headline on the front page, one huge word stretching across the entire page: HYSTERIA. The sub-reading read: FARMER CRITICAL AFTER BANK SHOOTING.

For a moment he considered buying the paper but the lights changed and he drove on. De Wit's psychic had arrived, he thought. Hysteria, indeed.

'I heard nothing, Captain,' Snyman said. 'The first I heard about it was when they gave the address of the place over the radio. I couldn't believe it. The bastard shoots a cannon and I heard nothing.'

They stood in a circle around the mortal remains of Oliver Sigmund Nienaber – Joubert, Snyman, Petersen, O' Grady, Basie Louw and two uniform men from the Wynberg Police station. Nienaber lay in the door of the lift, almost covering his attaché case, on his stomach, one bloody hand extended. The doors of the lift slowly, mechanically opened and closed, bumped against Nienaber's body, opened and closed . . .

'Someone must switch off the lift,' Joubert told one of the uniforms.

'Right away, Captain.'

'The security guard at the front entrance didn't hear anything, either,' Snyman said.

'Where is the woman now?' Joubert asked.

'She works for a computer firm here on the seventh, Captain. They called a doctor. She's suffering from shock. She says she took the stairs when the lift didn't arrive. When she got there . . .' Snyman pointed to the fire-escape which ran alongside the lift shaft, 'she saw him. She says she knew him. He always greeted her in such a friendly fashion.'

'No one saw anything?'

'I think the Mauser came in at the service entrance at the back, Captain. Security man says tenants are constantly leaving it open because there are too many people in the building who have keys for it.'

'How do you know it was the Mauser?'

Snyman took a small plastic bag out of his shirt pocket. There were two cartridge cases in it.

'Is someone watching the door for fingerprints?'

'Station's people, Cappy,' O' Grady said.

A man and a woman from the video unit came walking up the stairs. 'Why isn't the bloody lift working?' the man asked as he breathlessly climbed the last few steps.

No one said anything. The man saw Nienaber lying in the lift. The doors opened and closed, opened and closed.

'Oh,' the man said.

'I can't believe that I heard nothing,' Snyman said.

Joubert looked at Peterson. 'You were right, Leon. Nienaber was lying.'

'But now we'll never know what the truth was, Captain.'

'We'll find out.'

'Where are the photographers? I want to turn him over and see if he got one in the cock as well,' said O' Grady.

'You also think it was the Mauser?' Louw asked.

'Another Mauser?' Pagel, the pathologist, asked breath-lessly from the staircase.

'We think so.'

Snyman's hip radio crackled. 'Captain Mat Joubert, Captain Mat Joubert, please phone Dr Boshoff at the University of Stellenbosch. Captain Mat Joubert . . .'

'Is there a phone anywhere here?' he asked.

'In Nienaber's office, there, around the corner, Captain.'

He walked down the passage. Anne Boshoff – what did

she want? He dug in his inside pocket looking for his notebook with her telephone number.

Nienaber's office was luxurious – a big reception area with expensive furniture in pastel colours, a carpet with a thick pile, paintings against the one wall. Nienaber's newspaper advertisement had been enlarged and framed and hung under the big logo of his firm's name.

The end of an era, Joubert thought. The Great Predator wasn't scared off by success, didn't allow himself to be sidetracked by egotism and vanity.

He found a telephone on the reception desk, paged in his notebook until he located Anne Boshoff's number and dialed.

She replied by stating her name.

'This is Mat Joubert.'

'Matthew! How lovely to hear your voice. But you still sound old. Are you living yet, Matthew? When are you coming to see me?'

'I got a message . . . ?'

'And called back so quickly. Efficiency in the Civil Service always makes me feel so secure. It's about the psychic, Matthew. Madame Jocelyn Lowe. I do hope you're not the "old friend"?'

'The "old friend"?'

'Don't you read the papers?'

'I'm busy with a murder investigation, Dr Boshoff.'

'Anne.'

'Your adopted, middle-class homosexual struck again this morning, Anne.' He stressed her name, somewhat irritated, but she didn't react.

She whistled. 'He's speeding up.'

'Speeding up?'

'Do you know that most of the time you repeat what I've just said? Yes, he's speeding up. It's only three days since

MacDonald, Matthew. The time span between each murder
is getting shorter and shorter. Let me see . . .' Joubert heard
the rustle of paper. 'A week between the first and the
second. Almost, if you count the day of the first murder
as day one. Then four days until the third. Another four
days, then MacDonald. And only three up to today. Monday, Tuesday, Wednesday. Or two, if you exclude Monday.'

'That's true.'

'He's sick, Matthew. Very sick. He's getting out of
control. He needs help. This changes my analysis. I'll have
to go back to the books. Tell me, was the victim gay again?'

'It's Oliver Nienaber.'

'The hairdresser king?'

'The very same.'

She whistled again. 'He wasn't gay, Matthew.'

'He wasn't gay. But how do you know?'

'I know men. Matthew. And that one wasn't gay. You
could see it.

'I have to go.'

'I want to know about the psychic first. She says in the
Times . . .' The sound of paper again. ' "Let's just say I
came to help an old friend. Someone involved in the
investigation." Is that you?'

'No.'

'I'm so pleased. Be careful of those creatures, Matthew.
They lie like troopers. Martin Reiser, of California, did
scientific research on them. And you must know what he says:
"The bottom line is that they all did very, very poorly . . ."'

Gerrit Snyman appeared in the door, in an obvious
hurry.

'I really have to go,' Joubert said. 'But I appreciate . . .'

'Don't let it be words only, Matthew,' Anne Boshoff said
and put the phone down.

*   *   *

They rolled Nienaber over. There was a splash of blood on his chest, a neat hole through the designer tie.

'No, the family jewels were spared,' said O' Grady, sounding disappointed and bit off another piece of nougat.

'But it's definitely the Mauser. It isn't over yet.'

'Yup, it ain't over till the fat lady sings, as they say at the opera.'

And then Joubert suddenly knew where he would take Hanna Nortier when he asked her out.

'The attaché case is locked, Captain,' Snyman said from the floor.

'Let forensics check it for fingerprints and then take it to the office. Van Deventer can use his little screwdrivers on it.'

'He'll love that,' said O' Grady.

'Gerrit, we're going to Nienaber's wife. Let me know if anything crops up.'

'Very well, Captain.'

Joubert took the stairs followed by O'Grady, Petersen and Louw. There was a lightness in his step. Because he knew where he could take Hanna Nortier.

33

The bank robber liked the names which the media had given him. *Don Chameleon*, in the English press, *Sweetheart Robber* in *Die Burger*. But now he was unhappy. They thought he was the Mauser murderer. And an innocent man lay in the Panorama Clinic, shot through the shoulder because a constable had thought it was the Sweetheart Robber.

He hadn't wanted violence or anything approaching killing. He hadn't wanted all the publicity. All he wanted . . . but it didn't matter any longer. All he wanted now was to rectify the matter.

That was why he was going to rob a different bank that morning. Premier Bank's branches were getting too hot. Why had that constable been at hand in the Tygerberg branch? Were they setting traps for him? That big captain who had been on television. He looked somewhat absent-minded but he wasn't a captain for no reason.

Don Chameleon wouldn't allow himself to be caught. He would only rectify the matter. And then wait until the whole thing subsided.

He was a businessman this morning, a bearded, moustached businessman in a black wig, dressed in a charcoal grey, tailor-made suit with a white shirt and a blue and orange tie. He walked through the doors of BANKSA's branch in Somerset West, the furthest he could get from his other working areas. He walked straight to the teller, a short, middle-aged woman and took a white envelope out of his pocket.

'Good morning, sweetheart,' he said succinctly.

'Good morning, sir.' The woman smiled at him. 'Words like that can get you into trouble,' she said calmly and unsuspectingly.

'How so?'

'The man who robs Premier Bank. Can I help you?'

'What do you think of the robber?'

'They say he's the Mauser murderer. I hope they shoot him before someone else is hurt.'

'They're lying,' the robber said angrily. 'Do you hear me? They're lying.'

'Sir?'

He opened the left side of his coat. 'Do you think this looks like a Mauser?'

The woman stared at the black pistol under his arm, her eyes frightened now.

'I want fifty Rand notes. Quickly. And I don't suppose I have to mention the alarm.'

The woman nodded. 'Just remain calm, sir.'

'You remain calm.'

She took packets of fifty Rand notes out of her cash drawer and placed them on the counter.

'Put it in a bank bag, you moron.'

The sharpness of his voice startled her. He shifted the envelope towards her. 'See that the Police get that. Captain Mat Joubert.'

'Very well, sir.'

'What perfume do you use?'

'Chanel.'

'It disgusts me,' he said, took the bag and walked to the door.

*   *   *

Joubert stared out over the Cape Flats and the Hottentots-Holland Mountains but he had no appreciation of the view from the window in Oliver Nienaber's study. He was exhausted after the session with Antoinette Nienaber.

They had first gone back to Murder and Robbery to inform de Wit. The Colonel had smiled and phoned the Brigadier. Then they went to the big house in the wealthy suburb and knocked on the door.

The beautiful blonde woman had collapsed – collapsed and screamed: 'No, no, no,' an incessant shrill sound which penetrated the marrow.

Joubert had bent down and placed a hand on her shoulder but she had slapped it away, her face contorted with pain. She had jumped up and with both hands on his chest, had pushed him back across the threshold, outside, while she made wailing noises and slammed the door in his face. There he, Petersen, Louw and O' Grady had stood, their heads bowed, listening to the sounds on the other side of the door.

'Get a doctor and a policewoman,' Joubert had said and opened the door again. 'Tony, come with me.'

He'd walked in and walked in the direction of the sounds. A maid stood in the passage.

'I'm going to phone the Police,' she said.

'We are the Police.'

The black woman said something in Xhosa which he didn't understand.

'Mr. Nienaber is dead,' he'd said.

She'd called on her gods in her own language.

'Help us with her.' He gestured in the direction of the noises.

They had found her in the bedroom on the floor, a framed photo pressed to her breast. She hadn't heard them entering the room and remained unaware of their presence,

297

only making the noises – not the tearing sobs of grief but the wails of insanity.

They had stayed with her until the doctor and a police-woman arrived. They had stood there in the bedroom of the Nienaber's, next to the big double bed and tried to see nothing and hear nothing until the tall, slender doctor had eased past them, opened his black bag and taken out a needle and a small phial. He had tried talking to her first but Joubert had seen that she heard nothing. Then the doctor had given her an injection.

Now Joubert stood in the study, against the window and felt guilty – all he could think about was having a smoke, to take a deep draw of the rich, full flavour of a Winston and to forget about the message of death which he had brought and the abyss into which it had plunged Antoinette Nie-naber.

'Shit happens, Captain,' O' Grady said at the door.

Joubert turned and wondered how long the man had been standing there.

'Yes,' he said.

'It's part of the job.'

'Some job.'

O' Grady, now wordless, rummaged in his pocket for nougat. He took out a new bar, nimbly tore off the wrap-ping.

'It's all I can do, Captain.'

Joubert looked out of the window again, chewed on the fat sergeant's words.

How had he handled it in earlier days? How had he carried the black coat over his shoulders with such ease? How had he acted the angel of death then, without it gnawing at his vitals like a cancer? Had he been too young? Too stupid?

No.

It had been ignorance, pure and simple. Death had no capital letters, it was something that happened to other people's nearest and dearest. A phenomenon, a normal aberration, a source of excitement, the start of the chase, the sound of trumpets as the cavalry was called in. Have no fear, Mat Joubert is here – the great leveller, the long arm of the law, the restorer of the legal scale's balance.

And then came the death of Lara Joubert and he had tasted it on the palate of his soul for the first time.

It's all I can do.

'I'll have to go through the study, Tony.'

'I'll cover the bedroom, Cappy. The Lieutenant is talking to the maid. I'll get Basie to come and help you.'

'Thanks.'

O' Grady disappeared. Joubert turned and walked to the desk. He sat down in the armchair. A blotter and pencil set lay in front of him. The blotter was a monthly calendar with space for appointments but nothing was written on it. There was a telephone to one side. Next to the telephone was a new Cape telephone directory with two smaller books on top of it. He looked at the books.

Seven Habits of Highly Successful People.

Maybe he should read it.

Bottom-up Marketing.

Oliver Nienaber's books. Oliver Nienaber's keys to fame and riches. He shifted the telephone directory towards him. Had Nienaber sat in this chair and read? Had he used the directory to look up Alexander MacDonald's number, made an appointment? He opened the directory, paged to M, looked for MacDonald. *MacDonald's Fisheries* was underlined. His heart beat faster. F? He found Ferdy Ferreira's number but it wasn't underlined.

Disappointment.

W for Wallace. Not underlined, either. Wilson, D? Un-marked.

Had Nienaber spoken the truth about MacDonald? Joubert closed the guide and started at A. He paged with his middle finger, licking it occasionally.

Basie Louw came in. 'Need any help, Captain?'

Joubert looked up. 'Yes.' He wanted to open a desk drawer but it was locked.

'We must go through the drawers, Basie. Ask the maid if she knows where the keys are.'

When Louw left, Joubert paged on. The first name that was underlined, was *Oberholzer, C A, 1314 Neptune's View, Yates Road, Sea Point*. And a number. He stared at it. Why? When? He paged on, past MacDonald's Fisheries again. He pulled the telephone towards him, his insides clenching. He dialed the number.

A long, steady beep.

He looked up the number of Enquiries, dialed and asked them to check the number. They said they would phone back.

He paged on, as far as Z, but found nothing.

Louw came back. 'The woman says Nienaber had the keys, Captain.'

'See if you can get hold of Snyman, Basie. He'll have them.'

Louw walked to the telephone.

'No, use the car phone. I'm waiting for an urgent call.'

Louw nodded and left. Joubert got up, idled towards the window. He looked at Nienaber's newspaper and against the wall again, the smile, the neat hairstyle, the honest face.

'What did you know, Oliver?'

He studied all the certificates against the wall. ACAD-EMY OF HAIR DESIGN GOLDEN SCISSORS AWARD, CAPE COMMERCIAL COLLEGE BUSI-

NESS SCHOOL – *This is to certify that OS Nienaber completed the course in Small Business Management*; JUNIOR BUSINESSMAN OF THE YEAR. And the company registration certificate for Hair Today.

The telephone rang. Joubert reached it in two, long strides.

'That service was terminated, sir. This morning.'

He put down the receiver and put his hand into his pocket, looking for a cigarette. He remembered that he no longer smoked. Was his timing right for stopping? He didn't have the time to worry about it now. He hurried out to the bedroom where he found O' Grady on his knees, in front of a night-stand.

'I'm going to Sea Point. I'll radio them to send a car for you from the office.'

The elderly woman who opened the door for him, spoke calmly about her daughter's death. Next to her, in the sitting-room of number 1314 Neptune's View, sat her grey husband, thin and quiet, staring at the floor. They were both dressed in black, good clothes.

'The service was this morning, in the Sea Point church, but there weren't many people. Five or six who left immediately after the service. At least her boss went to the crematorium with us. This is the way it is in the city. Our neighbours could come but they've already gone home. We farm at Keimoes, Captain. Our son is in America, studying. He is on his way, but too late for the service.'

'Unfortunately I'll have to question you about her death, Mrs. Oberholzer.'

'I thought the Police had finished the investigation,' her husband said. 'They think it was an accident or something.'

'It must've been the local station, sir. I'm from Murder and Robbery.'

'She fell. Out of the window.' Rina Oberholzer pointed at a room leading out of the sitting-room.

'Do you think they made a mistake? The other Police?' her husband asked.

How could he even start to explain? An underlined name in a telephone directory . . .

'I don't know, Mr. Oberholzer. I'm investigating another case. I . . . Her name . . . It might have nothing to do with it.'

'There's so much evil in this world.'

'What kind of work did she do, Mrs. Oberholzer?'

'Secretarial, at Petrogas. For years now. There's no work for young people in our town, Captain. They all go to the city to look for work. We were always worried. It's such a big place. But we thought it was better than Johannesburg.'

'Did you know her friends here?'

'Carrie was a social person, Captain. She had so many. Her letters were always full of names. There were so many. But where were they this morning? But that's the city. Full of fair-weather friends.'

'Oliver Nienaber?'

They shook their heads.

'Alexander MacDonald?'

No. They didn't know. So many names.

Drew Wilson? Ferdy Ferreira? James Wallace?

They didn't react.

'Who are these people, Captain?' Carina Oberholzer's father asked.

'They're involved in another case. Did she have . . . a friend?'

Husband and wife looked at one another.

'Yes, a Portuguese.' The man's voice was disapproving. 'A Catholic.'

'Do you know how to get hold of him?'

'At work, probably. He has a restaurant in the harbour.'

'A fish and chips shop.'

'Do you know his name?'

Rina Oberholzer took her husband's hand. 'Da Costa,' she said as if the words were difficult to say. 'Julio da Costa.'

34

T hey had a conference in the parade room, Joubert's whole team, Griessel and some of his men, de Wit and the Brigadier.

' "Dear Captain Joubert",' Joubert read the bank robber's letter to his audience. ' "I wish to inform you that I am not the Mauser murderer. I also want to inform you that I won't execute a robbery at Premier, or any other bank, until you've caught the Mauser murderer. I'm sorry about the farmer, Scholtz, who was shot but I actually had nothing to do with it. Yours sincerely, Don Chameleon (the Sweetheart Robber)".'

Joubert turned the paper round and showed it to the others. 'Typed,' he said.

'Typewriter. Not a computer print-out. No prints,' Griessel said.

'Fuckin asshole,' Vos said. 'He fancies his name.'

'Do you believe him?' the Brigadier asked.

Griessel was firm. 'Yes, Brigadier. He and the Mauser make no sense. Too many differences.'

'I agree,' the Brigadier nodded. 'What are you going to do now?'

'I'm going to catch him, Brigadier,' Griessel said.

'I like your optimism.'

'I've got a feeling, Brigadier,' Griessel took a pile of photographs out of his file and got up. 'If we look at these pictures there's one similarity,' and he pinned them to the notice board with thumb tacks.

'Look carefully,' he said. 'Look carefully because I missed it at first.' He stood back so that everyone could see. 'One thing doesn't change.'

They all screwed up their eyes for a clearer vision.

'They all look different to me,' de Wit said pessimistically.

'Brilliant, Colonel. That's what I kept missing. They all look different. They don't look like the same person. Except when one looks very carefully. The nose. Look at the nose. Look carefully. It has a little twist at the end. You should be able to see it better from fairly far away because the photos aren't good. The same guy but he looks completely different every time. And that's how I'm going to get him.'

'Oh?' de Wit said, prepared for the possibility of being embarrassed in front of the Brigadier should Griessel be spouting nonsense.

'He's a pro, Colonel. Not of robbery, but of disguise. He knows what he's doing with the wigs and the moustaches and the other stuff. Look at this one where he's an old man. Hell, he looks like an old man. Look at the wrinkles. Look at the clothes. It's as if he's playing a role in a flick. Everything is just right. It's too much to fool only the bank cameras. That guy is a pro. He enjoys it. He knows it.'

Griessel turned back to his audience.

'It's his job, his profession.'

'Ahhh,' said the Brigadier.

De Wit rubbed his mole, pleased.

'You're a star, Benny,' Joubert said.

'I know. Because that's not all.'

They were all attention.

'He's got a grudge against Premier. Why rob just them? I don't mean the last one. That doesn't count because he's got cold feet now. I'm speaking about the previous ones. Clever guy like him wouldn't concentrate on the branches of only one bank. No, no, there must be a reason because he must know there'll be hell to pay if he focuses on only one. You don't have to be an Einstein to know that the cops are going to lay traps for you, unless you screw around a little more. He hits Premier because he's got a grudge.'

'You're simply guessing,' the Brigadier said.

'I know, Brigadier. It's a theory. But you must admit it has merit.'

'Whole fuckin' country has a grudge against banks,' Vos said.

'Also true,' Griessel hit back. 'But how many professional make-up artists can there be in the Cape?'

They considered the truth of this statement in silence.

'You're going to look for make-up artists,' de Wit said and grimaced.

'One after another, Colonel. To be honest I've already began telephoning. And they tell me I must start with the Arts Council. And then the film studios. There are about twelve or thirteen of those. They said he might be free-lance as well but in this profession everyone knows everyone else.'

'Well done,' said the Brigadier.

'So I'll ask to be excused, if I may. With my team.'

'With pleasure, Sergeant.'

Griessel walked out ahead of them and Joubert noticed the squared shoulders.

It's all I can do.

'Captain?'

All eyes were fixed on Joubert.

Joubert straightened the brown files in front of him, picked up the notebook and started paging. He cleared his throat.

'I think we're making headway,' he said, not sure whether he believed it himself.

'There is new information but we're not quite sure how it

all fits together.' He found his latest notes, hurriedly made just before the impromptu conference.

'But let me start at the beginning. Four of the victims have been connected in sets of two. James Wallace obviously knew Ferreira. Wallace's wife says she's certain Ferreira came to see her husband at home one evening but Ferreira's wife says she knows nothing about it. We don't know why he went there. Then we're sure that MacDonald knew Nienaber. Nienaber admitted that he was at the murder scene but . . .'

'Why do I only hear about this now?' the Brigadier demanded.

Petersen sank lower in his chair. De Wit's mouth opened and closed. 'I . . .'

'Nienaber had his attorney at the interrogation, Brigadier. We had to work according to the book. And there was simply too little evidence. He was well-known, an influential man . . .' Hopelessly Joubert tried to shore up his position.

'You should've informed me.'

'We should've, Brigadier. It was my fault. But we wanted to keep a low profile because we put a tail on him. We thought he was a suspect in the case. We wanted to see whether we could find a connection between him and the others. But because the relatives of the others couldn't confirm anything . . .'

'You should've told me . . .'

'You said there was new information,' de Wit said hopefully.

Joubert threw him a grateful look. 'That's right, Colonel. By chance we saw in Nienaber's telephone book that he had underlined a few names. MacDonald's. And a Miss Carina Oberholzer's . . . She fell out of her window on the thirteenth floor of an apartment building in Sea Point on Friday evening. Pathologist says there were no other injuries or bullet wounds. Sea Point's detectives say that there were no signs of a struggle. But I can't believe that it was coincidence. On Friday the Ferreira murder happened. On Monday it was MacDonald, where Nienaber also happened to be. The timing . . . Her boss . . . she was a secretary at Petrogas – says she was bright and cheerful on Friday as she always was. Her friend has a restaurant in the Waterfront. He said he'd spoken to her on the telephone that afternoon and she had said would come and lend a hand during the rush hour around nine o' clock. Later on he became worried and tried to telephone her, after ten sometime, and there was no reply. He could only go and look for her when he closed but by then she was dead.'

'So he has an alibi,' Vos said.

'Yes,' said Joubert. 'And he needed one. Carina Oberholzer was his sly. The bastard is married. And he says Oberholzer knew it.'

Detective Sergeant Carl van Deventer owed his promotion to Murder and Robbery by becoming the best burglary detective in Cape Town's police station.

He could, just before he left the city's station, say whether a burglar was a professional or an amateur simply by looking at the marks, or lack of them, on the locks of a house or flat's front door.

Like a fortune teller reading tea leaves, so van Deventer could look at the crime scene of a burglary and sometimes rattle off the name and the criminal history of the offender by the manner in which the drawers had been opened, the way the cigarette butts of the burglar had been placed an ashtray.

He had achieved his expertise through a deep-seated interest, hard work and study – not only for the official police exams but also at the University of the Street. By questioning those charged by asking them kindly but urgently to tell him how they had disarmed the alarm, how they had manipulated the mechanism of a lock.

And through the years he had built up a set of burglar's tools which had made him a legend.

If you worked at Murder and Robbery and the children flushed the house keys down the lavatory in a friend's house, you didn't phone a locksmith – you sent for Carl van Deventer. If you wanted to side-step the law of criminal procedure in a small way by searching a suspect's house or office without the necessary documents (or keys), you telephoned van Deventer.

If you had a locked attaché case and the combination had accompanied Oliver Nienaber to eternity, you asked van Deventer to bring his little screwdrivers.

Van Deventer was investigating a satanic murder in Durbanville when Detective Constable Snyman phoned him with the request.

'Leave it on my desk. I'll be there this afternoon,' van Deventer had said.

True to his word he set to work immediately when he got back to the office. He took his little black leather bag out of his jacket's inner pocket, chose the right implement, wiggled a bit here, pressed a little there and the two locks of the attaché case snapped open, exactly forty-four seconds after he had taken the tool out of the bag.

Van Deventer's reward for his work was that he was allowed to see the contents of the case. He lifted the lid, saw the Star 9 mm and he knew he mustn't fiddle with the contents because it could be the murder weapon. You didn't screw around with a murder weapon unless you were looking for early retirement.

He phoned Snyman but there was no reply. He phoned Mat Joubert but he wasn't in his office, either. Van Deventer did what the book told him he had to do with a potential murder weapon. He walked to Mavis Petersen at Murder & Robbery's reception desk, signed in the case at the door, walked to the safe and locked it away. Then he asked Mavis to tell Snyman or Joubert that it was open and ready for their attention.

He didn't know that the Star wasn't a murder weapon. Neither did he know that under the pistol, between all the other documents, there was a list of names waiting to be discovered. He didn't know that the name of the murderer appeared on the list.

But Carl van Deventer didn't have second sight, even if he could read ashtrays like tea leaves.

'No, I don't read tea leaves,' said Madame Jocelyn Lowe and smiled.

She stood in the parking area of the hotel in Newlands where James J Wallace had breathed his last. She was at the centre of a fairly large crowd of media people. The SABC was there and M-Net and a free-lance team which hoped to sell something to Sky News or CNN. The BBC2 and Thames teams were also present. The newspapers were there as well; local – with their wide range of languages – and those from other countries. The British tabloids were strongly represented.

Mat Joubert, Nougat O' Grady and Louw stood to one side. Louw's jaw had dropped in sheer amazement at it all. Joubert stood with his head bent. He didn't want to be there. He wanted to get on with other things. Like phoning Hanna Nortier and saying: Hi, Doc, what about a little boogie at *The Barber's* on Friday evening? But he had to be here because he had to get his evidence back. Madame Louw had personally spoken to the Brigadier and the Brigadier had personally asked Joubert to assist her.

Joubert could see why de Wit had been so keen on having the Madame. And he could see why the Brigadier was so keen to help the Madame.

She was a good-looking woman, in her forties, but tall and attractive with great dignity and a chest measurement to match.

'Gypsies read tea leaves and palms,' she said. 'I'm a psychic. Psychics don't read. They feel,' her voice light but strongly Oxbridge accented. 'I have acquired some pieces of clothing worn by the murder victim and will proceed to see if I can sense some vibrations of the tragic incident that transpired here.'

'Transpired here,' O' Grady mimicked her accent under his breath. 'Woman's a fucking charlatan. But she's playing them like a violin.'

Joubert said nothing because he wasn't sure of the meaning of 'charlatan.'

'There is such a strong presence. We must have some very talented people here,' she said. 'But I'll have to ask you to move away. I need space and silence to do my work.'

The press quietened down.

'If you could wait over there, please.' She pointed an elegant, be-ringed finger to the edge of the parking area. 'And please, Messrs. photographers, no flashes while I'm concentrating. There will be plenty of time for pictures later.'

The media scrum moved meekly in the direction which the woman had indicated, the television cameras in the lead to get tripods and Sony's ready before she started.

She waited patiently, then turned her back to them and went to stand on the spot Joubert had self-consciously pointed out to her. The bloodstained marks where Jimmy Wallace had lain were dull and black by now, like the many oil marks on the tar.

She took Wallace's bloody white shirt out of the plastic

bag, closed her eyes theatrically and pressed the piece of clothing to her breast. Her body stiffened and she stood stock still.

Joubert heard an unearthly noise – a low, monotonous sound. He realised that it emanated from the woman's mouth. 'Mmmmmmm . . .' A single, unmusical note. It kept on and on while she remained standing quite still, her back straight, her backside neat in the sober but fashionable dress.

'Mmmmmm . . .'

Joubert wondered whether de Wit had known her very well.

An old friend, Anne Boshoff had quoted the *Cape Times*.

They would be a very odd couple, he thought. The tall, sensual woman and the short, ugly little man.

No, Anne Boshoff had said de Wit hadn't even given anyone the glad eye at congresses.

'Mmmmmmmm . . .'

He had trouble in dismissing the image from his mind, the Madame naked on her back in her house in a spooky room with cobwebs in the candelabra and a black cat in front of the hearth. Bart de Wit grinning, while he played with that chest measurement and the Madame made an unearthly noise.

'Mmmmmmm . . .'

Why was he thinking about sex again? His stomach suddenly contracted. Was it in expectation of his potential evening out with his psychologist? Did he hope somewhere in the back of his head that he would get the opportunity to stroke the frail body with his big hands, to enfold her small, small breasts and slowly but surely ready her for love? To kiss her gently on that pretty lipstickless mouth, to let his hands slide to her shoulders, to touch her carefully . . .

Madame Jocelyn Lowe audibly blew out her breath. He

shoulders sagged wearily, her hands holding the shirt, dropped from her chest, her head was bowed. She stood like that while the seconds passed and the press shuffled uncertainly.

'Not enough,' she said with tired resignation. 'We'll have to move on.'

35

A convoy of cars moved from murder scene to murder scene, the Madame and her black chauffeur leading in a Mercedes-Benz, then the detectives in their Sierra and following, a caravan of press vehicles – from minibuses for television teams to cars for the print media.

While Madame was trying to pick up the vibrations of Fredy Ferreira's last moments, Joubert went looking for a telephone booth at the Old Ship Caravan Park. He looked up Computicket's number in the ragged directory and dialed. They said *The Barber of Seville* was indeed being performed on Friday night. Also on Saturday and the following Wednesday, Friday and Saturday.

He asked whether there were seats available for the coming Friday evening.

It depended on whether he wanted expensive or cheap seats.

'Only the best,' he said.

'There are quite a few expensive seats available. If you give me your credit card number . . .'

He hesitated for a moment. If Hanna Nortier didn't want to go with him . . . He saw himself and Benny Griessel sitting among the operagoers, two fucking stupid cops listening to sopranos and librettos and stuff like that. But then he decided he had to think positively. Nothing ventured . . .

He booked two seats, put the phone down and drove

down to the sea where the Madame was still going
'Mmmmmmm . . .'

'I have some interesting observations but you will have to
give me time to get my thoughts in order. I can do that while
we're travelling back to the hotel. Shall we call a news
conference at six o' clock?'

The press complained but they were long acquainted with
patience. They packed up and moved back to the vehicles
which were neatly lined up in the gravel parking area next to
the beach.

'World's biggest bullshitter,' said O' Grady as he
moved.

Joubert said nothing. He held the pieces of clothing which
the Madame had required for her work and thought about
his craving for a cigarette. His head felt . . . There was a
buzzing in his ears. Lord, he could *hear* his craving.

'I want to hear it,' Basie Louw said. 'May I attend the
press conference, Captain?'

'Yes.'

'I want to hear what she says. I want to hear whether she
knows that Wilson was queer. And whether she knows that
Wallace screwed around.'

Behind him walked the thin crime reporter of *The Argus*.
She heard Louw. Her trained ears were flapping in the
breeze but he said nothing more. She checked to see whether
any of the other media had heard him but saw that they
hadn't been near enough.

'Anyone want a lift back to the hotel?' she asked with an
English accent, loud enough for Louw to hear.

'You going back to the office, Captain?' Louw asked.

'Nienaber's house,' Joubert replied.

'May I come with you?' Louw asked the reporter.

'Of course,' she said.

*   *   *

'The boys are with the neighbours, Captain. I talked to
the eldest. He said his father's brother was on his way
from Oudtshoorn. The neighbours phoned him. The hospital says Mrs. Nienaber is still under sedation,' Snyman
said.

'And the desk?'

'These documents, Captain.' He pointed to a neat pile on
the floor. 'Nothing of importance. Family stuff. Marriage
certificate, baptismal certificates, children's school reports,
photos . . .'

'Good work.'

'What now, Captain?'

'Did you ask the boy about the other names?'

'He's never heard of them.'

'Oberholzer?'

'No.'

'Now we simply start all over again, Gerrit. I'll phone
Mrs. Wallace and Mrs. Ferreira. You take Wilson's mother
and colleagues. Ask about Nienaber.'

Snyman nodded and turned but Joubert saw that the
constable didn't agree with the connection theory. Then
Joubert walked to Nienaber's study, past the photographs
and the certificates, sat down behind the desk again and
took out his notebook. Dr Hanna Nortier. He would see her
again tomorrow. But then it would be official. Now it was
personal. He dialed the number.

'Hello. Unfortunately I'm not available right now. Please
leave a message after the beep. Thank you and goodbye.'
An electronic beep sound followed. He said nothing. She
was probably busy with someone. He cut the connection,
dialed again.

'Hello. Unfortunately, I'm not . . .' He thought she had
such a pretty voice. She spoke as if she was truly sorry that
she was unable to take the call. Her soft, melodious voice.

He could see her mouth moving, the pretty mouth in the pretty, angular face, the long, pointed nose. Did she sound tired? That slender body which had to carry the heavy weight of other people's problems. He so much wanted to help her to relax. He wanted to make things easier for her . . .

Softly he replaced the receiver.

You're in love, you fool.

He put his hand out to his coat pocket, to reach for a cigarette. It stopped halfway when he remembered.

Your timing is bad, he thought and watched his shaking hand.

Oh, dear God in Heaven but he was desperate for a cigarette right now.

Just smoke less. Four a day. Three would be fine. Three cigarettes a day, could, true as God, not do anyone any harm. One with his coffee . . . No, not before swimming. The first one in the office. At about nine o' clock, say. And one after he'd had his diet lunch. And one in the evening, with a book and a small drink. He would have to think about drink. He could no longer drink beer, it was fattening. Whisky. He would teach himself to drink whisky.

What will you drink, Mat, Hanna Nortier would ask him on Friday evening when she had invited him in to her house or her flat or whatever and they were sitting in easy chairs and she had put on some or other piece of opera music on her CD player, softly, with only the beautiful standard lamp in the corner lit, the room shadowy.

Whisky, he would say, whisky, please, Hanna.

Hanna.

He had never said her name out loud.

'Hanna.'

Then she would give a satisfied nod because whisky was a drink for cultivated operagoers and she would get up and disappear into the kitchen to get each of them something to drink and he would lean back, fold his hands behind his head and think of intelligent remarks to make about the opera and his blood brother, Rossini, when she came back to give him his whisky and sit down on the chair again, her legs folded under her, comfortable, her brown eyes under the heavy eyebrows fixed on him. They would discuss things and later, when the atmosphere and the feeling were right, he would lean over and kiss her mouth, lightly, to test the water. Then he would sit back in his chair again and wait until later . . .

He dialed the number again, filled with compassion for Hanna Nortier and her busy days and the dreams he dreamt about him and her.

'Hello. Unfortunately I'm not available at the moment. Please leave a message after the beep. Thank you and goodbye.'

'This is Mat Joubert,' he said softly, after the beep. 'I would like . . . I . . .' Earlier he'd known what he wanted to say, now he was having difficulty. '*The Barber* . . . I have two tickets for Friday evening . . . you might like to come with me. You can phone my home, later, because I'm still working and I still have to go and . . .' He suddenly wondered how much time there was on the cassette and ended abruptly. 'Thank you very much.' He put down the telephone and patted his pockets again and decided three cigarettes a day wasn't too much and dialed Margaret Wallace's number.

Her son answered and went to call her. He asked her whether her husband had known Oliver Nienaber.

'The hair person?'

'Yes.'

'He did.'

Joubert leant forward in a dead man's chair.

'How did he know him?'

'They were both finalists in the Small Business Man of the Year Award. Nienaber got it.'

Joubert looked at the certificates. He found the one he was looking for.

'We sat next to them at the awards ceremony. That was what . . . two, three years ago. His wife is such a beautiful person. We got on very well.'

'Did they have any other contact?'

'No, I don't think so. I don't think James liked the man very much. There was . . . tension at the table. But I suppose it was because they were adversaries, in a sense.'

Margaret Wallace was quiet for a moment. 'Don't tell me he's . . .'

'Yes,' Joubert said with sympathetic caution. 'He was shot this morning.'

He heard her sigh. 'Dear Lord,' she said resignedly.

'I'm sorry,' he said, and didn't know why.

'What does it mean, Captain? That Jimmy knew the Ferreira man and now Nienaber. What does it mean?'

'I'm trying to find out.'

'It must mean something.'

'Yes. Well . . . So you don't know if there was any other contact?'

'No. I don't think so. Jimmy never spoke about him again, afterwards.'

'Well, thank you, Mrs. Wallace.'

'Captain . . .' she was uncertain, hesitant.

'Yes?'

'How long did it take you . . . I mean, how much time, after your . . . your wife passed away . . .'

He thought. Because he couldn't tell her. He couldn't give her the bad news that it was more than two years and that he was still caught in the web of Lara's death. He had to lie, give the woman with the mismatched eyes hope.

'About two years.'

Dear Lord,' she said. 'Dear Lord.'

Griessel knew that the make-up artist of the Arts Council's drama department couldn't be the Sweetheart robber because she was a woman, an interesting woman without being good-looking. Her hair was very short and a deep auburn, her face open and intelligent. She smoked a long cigarette and gestured with her slender hands when she spoke.

'You're looking for a film make-up artist,' she said and her voice was deep. She pointed to the row upon row of photographs of actors and actresses against the wall. 'These were taken during productions or rehearsals. Look at the make-up. It's heavy. Look at the eyes. Look at the mouths. Look at the clothes. For the stage you need to do make-up differently. Strong, because the guy right at the back must also be able to see. Very well, there are some things which are the same.' She put a forefinger on one of Griessel's photos which lay on the coffee table in front of her. 'I would also be able to make him look old but my lines would be stronger. This was done with latex. I'd do mine with a pencil. Perhaps just a little latex for a double chin or something like that. This guy works for the movies. You can see it. Look here.' She pointed at the Elvis photo. 'You can see his cheeks are fatter. It seems as if his cheekbones are stronger. They can do it with rubber, press rubber strips inside his cheeks. If you do that for the stage, the actor won't be able to speak. And they must be able to speak on the stage, they have to project, because the guy up there must be able to see and hear. But with film they can re-record the voices later. And this one. That's not a theatrical beard. A theatrical beard or hair costs a fraction of what they use in films because the audience can't see it close up. If you stand next to an actor wearing a theatre wig, you can see it's a wig. The same applies to a beard or a moustache.'

The cigarette had been stubbed out and she lit another one.

'Are there any who work for the theatre and films?'

'No . . . Perhaps. But I don't know of any. The theatre world is pretty small. There are four or five of us here. And I don't know one who has worked in films. It's not something you can free-lance because it's an art of its own.'

'How many film make-up artists are there?'

'In the Cape? Can't really say. Four or five years ago there wasn't one. Now it's fashionable to come and starve in the Cape if you're arty. But I don't know how many there are now. Ten? Fifteen? No more than twenty.'

'Do they have a union or something?'

She laughed and he saw that her teeth were slightly yellow from the cigarettes but it didn't make her less attractive. 'No.'

'Where should I start looking?'

'I know a guy who has his own production house. I'll give you his phone number.'

'Production house?'

'Film makers. They call themselves production houses. Actually it's only one or two guys with a small company. They hire cameramen and make-artists and directors and lighting and sound and so forth. He'll probably have everyone's telephone number.'

'What does a film make-up artist earn?'

'In Hollywood they're probably rich. But here . . . Free lancing is a hard life . . .'

'That's possibly why he robs banks,' said Griessel and gathered up his photos.

'Are you married?' asked the make-up artist.

'Divorced,' said Griessel.

'Attached?'

'No, but I'm going to get my wife back. And my children.'

'Pity,' said the make-up artist and lit another cigarette. 'Let me get you that number.'

'Thank you for being here, ladies and gentlemen. We have all had a trying day and I will try not to waste your time. But please allow me a minute or two to explain something to you.'

Madame Jocelyn Lowe stood on a stage in one of the Cape Sun's conference rooms. In front of her sat sixty-four representatives of the press and one member of Murder and Robbery.

'The talent I possess, I did not ask for. It was given to me by the grace of God. When it comes to helping the police in solving a murder case, I do not ask them for money. It is my way of saying thank you, of making a very small contribution. On the other hand, not all people believe that my powers are real. There will be sceptics amongst you. All I ask is to be given a fair chance. Do not make a judgement until the case is solved. Only then will we know if I was of any help.'

Louw sniffed. Then it wouldn't matter any more, Clairvoyant, he thought. He and the English reporter had enjoyed talking to one another on the way from Melkbos. About the Madame. The reporter thought she was a rip-off. And he, Basie Louw, had agreed. Because the reporter might not be pretty but her ass looked good in the denim and if he played his cards right, he might strike it lucky tonight.

'Now let me get to the part I know you're here for.'

A few media people clapped sarcastically but the Madame merely smiled in a dignified manner.

'I can assure you that it wasn't easy. In some instances the tragic incidents took place some fourteen days ago. Time, unfortunately, diminishes the aura. It is like sound, travelling through space. The further you are from it, the weaker it becomes. Also, when a murder takes place in public places, such as a parking lot, a beach or an elevator, there are so many confusing vibrations. Again, to use the analogy of sound, it resembles a great many voices speaking all at once. It is hard to try and single out one of them.'

She's already making excuses, Louw thought. The press people shifted in their seats as if they agreed with him.

'I can see some of you think I'm making excuses already . . .'

Jesus, Louw thought. She can read minds.

'. . . but again, save your reservations for later, because I have absorbed enough to draw a pretty clear picture.'

It was suddenly so quiet in the room that only the air conditioning was audible – and the sound of the Sony Betacams turning.

'First of all, I sensed a lot of hate and fear. Even at the parking area in Newlands, the hate and fear were still palpable . . .' Press pens were scribbling frantically. 'Hate that has accumulated over many years, I can tell you, to be that strong. Fear that goes back into the mists of time. I see . . .' And Madame Jocelyn Lowe closed her eyes, her hands in front of her, somewhat defenceless '. . . a figure consumed, driven, overcome. The patterns are not rational, sanity is but a shadow. A figure is moving in the twilight, large and imposing, a predator hungering for revenge. He moves into a faint pool of eerie light. A hat takes shape, broad-brimmed. Features emerge slowly, blunt, contorted, the eyes beacons of hate. A beard, I think. I sense a beard light in colour, sandy perhaps, luxuriant, flowing from chin and cheeks, into the coat. His hands . . . They are huge, shaped by generations of toil in a harsh land. He is holding the strange firearm at his side, waiting, searching, indiscriminately, for those . . . A predator, a warrior, a throwback to a forgotten era, a ghostlike apparition. But he is flesh and blood, he is real, his hate is real, his fears . . .'

She opened her eyes, stood quite still for a moment then picked up the glass of water on the lectern next to her and took a small sip.

'You must understand. This is very tiring.' Another sip. Then calmly, without the theatrical intonation, but softly, only loud enough for her voice to reach every corner of the absolutely quiet room. 'I have reason to believe that the killings are politically motivated. Not, ladies and gentlemen, the politics that you and I know, but the politics of a slightly demented mind. Yes, I did sense a man. But a strange man, a special, strange creature. A man who feels his heritage heavy on his shoulders, who carries the weight of a nation.'

'Are you saying he's an Afrikaner?' a reporter of the *Weekly Mail* couldn't help asking.

Smiled slightly: 'I did not hear him speak, sir.' There was subdued laughter, a release of the tension which had accumulated in the room.

'But you said his beard was sandy. That makes him a white man.'

'Caucasian? Yes. That much I can say.'

'And he wears a hat?'

'Yes.'

Questions suddenly became a chorus. The Madame held up her left hand. The gems in her rings reflected the light. 'Please, I have almost finished. But I have something to add.'

325

Silence again.

'I sensed a hat. But that does not mean that he wears it every time he pulls the trigger. I also sensed a long, black coat. But again, that is just a vibration, that could merely imply that he favours these garments. But there was one other thing. He does not live in this city. He does not have a home here. If they want to find his home, they must look elsewhere. They must look for a place where the plains are wide and the sun is strong. They must look for a place where you can see no mountains, where the river runs dry. *There* this man is at home. There he nurtured his hate and fear. *There* he found the devilish energy which moved him to kill.

'Now I will gladly answer your questions. But please keep in mind, I have told you all I know.'

Hands shot up, questions were asked.

The reporter of *The Argus* turned to Louw and smiled 'What do you think? As a policeman?'

'I think she's talking shit,' Louw said honestly and was immediately sorry that he had used the word. Some women didn't like swearing and he didn't want to spoil his chances

'I think so too,' said the reporter and smiled again. 'Can buy you a beer?'

'No,' Louw said. 'I'll buy you one.'

Joubert's dinner was chicken stew: 60 grams of (skinless chicken, 60 milliliters of (fat free) gravy, 125 milliliters of mixed vegetables, and as much boiled (tasteless) cauliflower as he liked – and one bloody fat unit.

And after that, one full flavoured Winston, one tot of whisky.

His life, measured out in small grams.

But he looked forward to the cigarette and the drink. It suddenly made the bleak evening worthwhile. His reward

326

After he had phoned Gail Ferreira and she had given him negative answers to his questions, he drove to a liquor store and bought himself a bottle of whisky. Glenfiddich, because it was the most expensive, and he wanted to drink a decent whisky, not the cheap muck with spurious Scottish names marked as special offers on the shelves. And then to the cafe for a packet of Winstons which now lay on the table, unopened and full of promise. Oh, it was going to be good. Oh, that first drag which still tasted of matches (because he'd thrown his damn lighter away with the Special Milds that morning) which he was going to draw deep . . .

The phone rang. He jogged down the passage, swallowing a piece of cauliflower as he went.

'Joubert.'

'This is Hanna Nortier.' This time the weariness in her voice was unmistakable and he wanted to fetch her and tell her everything was going to be fine. 'I don't know whether it's a good idea,' she said and he was suddenly sorry that he had asked her.

He didn't know what to say.

'You're a patient.'

How could he have forgotten that? How could he have placed her in such a position? He wished for an honourable way out for her . . .

'But I need to get out,' she said, as if she was talking to herself. 'May I give you an answer tomorrow?

'Yes.'

'Thank you, Mat,' she said and put the phone down.

He walked back to the kitchen.

The reporter was as clever as a cageful of monkeys. She waited until they had started on their fifth beer in the ladies' bar of the Cape Sun. 'I hear the Wallace guy slept around.' Not a question, a statement, her English accent now

DEON MEYER

marked when she spoke Afrikaans because although she could take her drink, it wasn't easy to keep up with the policeman.

'You journalists always know everything,' Louw said with honest admiration.

That wasn't what she wanted to hear. 'I only know a little.'

'It's true, though. He was ever ready. Up to the very last. He was with a blonde in the hotel and when he walked out they blasted him.'

'But he was married.'

'That didn't stop him with the blonde.' Louw suddenly realised to whom he was speaking. 'You won't . . . you won't quote me, will you?'

'My lips are sealed,' and she smiled at him.

Tonight my luck's in, Louw thought. 'She was from Johannesburg. Worked in computers. And then Wallace screwed her, over lunch as it were. Van der Merwe. I've her name her somewhere.' He took out his notebook and paged, swallowed some beer, paged on. 'Elizabeth van der Merwe. But she wasn't a suspect. I could see that immediately.'

He emptied his glass. 'Another one?'

'Why not?' and she slipped into English again. 'The night is but a pup.' And gave Basie Louw a meaningful look.

36

Nienaber knew MacDonald and Wallace. Wallace knew Ferreira.

And Oberholzer. And Wilson, who didn't want to slot in.

The previous evening, after his gloom about Hanna Nortier, he had considered the information from all angles. Now, in the swimming pool. The pieces of the puzzle still wouldn't come together.

He knew the feeling: the awareness that everything meant something, but there just wasn't enough to unravel a premise, to put enough information together so that he could formulate a firm theory. It was frustrating because he didn't know where else to look. The answer might well be there already, right in front of him. It sometimes needed a fresh perspective, a new approach.

He had tried everything the previous night.

Mass mail distributor. Jeweller. Out-of-work carpenter. Fisherman. Hairdresser.

Forty years old, thirtysomething, fifty, forty, forty.

Success, so-so, failure, so-so, success.

Roving prick. Gay. Blue movie addict. Rapist. And he didn't know whether Nienaber had been faithful to his wife.

Oberholzer? Had she been involved? Really? She'd had a relationship with a married man. Had she earlier had a relationship with Nienaber? He made notes in his head while his arms pulled him through the water. Phone the hospital. Perhaps he could speak to Mrs. Nienaber this morning. Speak to Oberholzer's boss. Where had she worked before? Phone that hairy Walter Schutte at Wallace Quickmail again. Had he heard the name Carina Oberholzer?

What would Dr Hanna Nortier want to discuss this afternoon?

Dear Lord, he mustn't bawl again.

He had to steer her away from Lara Joubert. He couldn't discuss it today and take her to the opera tomorrow.

She could open him up. He knew it. She could peel him like an orange and reach the juice. She was too clever for him.

Perhaps he shouldn't go. Perhaps he should phone and say the Mauser affair was getting too hot and he couldn't make it. He'd be there on the following Thursday as usual and were they still going to the opera?

He pulled himself effortlessly out of the water, unaware of his even breathing and the great distance he had swum while struggling with solutions. He dressed, drove to Kasselsvlei, avoiding newspaper posters which screamed IT'S BOER WAR III, SAYS UK PSYCHIC. And *Die Burger*'s: SALON BARON'S LIFE CUT SHORT.

He saw them but his thoughts were too busy to take any notice.

Anne Boshoff said the murderer was out of control. And there was nothing he could do to stop it. When would he strike again?

Late afternoon. Late night. Early morning. Early morning. Early morning.

The after hours murderer. What do you do during the day, you bastard? Or couldn't you forecast the movement of your victims during office hours?

He drove his usual route, as he did every morning, without thinking about it, unaware of the big breakthrough which was waiting in the attaché case.

'Sarge van Deventer says he put the Captain's case in the safe,' said Mavis Petersen when he walked in.

He thanked her, asked her to fetch it, signed for it and took it with him to his office. He put it down on the table, took out his Winstons, put them next to the case, went to the tea-room and fetched himself a large mug of (bitter) black coffee. Then he came back, sank down in his chair, lit a Winston and drew in a deep lungful of smoke.

Lovely.

He swallowed the strong instant coffee, drew on the cigarette again . . .

GENUINE BUFFALO HIDE was written on the leather case.

He opened it. The pistol lay there, the safety catch on. He took out his notebook wrote: *Antoinette Nienaber? Always carried the pistol? Knew Oberholzer? Ferreira? Wilson? Faithful?????*

He put down the pen and the notebook, picked up the pistol and sniffed the barrel. Hadn't been fired in a long time, nor cleaned. Why carry the pistol, Oliver? He put the pistol aside, picked up the cigarette, drew on it again.

A black diary, reinforced with gold on the four corners of the covers. Diary and notebook. He paged to the date of the first murder. January 2. Nothing of importance. He paged on. January 3,4,5,6,7,8. Appointments with people unknown to him. *Ollie's birthday.* One of the sons. 9,10,11.

Then Joubert saw the list.

Mac McDonald. Incorrectly spelt. *Carina Oberholzer. Jacques Coetzee.* Space. *Hester Clarke.*

Mat Joubert forgot about the Winston between his fingers. He read the list again. He got up and walked to the door.

'Nougat,' he yelled down the passage, an urgent bellow.

'Snyman! Basie!' There was a new note in his voice. He shouted again, even more loudly.

He's sick, Matthew. He's out of control.

Anne Boshoff's words were his driving force now. He was going to stop the bastard. He would see to it that Jacques Coetzee and Hester Clarke didn't become dossiers as well. He was a drowning man who had been tossed a lifebelt, a nomad in the desert who saw the oasis reflected in a mirage. He was a combat general – the war had begun in earnest.

The parade room was a hive of activity. Joubert sat against the wall. Next to him, O' Grady. They distributed the list of names. The reinforcements which arrived from other police stations joined the queue. Two to a team. The order was to find the right Coetzee and the right Clarke. The only lead was the set of names and photos of the Mauser victims. And Carina Oberholzer.

'There are fifty-four Coetzees in the fucking directory,' O' Grady had complained when they held a meeting in Joubert's room and he had looked up from the directory.

'Here are hundreds of Clarkes with an "e",' Snyman had said.

'He made a spelling mistake with MacDonald,' Joubert had said. 'We'll have to tackle the Clarks without an "e" as well.'

'Another hundred,' Snyman had said despairingly.

'It doesn't matter,' was Joubert's reply. 'This thing ends today.' With finality in his voice.

De Wit had come in. Joubert had informed him of the latest state of the investigation and asked for reinforcements. De Wit, unashamedly excited, had trotted off to his office to telephone the Brigadier and the General.

Louw was late, with the smell of old liquor on his breath and a satisfied expression in his eyes. Joubert had given him the task of questioning the deceased's relatives about the new names. Then they went to the parade room to put the men available from Murder and Robbery on the trail of the J Coezees and H Clarkes. But Joubert knew initials were meaningless. 'Jacques' might well be a second name, the initial appearing after that of the first in the directory. But they had to start somewhere.

'Ask them to look at the photos. Read out the names to them. Watch them because they may lie,' was the instruction given to each team. Nienaber had lied about MacDonald and Wallace, and now he was dead. Why had Nienaber lied? Why the pistol? Had he always carried the pistol?

Feverishly Snyman made copies of the list of names, goaded by the Captain's tone of voice.

And now the detectives poured in – from Paarl and Fish Hoek, from Table View and Stellenbosch, some annoyed because they were busy with other important cases, some grateful for the change and opportunity of working on the sensational Mauser murders.

'Phone the hospital. Ask them if we can speak to Nienaber's wife yet,' Joubert told Gerrit Snyman, delivering the last pile of photostats.

Snyman scurried. Joubert and O' Grady dealt out more work.

'The doctor says she's conscious but she can't see anyone,' said Snyman when he came back.

'We'll see,' said Joubert. 'Take this. I'm going to the hospital.'

In Kraaifontein, on the open piece of ground between the Olckers High School and the railway line, there was a huge marquee. At the entrance to the marquee a banner had been erected. TABERNACLE OF THE REDEEMER. SERVICES: WED. 09:00. SUN. 09:00, 11:00, 19:00.

Next to the big tent, there was a 1979 Sprite Alpine caravan with a tent pitched in front of it. On the caravan's couch which could extend into a double bed, sat pastor Paul Jacques Coetzee. He was busy preparing for the following evening's service.

Pastor Coetzee was unaware of the fact that more than eighty detectives in the Cape Peninsula were looking for him because he didn't own a television set and didn't read the newspapers. 'Instruments of the devil,' he had called the media in many of his rousing sermons.

He was engrossed in his work, heard all the phrases which he would fling from the pine pulpit, heard the refrain of The Message which would re-echo from the loudspeakers.

From the heart come wicked thoughts, murder, adultery, corruption, theft, false witness, scandalmongering.

'Sergeant, I have the information you were looking for,' said the secretary of Premier Bank's district manager.

Griessel sat in his office, pen at the ready.

'I'm all ears,' he said.

'Of the fourteen names you gave us, there are five who have accounts with Premier. Carstens, Geldenhuys, Milos. Rademann and Stewart.'

'Yo?' he said when he'd finished writing.

'Carstens and Rademann are women. Of the three men remaining, two are problem clients.'

'Yes?'

'Milos and Stewart. Milos has overdraft facilities of R45 000 with sixteen incidents of repayment arrears in the past twenty-four months.'

Griessel whistled.

'His cheque account was frozen and he has no other account with us. Legal proceedings have already been instituted against him to try and recover the outstanding amount. Stewart's car was re-possessed two months ago after he had, for six consecutive months, failed to pay the monthly payment of R980,76. His cheque book and credit card have also been frozen. He still has a savings account with us. The balance is R543,80.'

Griessel wrote it all down.

'Sergeant,' said the woman with the sweet voice.

'Yes?'

'My chief asked me to remind you again that the information is absolutely confidential.'

'Absolutely,' said Griessel and grinned.

'I understand your position, doctor, but you must understand mine. Out there is a man with a Mauser who, according to the criminologists, is out of control. And in here lies a woman who can help to prevent more bloodshed.'

Joubert was proud of his choice of words.

'You don't understand, Captain. Her condition is . . . She's on a knife edge. My only responsibility is towards her.'

He played his trump card. 'Doctor, I can go to court and apply for an interdict.'

'Captain, the court will hear me too.'

Check. They stood facing one another in the passage of the private hospital. The doctor was short and slender with dark circles under his eyes.

'I'll have to ask her if she's willing to see you.'

'I'd really appreciate that.'

Joubert waited while the doctor opened the door and disappeared. He put his hands in his trouser pockets, took them out again. He was unhappy. He didn't have time. He turned, walked on the thick carpet. He walked back and forth.

The doctor came back. 'She says she owes you.'

'Thank you, doctor.'

'Five minutes, Captain. And be very gentle with her.'

He opened the door for Joubert. Antoinette Nienaber looked dreadful. The lines next to her mouth were deeply etched. Her eyes were sunken, her face the ghostly copy of a skull. She lay with her head deep in the pillows, the upper part of her body slightly raised. There was a drip attached to her arm, the tube snaking up to the plastic bag. She wore powder blue night clothes. Her blonde hair lay lifelessly on the pillow.

He walked to the bed.

'I'm sorry . . .' he said uncomfortably.

'So am I.' Her voice was remote. He saw traces of a narcotic in the unfocused eyes which stared at him.

'I have only a few questions. You must tell me when you're tired.'

She nodded her assent.

'Do you know if your husband knew Ferdy Ferreira or Drew Wilson?'

It took her a while before she shook her head. No.

'Carina Oberholzer?'

No.

'Jacques Coetzee?'

No.

'Hester Clarke?'

'No.' A thread of a voice.

'Did your husband usually carry his firearm in his attaché case?'

Her eyes closed. The moments ticked past. In the passage there were footsteps.

Had she heard him?

The eyes opened. 'No,' she said and a drop formed under her eye, ran down the pale cheek, fell onto the blue collar of her night-gown, lay there for a second before being absorbed into the material.

He was caught up in conflicting emotions. The urgency in him made him want to ask her whether her husband had been faithful but he knew he couldn't, not now. What about a euphemism? Had they been happily married? He saw her looking at him, the eyes waiting, a deer facing a shotgun.

'Thank you, Mrs. Nienaber,' he said. 'I hope you . . . I wish you well.'

Thank you. Her lips formed the words but there was no sound. She turned her head away, towards the window.

Joubert was back in the office, telephone against his ear.

Julio da Costa said that Carina Oberholzer may have mentioned names like Jacques Coetzee or Hester Clarke but he wouldn't have remembered. 'She talked a great deal, Captain. All the time. And laughed. She was a very lively girl. She liked fun and parties and people. Her job was only something to make money and to pass the day. She was a night person. That's how we met. She came in here one Friday night, after midnight, she and a crowd of friends.'

'And then?'

'Hell, Captain, you know the way it goes. One can't work all the time. And you know what it's like with a wife at home.'

Joubert said nothing. Because he no longer knew.

'It's not illegal,' Da Costa said defensively. 'And in any case, it wasn't her first time.'

'How do you know?'

'A man always knows, Captain. If you'd had her, you would also have known what I mean. Hot stuff.'

'Did she ever discuss it?'

'All she ever said was that she didn't want life to pass her by. She wanted to enjoy every minute.'

Joubert ended the conversation.

Carina Oberholzer from Keimoes. Who laughed and talked and lived her short life to the full. The willing girl from the farm, the sly of a Portuguese Catholic and who knew who else. Had no one known her well enough to know what she knew?

He got the number of her parents, dialled the long code and the number, waited. It rang for a long time. A woman's voice answered, a servant.

'The people aren't here now. They've gone to fetch their son in Johannesburg.'

He took the Tupperware container out of his drawer and opened it: 60 grams of fat free cottage cheese; four rice cakes; tomato, avocado pear and lettuce with a small portion of fat free dressing. He was going to die of hunger. At least the Winston was waiting, the high point of his day, his greatest pleasure.

Someone came running down the passage.

They've traced someone, he realised.

It was Louw. 'He shot Jacques Coetzee, Captain. Less than an hour ago. And someone saw him.'

The two school boys were in standard six and they were very keen to see the body but the Police wouldn't hear of it. The boys had to keep out of the way, stand between the guy ropes which kept the walls of the marquee upright, watching one police vehicle after the other arriving. But it was much better than the double Biology class they were missing.

One of the first detectives to arrive there came up to them with another man, a big one.

'These are the boys, Captain.'

'Thank you,' the big one said. He put out a huge hand. 'Mat Joubert,' he said.

'I'm Jeremy, sir.'

'Neville,' said the other one. He shook their hands.

'You'll have to tell me everything.'

'Weren't you on TV the other night, sir?'

He shrugged. 'May have been.'

'Then this is the Mauser thing, sir?'

'We think so.'

'Sheesh, sir, but that guy is blowing them away, hey.'
Great admiration.

'We're going to catch him.'

'We only saw his car, sir,' Jeremy said. 'We heard the
shots. We were behind the tractor barn when we heard the
shots but a train passed and we weren't sure. Then we
walked over to have a look. Then we saw the car.'

'What make?'

'That's a bit of a problem, sir.'

'You're the one who doesn't know one car from another.'

'I know cars. You should have your eyes tested.'

'Hey,' Neville said but without aggression, as if their
arguments were a normal ritual.

'It was a Uno, sir, a white one. I think it was a Fire but
I'm not sure. It wasn't a turbo because the turbos have
larney stripes and a louvre.'

'It was a Citi Golf, sir. White. I know a Golf's backside
because my brother drives one. He's also in the Police, sir.
In Natal. They shoot Zulus.'

'Hey,' said Jeremy. 'They'll lock you up.'

'You're sure it was a Uno.'

'Yes, sir.'

'And you're sure it was a Golf.'

'Yes, sir.'

'Registration number?'

'We were too late. We only saw his tail as he drove away.'

Joubert measured the distance between the school

grounds and the boundary fence and the road which the
vehicle had taken. 'You didn't see what he looks like?'

'No, sir.'

'Well, men, thank you very much. And if either of you
makes a different decision about the make, you'll let me
know. I'm with Murder and Robbery.'

'Of course, sir.'

He was about to walk to the caravan when Jeremy spoke
again.

'Sir.'

'Yes?'

'May we really not see the body?'

He suppressed a smile and shook his head. 'It's not a
pretty sight.'

'Lots of blood, sir?'

'Buckets.'

'And the bullet holes, sir?'

'As big as hub caps,' he lied shamelessly.

'Sheesh,' Jeremy said.

'Jeez,' said Neville. 'That Mauser is a cannon.' And they
walked away deeply impressed, with information worth a
fortune in their world.

37

It was one of the additional teams who found the body. 'We must've missed him by minutes, Captain. The blood hadn't even clotted.' The body lay in the caravan, driven back by the first shot which had ripped into Coetzee's skull just above the left ear. The other shot was through the heart, as in all the previous cases, except MacDonald's.

If only he had looked at the attaché case the previous day. But how could he have known? He walked to the Sierra, radioed O' Grady. They must try to recall the teams who were looking for Jacques Coetzee. The whole effort must focus on Hester Clarke now. He must try to save at least one life.

'There's an address on the telephone account, Captain,' Louw called from the caravan. 'Durbanville.'

At least, Joubert thought, the connection had been proven. They now knew that Nienaber's list meant something. And there was only one name left.

He called Louw and they drove to Durbanville to a dilapidated house in the centre of the town. The grass was long and untidy, the flowerbeds overgrown with weeds.

'I hope he was a better pastor than a gardener,' said Louw. He had brought a bunch of keys which had hung in the caravan door's lock and tried until one fitted the front door's.

They walked in. There was no furniture in the sitting-room, only a telephone which stood on the floor. In the kitchen there were dirty plates in the wash-up. An old ice chest rattled in the corner. The empty passage was uncarpeted. So was the first bedroom. The second held a single bed, a bedside table with no drawers. On the floor there was a pile of books. Joubert picked up one. '*Praise his Name*.' The second one was also religious. All the others as well.

On the bed table there was an opened envelope. He picked it up and took out the contents:

SMUTS, KEMP AND SMALL, ATTORNEYS AND NOTARIES.

> *Dear Mr. Coetzee*
> *According to our client, Mrs. Ingrid Johanna Coetzee,*
> *you are still in arrears with regard to the alimony set out*
> *in the divorce decree . . .*

Griessel was hot on the trail of George Michael Stewart.

He found no one at the man's flat in Oranjezicht but the caretaker there said the suspect worked part-time as a waiter at Christie's, the restaurant in Long Street.

He couldn't find a parking space, eventually parked on a loading zone in Wale Street and walked around the corner. The restaurant was virtually full for lunch, with yuppies very much in evidence. He was received at the door by a tall, refined man with a tense smile who quickly led him to a table at the back, near the kitchen door and pushed a menu into his hand.

Griessel sat down and felt people looking at him. He didn't fit in here. He looked self-consciously at the dishes on the menu and saw that he wouldn't be able to afford much. He decided on the pumpkin soup and looked up again. There were only two men serving, both white – the refined one who had taken him to his table and another one of average height and build. Both were dressed in the same outfit, a pair of black trousers, white shirt and black bow tie. Both had short dark hair and were clean-shaven. Both their noses looked somewhat like the bank robber's.

Mr. Average made a beeline for him, notepad and pen in his hand.

'May I tell you about our specials, sir?' he asked mechanically, without really seeing Griessel.

'What's your name?'

'Michael Stewart,' said the man and looked with closer attention at his client.

'I would like to have the pumpkin soup. please.'

'Yes.' He wrote it down 'And then?'

'That's all, thank you, Mr. Stewart.'

'You're welcome.' The man hurried away, into the kitchen.

He speaks English, Griessel thought. The robber speaks Afrikaans. A smokescreen?

He leant forward, his elbows on the table, his hands under his chin. He looked at the people around him. Men, mostly, a woman here and there. They were close to the Supreme Court and Parliament, he thought. Important people, these, with BMW's and Jettas and cell phones. At the table next to him a man swallowed a beer with great enjoyment, the glass tilted, the adam's apple moving up and down, up and down until the last foam slid out of the glass and he put it down on the table and wiped his mouth with a napkin.

Griessel imagined the warm glow the liquor would cause in the man's stomach, how it would spread through the body, to the head, warm and easy and pleasant – a tingling, a tide of pleasure, a smoother of sharp corners and edges.

He looked down, at the salt and pepper pots on his table, put out his hand, picked up one. His hands were sweating.

George Michael Stewart hadn't reappeared from the kitchen, he realised he smelt a rat.

He fingered the Z88 fastened to his belt. He shouldn't have asked the man for his name. He looked at the kitchen door. How long had it been? Five minutes. It was only Mr. Refined who hurried between the tables, removing an empty wine bottle at one, asking whether the food was to their satisfaction at another.

Where was Stewart?

Minutes went by during which his uneasiness grew. If the man had suspected something and escaped through the back door, he could be at the station by now, Griessel thought.

Soup couldn't take that long.

He made a sudden decision, got up, his hand on the grip of the firearm and walked hurriedly to the kitchen door, a metal door which swung open easily. With his back against the door and his pistol in his hand, he banged open the door with some force and walked straight into George Michael Stewart and a plate of bright yellow soup. The hot liquid splashed on Griessel's shirt and tie, Stewart staggered back, fell and sat down on his backside. With his eyes huge, he looked at the square figure who loomed over him with a pistol.

'My service can't be that bad!' he said nervously.

Attorney Kemp, nattily dressed in a dark-grey suit and a fashionable tie, was as big as Mat Joubert. He sat on the edge of the untidy desk with Joubert and Louw in the chairs in front of him. The attorney was busy telephoning East London because that was where his client, Mrs. Ingrid Johanna Coetzee, lived now.

He had immediately been willing to help the detectives. He was a hasty, efficient man with a deep voice and hair painfully neatly barbered and combed.

Joubert looked at the man's clothes again – the double breasted coat, the fine stripe in the texture of the material.

Joubert had no clothes for tomorrow night's opera. He would have to buy a suit like that. He would have to have his hair cut. Everything had to be just right. If Hanna Nortier told him this afternoon that she was going with him. If he managed to get to Hanna Nortier this afternoon.

'I see,' said the attorney into the receiver. 'I see. Fine. Thank you. Goodbye.' He put the phone down. 'She's on holiday. Gone diving. I didn't even know she was into diving. Small, colourless, little woman.'

The attorney walked round to the big chair behind his desk. 'I didn't want to mention the man's death.' He wrote on a large notepad, tore off the page and handed it to Joubert. 'That's where she works. The accounts department. They said she would only be back in the office on Monday.'

'You'll have to fly,' Joubert said to Louw. Then he looked at the attorney. 'Why were they divorced?'

'His religion,' said Kemp. 'He used to be a television technician or something. Here in Bellville at a repair shop. and then suddenly turned holy and lost his work because he spent the whole day in church, one of those charismatic ones where they spend every evening saying hallelujah and amen and clapping their hands. She couldn't bear it any longer. Luckily there were no children. He didn't want to divorce her at first. Against the Law and the faith. But we gave him merry hell. And the alimony . . . She had never worked. He wanted her to stay at home, be mama and do housework. He was never quite all there . . .'

'Then he started his own church?'

'It was after the divorce. I only know a part of it, what she told me over the telephone. She couldn't believe he could preach. He had always been a silent, sulky man. But there

345

you have it, cometh the hour . . . He fell out with all the other churches and founded his own. Lot of money in it, you know.'

'The place where he worked?'

'I don't know. You'll have to ask her.'

Thank you very much.' Joubert got up, so did Louw.

'It's a pleasure. I like to help the legal process when I can. Will you get the Mauser man?'

'It's a matter of hours.'

Joubert turned back at the door. 'If I may ask, where do you buy your clothes?'

'Queenspark,' the attorney smiled. 'But I must confess. My wife does the buying. I'm too damn stupid at it.'

Christie's was empty now. Griessel sat at his table, his shirt and tie reasonably clean but very damp from repeated applications of a wet cloth. Stewart sat opposite him. They were smoking Stewart's Gunstons.

'I don't rob banks,' said Stewart and his Afrikaans was reasonable but not without an accent.

'Can you prove it?'

'Ask Steve,' and he pointed his cigarette at the other man in a bow tie. He was still clearing tables with a few black women. 'I'm here every day from ten in the morning until midnight.'

'My brother Jack lies just like I do . . .'

'Hell, Steve owns the place. He makes the money. Why would he lie?'

'Why are you working here?'

'Because there's not enough make-up work in the Cape. I should never have come.'

'Why did you?'

'Followed a woman. And for the mountain and the sea and the atmosphere. Now she's dropped me because I don't

have any money. I owe the bank and the make-up jobs are
few and far between. The last one was two months ago.
French team, came to make a television ad. But my car . . .
I'm still paying it off even if it's in the scrap yard . . .'

Griessel took a photo out of his pocket. Elvis. 'Do you
know him?'

Stewart looked. 'He's . . .' He searched for the word.
'Careless.'

'Oh?'

'Look at the sideburns. The gum is visible here. Perhaps
because he does his own make-up. It's quite tricky. I've
never tried it.'

'Do you know him?'

'No.'

'Heard of Janek Milos?'

'Mmm . . .'

'You don't know him.' Griessel didn't ask – he stated.
With disappointment because he had hoped Stewart was
going to be his man. Because Janek Milos didn't sound like
a decent Afrikaans boy who robbed banks politely and
called tellers 'sweetheart.' Because his nice theories were
crumbling.

The detectives came back for more names and addresses
and Joubert's heart sank with every new pair who walked
into the parade room after another fruitless effort. They had
reached Clarke without an 'e', were at R and S for initials
but had found nothing.

He looked at his watch. His appointment with Hanna
Nortier was getting closer and closer. He still didn't have an
excuse.

Louw had come to say goodbye. He had found a seat on
the half past six flight to Port Elizabeth and East London.
They again went through the possible questions which

Joubert wanted answered. Louw had left, his eyes droopy from his hangover.

Another two detectives arrived, shaking their heads.

'Telephone, Captain,' Mavis called from the door.

He got up and walked hastily to Reception. 'Joubert.'

'Bertus Botha, Captain. We've traced a Hester Clarke. But she's dead. Died of cancer. Early in December.'

'Where are you phoning from?'

'Her sister's house, Captain. Fish Hoek. Deceased was fifty-three. Spinster. Artist. Designed Christmas cards and stuff for a publisher in Maitland but they worked from home. Developed cancer of the spine. The sister says it was due to sitting all day long, no matter what the doctors say. She says all she knows about the Mauser murders is what she's read in the newspapers and seen on TV.'

'She's quite certain?'

'Yes, Captain. We showed her the photographs 'n everything.'

'Her sister never had any contact with Oliver Nienaber?' He hoped, hopelessly, because there couldn't be that many Hester Clarkes in the Cape and he was desperate, there had to be an end to it.

'She says they never went out. She says the streets aren't safe. She knew everyone her sister knew.'

Joubert's mind dug around for more possibilities.

'The doctor who treated her sister – get me his name. I'll hold on.'

He heard Botha putting down the telephone and the sounds of talking in the background. Then Botha came back with the information. Joubert wrote it down. Groote Schuur. He thanked Botha and looked at his watch again. Just enough time to touch at the hospital and then drive to his psychologist.

38

The doctor remembered Hester Clarke's illness very well. 'She never complained. Strong woman. It must've been extremely painful, especially the last few months.'

When was the cancer diagnosed?

Three or four years ago. They had tried everything.

Her mental state?

Strong woman. I told you.

And so Joubert fished, in a useless effort to catch something which would cast some light. He knew it was a dead end street.

He drove to the city, spoke to O' Grady on the radio.

No news about Hester Clarke, O' Grady said. Most of the teams had returned. But Pastor Jacques Coetzee's caravan was proving to be interesting. They had found R40 000 under the seat. In hard cash. And bank documents which indicated that the church was financially very well-placed. Lists of members, deacons, elders . . .

Bring it to the office, Joubert said. And sent Bertus Botha's team back to the sister of Hester Clarke. Find out to which church they belonged. And telephone the relatives of the other victims again. Ask Nienaber's children. Had they heard of the Tabernacle of the Redeemer.

While he drove, a feeling of optimism took hold of him. Each case, each dossier was a mountain to climb. Sometimes the hand- and toeholds were easy and you had a fast ascent to the summit where you handed over the warrant of arrest, a neat parcel of motive and evidence, cause and effect. But sometimes, like this one, the mountain was smooth and slippery, without crevices for hands and toes to grip. You climbed and slipped, climbed and slipped without progress, without a way to the top.

But now things were beginning to change. Eventually, something for which someone was willing to commit murder. To blow six people's brains and bodies to kingdom come.

Money.

The root of all evil. The driving force, the urge which made them steal and shoot and hit and chop and set alight.

The adrenaline was flowing freely when he walked into the waiting room and sank down on a chair. They were close now. They were very close. He was going to solve the case. Today.

Hanna Nortier opened the door and there was a smile on her face.

'Come in, Captain Mat Joubert.' Her voice held a gaiety and he rejoiced because he knew she was going to accompany him to the opera.

'I think we must discuss tomorrow night first,' she said as she opened his file. 'So that we can put it behind us. I'm not allowed to go with you. It's ethically wrong. It's unfair to you because we still have hard work ahead of us. I can't justify it in any way at all.'

He looked at her while he kept the disappointment out of his face with great difficulty.

'But there is the other side of the coin. I'm flattered that you've asked me out. I can't remember when last I went anywhere with a big, strong man. I want to very much. I badly want to see *The Barber of Seville*. I want to go out. I'm in a rut. I believe I can separate my private and professional life. I must be able to do it. But not at your expense.'

She spoke quickly, urgently, a Hanna Nortier he hadn't seen before, her slender hands dancing to stress her words, her pupils large and black, her beauty so perfect that he was unable to look away.

'Can you separate the therapy and the personal . . . togetherness, Mat?'

Not too fast, he warned himself. Not too keen.

'I think so.' Nice and even, thoughtful.

'You must be quite sure.'

'I am sure.' Too quickly.

'If you change your mind you can still phone me tomorrow.'

Was she going with him?

'I'll write down my home address. At what time does the opera start? Eight o'clock?'

He nodded.

'I'll be ready by seven thirty.'

'Thank you.' Why did he thank her? Because he was so grateful that his stomach muscles were clenching.

'How's the investigation going?'

He didn't react immediately, first had to accommodate the change of gears.

'Well. Very well. We're close.'

'Tell me.'

'There was another murder this morning. The pastor of a marquee church in Kraaifontein. They . . . We found money in the caravan. I think it could be the motive. And then it's just a question of time.'

'I'm so pleased for you,' she said sincerely and tidied the file. Her words moved into another tempo. She looked straight ahead. Gently she said: 'I want you to tell me about the disciplinary enquiry.'

He did not want to think about it.

It was four months after the death of Lara Joubert.

But he didn't tell her that. Let her work it out on her own.

She had changed from personal to professional too quickly. He wasn't ready. He had expected a slower landing and now he had to think back, open the doors and hear the voices, the blackness of his feelings then, the dark, a flawless black night, pitch black, the incredible weight, the feverish dreams as thick as molasses, while seconds ago his heart had been as light as a feather, a bird in flight.

He closed his eyes.

He did not want to think about it.

Reluctantly he searched for the images in his mind.

Blackness.

He had been in bed. Winter.

The images. Slowly. Tiredly it flowed back, uneven and confused. It was late at night, in his bed, he remembered, slowly recalled even the taste in his mouth, the weight of the blankets, the dream world, visiting his wife in the realm of the dead, her laugh, her sounds, *uhm, uhm, uhm, uhm,* a telephone ringing Captain Joubert to Parow cold and wet Northwest wind.

A house with cement walls and a garden gate and a path between flowerbeds and a small fountain in the centre of the lawn; the blue lights turning in the street; the neighbours in their dressing-gowns against the cold, curious, staring; the uniform who told him the man was inside, he had shot his wife and he wouldn't come out; the neighbours had heard the sound of the shots and went and knocked and then he shot at them and shouted at them and said that tonight he was going to blast them all to hell and gone; the neighbour's cheek was bleeding from the glass slivers of the front room's window.

He went to stand in front of the door; the sergeant of Murder and Robbery had shouted, no Captain, not in front of the door; the book says stand against the wall; but

Joubert's book was covered in soot. I'm unarmed, I'm coming in and I put my service pistol down on the slate stoep and I opened the door and walked in; no, Captain, jesus god, he's fucking crazy.

He had closed the door behind him, the wind audible in the house.

'Are you mad?' The big .375 Magnum pointing at him, the man in the passage virtually insane, terror-stricken. 'I'm going to kill the lot of you.'

He remained where he was and looked at the man; his eyes were unblinking, he waited for the lead to penetrate his brain and let the curtain fall. 'You're mad, go away.' The man's mouth spat saliva, his eyes were those of an animal, the big revolver shook. He didn't move, simply stood there, gazed, uninvolved.

'Where is she?' his own voice emotionless.

'In the kitchen. The whore. She's dead, the whore. I killed her. Tonight I'm going to kill you all.' The weapon was aimed straight at him again; the man's breathing was ragged, his chest heaved, his body shook.

'Why?'

A sound – a sob and a cry and disgust, intermingled; the weapon dropped a few millimeters; the man's eyes closed, opened.

'Kill . . .'

The wind and showers of rain against the windows, on the corrugated iron roof; light scurrying across the walls, the shadows of windblown shrubs. The man's body tipped up to the wall, the revolver still held high, his shoulder against the wall; then the sound, another one, long-drawn, a wailing; the man sank down to the floor; his legs were bent, his eyes unseeing; a bundle, crouching, sitting, arm on one knee; the grip on the firearm loose, a sound like the wind, as comfortless as his own soul.

Breathing slowed.

'What could I do?'

Weeping. 'What could I do? She didn't want me any more. What could I do?'

Shoulders shaking, spasms.

'She's mine.' Like a child. A high whimpering voice.

A silence which stretched and stretched.

'She said to him: "You know I'm yours." I stood here – she didn't know – I stood here and I heard her saying, "All yours."' The last words were a cry again; the voice jumped an octave, uncomprehending.

' "You know. Like last night," she said. And I hit her and she ran. To the bathroom at first . . .'

He looked up, pleading. 'I don't even know who he was.' He got no reaction.

'What am I going to do?'

In the passage: he standing, the man half-lying, half-sitting against the wall; the revolver hung against his leg; someone outside called Captain, Captain, silence again, only the wind and the rain and the sobs, now soft and even, the man's eyes on the firearm.

An awareness of a possibility, of a way out, a comfort; consider, count the cost, the future.

A slow decision.

'Will you go out?'

Yes, because he knew the yearning, the decision, he knew the darkness; turned round, towards the door; opened it, cries outside, Captain, jesus you're OK, what's the fucker doing; the sound of the shot inside; he didn't move, simply stood there, his head bowed until they realised and ran past him, through the door.

'The sentence was suspended.'

He looked squarely at Hanna Nortier. She had wanted to ask. She had wanted to know. She wanted to sail the soul of

Mat Joubert like an unknown sea, map the contours of the
Coast of the Dead, describe the landmarks, name them. Ask
me Doc, ask me. I'll tell you how close to it I was that night,
back at home, to blowing my brains all over the living-room
carpet with a service pistol. I could see and feel the release of
my friend in Parow, touch it, with my service pistol in my
hand, my thumb on the safety catch, on my way to Lara.

Willie Theal had hammered on the door. Mat, dear boy,
dear boy. The thin arm around his shoulders. They stood on
the front veranda, his head against Theal's chest, the pistol
pointing to the ground, the moment past, the intensity lost.

Ask me, Doc.

Hanna Nortier evaded his gaze, wrote in the fucking file
which he wanted to grab and read, aloud, let's see what the
clever Doc thinks . . .

'And the petition?' She spoke softly again, like the previous times, her gaiety gone, dissipated by the black cloud
that was Mat Joubert, the world's only intelligent black
cloud who cast shadows wherever it went, who blotted out
the sun, quenched laughter.

'They thought the punishment wasn't severe enough. Van
der Vyver, the sergeant at the house in Parow. He said I'd
endanger lives again. He told the others. He was right. They
went to Theal. My commanding officer. But Theal said I'd
be OK, they were in too much of a hurry. Then they drew up
a petition, took it as far as the assistant district commissioner who had known my father and stopped the whole
thing and said loyalty kept the Force together. My father.
Gave me from the grave what he couldn't give me in life. It's
ironic, isn't it Hanna?'

He used her name for the first time, without respect. She
could've dropped it today. She could've discussed other
things today, this and that, because he was getting his act
together. I'm busy getting my act together, Hanna, and now

you're fucking with my head. Doc, I'll be fine, I promise you, tomorrow evening my head will be just fine . . .

She blew her nose and only then did he see the wetness in her eyes and he half rose from his deep chair.

'Life is ironical,' she said, her voice under control. 'That's enough for today.'

Then he knew that he had touched her and wondered how and he wondered what it meant.

Janek Milos opened the door and Benny Griessel knew he had his man.

'It's your nose,' Griessel said.

Milos turned and ran into the house. Griessel swore and sprang after him, hoping that he would catch him quickly because after a hundred meters or less, he wouldn't have a hope.

Milos shut doors as far as he went but the back door was locked and in his feverish haste he couldn't get the key to turn. Griessel struck the man's back with his shoulder, forcing him against the door. The wood splintered, breath woofed out of the man's mouth. Griessel was on him, his knee against the man's back forcing him to the ground. He jerked his arm back and twisted it towards his neck. Handcuffs on the right hand. Click. Found the other hand. Click.

'Hello, sweetheart,' said Griessel and kissed Janek Milos on the back of his bald head.

'If you don't sue *The Argus*, I will,' said Margaret Wallace's mother over the telephone, her voice shrill with agitation.

'Why, Mom?'

'I don't want to tell you. It's horrible the way they lie.'

'What is it, Mother?'

'It'll upset you.'

'Mother, please.'

'They say . . . Heavens, my dear, it's a pack of lies. It's just that I'm so . . . so . . .'

'Mother!' A desperate order.

'They say Jimmy was with another woman. The day he died.'

'You must be fucking joking,' said the Brigadier who was pacing to and fro in the parade room. 'The Minister is shitting his pants and you tell me the thing still doesn't make sense. You tell me there's R40 000 in the priest's caravan and it's just fine because he banks on a Saturday. You think the church is the answer and relatives have never heard of it.' He stopped and glared at de Wit and Joubert. 'You must be fucking joking.'

They stared at the floor.

'Have you any idea of the pressure? The General is too scared to answer his telephone and I had to flee my office because the press are camped out in the street. And the bastards are everywhere. Here, at the gate, a uniform virtually had to save me from the vultures and you tell me the thing doesn't make sense.' He started pacing again, his arms swinging. His face was scarlet, the veins in his neck swollen. 'The Minister says we're the laughing stock overseas. We simple Boers are so stupid they have to send us a clairvoyant. Whose idea was that? You have a list of names the motherfucker wants to kill and they're still dying like flies. And now you look so grateful that the names on the list are coming to an end.'

He took a kick at a chair. It fell over backwards, hit the wall, sprang back, clattered over the floor and lay there.

'Doesn't anyone have anything to say?'

'Brigadier,' said de Wit, his smile sickly and askew.

'Don't you "brigadier" me. Never in my forty years in the

Force have I come across such a sorry bunch of asshole dumb policemen. You couldn't catch a dead locust in a jam jar, if you ask me. What else do you want the motherfucker to do? Walk in here and mount his goddamn Mauser against the wall and say: Catch me, please? By this time all the policemen in the province are here to help. What else must we do? Get Gauteng's as well? What about the Defence Force? Let's call them in as well, tanks and bombers and the fucking Navy. Let's not play games here. Let's make real cunts of ourselves. Let's phone the Chinese. They've got clairvoyants for Africa. And the Japanese. And we get Hollywood to come and film you because only their cameras are still missing.'

Another chair tumbled, clattered.

'Jesus Christ.'

They stared at the floor. De Wit, Joubert, Petersen, O' Grady, Snyman and Vos.

The Brigadier's hands made signs but he seemed incapable of further speech.

The door opened. Heads turned. Griessel came in.

'Ladies and gentlemen,' he said proudly, 'meet Sweetheart,' and taking the man by his shirt, pulled him into the room.

39

'January 10, 19:17. Interrogation of suspect, SAP two slash one slash nine five slash fourteen, Murder and Robbery, Bellville South. Investigating officer: Detective Sergeant Benjamin Griessel. Observers: Colonel Bart de Wit, Captain Mat Joubert, Captain Gerry . . . e . . .'

'Gerbrand.'

'Captain Gerbrand Vos. First question to suspect. Full name.'

'Janek Wachlaff Milos.'

'Nationality?'

'Eskimo. You can hear that. I speak fluent Eskimoose.'

'Nationality?'

'South African.'

'Identity number?'

'Five nine zero five five one two seven zero zero one.'

'Address?'

'Seventeen Iris Avenue, Pinelands.'

'You are aware of your right to have a legal representative present. If you don't have a legal representative, or cannot afford one, the State will appoint such a legal representative. At any time during the proceedings you may ask the State to appoint an alternative legal representative, upon which the case before a magistrate of the district court or a higher court . . .'

'Spare me. I don't need an attorney.'

'You're going to need an advocate. We're hitting you with armed robbery, Wachlaff.'

'It was a toy gun.'

'Pistol.'

'Whatever.'

'Do you admit that you're undergoing this interrogation of your own free will, without any pressure or encouragement by the South African Police . . .'

'South African Police Service.'

'Sorry, Colonel. Without any pressure or encouragement from the South African Police Service.'

'Yes.'

'Where did your name originate?'

'Good old Eskimo name.'

'You're a funny one, Wachlaff.'

'My father was Polish, OK?'

'Is your mother Afrikaans?'

Silence.

'Will you speak? For the sake of the tape recording.'

'Yes, she was. What has that to do with anything?'

'Profession?'

'Housewife.'

'No, yours.'

'Make-up artist. Free-lance.'

'Not very successful?'

'Not my fault. Blame the SABC. The more they dub, the more we die of hunger.'

'So you decided to rob a few banks.'

'Only Premier. The other one was to send him the message.'

'For the record, the accused is referring to Captain Mat Joubert. Why Premier, Wachlaff?'

'They owe me.'

'They owe you?'

'I wouldn't have taken more than R45 000. That's what they owe me.'

'Why?'

'My house?'

'Your house?'

'They approved the loan. No problem, Mr. Milos. We're happy to assist, Mr. Milos. Just sign here, Mr. Milos, we'll let you have it at quarter percent less.'

'And?'

'Then they withdrew the loan. Because their assessor hadn't seen the structural defect until I told them about it.'

'Structural defect?'

'The entire back of the house is fucking slowly sinking into the sand but the contract says the seller is not responsible and I had already signed. "We're sorry, Mr. Milos, but there's not enough security for the loan. No, it would be overcapitalising to have the defect repaired, Mr. Milos. We're transferring the loan to overdraft facilities. Do look at paragraph so and so, sub-paragraph this and that, the interest is just slightly higher." And then the SAB fucking C rationalised and what could I do? Phone Murder and Robbery?'

'Then you began to rob banks?'

'I looked for work.'

'With no success.'

'No, sir, I was snowed under by offers. Twentieth Century Fox, MGM, Warner's. They queued. But I really don't want to be a millionaire at thirty-two.'

'You are funny and sarcastic, Wachlaff.'

'You try looking for work with your white skin, pal. "What experience do you have, sir? Make-up? We'll phone you, sir. We're actually busy with affirmative action right now".'

'Then you started robbing banks.'

'Then I went and took back what they owed me.'

'It's known as armed robbery, Wachlaff.'

'My name is Janek. It wasn't a weapon. It was a toy.'

'Do you admit that you robbed branches of Premier Bank of January 2 and 7 of R7 000 and R11 250 respectively. And that on January 11 you attempted to rob the bank's branch in Milnerton. And that on January 16 you robbed a BANKSA branch in Somerset West of R3 000? Each time by threatening the employees with a firearm?'

'You saw the fucking gun. It's a toy.'

'Can you prove that the toy pistol is the same one you used during the armed robberies?'

'No. But hell . . .'

'Yes?'

'I didn't want to hurt anyone. I was polite and civilised, up to the moment you started fucking around with the Mauser thing.'

'What Mauser thing, Wachlaff?'

'My fucking name is Janek. You know very well which Mauser thing I'm talking about. The guy who's wiping out the whole Peninsula.'

'What do you know about the Mauser thing?'

'What I and the rest of South Africa read in the newspapers.'

'Where do you keep your Mauser?'

'Listen, I'm prepared to cooperate but I'm not prepared to listen to shit.'

'You started the Mauser thing when you mentioned it in Milnerton. I quote from the statement of Miss Rosa Wassermann. "And then he said: Seems I should've brought my Mauser."'

'The fat bitch wouldn't cooperate. I wanted to give her a fright.'

'There are twelve detectives busy searching your house at this moment. If they find the Mauser . . .'

'They won't find anything.'

'Why, Wachlaff? Have you hidden it somewhere else?'

'I don't have a fucking Mauser. How many times must I repeat it? I wouldn't even know how to get hold of one. I bought a toy gun which looks like the real thing and I never took it out of my pocket because I was afraid people would see that it was a toy. OK, OK, I admit I stole the money. But it wasn't robbery. And it wasn't theft. It was my money which I took back. I would've returned BANKSA's money but I had to get it from Premier first. OK? You can't force me to admit something I didn't do.'

'Where's the money, Wachlaff?'

'Janek.'

'Where's the money, Janek?'

'It's my money.'

'Where is it?'

'Fuck you all. I'm going to jail in any case and when I get out Premier is still going to screw me for the money. Plus fucking interest. So what's the use?'

'The judge will regard it in a very positive light if you return the money, Janek.'

'It's my money.'

'Where is your money, Janek?'

(Silence)

'Janek?'

'In the ceiling. Under the hot water cylinder.'

They had a conference in de Wit's office, the commanding officer now a member of the team, a frail camaraderie created by the Brigadier's tirade.

Joubert's mouth was dry and tasted of old cigarettes. In the interrogation room he had discarded his resolution of three a day – simply to get rid of the intense hunger and the headache which throbbed behind his temples. He had kept up with Griessel, one cigarette after the other and he wanted another one now but de Wit's sign stopped him. I CHOOSE NOT TO SMOKE.

They went through the dossiers line by line, bit by bit, studied the shapes of the puzzle, the holes bigger than the small pieces which fitted. They started from the beginning, built theories which others demolished with one question, shuffled again, built, broke down, until they realised the core simply wasn't there, the angles and corners still made no sense.

At quarter past eleven they decided to wait for Basie Louw to return after he had traced Ingrid Johanna Coetzee.

Perhaps the new day would bring a new perspective.

Joubert drove home, tired in body and soul, hungry, thirsty. The events of the day ran through his head.

A car was parked at his gate.

He stopped in front of the garage, got out and walked to the car. A BMW, he saw by the light of the street lamp.

A movement on his veranda.

His hand reached for his service pistol, instinct took over. The Z88 was in his hand, adrenaline pumped, the tiredness was gone, the mind clear.

'You bastard.'

He recognised the voice.

Margaret Wallace walked purposefully towards him, taking no notice of the pistol. 'You bastard.'

He walked to meet her. His mind was having trouble fitting her into the scheme of things. He saw she wasn't armed. Then she was on him, hitting his chest with both hands.

'You never told me.' She hit him again. He retreated, dumbfounded, the firearm in the way when he wanted to ward off her blows. Her hands were clenched, clumsy against his chest. 'You never told me, you bastard.'

'What . . .' he said and tried to catch her hands, but they hammered on his chest. He saw her contorted face, the dignity gone, filled with hate and pain.

'I had a right to know. Who are you to keep it from me? Who are you?'

He managed to catch her right hand, then her left. 'What are you talking about?'

'You know, you bastard.' She struggled to free herself, bit the hand holding hers. He dropped her hands with a cry of pain, tried to get away from her.

'I don't know what you're talking about.'

'The rest of the world does. The rest of the world knows. You tell the newspapers but you don't tell me. What kind of a man are you?'

She hit him again. A blow caught him on the lip and he felt the warm blood running into his mouth.

'Please,' he said, a cry which stopped her. 'Just tell me what you're talking about.'

'You knew Jimmy was with another woman,' she said, and then she cried, her fists in front of her as if she wanted to defend herself. 'You knew. You. You with your sad story of your wife. To think I felt sorry for you, you bastard. To think I felt pity for you. You don't deserve it. What kind of a man are you?' Her fists dropped, hopelessly, exhausted. Her pain overwhelmed the words.

'I . . . I . . .'

'Why didn't you tell me?'

'I . . .'

'Why did you have to tell the newspapers?'

'I didn't tell the . . .'

'Don't lie to me, you bastard.' She came at him again. He yelled at her: 'I didn't tell the newspapers. It was

someone else, dammit. I didn't tell you because . . . because
. . .' Jesus! Because he knew what it felt like and he had been
sorry for her in her yellow pinafore and her grief. She didn't
know what it was like – the messenger of Death, the bringer
of the bad news . . .

'Because I didn't want to hurt you . . . more.'

'Hurt me? You didn't want to hurt me? And now? Now
I'm *not* hurt, you stupid bastard? Do you know what it feels
like? Do you know?' They were standing on the lawn where
the dew sparkled like diamonds in the street light. His house
was dark, the street quiet. Her voice carried.

'Yes, I know,' he said softly.

'Rubbish,' she said with renewed anger.

'I know.' Softly, so softly.

'Rubbish, you bastard. You don't know. You can't
know.'

It wasn't the long day, the exhaustion and his raw nerves
after hope and the severe reprimand of the Brigadier and
the murder and his painful session with Hanna Nortier. It
was the yearning inside him to let it all out, twenty-six
months' worth of a witches' brew which wanted to boil
over, the pleading of his soul to be cleansed, to lance the
abscess, filled with the pus which was straining against the
septic skin. He made a cut with the scalpel with a light-
headedness, an emotion between anger and panic, between
relief and fear.

'I know.' He yelled. 'I know.' He walked over to her, his
shoulders hunched, his head bowed. 'I know, just as you do.
More, much more. I know it all.' He leaned towards her,
wanted to snarl at her, wanted to punish her. 'I know it. I
wanted to keep it from you. Did you say goodbye? When
your husband left that morning. Did you say goodbye? I
didn't. I never even said goodbye. She was simply gone. I
woke up and she was gone. Simply gone.'

He heard his words echoing against the wall of his house, then only heard his breathing, too fast, in, out, gasping, and he saw the abyss ahead of him which he would have to cross now. He saw its deep darkness and he was frightened. God, he had to get across it like a high-wire artist, and there was no safety net. The fear began in a small way, somewhere in his belly and then it increased, hugely. It drove him back. He closed his eyes. He knew his hands were shaking but he put out a tentative foot and felt for the wire which stretched ahead of him. He couldn't turn back now.

'She was just gone.' His voice was low but he knew she could hear the fear.

Breathe.

'Sometimes in the middle of the night I would reach out to touch her shoulder or her hip. It was always so warm.'

He sighed deeply.

'It was my . . . my . . . haven in the dark, to know that she was there. She could fall asleep so easily. I never knew. She worked for the drug squad. Sanab. I asked her what she did for them. The she laughed and said she was undercover. But at what? She wasn't allowed to tell. Not even me. And then she slept like a child with a harmless secret. Maybe there was something I missed. If I'd paid more attention. If I'd only asked more questions, if I wasn't so busy scheming myself and hadn't been so deeply impressed with my own search.'

His derisory laugh was aimed at himself, a sob. It gave him the courage to give the next step even if the long, thin wire was swaying over the abyss.

'I thought that if I only played drug games for Sanab I would also be able to sleep. So superior. During the night, next to Lara, I tossed and turned and I was so superior.'

Margaret Wallace stretched out her hand to him, let it rest on his forearm. For a moment it was a lifebelt. Then he drew his arm away. He had to reach the other side on his own, that he knew. He suppressed the emotion, the self-pity, the weeping.

'I was so self-satisfied.' As if it explained why he didn't deserve her hand.

'It's so strange,' he said, almost with amazement. 'We only live inside our own heads. Like prisoners. Even if our eyes look outwards, we live just here, inside this bony skull. We actually know nothing. We live with other people, every day, and we think we know because we can see. And we think they know, because they can see. But nobody knows. I was so satisfied, in my own head, with my own task, so important. So clean.'

He grimaced in the dark but he didn't realise it. His hands were still shaking, hanging next to his body, his eyes were still closed.

'That's the problem, when you can't get out of your own head. You think you're so clean. Because Silva was so dirty. We think in terms of black and white. Silva was a killer, dirty and black as sin. And I was the clean, white light of justice. And they encouraged me. Get him. They made me even cleaner. Get Silva for the girls, the two women he had thrown away on a rubbish tip like so much human garbage. Get him for the cop of Murder and Robbery with the hole in the forehead. Get him for the drugs, for his invulnerability, for his dirty, black soul.'

Joubert looked back and saw that he had made progress on the thin wire.

He gave a longer step.

'It's against the law to plant microphones. We're not allowed to. But if you're clean, you have power. I hired the stuff in Voortrekker Road from the big private eye with the red face and I drove to Clifton and I waited, that morning, until it was safe. Such a beautiful morning, without wind or cloud, in Silva's flat which overlooked the sea. There was a telescope on the balcony. Everything was so white. And expensive. I was scared, I have to admit. I hurried. One makes comparisons while you plant the small microphones. You think about where you live and you look at the stuff that money can buy. One at the telescope, one in the small bar, one near the bed, one in the telephone. And R250 of my own money for the supervisor of the building to put the receiver and the recorder in the cellar's electricity box.'

He didn't look ahead because he knew instinctively that the wire was going to sway, the cable ahead of him become threadlike and impassable, and now he wanted to turn back. He walked faster, killed his fear with words.

'Lara didn't come home that night. I phoned Sanab. They said she was working. What kind of work? "You know we can't tell you." It's my wife. "She's undercover, Joubert. You know how it works". Then I walked through the house and I smelt her, saw the magazines in the living-room and in front of her bed. And I thought about my scheming, about the microphones and the recorder, and I wondered if the little tape was turning. I slept badly – it was a long night and a long morning. Then I drove to Clifton again and I walked down the stairs and in the cellar it was dark.'

He wanted to shout because the wire below him shook, swung. He wanted to fall. He saw the abyss, below him now – his arms swung and grabbed for balance, his whole body was shaking. He no longer knew whether he was speaking or whether someone could hear him. All he had to do was finish.

He had unlocked the electricity cupboard in the dark, put on the earphones and wound the tape back. PLAY. He leant his head against the metal edge of the cupboard and he heard the noises on the tape. His head wanted to create images of it – he was the white light of justice. Silva was black. He heard a door opening, closing. *So, what do you think?* Silva.

It's lovely. What music do you have?

He jerked upright, his head banging against the ridge of the electricity cupboard. God, it was Lara. Was it?

What would you like to hear?

Rhythm.

Shuffling, rock music, earsplittingly loud, inaudible voices, music. Minutes, minutes, minutes passed. The tension in his shoulders and neck. What was happening up there? He couldn't hear. Lara laughing between two short cuts, carefree. Silva, *ooh baby*, Lara laughing, music. He fast forwarded the tape, small bits at a time, the lyrics, the rhythm his guide, silence between cuts. Twenty, thirty minutes later on the tape: the music changed, slower, softer. He played the tape back, found the cut-off point of the rock music: sudden, deadly silence, a shuffle. Ice tinkling in a glass. Silva *uh*, slow music, louder, then softer, silence, creak, he knew it, bed, Silva's bed, big bed, white, *great body, baby, you can dance but can you love*, ice in the glass, tink, tink, *don't drink too much baby, I want those tits show me more show it all, baby.*

Watch me. His Lara, he saw his Lara, he knew his Lara, knew the huskiness of her voice, the slurring of her tongue. He wanted to stop her. Not for him, my Lara, not for him. *Jesus, baby, your body, hot bod get that out, baby, yes, yes, come here . . .* Lara laughing: *There's lots of time.* Silva: *Now, baby, no, now, c'mon, baby.* Lara's laugh. Silence. The bed, the bed sounds, sounds. *Ah, good, take it, yes, take it, jeez, good, now, uhm, jeez, baby, uhm, uhm, jeez, you're alive, baby, uhm.* It was his, his, his noises, his Lara, his Lara. He wanted to tear off the earphones, run up the stairs, stop it. But this was last night, not now. The voices on the tape. *Uhm, uhm, uhm.* His cell, his icy cell. *Yes, move me, yes ride*

*me, yes, baby, jeezus, uhm, jeezus, uhm, jeezus, yes, baby, I'm
there, I'm there, oh, uhm, come, baby, come baby, uhm, uhm.*
Faster and faster. His Lara, he knew his Lara, knew her,
knew her, knew her. The music had stopped. Only the
breathing remained – slower, slower, quiet, even, quiet.
Sounds, the noise of the bed. Silence. A crackling noise.

. . . are you going?

Sleep.

Come back.

In a moment.

What are you doing? An exclamation, worried.

Checking something out.

Silence.

Let's have a look.

What are you doing . . . That's mine. Frightened. His
Lara.

What have we here?

The bed creaked sharply. *That's mine.* His Lara.

It was too easy, baby. I knew it was too easy.

Dully, the sound of Silva's fist. *Thud!*

Ah. His Lara. A small sound. *Ah.*

*You bitch, you were going to shoot me, you think I'm stupid,
bitch, who do you work for, you think I'm stupid. It was too
easy, never trust an easy fuck, baby, you're going to die.*

*You're crazy, Silva, I always carry it with me, you know
what the world is like, Silva, please.*

*Never trust an easy fuck, my mother taught me, you're a
plant, baby. You think I'm stupid, you came on too strong,
you think if I drink I'm stupid, baby. Who sent you?*

You're mad, Silva, I don't know why you, ah . . .

*I'm going to fucking kill you, bitch, who sent you, not that it
matters, I'm sending you back, look at me, baby, you've
fucked your last fuck, look at me . . .*

No, Silva, please . . .

DEON MEYER

. . . look at me . . .
. . . please, please . . .

The shot tore through him, tore through him, tore through his flesh and his blood and his soul and tumbled him down, his life, his life was falling, tumbling, he, down, with all the broken pieces, the remains, tape clicking, the yellow light dead, the tape turning, shirrrrr, back, to the beginning, his body jerked, jerked, jerked, and now he stood on the lawn and he shivered because the cold was so deep and Margaret Wallace was holding him, the tape which stopped and turned, the yellow light, a door opening, steps *so, what do you think; it's lovely what music do you have*, Margaret Wallace who held him, more and more tightly to stop the spasms, shaking with him, the two of them drowning, weeping, among the shrubs in his garden.

40

'They found her at the river, at the same place as the others, and they went in and he pulled a gun and they shot him.'

They were drinking his coffee – dark, strong, sweet coffee – and he looked at Margaret Wallace across the kitchen table.

'And you?' she asked.

'I don't know, there's a blank there. Somewhere. And then I was sitting on the beach and people were walking past and staring at me and I got up, went back to the private detective and I threw his stuff at him and I hit him and I walked out and I kept on walking, down Voortrekker Road and I walked home and then they came and they told me and I couldn't tell them that I knew. That was a bad part: I couldn't tell them . . . They stayed with me for the night.'

Coffee, cigarette.

'I didn't cry then. This is the first time.'

The truth of it came over him. 'This is the first time I've cried for her.'

So they sat in silence, in the late night, until the coffee was finished and she got up.

'The children . . .'

He nodded and saw her to her car. She looked at him but found no words. She switched on the engine and the lights, touched his hand once and then drove down the road. He watched the rear lights disappearing and stood on the pavement, empty. The abscess had been lanced; the wound was bleeding, scarlet, clean. The blood ran in a stream, a flowing stream, through him and he looked up at the stars, now burning brightly. He went into his house, switched off the lights, walked to his room in the dark, took off his shirt and tie, his shoes and socks and his trousers and lay down on the bed and thought about Lara, all the doors in his head open. Lara, Lara, Lara. Until daylight glowed behind the curtains.

Then he got up, drew a deep, hot bath, got in and waited for the cold to be driven out. He washed every inch and crevice of his big body with great seriousness using a great deal of sudsy lather. Then he rinsed off and dried himself until his skin was red. He put on clean, freshly-ironed, clothes – white shirt, grey flannels, striped tie, navy blazer. He walked to the kitchen, took out brush and polish, shined his shoes and put them on. He locked the front door, got into the car and switched on the windshield wipers to remove the dew. He drove his usual route.

At Murder and Robbery Mavis greeted him as he walked past. He smiled vaguely, walked up the steps, down the passage to his office, sat down. Reality was unreal, slightly out of focus.

His fingers massaged his temples, rubbed his eyes.

Mauser.

He leant forward, elbows on the desk. The palms of his hands pressed against his eyes, his tired eyes. He looked for concentration, looked for focus. Basie Louw. When was he going to phone?

There was nothing more he could do. Only wait. No, he must do something. Had to do something.

Wallace, Wilson, Ferreira, MacDonald, Nienaber, Coetzee.

And Oberholzer.

Phone her parents about Coetzee, the church.

Slow, almost sub-conscious movements.

'Hello?'

'Mrs. Oberholzer, it's Joubert here from Murder and Robbery in the Cape.'

'Good morning.'

'I still have a few questions, Mrs. Oberholzer.'

'It's about the Mauser murders.'

'Yes, Mrs. Oberholzer.'

'We recognised the names, the next day.'

He felt guilty. He should've told them.

'You must be phoning about the man yesterday. The minister.'

'Yes, Mrs. Oberholzer.'

'I looked through her letters. There's nothing.'

'Nothing about his church?'

'No.'

Dead end street. 'Thank you, Mrs. Oberholzer.'

'It was an accident. The whole thing. We know it was an accident.'

'Yes, Mrs. Oberholzer.'

'Very well then.'

'Thank you,' he said and then remembered the other question which he'd tucked into his head somewhere and not asked yet. Leave it, maybe it was a dead end, too. He asked it in any case, dutifully, in passing.

'Just one more thing. Where did she work before Petro-gas?'

'Sea, sea, sea.'

He didn't catch it.

'A college.'

'CCC?' Grasping.

'Cape Commercial College. They offered business

courses, I don't know whether they're still in existence. Carrie said they were too mean, so she left.'

Cape Commercial College. He tasted the name, wanted to slot it in somewhere, somewhere it wanted to fit but he couldn't identify the space.

'Thank you, Mrs. Oberholzer.'

'Goodbye.' Stiff, as the whole conversation had been. They were inimical towards him, the disbeliever who wanted to change their perspective of accident and tragedy.

Cape Commercial College.

His thoughts darted in all directions looking for a connection. He said the name again, aloud, rolled his shoulders a few times to loosen the stiffness. His thoughts were a jumble, he lit a cigarette, sank back into his chair, tried to organise his thoughts. Start from the beginning. Think through Wallace, Wilson, Ferreira, MacDonald, Nienaber, Coetzee. He found nothing. He was making a mistake. He was tired. There was nothing, it was his imagination.

A bright moment of insight – it was there. Desperately he took out his notebook, paged through it. Nothing, nothing, nothing.

He got up, stretched, killed the Winston and walked down the quiet passage, still too early for the others. He wanted to go to the tea-room for something hot and sweet – and remembered, in the passage. He halted, breath held, too frightened to hope, too scared to think. There had been certificates against the wall of James J Wallace's office but – idiot – he hadn't looked at them properly. He turned and hurried to his office and before he could pick up the telephone he remembered what Gail Ferreira had said about her husband, Ferdy: 'He always said he had to work for himself. But he was too useless. He even went on a course once to start his own business but nothing . . .'

His heart knocked against his chest wall, almost daunted

In Nienaber's study, against the wall: CAPE COMMER-CIAL COLLEGE BUSINESS SCHOOL – *This is to certify that O.S. Nienaber completed the course in Small Business Management.*

He put out his hand for the telephone. It rang.

'Joubert,' he said, but he was barely listening. His thoughts were a maelstrom.

'This is Margaret Wallace.'

He was astonished by the coincidence. 'Why did you call?' he asked excitedly, tactlessly.

'To say I'm dreadfully sorry.' Her voice still bore the night's scars.

'I've found something,' he said because he didn't want to discuss that now. 'Your husband. Did he do a course? A business course, at Cape Commercial College?'

She was quiet for three heartbeats. 'It was a long time ago,' she said and he heard how tired she was. 'Six or seven years. Eight?'

'But he did.'

'Yes.'

'I need a date. And an address and names. Anything.'

'Why? I mean, it was so long ago.'

'I think it's the connection. I think it might lead to what we're after.'

For the first time she was aware of his urgency, the vitality in his voice. 'I'll have a look. I'll call you.'

'Thank you,' he said but the connection had been broken.

He looked up the number in the directory. *Cape Commercial College, 195 Protea Rd. Woodstock. Box 214962, Cape Town.* He dialed. It rang for a long time. He checked the time. Twenty past seven. Too early, he would have to wait. He phoned Gail Ferreira, but there was no reply, either. She must be between her home and work. Why was his timing always so terrible?

No one to send to Wilson's house and MacDonald's boat, no people anywhere to answer telephones. He knew he had it, still didn't know what it meant but he was right – there was a connection. He was right, ladies and gentlemen, Mat Joubert wasn't stupid, only storm damage, a little storm damage – OK, OK, a great deal of storm damage, but it could be repaired. The grey matter was still in working order, ladies and gentlemen and he was going to end this thing today and tonight he was taking Hanna Nortier to *The Barber* and, ladies and gentlemen, the repairwork would begin in all seriousness. Because he was free – the wound was bleeding but it was free of pus.

He wanted coffee and a Wimpy breakfast with eggs and bacon and sausage and fried tomatoes and toast with butter and coffee, and a Winston – life wasn't so bad – and then he would return to his diet and he would get very thin and fit and become a non-smoker. He got up, the tiredness thrown off his shoulders like a useless garment. When he went to fetch coffee, he was in the passage when he heard his telephone ringing and ran back.

'It was in 1989,' said Margaret Wallace. 'Three months in 1989 – August, September and October. I remember now. He took evening classes and then the whole group went away, at the end, for a few days. There's a certificate on the wall, and I found a curriculum and a prospectus. They're in Protea Road, in Woodstock. The man who signed the letters of confirmation was Slabbert, WO Slabbert, the registrar. It was seven or eight years ago, Captain . . . What on earth could it mean?'

'I'll let you know before the day is over.'

Petersen was the first to reach the office. Joubert sent him to Hout Bay to MacDonald's boat. Then O' Grady arrived and also got an immediate order. Snyman was late. 'I recall something like that in Drew Wilson's wardrobe, Captain, a certificate, among the other stuff, at the back, behind the photo albums, but I didn't think it was important.'

'I wouldn't have, either,' Joubert said. 'Fetch it for me.' De Wit was pacing to and fro in Joubert's office, finger nervously next to the nose. Vos was drinking tea, then said calmly: 'Now you're going to nail him, partner.'

The telephone rang. O' Grady calling from Nienaber's house. 'Certificate's date is 1989, Captain. This is it.'

They waited, talked, speculated. Half past eight. He phoned Gail Ferreira's work number. 'Yes, it was in 1989, Captain. Late in the year. Late in Ferdy's life. He was useless by then.'

'Seven years,' said de Wit. 'It's a long time.'

'Indeed,' said Joubert.

Telephone again. 'This is Basie Louw, Captain.' His voice was weak, like an old man's.

'What's the matter, Basie?'

'Jeez, Captain, I had to go out in a boat to find them.'

'And?'

'Seasick, Captain. I get horribly seasick.'

'Is Mrs. Coetzee with you, Basie?'

'Yes, Captain but she says she doesn't know the others. She's never heard of . . .'

'Basie, ask her if Coetzee did a course in Small Business Management in 1989 at the Cape Commercial College.'

'A course in what, Captain?'

'Just ask her whether he was at the Cape Commercial College in 1989.' He said the name slowly, pronouncing each word clearly and distinctly. He heard Louw putting his hand over the mouthpiece, and waited.

Louw replied, surprised: 'He did, Captain. He . . .' Joubert heard the woman interrupting Louw but couldn't make out what she was saying. He heard Louw saying impatiently 'yes, yes, yes.' Then Louw spoke into the receiver again. 'She said it was that Christmas that he became so involved with the church, Captain. Christmas of '89. She says that's when all the trouble started.'

'He said nothing about the course? About the people who were with him?'

Again an indistinct conversation with the woman. 'No Captain, he didn't say anything.'

'Thanks, Basie.'

'Is that all, Captain?'

'That's all, Basie. You can . . .'

'The College, Captain . . . is it a new thing?'

'It seems they were all there, Basie.'

'Fuck my duck.'

'You can come back, Basie. Take the boat.'

'Captain?'

'Joke, Basie.'

'Hu, hu,' Louw laughed without humour.

Leon Petersen came back from Hout Bay. 'There's nothing. Not a certificate, nothing.'

'His men?'

'They say they don't remember anything like that.'

'It doesn't matter. MacDonald is already involved, through Nienaber.'

'What now?'

'Now we're going to the Cape Commercial College.'

41

WO Slabbert, the registrar, principal and only share-holder of the Cape Commercial College, was a bullfrog of a man with multiple double chins, a wide, flat nose, a broad, open forehead and big, fleshy ears. He had a crew cut. He looked pleased with the deputation from Murder and Robbery who came into his office in a single file – Joubert leading, then O' Grady and de Wit, with Petersen bringing up the rear.

'Call me WO. You probably want to take a course,' he said, pen in hand, after they had introduced themselves and found a seat. He sniffed and his nose made a little curve just above the left corner of his mouth.

'No,' Joubert said.

'You don't want to take a course?' Sniff. Again the strange movement of the one nostril.

'We're investigating a series of murders which were committed in the Peninsula in the past fortnight, Mr. Slabbert.'

'Oh.' Disappointment.

'We've been informed that Miss Carina Oberholzer worked for you.'

'Yes?' Tentative.

'Tell us about her.'

'Is she dead?'

'She is.'

'Carina dead,' he said as if he couldn't believe it and

381

sniffed again. Joubert wished the man would blow his nose.

'How long did she work for you?

'Four, five years. Who . . . How did she die?'

'What kind of work did she do here, Mr. Slabbert?'

'She was in administration. Received the applications and the registrations, sent out the lectures, saw to it that the lecturers received their subject matter. We don't have lecturers here – they're part-time, do other work as well.'

'And that's all she did, the administration?'

'She was only the third or the fourth person I'd appointed. You can imagine, we were very small. Carina grew with the place – bit of this, bit of that, admin, secretarial, answering the phone, doing a little typing.'

'And then she resigned?'

'Yes, she left to join some petrol concern.'

'Why?'

'With Carina it was always money. She was a pretty little thing and a good worker but she was always talking about money. I said: "You must be patient, Carrie." But she always said that life costs money. She was such a pretty little thing, always laughing and talking. And I had to take her off the switchboard because of the endless personal calls.' Sniff.

'She was working for you in 1989?'

'Yes, I . . . Yes, she was, from '87. Shame, her parents farm in the Northwest. I met them once or twice . . . They must be taking it badly.'

'Does the name James J Wallace mean anything to you?'

'No, I can't say . . .'

'Drew Wilson?'

'I can't . . .'

'Ferdy Ferreira?'

'Aren't these the Mauser . . . ?'

'Alexander MacDonald?'

'If it's the Mauser people, why didn't I read anything about little Carina?'

'Do the names mean anything to you, Mr. Slabbert?'

'Yes, I've heard of them. That hair salon chap as well – what's his name?'

'Nienaber.'

'That's him and the one yesterday, the reverend . . .'

'Pastor.'

'Yes, the pastor. But . . . was there another one today? Little Carina?'

'No, not today. How do you know about the Mauser, Mr. Slabbert?'

Sniff, curve. 'One could hardly avoid it. The newspapers are full of it.'

'You only heard the names in the media?'

'Yes.'

'Do you know a Hester Clarke, Mr. Slabbert?'

'Yes, I know Hester Clarke. Don't tell me she . . .'

'Hester Clarke from Fish Hoek? The Christmas card designer?'

'No, I don't know whether she designed Christmas cards.'

'Fifty-year-old spinster?'

'No, not our Hester – she was a small little thing, young. Young girl.'

'She was?'

'Yes, we don't know what became of her. Had simply disappeared when we looked for her again. Changed her telephone number or something. Never heard from her again.'

'What was your connection with her?'

'She gave our self-actualisation courses. Cute girl, just out of university. We advertised and she came to see me almost immediately. Clever girl, full of bright ideas . . .'

'Your self-actualisation?'

'We started the business school for the small businessmen, you know,' sniff, 'evening classes. We'd started the
evening classes by then but only in the Cape – the corre-
spondence courses for the other stuff, evening classes for
creative courses and the business school. First, how to start
your own business, the legal aspects, the ways and means,
the books, the stock . . . all those small things. Then we saw
we needed a last rounding off to send them out into the
world. Self-actualisation. Norman Vincent Peale, Dale
Carnegie – how to make friends and think positively, that
kind of stuff.' He sniffed again and Joubert wondered
whether he should offer the man a handkerchief.

'She gave a course in self-actualisation in 1989.'

'Yes.'

'With evening classes.'

'No, it was little Hester's idea to take them away for two
days, Friday and Saturday to the Berg River. There's a little
guest farm between Paarl and Franschhoek. It was her idea
– she said they were too tired in the evenings during the
week. They had to get away, be fresh, out of the usual
surroundings. She was full of plans. We still do it in the last
part of the course. There are usually ten or twelve in the
group and then they finish and we hand out certificates on
the Saturday evening.'

'How often did you go away like that?'

'Oh, just once a year. Look, the course is three months of
theory in the evening classes because people work during
the day. You can't get them to class every evening – they
don't want it.'

'And that's all that Hester Clarke did? Two evenings in a
year?'

'No, she wrote lectures as well for the creative sections.
We still use them. All the introductory lectures about what

"creativity" is and she checked the little projects set and drew up the little exam papers.'

'Here, in the office?'

'No, I don't have the money to keep lecturers here. She worked from home.'

'Where did she live?'

'Stellenbosch. I think she was studying part-time as well.'

'And then she disappeared?'

'I won't say "disappeared". But it was very strange. When we tried to find her in the new year, her telephone wasn't working or someone else answered the phone. . . . I can't remember any longer. We sent letters and telegrams but she was simply gone. I had to find someone else in a hurry. I thought she would probably come back – on holiday or something like that. But later we gave up.'

'Who gives the self-actualisation now?'

'Zeb van den Berg. He was in the Navy for years and it's his retirement job. But little Hester's stuff . . . We're still using it.'

'Carina Oberholzer? Did she have anything to do with it?'

'She organised the stuff, the accommodation and the lecture hall and the prizegiving. She went to the guest farm on the Saturday.'

They chewed on this until Joubert asked: 'What year did Hester Clarke disappear, Mr. Slabbert?'

'I'll have to think.' Sniff. The nose performed its impossible action again, a small muscle spasm. 'Let me see . . .' He counted, using his fingers. Seventy-eight, eighty-eight, eighty-nine . . . 'Yes, ninety because we got someone from the Mutual who was doing their training just for a month. But it didn't work – they wanted too much money.'

'So Hester Clarke did her last self-actualisation in 1989.'

'Got to be.'

'Mr. Slabbert, we're reasonably sure that all the victims

of the Mauser murderer were in the 1989 group of your
small business course. Have you . . .'

'No!'

'Have you records of that year's students?'

'Were they students?'

'Do you still have the records?'

'All students?'

'Mr. Slabbert, the records?'

'Yes, we keep the records . . .'

'May we see them?'

Slabbert returned to reality. 'Of course, of course. I'll
show you.' He opened one of his desk drawers, took out a
bunch of keys.

'You'll have to follow me.'

'Where to?'

'Oh, there's far too much to store here. I have a little
warehouse in Maitland.'

They followed him, through the door, past the desks of
the administrative personnel, past fourteen women, black
and white, at tables on which stood piles and piles of
documents.

'There'll be a photograph as well,' Slabbert said when
they were outside.

'Of what?'

'Of the group, with their certificates. But to find it, that's
the problem,' said Slabbert and he sniffed.

42

The 'little' warehouse in Maitland was the size of a Boeing hangar, a dirty, rusted steel construction between a scrapyard and a panelbeater. Slabbert pushed open the huge wooden sliding door with difficulty and disappeared into the dusk. They heard the click of a switch and then lights flickered and steadied against the high ceiling of the warehouse.

O' Grady turned 'shit' into a three syllable word. The others simply stared. Piles and piles of brown cartons ran from the front to the back, from side to side, stacked seven meters high, neatly packed on shelves of metal and wood.

'The problem,' Slabbert said when he'd indicated that they must come in, 'is that in the beginning we didn't think that it would grow to be so much. Then people started asking for re-marking and records of scores and copies of certificates and then we realised we'd have to store everything. But by then there was so much stuff that we only began a filing system in '92.'

'And before that?' Vos asked anxiously.

'There's a bit of a problem.'

'Oh?' Joubert said and his heart sank.

'It hasn't been filed. There are simply not enough hands. Hands cost money. Besides, we seldom get any queries for before '92.'

'Where would the '89 records be?' Joubert asked.

'In this row.'

'Where in this row?'
'To be perfectly honest, I have no idea.'

Bart de Wit radioed for more help, this time only from Murder and Robbery because he wanted to avoid the Brigadier at all costs. The others rolled up their sleeves and started taking down cartons. They developed a system and when the reinforcements arrived, extended it.

Carton after carton was unpacked, opened, passed on. Another team took out the contents, put it on the floor where Joubert, Petersen, Vos, O' Grady and later, Griessel, paged feverishly through the documents looking for dates, names, subjects.

'Who's going to put it all back?' Slabbert asked with a sniff of annoyance.

'Your administrative personnel,' de Wit said with finality.

'Time means money,' Slabbert complained and he took a hand as well, dragging cartons which had been searched into a corner.

Progress was slow because there was no system in the manner in which the material had originally been packed – documentation on computer repair courses lay next to *Introduction to Journalism. Basic Welding* was in a carton with *Painting for Beginners.*

De Wit had lunch delivered – Kentucky chicken and Coke – and they ate while they worked, swore, laughed, had serious discussions. One carton after another was checked without a break. The afternoon slowly wound to an end, the cartons slowly became less. Just after three they were half-way, with no success. Ties were off, sleeves were rolled up, shirts had become untucked, the firearms in their leather holsters were in a neat row next to the door. There were dust marks on their clothes, arms and faces. Occasionally a few words were exchanged while time marched inexorably on.

Joubert and Griessel took a break, stood outside in the sun, their bodies stiff. Exhaustion was stalking Joubert again.

'I'm going to ask the Colonel for leave,' Griessel said and sucked on his Gunston. 'I want to take my wife and children away for two weeks to see if we can make a fresh start.'

'That's good, Benny.'

'Perhaps ask for a transfer. To the platteland. Station commander in a village somewhere where all you have to do is lock up the drunks on a Friday night and try to solve a few stock theft cases.'

'Yes,' Joubert said, and wondered how he was going to make a fresh start.

Then they walked back to the hive of activity inside, sat down on the cold cement floor, licked their fingers and started paging again – Joubert with urgency because he had an impending appointment and he was developing a strong suspicion that he wouldn't be able to make it. He wondered whether there was still time to ask them to exchange the tickets for the following night and whether Hanna Nortier would be available then. *I want out. I'm stuck in a rut.* In what kind of a rut could such a woman be stuck, he wondered while his fingers flipped, flipped, flipped and his eyes skimmed. He shifted from one buttock to the other when they put more documents in front of him.

They had started arguing about supper – pizza opposed to fish and chips, anything as long as it wasn't chicken. They complained about wives who were going to be annoyed about the long hours again. Couldn't Mavis start phoning and explaining? It was nearly seven o' clock.

Then Benny Griessel shouted triumphantly: 'Ferreira, Ferdy,' and held the documents above his head. They all came to a halt, some applauded.

'Wilson, Drew Joseph. They're here.' The detectives walked towards him. Griessel took out one parcel of documents after the other – each individual's entry form, assignments, examination papers, score sheets, receipts, letters of enquiry and replies, final score sheets. All stapled together.

'MacDonald, Coetzee, Wallace, Nienaber. They're all here.'

'Is there a photo?'

Griessel searched.

'No,' he said. 'Where's the box this came out of?'

WO Slabbert came steaming up from where he was trying, with great difficulty, to replace the cartons. 'The photo will be in one of their parcels.'

Hands grabbed at the stapled documents of the individuals, fingers paged quickly.

'Here,' Griessel said on whom the gods were now smiling. He got up, stretched, extracted the staple, dropped the other papers to the floor, carefully held on to the photograph. He stared at the faintly yellowed print. Joubert got up, walked to Griessel, tried to peer over his shoulder.

'How young Nienaber looks,' Petersen, next to Griessel, said in surprise.

Joubert held out his hand for the photo. For a moment he thought he'd seen . . .

A black and white image. The men stood in a semi-circle wearing jackets and ties, each one with a certificate in his hand. Wilson's eyes were closed at the moment of flash and shutter. MacDonald, his smile wide, towered above the rest. Coetzee serious. Ferdy Ferreira's shoulders were angled towards the limp, his eyes didn't look at the camera. Wallace's hands were folded in front of him; there was a space between him and Ferreira, a detachment. Mat Joubert saw nothing of this.

He stared uncomprehendingly at the small, slender figure

of the woman in front of them, a head shorter than the shortest man. He looked, without assimilating what he was seeing. Time stood still. Solemnly he took the photograph out of Griessel's hand, held it to the light, still not looking for an explanation.

She wasn't smiling. He knew the frown between her eyebrows, the contours of her head, the nose, the mouth, the chin, the narrow shoulders. Seven years ago her hair had been longer, hung over her shoulders down to the small breasts. The dress, grey on the black and white photo, reached to below her knees. She wore flat-heeled shoes. Serious. She looked so serious . . .

'That was little Hester,' Slabbert said behind him. 'Small little thing.'

It was an old house in Observatory, restored and painted in a strong, earthy colour on the outside, dark brown. The wrought-iron lattice on the wall was white and neat. The garden gate opened soundlessly. He walked down the cement path, two rows of flowers on either side of him, the little lawn so small and tidy. The door had a brass knocker but he used his knuckles, knocking softly. The photo was in his left hand.

'You know her,' Griessel had said when he saw the paleness of Joubert's face. Suddenly everyone was staring at him. He said nothing. He remained staring at the photo, a moment of life seven years ago. He couldn't even begin to formulate questions because of the impossibility of her, there, among the dead, was too overwhelming.

'I know her,' he had said eventually and didn't hear the voices asking 'where?' and 'how?' and 'when?' The photo trembled lightly in his hand. Life seemed unreal to him like one of his dreams in which someone appeared where she didn't belong, suddenly, so oddly that you wanted to laugh, shout: My, Mat Joubert's peculiar mind! But this was no dream, this was reality.

'I'm going alone.'

De Wit had walked to the car with him. 'I owe you an apology, Captain.' Joubert was silent. 'You'll be careful?' He heard the concern in the other man's voice, understood something of de Wit at that moment. 'I'll be careful.' He had said it to himself. Not arrogantly but with gentle determination.

Now there were hurried steps on the wooden floor inside the house, the door swung open and she stood there.

'You're early.' Her rosy mouth was smiling. She wore lipstick, just a touch. He had never see her wearing it before. Her hair was drawn back into a plait, her neck open and white and defenceless, the black dress off the shoulder. He captured the image with the camera of his mind until her face changed when she saw that he was jacketless and tieless, saw the dust on his shirt, the rolled up sleeves.

Wordlessly he held the photograph out to her. Her smile disappeared, her face was expressionless. Her eyes searched his for an explanation. She took the photo and looked at it. He saw the shadow which fell over her, her eyes which closed, then opened, still fixed on the picture. She dropped it on the polished wooden floor and turned away, now almost unaware of him.

She walked down the passage. He saw the shoulders, the pretty shoulders with the bone and muscle so boundlessly perfect. The shoulders carried a heavy burden. She walked slowly, with dignity, her back to him as if he didn't exist. He followed her, one, two, three steps on the wooden floor, then stood in the passage where a light was burning. Her odour was in his nostrils, a faint, feminine perfume. She had disappeared at the bottom of the passage. He remained where he was, hesitant.

He heard a sound in the silence of the house, a whisper of activity. Then she returned, walking up the passage, the firearm in her hands, the slender stock in the palm of her right hand, the slender fingers of the left hand holding the long barrel. She carried it like a sacrifice, the scale of the pistol wrested out of context by her frailness. She stood opposite him, a space between them. She remained in that position, holding the pistol as if the weight was too much for her. A corner of the magazine pressed against the black material of her dress, against her stomach. Her head was bowed as if he was an executioner. Her eyes were closed.

He couldn't prevent his mind from completing the puzzle. It was a mechanical process, involuntary expertise, irreversible, even had he wanted to reject it. But he was too empty. He stood there while the gears in his head slowly meshed, one after the other. This is the case for the prosecution, your worship – conclusive proof, at last, conclusive proof, the chase ended.

'Why?'

She didn't move.

He waited.

An almost invisible movement of her breast, the breath shallow, in and out. Otherwise there was no movement.

He walked carefully towards her, slowly, put his hand on her shoulder, felt her cold flesh. His big hand folded over the collar bone, pulled her nearer, led her up the passage. She came with him like flotsam. He steered her to the right, to a room where there were a couple of big chairs, the floral material colourless in the dusk. The carpet muffled his footsteps. The paintings against the wall were dark squares. He made her sit down in a deep chair with soft cushions, her eyes open now, in the dusk. She sat up straight, the Mauser on her lap gripped with both hands. He sank down on his knees in front of her.

'Hanna.'

She forced her eyes towards him.

He put out his hand, wanted to take the weapon away from her but her grip was too strong for the softness of his heart. He pulled his hand away.

'Hanna.'

Her lips parted slightly. She saw him. The corners of her mouth contracted as if she wanted to smile. She looked at the object in her hands.

'It's so strange,' she said, so softly that she was barely audible. 'I was always so afraid of it. When Grandfather took it out of the leather holder. It looked so evil. So big and ugly. And the smell . . . When he opened the holder I could smell it. It smelt of death – an old, dead smell, even though he cleaned it. I didn't even hear what he was telling me. I just wanted to look at the pistol, looked at the pistol the whole time until he had finished and put it back in the holder again, then I could look at him. I wanted to be sure that he had put it back, closed it.'

She looked at him again. The corners of her mouth had drooped again, forming a half-moon.

'I found it among my father's things. Two piles. What I wanted to keep on one side, what could be given away on the other. There was so little that I wanted to keep. Photographs of him and my mother. His bible, a few records. His watch. I put the pouch on the other pile at first. Then I transferred it. Then back again. Then I unfastened the buckles and the smell rose up and I remembered my grandfather and I moved it back.'

Her eyes had wandered, somewhere in the dark, then suddenly looked at him again.

'I never thought that I would need it. I'd almost forgotten about it.' Then she was quiet, the grip on the weapon relaxed and he considered whether he should try to take it away again.

Her awareness of his presence wandered again.

He said her name again, but she didn't move.

'Hanna.'

The eyes slowly blinked.

'Why?'

She gave a deep, long, slow breath, preparation for a last, all-embracing sigh.

Then she spoke.

43

I nside they were laughing, systematically more and more
loudly, with greater exuberance. Outside it was clear
and quiet, a night without imperfections. The moon was
bright and in full sail, the stars were a sweep of glittering
dust from horizon to horizon. It was cloudless, balmy,
warm. She was standing on the little stoep of the lecture
hall. The river murmured below, the moon was a yellow
stained glass design on the water. Only a layer of wine
remained in the glass she brought to her lips. The wine was
very dry but she could taste the sun in it. She took a tiny sip
because she only allowed herself one glass. Perhaps another
half when she went to her room as a reward for good work
done. It hadn't been an easy group. The differences in
personality, in seriousness, in intelligence and in application
had demanded a great deal from her, more than usual, she
thought. Even so, it had been a success. Everyone had
discovered a piece of himself, everyone had grown – some
very little, she had to admit, but their growth potential had
not been formed by her.

Perhaps another year or two of this, then bigger, better
things. She regarded the College as a step on a ladder, a
temporary pause, but she felt no guilt. Slabbert got a great
deal of value for his money. He got integrity and work ethic.

Another year or two.

She tasted the last of the wine on her tongue, let it slip
gently down her throat, looked forward to her room. The

others had been housed two to a cottage, she and Carina had the privilege of single rooms. She had insisted on that – her time was too precious. Her book and music waited in her room. This evening she was going to listen to *Il Trovatore*, perhaps the first two acts. 'So much death?' they had asked, even in Verdi's time. 'But is all life not death?' the maestro had replied. She smiled at the moon, turned, slid open the glass doors and walked in.

They were sitting around a table, talking with great verve, each one with a glass in front of him. Nienaber was holding the floor while MacDonald, Ferreira and Coetzee listened. Wilson, her star pupil, the one for whom she had a soft spot, sat a little outside the group. Wallace and Carina Oberholzer were having their own conversation at the end of the table.

No one else was evidently drinking dry white wine. She found the bottle easily between the full and empty beer bottles, the open brandy and whisky, liter bottles of mixers and a big ice bucket. She poured herself exactly half a glass.

'I'm going to excuse myself,' she said as they looked up when she came to stand next to the table.

They protested. She saw the alcohol had filmed their eyes.

'I'm coming with you,' said MacDonald. The other laughed, exaggeratedly.

'She's too thin,' said Ferdy Ferreira slyly but she heard it with painful discomfort.

'The closer the bone . . .'

Suddenly she was in a hurry. She gave a weak smile, said they must enjoy the rest of the evening and she would see them and say goodbye at breakfast.

They said goodnight and sleep well. 'Hands above the blanket,' Ferdy Ferreira called out before she had gone through the door and one or two laughed loudly. When she was outside, she shook her head. A rough diamond, that one.

She walked through the sounds of the night – insects, the river, a dog barking somewhere, a lorry roaring its way up a hill. The voices behind her faded as the distance increased. She focused on what was waiting, everything placed exactly where it should be, late that afternoon while others were dressing for the certificate ceremony. She had uttered a few words of encouragement, handed over the certificates. MacDonald had insisted on kissing her when he received his. They clapped hands for one another, made senseless remarks. Then the photograph: Carina Oberholzer had made them stand in a semi-circle and taken one, two, three photos.

She unlocked her bedroom door. The bedlight was burning. Everything was just so. She shut the door, leant against it and gave a gratified sigh.

First of all she pressed the button on the radio and cassette player. The music filled the room. Bent the knee of her right leg, lifted the ankle up to her hand, removed the shoe. Then the other one. The start of a ritual. She placed the shoes next to one another, symmetrically, at the bottom of the single door wardrobe. She unbuttoned her blouse from the top, watching herself in the long mirror on the inside of the cupboard door. She didn't want to do the usual self-evaluation now, didn't want to consider the meaning of the sequence and every other step of the undressing process – even if it was only a game, a vague, cynical, rueful smile, a game she played with herself almost every evening. She put the blouse on a hanger in the cupboard, then reached behind her for the button of the skirt, pulled down the zip. It cost only one smooth movement to remove each leg from the garment. Her hands randomly brushed the fabric to remove imaginary threads from the skirt. She hung it next to the blouse.

Her underwear was delicate. While she listened to the

music, she unhooked the front fastening of the bra, saw her small breasts in the mirror, the whiteness of the skin. She smiled involuntarily because the decision not to be caught up in self-argument about size and shape at this stage, had been a deliberate one. The music was too beautiful, her mood too light and elevated.

The soft material of the night-gown slipped over her head. She adjusted it over her almost boyish hips and knew that the texture was a small sensation against her skin. She gave one last pleased look at the tidiness of the cupboard – she could be packed in minutes the next morning. She switched off the main light, pushed the pillows against the bedhead and slid between the sheets. She picked up the biography on the little bedside table and didn't consider her incapacity to enjoy fiction but made herself comfortable and opened the book.

Then she read.

Twice noise of the night's party disturbed her concentration. The first was a shout of resounding collective laughter which even rose above the sweetness of the aria and briefly she shook her head. They should take it easy, she thought, and then focused on the words in front of her again.

The second time was more disturbing. In the silence between aria and recitative, their cries had become a barometer of their inebriation. She recognised MacDonald's voice, maybe Coetzee's. Swear words were shouted. She immediately discarded the possibility of getting up and warning them – they were adults. He eyes looked for the words on the paper in front of her but the level of their intoxication remained a vague worry for a while until she lost herself in the life between the pages again.

At first sleepiness was an invader, then a friend.

She waited until the aria ended, then pressed the button to halt the tape. She shifted the bookmark against the spine of the book, placed in on the bedside table and reached for the switch of the bedlight. Then she turned, shifted onto her left side, lay like a foetus between the blankets, and closed her eyes.

The sounds of the revelry slowly penetrated her sleep. The vague laughter and single cries of nearly recognisable words cut sharply through the night sounds of the insects and the river's flow. Were they still at it? What was the time? There was a supervisor who might complain. Sleep had fled before the pressure of anxiety.

She got up, annoyed, walked to the window and drew aside the faded floral curtains. Would she be able to see what was going on up there?

The moon was high in the sky and bright. The trees, shrubs and lawns were bathed in a ghostly light. She peered in the direction of the small hall where the lights were still burning. She knew there was movement which had to accompany the sounds but she couldn't see anything.

Something moved outside, close, against the river. She focused on it.

A singe dark animal, square-shaped and strange. Until she looked more closely. A human figure. Two. An embrace. She looked away, took a small step back from the window, a convention. Another anxiety. It was Carina out there. She looked again, indignant. Carina and Wallace. He was kissing Carina next to the water. His hands were on the Rubens curves of her rump, her hands were around his neck. Their mouths were wide open, the tongues deep. Genitals against genitals, the drunkenness a close bond.

They had to stop. It was her responsibility to make them stop.

He pulled up her skirt, pulled away the elastic of her panties and placed his hands on her bare buttocks. He kneaded the softness, the flesh, thrust a finger into the cleft.

Her one hand came away from his neck pushed in between them, etched the cylinder of his cock against his pants, looked for the head with an experienced finger and thumb, rubbed and stroked it. Their mouths were busy. His one hand suddenly reached up, pulled the shirt out of the skirt. While the other hand remained at the back, the other was in front, under the bra. He pushed it up, looked for the nipple, took the whole breast in his hand.

She looked away, deeply shamed. It was her fault. She looked back, spellbound.

Carina's hand looked for his fly, unzipped it. Their mouths were together, the bodies slightly separated, a space created. Her hand slipped into his underpants, gripped him, pulled his cock through his fly. He knew what was coming and let her go, his hands next to his sides. She was on her knees, her tongue on the head of his prick, licking, tongue probing for its small mouth, licking, sucking it all in, sucking strongly, a slurping noise. He bent down. Her hand was jerking up and down. No, he said, his hands against her head. He pulled her up, placed an arm around her shoulders and steered her away from the river. His lust preceded him, still out of his trousers. Carina gave a brief laugh.

The scene held her captive. Her disgust and her indignation were slightly diluted by another minor anxiety. Wallace was married. There were children. And Carina Oberholzer knew it. She closed her eyes, waited until she knew they were beyond the window, outside her field of vision. She opened them again, stared at the shadows, now lifeless.

It was their lack of self-control, of civilised behaviour, of small loyalties which disturbed her so much. And her own inability to look away.

More movements in the night.

What were these people doing?

The spectators were dodging after the couple, drunk, clumsy, wordless, the eyes fixed, the brains switched to a primitive mode.

MacDonald and Ferreira, Coetzee and Nienaber, Wilson reluctantly in the rear.

She saw them – clumsy shadows – walking in the direction of Wallace and Carina. MacDonald was staggering. Their inebriation, she knew, was total.

She drew the curtains quietly and carefully until the moon was completely blotted out. She turned away from the window in the darkness of the room and knew that they had disturbed her peace, she did not want these memories. It was going to take an effort to forget them, sleep now forgotten. She switched on the bedlight. She pressed the button for the music again. Let them know she was awake. Let them come to their senses.

She sat down on the bed.

What were they doing? They were like children. She got up, opened the curtains of the other window a chink.

They stood outside the window of a cottage, in the pool of light shining from inside, quiet and intense spectators. It was Carina's bedroom and she knew what they were looking at even before she saw Ferdy Ferreira, his cock in his hand. She closed the curtain. Nausea rose in her until she struggled to breathe and tasted the vomit. She mustn't vomit now. She should have walked up earlier and acted firmly. She sat down on the bed again. Let there be an end to their lust. Lord, how primitive humans were. She raised the volume of the music.

It was the liquor. Liquor wouldn't be permitted again.

She picked up the book, sat up against the pillows and tried, with the greatest possible effort, to concentrate. It was going to be so difficult to erase the images. She read half a sentence, still aware of nausea. There were footsteps outside – they were going now, eventually they had had enough.

MacDonald crashed open the door, saw her lying there, saw her jerking the book away, the fright on her face. 'Come on, Hester, let's fuck.' He pulled Wilson inside as well. MacDonald was on her, threw the book aside. His hand was on the blanket. She cried out in sudden anger, sudden fear. She tried to stop him with her hands, saw the total, wild drunkenness on his red face, smelt the sour stench of his breath. He weighed her down with his big body, his hand held hers above her head. She jerked to and fro, she struggled. His other hand was under her night-gown, pulled it up, bared her breasts. 'At least there's something there, Hester.' She didn't hear it, she screamed. Her legs wanted to wriggle out from under him, shake the animal off her. He was too heavy, pressed down on her. 'Come on, Hester,' he said impatiently. He shifted his body down towards her knees, had to stretch to keep her hands above her head. She wanted to bite him, turned her head to bite the thick wrist. He wrenched her panties down, tore them. 'You're fuckin' small.' She sank her teeth into hair and skin. He yanked his hands away, smacked her against the side of her head. 'Fucking bitch, you bite.' He slapped her again. 'No,' Wilson said. The others entered the room. 'Me too,' said Ferreira, his prick in his hand. 'Jesus, Mac,' said Nienaber. His voice was slurred.

MacDonald had captured her hands again. A thin stream of blood was running from her nose. Her struggles were weaker, stupefied by the knowledge that was taking shape in her. He opened his pants, forced a knee between her legs. She jerked, wanted to get away, kicked. He weighed her down, his full weight on her. 'Open up, Hester.'

'Mac,' said Wilson, swaying.

'Fuck off,' said MacDonald and looked back over his

shoulder. 'Your turn is coming.' He grinned at the audience, forced her legs apart with his hips, his cock searching briefly for the opening and then he thrust it in, pressing inhumanly hard.

She felt the tearing, no pain to begin with, felt the tissue tearing. Then the pain came. Her consciousness fled, strength flowed out of her. He experienced it as acquiescence, dropped her hands, lifted himself slightly, looked back. 'She fucks too. Just like the other one.'

Her consciousness came and went. A fire burned down there, a hellish fire, consuming pain.

He slipped out, swore, pushed in again. 'Ha, ha, ha, ha.'

'Come on, Mac.'

'In a minute.'

Orgasm.

'Ferdy.' MacDonald got up, offered her.

Coetzee was faster, his pants down to his knees already. He kneeled in front of her, rubbed his hand over her stomach, rubbed her from side to side, pushed himself in and came suddenly. He stood up, surprised. Ferreira pushed him out of the way, licked Hester Clarke's breasts with long swipes of his tongue. The saliva left trails on her skin. He licked her stomach, licked downwards, licked her pubic hair. His hand jerked up and down between his legs. The yellowish fluid sprayed over her, over the bed.

'Ollie.' An order from MacDonald. Nienaber grinned, shook his head.

'Drew. Where's Drew?'

Wilson was outside, vomiting against the wall, on the lawn.

'What are you doing?' Wallace and Carina Oberholzer came stumbling up.

'You've had your fuck. We saw you having your fuck. It's

Drew's turn,' said MacDonald his big hand on Wilson's neck. He pulled, dragged him inside.

Wilson's throat wanted to rid itself of more fluid. The words were stuttered between retching noises: 'I can't, I can't.' MacDonald pushed him into the room, towards the bed.

The red of the fire was deep, all round her, she floated through the flames, light as a feather, without gravity, the pain an armour.

'You're a queer, Drew,' MacDonald hit him against the back on his head. Wilson staggered. 'Fuck her.' MacDonald grabbed Wilson's shirt.

'Mac, no,' said Wallace. Carina Oberholzer stood in the door, staring.

'Fuck off, Wallace. We saw you screwing like fucking dogs.'

He jerked Wilson upright. 'Fuck her, queer.' Wilson tried to defend himself with his hands but the knuckles were in his neck. She was lying there. Her eyes were open, wide open – she stared at the ceiling. He couldn't, he couldn't. He had trouble with his trousers, managed to undo the belt. He was soft, small, hid it from MacDonald, pressed it unwillingly against her.

'Put it in, you fucking queer.' MacDonald was at the bed, an eagle eye. Red face under the red hair. Red nose.

Wilson made the movements, felt his penis slipping in the blood.

'I want to see you come.'

He pretended, wanted to survive. MacDonald pushed him from behind. MacDonald's hands pushed him in and out, up and down. Wilson threw up, couldn't help it. He vomited again, over her.

Joubert got up off his knees.

She spoke mechanically, her voice dead, her body perfectly quiet in the chair, her gaze nowhere. He wanted her to stop.

'I was woken by the birds the next morning and the sun shining. Just another day. I just lay there. At first I could only hear. The birds. I couldn't smell. I couldn't feel. I lay there for a long time. When I moved it hurt. Then I looked. It wasn't my body any longer. I no longer knew it. They weren't my breasts, and my stomach and my legs. I didn't want to wash it because it wasn't mine. My body is clean.'

He went to sit in the chair opposite her. He was very tired.

'They had all gone. It was so beautiful and so quiet, in the morning. Only the birds.'

Then she was quiet and he was grateful.

He sat looking at her for a long time. It was as though she wasn't really there, he thought.

Why did he no longer want to touch her?

She hadn't finished. 'They wanted a blood test, last year. Everyone who was appointed had one. The doctor found it so difficult to tell me, to soften it.'

He didn't want to hear it. He knew, he understood immediately but it was too much.

'He wanted to draw more blood. He thought it had to be a mistake.' She smiled. sitting opposite him. He could barely see it but he could hear it in her last words – not a rueful smile but a genuine one.

'It's such a funny name. HIV-positive. Positive.' Still the smile, the last word almost a laugh.

'It was then that I bought the Smith & Wesson.'

He felt so heavy. He felt the weight pressing him down in the chair. His whole body felt the weight pressing down on him.

Her smile took a long time to disappear, bit by bit.

He had to take the pistol from her.

He remained seated.

He heard a car stopping outside. He knew. But the expected sounds of doors slamming didn't come.

'Your name,' he said and it sounded too loud in the silence.

He didn't know whether she had heard him.

Her finger clenched the barrel of the Mauser more tightly.

'They killed Hester Clarke.'

He didn't want them, in the car out there, to come inside.

He didn't want to ask the questions which now wanted to tumble over his lips. He wanted to leave her here and go away. He also wanted Hester Clarke to be dead.

But he had to know.

'When you received my file . . .'

Now she looked at him. For a long time, a journey to the present. 'I didn't know that it was your investigation.'

He hadn't wanted to ask it.

'I didn't invite anyone else to the music. I knew by then.'

He wanted to get away.

She was still looking at him. The left hand came away from the pistol, the right hand stiffened, a finger through the trigger guard.

'Will you go outside?'

He wanted to look at her for the last time. Alone. For a brief moment disappear into a future which might have been different. Then he got up, moved.

'No,' he said, because she had helped to heal him. He took the Mauser from her hand.

44

He used one of the side doors of the Supreme Court building to evade the press. After the crescendo of the arrest, the case had moved to the centre pages and then disappeared. But in diaries dates of the court's sitting had been noted and now they were back in full cry.

He heard the voice behind him. 'Captain.'

He waited on the stairs for her to catch up with him.

'How are you?' he asked.

'It's a long process. And you?'

'I'm all right.'

He saw that she was looking pretty, the mismatched eyes clear. He didn't want to go back to the office.

'Would you like to have coffee somewhere?'

'That would be nice.'

They walked next to one another on the pavement in the grey August light. Neither wanted to talk about the wordless, quiet figure in the dock, each for a different reason.

On Greenmarket Square there was a small coffee shop where he held the door for her. They sat down, ordered coffee.

'I didn't want to come. But I wanted to see her. Once. I wanted to tell her, somehow, that it was all right.'

He wanted to tell her that it would make no difference. He had heard the rumours of the psychiatrist's report. It would be laid before the Bench that afternoon.

'But she looks so remote.'

'Yes,' he said.

'You've lost weight.'

He was pleased that she had noticed it. 'You think so?'

'Yes.'

Their coffee came.

'So what have you been doing with yourself?'

'Working.' It was true. Just working. First to hide. From everyone, from himself, from Anne Boshoff – who telephoned twice and then gave up – and from the new psychologist. Later he had worked as part of his therapy, seeking a balance, step by small step.

'And I've given up smoking.'

'That's wonderful.'

'How are the kids?'

'They're better now. But still . . .'

'I've sold the house.'

'So have I. We're in Claremont now. Ashton Village. It's quite charming.'

'I'm in Table View.'

'Another house?'

'No, it's a . . . ' He searched for the English word, achieved it. 'A townhouse.'

'You can speak Afrikaans if you like. Mine isn't very good.'

'It sounds fine to me.'

Silence.

'Have you ever been to the opera?' he asked.